Book One of The Keeper Chronicles

# THE KEEPER
# AND THE COMPASS

By Katie Baker

Printed in the United States of America

Cover design by Mandie Manzano

Editors:

Arlyn Lawrence at InspiraLit

Grace Bridges at Splashdown Books

Proofreaders:

Grace Bridges at Splashdown Books

Heather Titus

*Acknowledgments*


For AK, EM, JC, and CB—

who are my greatest adventure and best story ever told.

# Prologue

*In a land far, far away*

A single candle illumined the gaunt woman who sat at a dressing table in the corner of a stark room. Agatha tapped her chin with one finger while chipping away at the table's flaking paint with another. In the silence, her mind spun out threads she intended to weave into the intricate and delicate plot she had already set into motion.

She lifted her second-most-treasured possession, the handheld mirror she kept hidden in a secret compartment of the dressing table's top left drawer, bringing it closer, alert for any details to aid in her endeavors.

Instead of her own reflection, the mirror revealed a room with wooden floors and a zigzag-patterned rug, without clutter save several stacks of books. The bed was neatly made with a thick white duvet and a decorative green pillow. Bright lamps that needed no candle or flame lit the room with a warm glow. Neither a fireplace nor a chamber pot could be seen. Agatha tapped her chin again. "She's too wealthy to be using the woods, so she must have a separate toilet. Oh, how I'd love a second toilet." She sighed at the thought. "One day. One day I'll have it if all goes as planned."

The room in the mirror was much different than Agatha's, as was the girl who lived in it. She was currently sitting in her odd-shaped swiveling chair, one elbow resting on a roll-top desk and the other propping a book on her knee. "She has more hair than every neighboring noblewoman in Nottingham combined," Agatha sneered, working on a tangle in her own long, straight tresses. "I always wanted curly hair."

Months ago, when Isaac had first started visiting, offering to be her tutor, he had mentioned the girl, his affection for her unmistakable. So Agatha kept a close eye on her, studied her, considered her strengths and weaknesses. And now, she knew where to find her.

The girl in the mirror lowered her book and grinned at another person entering the scene. "Ah, the black-haired boy again," Agatha said to herself. "He does have a strange look about him—I've never seen eyes shaped quite like that. He'll grow to be a handsome one, he will."

She had spied on the two spending many afternoons together, studying, talking, giggling. He seemed to prefer the chatting and laughing part, but the girl was studious, her nose in books with a pencil behind her ear, urging him to complete his studies. "Who is he? And what are they talking about?" If only Agatha could go there, see for herself, hear their conversation. Then the plot would move forward more quickly.

Her fingertip moved to her first-most-treasured possession—the little hourglass hanging from a chain around her neck. The tiniest grains of sands filtered through it, one at a time. She couldn't flip it yet, not until the

5

final grain of sand fell. It was beyond her power to speed the process along.

Her stark room trembled, and a breeze tickled her neck. She blinked, and a man appeared, sitting on the dressing table, legs crossed at the knee. Six feet tall, trim, and pleasant to behold, he caused her heart to skip in her chest.

"Hello, Agatha!" he said. "Ooh! What have we here?" He snatched the mirror from her before she had time to hide it.

"Isaac! That's private!" she said, flailing after it. He held it well out of her reach with a wink and a grin. "Give it back!" she screeched.

"What? This?" He stood on the dressing table, hunched to avoid the low ceiling. "What's so special about a wee mirror? Will it show me the future, perhaps? Or who is the loveliest in the kingdom?" His jovial laughter ricocheted off the walls of the small room. "Mirror, mirror in my hand, who's the fairest in the land?"

But when he gazed into it, he grew still. "What is this?" The color drained from his lips, and he licked them. "Agatha, what is this? Why is *she* in your mirror? And how did you …?" The answer dawned on him, and he growled. "You used me." His booming voice reduced to a whisper and heat bloomed in his cheeks. His eyes flashed.

Words failed her. He'd never been angry with her. Never. Through all their lessons and conversations and sometimes heated discussions, he had always remained cordial and kind. This time, though, she probably deserved it. A line had been crossed. "I'm sorry," she said, more for displeasing him than for spying on the girl. "I didn't mean to anger you. I—I can explain."

He stepped off the dressing table, standing to his full height. The silver pendant he always wore hummed and vibrated, sharing in his rage.

The necklace captured her attention, as it often did, candlelight reflecting off its shiny metal casing, mesmerizing her even amidst her current tempestuous circumstances. Her peripheral vision blurred, the pendant demanding every ounce of her attention.

"Agatha!" The momentary spell broke when he barked her name. He hid the necklace beneath his palm. "You stay away from her," he said through clenched teeth. "Stay away from my niece!" He raised the mirror higher and flung it to the ground.

"NO!" Agatha screamed. She fell to her knees, broken bits of glass lying between her and Isaac.

"Our lessons will not end in a few months as planned," Isaac said. "They end today. They end now."

"Today?" She trembled, his words sinking in. "You mean, you're going?" She'd expected him to be angry, sure, but to abandon her altogether? Her desperation turned to anger. "To spend more time with your *beloved*?" she spat. A thrill traveled along her spine at his reaction to her revelation, when his skin paled and sweat soaked into his collar. "Yes, I know about her too."

"First my niece, and then … you know too much. You've betrayed my trust. I've put them both in danger. And I'm leaving before I do something I regret." He shook with emotion, but his voice was quiet.

"Don't you leave me!" she screeched, the shards of glass rising off the ground, their sharp points rotating towards Isaac.

"Whoa. Agatha. What are you doing?" He raised his hands in defense. "Dulci distinet a domo …"

Razor-sharp glass arrows shot forward, slicing his skin in a dozen places and rendering him momentarily speechless. In one quick motion, the shards reversed and reformed in her hand, the mirror intact and functioning once more. The girl and her friend reappeared.

Isaac's eyes widened, shocked at what he had just witnessed. His injuries, though not serious, still caused him pain, and he grimaced. "Dulci distinet a domo domum!" he said, teeth gritted together and wiping blood off his ear. She leapt for him. His pant leg scrunched in her grip, and, together, they disappeared.

She slammed into a hard wooden floor and moaned. He touched down with unusual ferocity, shaking her off his leg. The clunk, clunk, clunk of his boots echoed in her ears, close but moving farther away. Blood from his forehead trickled to his temple, and he swiped at it, scrutinizing his red fingertips and then Agatha's crumpled form. "I've been a fool," he breathed. "Clearly there is more to you than meets the eye, Agatha. I'll return soon and figure out what to do with you."

"Dulci distinet a domo domum," he said again, and this time, unable to reach him in time, she remained on the floor while he disappeared.

Her body ached, both from the fall and the frustration that built inside her. The mirror, cold against her skin, clattered to the hardwood when she tried to move. His callousness with it, this second-most-treasured possession, added to her anger. "How dare he!" Summoning all her strength, she rose to her feet, the mirror firm in her grip, swaying with a wave of dizziness. She steadied herself on the edge of a table and allowed things to come into focus.

He had dropped her in a large, open room with stone walls and thick rugs. A large, four-poster bed adorned one corner. Canopy curtains draped the bed's headboard, and it was made up with lavish bedspreads and pillows.

Opposite the bed sat an elegant table ready for two people, and behind it, a small, tidy kitchen. A sitting area, with deep couches and overstuffed chairs, cozied up to a large hearth. "Well, not the worst place to be stuck for a while. That was kind of him."

Plopping into one of the chairs, she sighed, her temper starting to cool, gazing into the mirror once more. The girl was gone, her room dark. "Maybe she's using the chamber pot elsewhere. Hmph. Must be nice. She'll be back." Agatha placed her second-most-treasured possession on the armrest. "And I'll be gone." Her heel tapped the floor. "Now to find the door."

Minutes later, she returned to the chair and kicked it hard before sitting once more. "How can there not be a door? Even a *locked* door is preferable to *no* door." Her fingers again found the hourglass necklace, and she twisted her thumb around the chain, pressing the link into her skin. So many grains of sand remained before she could flip it—before she could have everything she had ever wanted and more. "Why must you move so slowly?" she huffed at the necklace, flopping backward in a most unladylike manner, sinking low in her seat.

From her new angle, something caught her eye.

Hanging above the hearth were several portraits of a girl with quite the coiffure, braids wrapped and twisted into a fancy up-do. "Another girl with immense hair," she said. "I wonder whatever happened to her."

Birdsong drew her to the largest window in the apartment. She had ignored it earlier since every window was barred with heavy, metal grates. But this one had fooled her. The grate on this window attached to the sturdy shutters, not the frame itself. How had she missed that? "Ooh, and no lock!" She pushed the shutters apart. Leaning out for a better view, her heels lifted off the floor.

Sunlight streamed in, and, with a gasp, she staggered away from the window, pressing into her chest, swallowing the rising bile. It made her cough and gag. Very few things frightened her, but that view made her knees tremble.

With a few deep breaths, she tried again, this time inching closer to the window where she placed her hands on the sill to survey the vista, holding on for dear life.

Mountains rose in the not-too-far distance. The sound of distant rushing waters tickled her ears. Several birds danced and flitted about the window, and a flowerbox overflowed with blossoms, herbs, and ivy. Trees grew thick and lush in the forest far below her. Clouds floated in the sky so close, she was sure she could touch them were she daring enough to release the window sill for anything longer than a second. She brushed a loose stone from it and watched it drop story after story after story, disappearing into the forest canopy. The air chilled her skin.

Pushing away from the window and leaning against the table, she crossed her arms and tapped her toe, then marched to retrieve the mirror. The girl had returned to her room with a plate of food and now sat at her desk drawing—her other favorite pastime. Agatha stared, spinning out more threads for the ever-thickening plot.

Everything hinged on the girl. She was the key—the key Agatha must turn to blow the doors wide open and get everything she desired. Everything she *deserved*. Her third-most-treasured possession, a journal in the top right vanity drawer at home, had instigated the plot. Thanks to Isaac and his lessons, she could read it. And, stupid man, he had left it in his unfastened bag for her to take. It was like he *wanted* her to have it, to read it. Why else leave it so easily accessed? Stupid, beautiful man. He had started this—it was all his fault.

One day she would tell him, once he was hers, along with that pendant he wore. She would tell him how she had maneuvered each piece of the board to achieve her endgame. The pendant would be hers. *He* would be hers, and his beloved, the one whose story filled page after page in his journal, whom he adored with such passion, would end up at the bottom of the sea where she belonged.

Agatha slammed her fist into her palm.

The girl in the mirror was the key. She connected all the pieces, and Agatha would play her like a pawn on a chessboard. Isaac had taught her chess too. Stupid man.

He was right about one thing, though. She *did* know too much.

Another grain of sand dropped in her hourglass. She must be patient. She must be cunning. She had no other choice.

A flash in the mirror garnered her attention. It was raining at the girl's house. It had rained there all day. Lightning had flashed in her room, yet she still sketched on her bed, unconcerned. She had no idea of the storm brewing.

Agatha returned to the window, her hands on her hips. Isaac would reappear soon, still angry, for sure. She must escape before he returned or threads might begin to unravel. "I don't have time for frayed threads."

11

But how? How could she escape?

She stared at the ground, hundreds of feet below. A new depth of power crackled beneath her skin. "It took Rapunzel eighteen years to break free from this tower. I have only a few hours. But then again, I'm no Rapunzel." Her maniacal laughter rang from the tower, and the little birds flitting about darted away to hide their faces beneath their wings.

# Chapter One

A bit closer to home

Sunlight poured through the window onto Jenny Fletcher's sketch-book, illuminating a rough depiction of the Shire spanning two pages. She lifted her head and blinked a few times. Her vision blurred, unaccustomed to the warm light trickling in through breaks in the dense, autumn clouds. It had stopped raining!

She tossed her well-worn pencil onto the rolltop desk, shot out of her chair, and pulled on new boots, bumping into her bedside table in the process. The pile of books stacked on it scattered across the floor. Grabbing the nearest one, she glimpsed its title. "Perfect," she said, voice scratchy from underuse. One quick cough cleared her throat, and she snatched her cell phone from the bed, clicking it on for the time. "How long have I been up here? Oy. A while."

With the phone shoved in her pocket and book in hand, she did a quick turn in the mirror hanging on her wall. "Oh holy hair," she said, pressing against her curly, auburn locks. They sprang to their original position when released. "Dangit." She scrunched her hazel-green eyes and sighed.

In the mirror, she saw the little plate on her desk, with a few crumbs still scattered on it—remains of the quick sandwich she'd had earlier. *Oh, lemme grab that too.*

Long legs carried her from the room and down the stairs two at a time. A tiny, white poodle called Moose raced her to the kitchen.

There, she found her mom, Constance Fletcher, closing yet another classic novel in their sunlit breakfast nook to pet the poodle now in her lap. The elegant bun and "cardigan with khakis" attire failed to hide Connie's athletic build. "Well, hello! Long time, no see. Wow, Jen-bug, your hair! It's really something."

Jenny clinked the plate into the sink and ran her fingers through her mane, cringing at her mom's comment and the use of her silly nickname. "It's the humidity. I've decided to embrace it. Go big or go home, right?" Her mother preferred it tamed, pulled up, less large by any means possible. She also favored turtleneck sweaters and pencil skirts—a far cry from Jenny's unique, more colorful style.

"Come on, Mom! Embrace it with me, like you did vintage t-shirts and skinny jeans. Embrace the big hair." Her voice lowered to sound more commanding, then she giggled and shook her curls, poofing them even more. "And anyway, my hair goes great with these boots." A kicked-up heel demonstrated how the deep brown leather complemented her reddish-brown locks. "Thank you for them, by the way. Very cool choice."

Connie softened. "You are more than welcome. They are really cute."

Grabbing her raincoat, Jenny beamed. "Aren't they?" One foot out the door. "I'm heading to read in the tree!" And she darted, not waiting to argue with her mom about why fifteen-year-olds might be too mature to climb trees. Halfway to her favorite reading spot, Connie called from the entryway, "Fifteen-year-olds might be too mature to climb trees!" Jenny kept going. "It's still really wet! Don't ruin those boots!" A quick thumbs up towards the house calmed her mom down, and then she arrived at the tree.

Sun rays pierced through the leaves. She hauled herself into the branches, to the perfect reading spot. Her dad teased her, dubbing her a tree-hugger, and her mom thought she ought to keep her teenage feet on the ground. But she had always loved the view from their tree, and neither Hunter Fletcher's opinion regarding her "hippie ways" nor her age nor the wet day were going to keep her from it.

From the familiar perch overlooking Willowbend Lane, she perused all the neighboring houses on her street, most of them quaint cottages or larger brick homes. The residents of Willowbend Lane spent lots of time outside, planting flowers, chatting with neighbors, and sharing the harvest from their gardens and backyard beehives. Today, however, the Lane sat quiet save the gentle wind plucking damp leaves from rattling branches.

Leaning against the trunk, Jenny opened her book—*Sense and Sensibility*. Chapter one pulled her in, and the rough tree and dripping foliage disappeared. Her chest ached more and more with each passing chapter and difficult circumstance Eleanor, the heroine, faced. The family's dwindling social status. A beloved sister's illness. Lost love and heartbreak.

Tears dripped off her chin, cold against her skin in the early autumn air, through the final chapters, resolving with elation. She cheered at Eleanor's eventual happy ending, picturing the heroine's beautiful, joyful countenance with which the story concluded.

With a deep, satisfied exhale, she shut the book and stretched, groaning when she moved her legs, followed by a muted chuckle, refusing to let stiff joints and a sore backside ruin a well-spent afternoon.

Distant but familiar sounds drifted through the tree. Several houses over, Josh Park, raking the abundance of debris in his family's yard, whistled while he worked.

*Man, that's a lot of leaves. Looks like sweaty work. Sweat'll make my hair even bigger.* A quick huff blew a stray curl off her nose. *Oh, what do I even care about bigger hair? Josh needs help!*

Tucking the book in her waistband and, with measured movements, she traveled from branch to branch, traversed Mrs. Hamilton's roof to another tree, then bridged into Mr. Hall's yard and onto his roof.

There, she squatted, distracted by the sprawling, mysterious house on the hill at the end of Willowbend Lane. It stood taller than its neighbors—prouder, less cheerful, and much more private. A high fence surrounded the large property, gated at the front with extensive security. Its black door and pruned shrubbery added to the mansion's still and stoic facade. Rumors floated through the neighborhood of its epic library and art collection, always piquing her interest.

Mr. Curtis Neil lived there and shared many of its traits: tall, quiet, proud, a little frightening. Unlike the other neighbors, he didn't often work in his front yard. The few times she'd seen him and said, "Hello Mr.

Neil! How are you?" he had answered with a curt, "I'm fine," and found something else to do. The other neighbors he greeted with kind hellos and handshakes. Perhaps he didn't enjoy teenagers. *Maybe when I'm older, we will be friends, and he will show me the books and the art.*

Negotiating the rest of Mr. Hall's roof and climbing into the final tree on her journey, she edged along the lowest branch. It extended past Josh's massive leaf pile and belonged to the tree responsible for most leaves in it, leaves which ought to lighten her landing if she chose to utilize them. *Now, what kind of entrance do I want to make?*

Jumping into the pile unannounced might scare the living daylights out of him. Getting whacked with a rake did not rank high on her list of objectives for the day.

He worked below her. His jet-black hair soaked in the autumn sun and strong arms made raking appear effortless, even with the soggy leaves.

When he rested the rake against his elbow to wipe his brow, she took advantage of the moment and jumped. Alighting on both feet deep in dank vegetation, she dusted off her hands on her jeans and straightened. "Hey buddy!"

The boy grinned. "Hi, Jenny!" Then, he ran off towards his house.

"Oh!" she said. "Okay, bye?" In a panic, she patted her hair for any hitchhiking debris, checked the zipper on her pants, and wiped her nose. *Man, did I scare him off?*

But he returned twenty seconds later. "Here." Offering her a second rake, he wilted a little. "I need help," he said, resuming his work.

"Couldn't you wait until this stuff dried a little?" she said, pawing at the ground with the rake.

"My mom is really mad I didn't do it before the storm, so I'm trying to make it up to her," he said. "I came to your house earlier instead of raking. It's kind of your fault." He winked at her.

"Ohhhh, oops. Well, happy to help. Anything to appease Amelia Park."

"Thanks. Maybe we could go to the quarry after this—give her a little space."

"Oh yeah, let's do it. I have no other plans. All I've done today is read and draw and read some more. No homework to finish." Sweat beaded on her forehead, and she took a second to pull her hair into a messy ponytail.

"I wish I was homeschooled," he said. "No homework sounds awesome."

"Uh, if you're homeschooled, it's all homework."

"Oh, ha! I guess you're right. Well, it still sounds better than regular school," he said, making some headway with the yard trash, the pile growing in size.

"Hey, speaking of school, is Liddy coming home anytime from her amazing university?" Jenny said. "I promised to take her swimming the next time she's here, but I think it'll be too cold for the quarry. We'll have to go indoors. My dad said this will be the last warmish weekend we have."

Josh wiped his face on his sleeve. "Um, I don't think she'll be here until Christmas, when her program goes on break. I've never seen her swim. I don't even know if she can. You know, her childhood is kind of, uh, shrouded in mystery." His parents had adopted Liddy five years before when she was eighteen. She now studied history in London and wasn't able to visit very often. They all missed her.

Jenny opened her mouth to tell him how much she liked Liddy

18

when her mom's voice, requesting her presence, echoed through the neighborhood. "Oh, I gotta go. My mom prefers hollering to texting, apparently. Hey, let me know about the quarry later."

"I'll check with my mom, but she should be fine with it. 4:00?"

"Sure," she said and handed him the rake, pulling her phone from her pocket. *Sense and Sensibility* dropped to the ground, and he bent to pick it up for her, perusing the title and drying a few water spots.

"Good book?" he said.

"Oh yeah. I just read it for like, the tenth time or something," she said, taking it from him.

"The whole thing? Today? Just now?"

She reddened. "Uh, maybe?"

"Wow, strong work," he said, and she stuck the book under her arm to unlock her phone.

"I'll text you a reminder about the quarry," she said, and his phone dinged from a chair by the house. "There it is," she said and took off toward home, climbing the fence and shouting, "Great to see you! Hope your mom chills out."

Once in the door, she dashed to change her sweaty shirt before helping with dinner. Throwing one shirt in the hamper and sticking her arms into another, she spun on her heel. "Hey, where's my mirror?" An empty space on her wall where the mirror had hung glared at her. "Well, that's strange."

Heading to the kitchen to ask her mom about it, hushed voices filtered through the foyer and met her ears. Hesitating, she stopped and listened. *Who's in there? Surely Mom didn't call me home then continue on in some secret conversation with person or persons unknown.*

Unable to decipher any of their words, tired of standing on the bottom step doing nothing, and super curious about the whereabouts of her mirror, she sauntered into the kitchen, rapping a knuckle on the wall to warn the whisperers of her presence. There, with her mom, stood her favorite uncle, head to toe in a trench coat with leather boots peeking below his hem. A meticulously trimmed beard and small, round glasses added to his hipster-professor look. However, the seven bandages covering his cheeks, forehead, and ears distracted from his usual style, as did the large mirror tucked snug under his arm.

"Isaac!" she said. "Your face! What happened? Are you alright?"

With tentative fingertips, he tapped a few of his bandages and grimaced. "I'm okay. Just a run-in with something rather … prickly."

"Wow, sorry. Um, what are you doing with my mirror?"

He put the mirror on the counter, face down. "I'm sorry Jenny. I have to take it back. I'll replace it with something even better. Bigger. Gilded maybe." She giggled—a gilded mirror was *so* not her style.

Moving to give her a hug, Isaac pulled his coat in tight then embraced her with warm arms. "It's good to see you, my not-so-little-niece."

Something pressed into her shoulder when he gave her a squeeze. Pushing away to investigate the source of it, she rubbed the spot it had pinched. *Ow! What in the world poked me?* Examining his clothing for any answers to her unspoken question, she considered the options. *A button? Sunglasses? An oddly shaped pen?* A tiny silver chain snuck out beneath his collar. *A necklace? Huh. Isaac wears a necklace? How 1995.*

Buttoning his coat despite the warmer weather outside, he gathered the mirror once again. "I'm actually just leaving," he said. "I'll replace it. I promise." The clocked chimed. "Oh my, I need to be going. Ta-ra, you two."

"How are you getting home?" Jenny said. "I didn't see your car."

"Oh, um, I, uh …"

"Uber," Connie interjected. "They are coming in two minutes. I ordered one for you ten minutes ago."

"Oh. Of course. Uber is very prompt. I used them in London all the time. Far faster than the black cabs. I'll wait in the drive. You two carry on cooking or whatever it was you were planning to do." He waved and called out, "Ta!" The door clicked behind him.

"Bye," Jenny muttered, facing her mom with a head shake and eye-roll. "That man. I'll never understand him. And Mom, you can order an Uber? Good work. I didn't know you were so up-to-date."

Connie chuckled. "I'm trying. Jenny, I'll hold him to his promise about a replacement. Don't you worry." She gestured to the ingredients for dinner prep already on the counter. "Ready to cook?"

Jenny nodded. "Josh wanted to hike around 4:00. That okay?"

"Sure," her mom said, washing some peppers. "And how is Josh?"

ooooo 🎕 ooooo

They met at 4:00 as planned and hiked until dinner. Every weekend following, for the next month, found them at the quarry or exploring in the woods. More and more leaves dropped from the trees and crunched under their feet. Additional clothing became necessary with each passing week.

One blustery day, when Josh returned from soccer practice, Jenny met him at his house with a "Happy Birthday" sign and a backpack. "Mom, I'm heading to the quarry with Jenny," he yelled from the door. They jogged to the left, through the woods by Mr. Curtis Neil's high privacy fence, and along the worn path.

"So, how does it feel to be sixteen?" she said. They marched along in single file, Josh in the lead.

"It's fine," he replied. "Doesn't feel real yet. Except for this!" A shiny driver's license flashed in his palm.

"You got it! Ugh, I'm so jealous."

Sticking the license in his pocket, he continued walking. "Now I can drive alone! I'll take you somewhere! Honestly, though, it was kind of weird at school. I didn't tell anyone it was my birthday, so everything was really normal."

"Why not?" she said, stunned that anyone would not want to proclaim their birthday from the mountaintops.

"I dunno. Just wanted it to be quiet, I guess." Emerging from the trees and through a break in the quarry walls, they both slowed and stopped talking. Cliffs rose high above them, long drill lines in the rock from the top edges to the water line and beyond, into the depths below. The water, still and dark in the dreary months, hid secrets they both tried not to consider, but any mysteries the quarry possessed could not detract from the beauty surrounding them.

A dock floated in the water by the beach where people swam and went paddleboarding in the summer. Today, it served as the perfect stage for Jenny's plan. "Get comfortable," she instructed him, the dock wobbling beneath them, "and no peaking." With everything laid out, she gave him a poke. "Okay, you can look!"

Josh brightened. She had spread out a picnic blanket, placed a platter with four decorated cupcakes at the center, and filled two cups with sparkling grape juice. Four candles burned on each cupcake. "Make a wish!" He obeyed, and, a moment later, blew out his sixteen candles in one puff. She cheered and clapped and high fived him.

They ate their cupcakes in silence, soaking in the easy quiet. Midway through cupcake number two, Josh took a swig of juice. "Hey, glad we're friends, Jenny. It's pretty fun."

"It *is* pretty fun. Here, I got you a little something," she said. From her satchel, she pulled a crisp, wrapped gift and placed it in front of him. "Hope you like it."

The paper fell to the wayside, and he held up a stack of books. "*Treasure Island, Gulliver's Travels,* and *A Wrinkle in Time.*"

"Have you read them?" He shook his head, examining the synopses at the end of each book. She exhaled. "Oh good! They're all books about people who had amazing adventures. I thought … I thought you might find this kind of book appealing."

He went for another high five. "That's so thoughtful. I can't wait to read them."

*Eek! Two high fives in three minutes. That's good, right?*

"You really like them? I wasn't sure how much time you'd have for extra reading," she said. "Especially books that are about something other than soccer."

The quarry magnified the sound of his laughter, and he slapped his thigh with *Gulliver's Travels*. "You're funny, Jenny," he said between hoots. Once he composed himself, he piled his books on the dock. "These are very cool gifts, Jenny. I'll squeeze them in between soccer games. I promise."

Relaxing, she pulled her knees in and rested a cheek against them. "Now that you're sixteen, where you gonna go?" she said, taking a lick of lemon icing. "Oh man," she moaned, rolling back to stare at the sky, slain by the savory sweetness on her tongue. "That's delicious." He cleared his throat. "Okay, sorry, sorry. Please, answer the question."

While she munched the soft, spongy cupcake, Josh talked about how he hoped for more freedom from his folks. A trip to the mountains for a backpacking trip or traveling the opposite direction to the beach to go surfing topped the list of places to go.

"I grew up going to the beach a lot," he said, "but not as often now that I've gotten older. I miss it. But there's also soccer, which takes a lot of time, and if I can make the League team, that'll be even more work."

She had shut her eyes while he described his plans, visions of the beach rolling through her head, but when "soccer" came up, she balked, and the afternoon sky came into focus once again. Josh loved soccer, but the idea of him being even busier made her want to throw cupcakes into the dark waters swirling below them.

To keep from dampening the mood during his mini birthday party, she steered the conversation to joint future adventures they might have now that he had a license. They spent the rest of the day discussing the places they dreamed of visiting. Their laughter bounced off the rising walls and to the clouds above.

ooooo 🕱 ooooo

The days soon got too cold to enjoy the outdoors for any length of time, so they spent evenings climbing at the indoor rock wall, running laps through the neighborhood in long pants and vests, and practicing soccer drills in Josh's garage. Every day they talked, giggled, and spent their free hours together.

But when the League soccer season started, he made the team.

# Chapter Two

Sitting in the center of her bed, Jenny dropped her phone onto the duvet. The text from Josh confirming his place on the League team faded into black. Her knees pressed against her forehead. *Why does he have to be so good?* A tear dripped onto her leg and left a streak on her thigh.

Based on the games she had seen him play during the fall soccer season at his school, he deserved a place on the League team. Soccer came easy for him. He joked how he had inherited his skills from his Korean dad since Koreans love soccer. But in fact, his hard work, dedication, and ridiculously fast mile contributed more to his ability than anything else.

Despite his talent being put to good use, and his elation at making the team, she had to fake being excited for him. The time commitment for practice and games meant less time for anything else, including her. *So long, friend. Nice knowing ya.* The duvet served as the perfect wiper for her tears. *Or maybe you'll surprise me.*

The League season started after Thanksgiving, and she saw less and less of him as Christmas approached. Their adventures dwindled. Each time she knocked on his door, his mom, Amelia, answered, apologized, and explained his absence, citing practice or a team meal or out with the guys. She always invited Jenny in to chat, and they forged a bond over their love of books and Christmas cookies. But Josh never arrived home before Jenny had to leave.

At first, he texted to say sorry for missing her, but even those stopped after a few weeks. Her "Merry Christmas" text was met with an ornament emoji.

A generic happy birthday message from him arrived a day late, and he failed to respond to her reply. She waited for hours, forcing herself to not pick up her phone every two minutes to check for a response. When bedtime came, and he still hadn't texted, she tossed the phone into her desk drawer and slammed it shut, dropping into her chair to cry.

In a last-ditch effort to see her friend again, Jenny decided to go to one of his games. With a front row seat, she wavered between anticipation at seeing him play and apprehension about seeing him at all. When he and his teammates swaggered to the field with quick waves to their families in the stands, she pushed her curls to the side and caught his eye. Surprise and near panic crossed his countenance, but he managed to give her half a nod. She returned with a wave. One of his teammates nudged him. "Who's that with the hair?"

"Just a girl from my neighborhood," he said loud enough for Jenny to hear, continuing onto the field without another glimpse in her direction.

The breath rushed out of her, and the bleachers shook when she dropped onto them, hands pressed against her aching chest.

Raindrops began to fall—cold, yucky, late winter rain. They soaked into her skin and polar fleece.

*Ugh, what am I even doing here?* She stood, scowling, and clenched her fists. Grateful for the rain on her face to hide the tears, she left. *If he doesn't want me around, then I won't be around anymore.* Stomping to her truck, the puddles splashed up her legs. *And I will* stop *being so pathetic.*

∞∞∞∞ 🝮 ∞∞∞∞

At home, she sat in her room. Rain rapped on the window panes. "Ugh, I can't just sit here," she said and grabbed her sketch pad. Soon, raindrops on glass, bare trees in winter, and gray landscapes filled the pages.

When she tired of sketching, she lost herself in a book for several hours, speeding through the chapters. Even a captivating story failed to erase her hurt, and once it ended, sadness flooded in again.

Phone in hand, she scrolled through her other friends' numbers, but no one she knew wanted to run in the muddy woods or go bouldering. Her girlfriends shopped and drank expensive coffee and talked about the boys who had caught their attention. They wore fancy workout clothes but never set foot in a gym of any sort. Rock climbing might damage their manicures. And anyway, she'd lost touch with them the last few months, spending most of her time with Josh.

Pushing off her bed, she paced in her room. "Maybe food will help." With quiet footfalls, she wandered along the hallway toward the stairs, past the closed door of the guest room.

With her foot on the top stairs, something caught her eye, and she stopped, spun, and examined the guest room door. "Did a light just flicker in there?" Shaking her head in disbelief, she huffed at her jumpiness, certain she had imagined a flash illuminating the crack under the door.

Returning to the task of obtaining food, she took the next stair. A thump sounded from the guest room. She jerked, socks sliding on the wood floors, blood coursing through her veins, throat tight.

Creeping closer to investigate, she reached for the doorknob. The door creaked open, and a face appeared in the crack.

Screaming, she kicked the door full strength. It smashed into something solid, eliciting a loud yelp followed by hysterical laughter. Recognizing the sound, Jenny groaned. "Isaac!" The door swung open, her uncle standing there, rubbing his forehead. "Dude!" she groaned. "Why? Why do you insist on terrifying me?" His chuckles were infectious, and she fought to keep a straight face while chastising him. "Isaac, what are you doing here?"

His snickering slowed, and worry flashed in his eyes. "I, uh, arrived just a bit ago from London. My place here is, um, under some renovations, as it were. Your mom said I could stay with you guys a night or two." Isaac split his time between his nearby apartment and a flat three blocks from Parliament, and he always sounded like a jovial British pensioner upon his return from the Motherland.

A ray of gray light from the hall window glinted on the same silvery chain around Isaac's neck she'd spotted during their last encounter, resting against his collar. She cocked her head for a better view, but he pulled at his shirt and straightened his jacket, and the chain dropped out of sight. "Hey, I wanted to ask you about your ..." she started to say, attempting to inquire about his necklace.

"I'm famished. Haven't eaten since yesterday. Fancy a sandwich?" he interjected, cutting her off.

"Oh! Um, okay? I, uh, was actually headed that way," she said, confused by her uncle's scattered behavior, his usual composure not quite in place. The thought of a sandwich and her uncle's company did sound nice considering her foul mood. She allowed him to escort her to the kitchen for a snack. The entire way there, he prattled on about the latest novel he had read, distracting her for a moment from their odd encounter in the hallway and the current dismal circumstances regarding her former best friend.

∞∞∞ 🌂 ∞∞∞

In the following weeks, after her uncle had left for his apartment, loneliness crept in. Between sulking in her room and wandering about the house with Moose at her heels, her mother attempted here and there to lift her sad mood, something Jenny both loved and despised.

First, Connie offered to pay for piano lessons, or guitar, or flute. Perhaps volleyball or dance, snorting with laughter when Jenny gagged at the mention of wearing a tutu.

"What about rock climbing?" Connie offered one morning. "Maybe some lessons there with the pro? Would that, you know, cheer you up?"

Jenny stopped chewing. "Mom!" she said, exasperated, ready to fight against another of her mom's suggestions. But, as "rock climbing" registered in her mind, the edginess left her voice. "That's actually a really great idea." A genuine smile pulled at Jenny's cheeks. *Wow. I'd almost forgotten how to move my face this way.*

"Really? Well, let's do it!" Connie sagged with relief.

During her first lesson, the instructor, Jesse, knowing Jenny already possessed some climbing skills, took her to a more advanced route. Staring

30

up at the imposing wall, she guffawed at him. "Seriously?" she said, blowing a lock of hair off her forehead.

"You can do this, Jenny, and if you fall, you'll be on belay and safe. And you will try again."

With an exhalation to calm her nerves, she grabbed her first hold. *If Sam could carry Frodo up the side of Mount Doom, I can get myself up this wall, maybe.* "Climbing." She swallowed.

He checked his equipment and responded, "Climb on!"

Scrutinizing the wall, calculating, searching for the next hold, she ascended. Jesse cheered for her, coaching her on where to reach next. With each successful hold and vertical distance achieved, she dug her way to the top of the depressing pit she'd been wallowing in. A few times, she rested, reassuring herself and determining her next move. When she made it to the top, she slapped the bell with a joyous "Whoop!" Jesse, her one-man audience below, shared her enthusiasm.

"That was awesome!" she said once her feet touched the ground.

"Totally," he said, encouraging her to do it again, but not before another girl, Rae, congratulated her on a first-rate climb.

"I'll be here tomorrow," Rae said. "Want to climb together?"

"Oh! I would love to!"

"I can pick you up anytime if you need a ride," Rae offered.

Having gotten her license a few months before, along with her beat up, rusty pickup truck, Jenny didn't need a ride, but she did need a friend. "I'd love that," she said. "Here, give me your number. I'll text you."

Soon, the fun and straightforward Rae Gray became a source of both friendship and fun, and, after some time, someone Jenny confided in. She didn't tell Rae about Josh right away, keeping her cards close, but, when Rae asked for the twentieth time who lived in the house Jenny always glared at as they drove by, she answered, "Just a boy from the neighborhood."

Rae laughed. "I don't believe that for a second. You shoot daggers in his direction every time we drive past."

So, with care and caution, Jenny explained her history with the boy from the neighborhood and how he had ghosted right out of her life.

"He turned me into a pathetic, saggy sop of a person," Jenny said, a little disgusted at her clingy behavior when his soccer season had started. "And when he was gone, I was so sad. Like we had broken up or something."

"But you were just friends, right?" Rae said as they pulled into the climbing gym, putting her trusty Volvo into park. "Right?"

"We were *just* friends. But even friends will break your heart."

ooooo 🦋 ooooo

Summer arrived, and homeschool slowed to a crawl. Jenny set a few goals to work towards through the hot months. Run a 10k race, finish a 5.10 rated climb, draw most days of the week, and, under heavy influence from her mother, read three classic novels. A calendar taped to the wall planned her runs and climbing sessions each week with reading and drawing penciled in daily.

One balmy morning, the damp air condensed on her skin while she loaded gear into her pickup in preparation for a difficult climb with Rae. Carabiners scraped against the truck bed, causing her to cringe at the sound. A peek at her watch urged her to move with a bit more intention—

Rae would arrive in less than five minutes, always on time.

The short but detailed list of obligatory gear dominated her thoughts, so when a voice behind her said, "Hey Jenny," she froze.

Her mind blanked. Blood pounded. Palms grew damp. A familiar voice, though deeper than the last time they'd talked. A thousand emotions flooded in along with as many questions. Should she be nice? Should she play it cool? Should she be angry at him for the hurt she still felt, being pushed aside for soccer and dudes?

A slow spin brought them face to face. The metal truck felt warm when she leaned into it. Arms folded on her chest, she studied him, long and hard. One quick movement raked the curls from her face. *Please don't cry.* "Hey," she said.

Josh eyed the gear still dangling from her grip. "Going climbing?"

"Yes."

"Cool. I miss climbing. I'd ... love to go again. Maybe ... I mean, do you have any extra room today? Possibly?"

"No, and anyway, don't you have *soccer*?" She growled the last word, turned her back to him, and dumped the last harness in the pickup with several loud clanks.

He shifted his weight from foot to foot, the ground grinding beneath his shoes. "I quit last week. I texted you about it."

Her mouth dropped open, but she snapped it closed, reaching for her phone and scanning her texts, still not facing him. "I didn't get it." An aggressive shove pushed the phone back into her pocket. "Why?"

"Uh, I don't know. I mean, I sent it. I promise. Sometimes my phone like, eats texts or something. Maybe that's what happened?"

"Why'd you *quit*, Josh?" A quick one-eighty and she glowered at him.

"Oh, ha. Sorry. Um, it just got too busy. I missed … I missed the rest of my life."

Her icy glare wilted him. "Well, the rest of your life missed you for a while, but it moved on and found other ways to fill its time." Intending to say more, she lost the chance when Rae's Volvo pulled to the curb, prompt as usual. Considering Josh with suspicion, Rae strutted to Jenny's truck and dumped her trad rack in, then raised an eyebrow toward her friend. "I have to go," Jenny said. "I only have two seats."

With her fingers on the door handle, she sighed. "I'm running at six tomorrow. Five miles. You are welcome to come if you don't mind going with just a girl from your neighborhood." Forcing herself to maintain eye contact, her ribs quivered from the pounding in her chest. *Oh man, is he tearing up? No! I don't want to feel sorry for you!*

He cleared his throat. "Six—as in a.m.?"

"Yes." The grimace she received upon confirmation of the early hour delighted her to her toes. *Oh good, I don't feel too sorry for you.*

"Okay, I'll be there. I promise." The car door began to close. "Oh! Jenny! I read the books you gave me for my birthday. Do you have any more? Adventure books?"

"Maybe," she said, shutting the door and leaning her head against the seat, white-knuckling the steering wheel. When she cranked it up, a satisfying vroom broke the silence.

"That Josh?" said Rae, watching him amble away.

"That's Josh," Jenny replied, throwing the truck into reverse.

"He's cute."

"Shut it, Rae," she said, pulling into the road, focusing ahead, refusing to glance in the rearview.

∞∞∞∞ ❦ ∞∞∞∞

Morning arrived sooner than she expected. Downing some orange juice and a banana, her foot tapped on the hardwoods glowing in the harsh fridge light. Would she be running alone or not? Another swig of juice. "Guess it's time to find out."

Hints of sunrise illumined the lane—the air thick with dew and apprehension. The beep of her watch indicated 6 a.m. There he stood at the bottom of her driveway, stretching his quads.

"You're here," she said.

"I'm here. And Jenny, I, um …" He studied his fingernails. "I owe you an apology. A huge one. I got so focused on soccer and those stupid guys on my team who were total turds. And I was too. I hurt you, I know it. I feel awful about it. I'm so sorry. You were *never* just a girl from the neighborhood. I knew as soon as I said it that it was a lie. And I wanted to call you after the game to talk, but when we won and went out afterward, Julia was there and … I don't know. Anyway, I was stupid to say it. You are far more than just a girl from the neighborhood."

For a long twenty seconds, she stared at him, hands on her hips. Nothing moved—no wind, no cars, no other people. A dog barked on the next block.

"I know I am," she said, her voice strong and matter-of-fact. "Since you are here, and I know how much you hate early morning runs, apology

35

accepted." She offered him a handshake. "Welcome back into my life, Josh. You have some rebuilding to do. I need you to know that. A *lot* of rebuilding. It can't be like it was, at least not right away. But, I'd like to be friends again."

"Yes. I totally understand. I'll make it up to you. I was such a tool. I'm so, so sorry."

She knelt to tighten her laces. "So, who's Julia?" she said, pulling them into place with vigor.

Josh kicked at the loose rocks on the street. "I don't know—a girl I was talking to for a while, but she decided to go after one of my *former* teammates."

"Is that why you quit?"

"No, and we ended it two months ago. She's ancient history. I quit because … I quit because soccer was turning me into someone I didn't like. That's the truth."

Jenny stood. "Ready?"

They ran hard and fast. Hearing him sucking wind a few yards behind her while she covered the ground with long, easy strides spurred her on, and she picked up the pace. Even when he attempted to sprint to the finish line at the edge of her driveway, she held him off, offering him a high five once he crossed the line after her. "That was fun," she said.

Panting hard and hunched over, he chuckled. "Yeah, fun, if you've lost your ever-lovin' mind."

The front door to her house opened and her dad, Hunter, appeared. He cut an imposing figure with broad shoulders and dark features, even in plaid pajama pants and sipping coffee. "Josh," he barked, "Come with me, please." Worry flashed on Josh's face.

"You'd better go," she said, suppressing a grin. They disappeared into the garage for several minutes.

When he reappeared, waving goodbye to Hunter, he asked her to walk home with him. It took a minute for him to speak. "Your dad is … intense."

"Ha, tell me about it. What did he say?"

"First, he offered to teach me to use a bow, which seemed kind of weird."

"Yeah, that's weird. But he's skilled, and he's a decent teacher. He taught me. You gonna do it?"

"It's hard to say no to him."

"Yep. It is. Did he say anything else?" Her dad may have given Josh a stern talking to.

"He did."

"Okay?" She bit her lip, worried about what he may have said.

"Let's just say that he loves you very much and doesn't want you to get hurt again, by me, in particular." Another gap in the conversation and he halted. "Jenny, I didn't realize how much I hurt you. You were a great friend, and I ditched you. Hard. I feel so bad about it. And I'm sorry."

"You already said sorry. You don't need to apologize again." In a rare moment of emotion, Josh hugged her, told her a quiet farewell, and disappeared inside.

Her mind reeled. *Too good to be true, or will he be a total jerk tomorrow?* Her head ached, and she pushed on her temples. *Can I do this again? It's a risky thing. And it's not like we were dating or anything. We were just friends, and still, it hurt so bad.*

But the next day, he texted and asked her to go to the climbing gym with him. "My dad is taking me," he said. She replied a quick yes, asked if she could invite Rae to meet them there, grabbed her stuff, and tied a bandana on like a headband. Her hair bounced with excitement when she bounded down the porch stairs and into Dr. Park's old, restored Jeep, heaving her bag into the seat with her. Dr. Park greeted her with a deep "hello" and made sure she buckled up before hitting the gas. The Jeep rumbled and rolled, much like its owner's voice. Muscled and tanned, similar to his son but with gray-speckled hair, he wore expensive sunglasses and cargo pants.

"Good to see you, Jenny, and your hair," he said, glancing in the rearview mirror at her wind-tossed mane. She giggled and made no effort to tame it.

A hint of Dr. Park's Korean roots lingered in his accent. "Looks like you brought plenty of gear," he said, motioning to the bulging bag in the seat beside her.

Heat crept into her cheeks. "Yeah, it might have a few, uh, books in it, in case I have to wait around at the gym. And actually ..." The books clunked while she dug in her bag. "Here. Another adventure book for you, Josh."

*"Around the World in 80 Days."* Josh traced the title on the book cover with his index finger.

"Nice choice," Dr. Park said.

They drove past Curtis Neil's imposing house on their way out of Willowbend Lane and saw him by the gate with his massive Doberman. Dr. Park stopped the Jeep and waved hello. The older man approached them. "Well, well, Tom and Josh Park, how do you do?" His Scottish accent hummed in her ears, but Jenny remained quiet, their short, awkward interactions in the past flashing in her mind. "Oh, and wee Jenny Fletcher in the back. Hello there." She offered him a hesitant wave. "Ah, I spot some carabiners. Heading to the climbing gym, eh? Enjoy the time, then. Klaus and I are headed out for a stroll." The Doberman sat on his haunches, still and alert. "Ta!" he called. They returned his waves and drove off.

"Mysterious fellow," Dr. Park said. The old man and his dog disappeared behind them, and Jenny turned forward again.

"So, Dr. Park, how's the world of Internal Medicine?" she said.

"Internal Medicine is stressful, to tell you the truth. That's why I asked Josh to climb with me today, to take my mind off things. I need a bumper sticker that says *I'd rather be climbing.*"

"Or how about *Your problem is—you aren't reaching for the skies?* Or, oh, I don't know ... *Take two of these and call your nearest climbing gym?*" She snickered at her own joke, which elicited a hoot from the driver.

"Those work too!"

"Dad does some pretty highly rated climbs," Josh said. "He did it years ago in the Korean army, and now he's getting back into it. We're planning a trip to the Rockies toward the end of summer."

"That sounds awesome!" she said. What possible vacations with her parents might involve rocks and ropes? *I will bring it up over dinner.*

Their morning flew by. They supported one another in increasingly challenging climbs at the gym. Rae met Josh, holding back, not so willing to trust him yet, though she belayed him a few times and didn't let him crash to the ground and even suggested a few holds for him to try.

With shaky arms, it took more effort for Jenny to pull herself into the Jeep once they were done, and she groaned. "I'm gonna be sore," she said, stretching her deltoids and peering at the clock. "Oh, I think we will get back just in time to greet my Uncle Isaac. He's coming into town today to celebrate my birthday."

"He's a little behind." Josh flared his nostrils in disapproval.

"That's how it goes with Isaac. He operates on a different timeline than the rest of us, but he gives thoughtful gifts, so I just deal with it. And anyway, you forgot it too."

"No, I texted you," he said, defending himself.

"Kind of," she retorted. With no desire to embarrass him in front of his dad, she hammered out a message on her phone. *You never replied*, she wrote and hit send. When Josh read it in the front seat, she saw him droop. *It hurt*, she sent.

*What can I do to make it right?*

"You're doing it," she whispered in his right ear, away from his dad, who remained oblivious to their silent conversation.

"So, you are fifteen now?" Dr. Park said. "You'll be driving soon."

"Sixteen, actually. My birthday was a month after Christmas. So I've been driving for a while now."

"Is that pickup in front of your house yours?" he said, and she nodded in his rearview mirror. "Did your dad find it for you?" Another affirmative. Dr. Park grinned and chuckled. "That Hunter Fletcher always finds the coolest stuff. Tell him I said hello. Good to see you, Jenny. Enjoy your day with your family."

"Thanks, Dr. Park, and Josh, thanks for letting me crash your father-son climbing party. See you guys later."

At the front door, she hesitated, listening. Dr. Park's words carried through the open car window and towards her stoop. "Jenny's gotten so tall, and she's a strong climber."

"Yeah, she's pretty awesome," Josh said. "Thanks for letting her come today, Dad."

She didn't turn or let them know she'd heard. Josh didn't need to see her giant smile yet anyway.

# Chapter Three

With a grip on the doorknob and about to enter her house, she paused, listening. A sports car careened onto the Lane, squealing its tires. The classic two-seater convertible pulled in the drive and stopped with a lurch. She released the door, dropped her climbing stuff, and ran to hug her uncle.

"Jenny!" he boomed. "Lovely to see you. Happy birthday! I'm sorry I'm so behind. The last time I saw you, I had completely forgotten it had happened. I was a bit, you know, out of sorts, with my flat and all."

"You did seem a bit distracted. Don't worry, we got another cake. It says, 'Happy Almost 16.5 Birthday.' I'll happily take an extra present to make up for it, like maybe a new mirror?" She craned her neck, inspecting his car for any hint of a gift or two. A large conch shell perched in the front seat. *That's odd. Probably not for me. What would I do with a shell?*

He always gave special gifts along with a book, usually a classic like *The Lion, the Witch, and the Wardrobe* or *The Swiss Family Robinson.* What might he bring for a sixteenth birthday—one of the most important birthdays ever?

"Indeed," he replied, blushing before marching to the front door, hugging Connie and calling a warm "hello" to Jenny's dad, Hunter. Connie returned the hug with such ferocity, her knuckles blanching, and she gave him a quick once over.

"Glad to see you are still in one piece," she said. The concern in Connie's voice was unusual, and Jenny frowned. *Why is my mom so concerned?*

Hunter, always strong and quiet, pulled Isaac into a sincere hug. Moose, last year's beloved birthday present, jumped and yapped.

"What, Moose, did you think I'd forgotten you?" A large dog treat appeared, and Moose darted off to a corner, chewing on his gift. "Well now, the dog has gotten his treat, but what of the birthday girl?"

"You know I don't say no to presents."

Isaac made a show of searching his various pockets. "Now where did that thing go? Ah-hah!" He extended both hands, one holding a large envelope and the other in a fist, containing something tiny. "Which one first?" he said, a mischievous gleam in his eye.

She tapped his closed fist first. When he opened it, a glare reflected off its contents, causing a momentary glow, and she gasped. There, curled and twisted, lay a delicate, silver chain with a circular pendant—the chain identical to the one she'd glimpsed from her uncle's collar in the kitchen and hallway during their most recent encounters. *Could it be the same one?*

With careful fingers, she lifted it and studied the pendant hanging in front of her. Its intricate star, inlaid silver and gold, shimmered in the soft light. "Oh, it's a compass!" Laying it flat in her hand, she waited for the needle to move toward north, recalling her dad's orienteering lessons. But the arrow remained still. She jiggled it. No dice. "Am I doing it right?" she whispered to Isaac.

"Sort of," he said, also whispering. "This one doesn't always point north."

"Oh, uh, okay. Worn out from years of directioning?"

"Ha! No, it's ... persnickety. Do you still want it?"

"Of course, I do! It's gorgeous. I love persnickety."

"Be sure to keep it safe. It's yours and only yours to wear. It's quite valuable, has an amazing and sordid history, and has been in the family for years, so take care of it. I'll fill you in on its story tomorrow when I take you to tea."

"Is that a promise?" Her mouth watered at the thought of proper English tea and biscuits. Isaac's company promised to leave her sides aching from laughter and her head full of fascinating information.

Once she slipped the compass over her head and it dangled against her chest, a shiver traveled through her, goose bumps popping up on her arms. Rubbing them, she examined it again. Minute, neat words, engraved on the flip side, were framed with other swirls and decoration. *Dulci distinet a domo domum.* "Latin for something like 'home sweet home,' I think?"

"Yes, very good, Jenny," said Connie.

"Okay, next part," Isaac said, passing her the envelope he still held. "I apologize for the wrapping. This traveling hasn't allowed for much else."

"Ooph! That's heavy. Whatever could it be?" Feigning ignorance, she shook it, smelled it, pretended to lick it. "Another puppy?" Moose barked and wagged his tail, eliciting a few giggles. "Sorry buddy, I don't think it's a puppy."

From the wrapping slid a thick, leather-bound book with worn edges and folded corners. The dark leather smelled oily and musty. "Oh, that's beautiful," said her mom. "And an antique, I think."

"What's the title, Jenny?" said Hunter.

"*Fantastical Fairy Tales, Fables, and Legends: Not for the Faint of Heart.*" She read the title aloud. "Sounds exciting, and ominous."

"These are not ordinary fairy tales, and you can't find this book at the library or bookstore. There are only a few copies of it left, in fact," her uncle said.

"Uh, how scary are these stories?" A quiver tingled the length of her spine.

Isaac held each of her shoulders. "Oh, Jenny. You are braver than you think. I wouldn't give you anything you couldn't handle." The sincerity in his voice went far beyond comforting a few jitters about a scary book.

She furrowed her brow. "Uh, thanks. I'll probably be fine. I mean, it's just a book."

"Yes. You will, I have no doubt. You must be." The last words were a whisper. He seemed to forget she was there. Straightening and releasing her arms, he moved past the intense moment between them and clapped his hands together. "Now, I heard something about cake?" he said, striding into the kitchen, leaving her alone with her gifts.

The book was heavy in her arms, and she pressed her back against the wall. His strange, penetrating words left her perplexed.

"Ouch!" The skin on her neck pinched under the weight of the compass. Still focused on her uncle, she ran a finger under the chain to loosen it up and cocked her head. "What is that?" The whirring she heard stopped a moment later, and with a shrug, she followed everyone else into the kitchen, the pendant heavier than she had anticipated.

ooooo 🐾 ooooo

Kissing her parents and uncle goodnight, Jenny trudged upstairs early to read. Her room above the garage glowed with moonbeams from the skylight cut into the slanted ceiling. A black, metal-framed bed rested in the corner of the room, and opposite it, an ancient rolltop desk her parents had bought at a garage sale where she kept her favorite drawing pencils and sketch paper. Several books were scattered on the desk too, waiting to be read. Muted wood, white, and black tones suited her austere taste in decor, accented by several framed charcoal drawings, green pillows, and knickknacks.

With her newest book on the bed, she flipped through a few pages. Words like "horror" and "witch" and "death" jumped off the pages. She thumped it shut, saving it for a sunny day outside, not a dark night alone in her room.

Instead, she picked one of her favorites, a lesser known version of *Robin Hood*. In her comfiest black leggings and a long, gray tank top, she snuggled into her overstuffed chair by the window, pulling a tan and green plaid blanket across her legs. Opening to the first page, she read the familiar first lines. *Long ago, in the deep, dark wood of Sherwood Forest, Robin of Loxley came upon the wagon of the local butcher, laden with choice meats, lumbering on toward the home of the onerous Sheriff of Nottingham.*

Something hummed against her sternum, interrupting the story, and she palmed the compass, feeling it vibrate. "What in the world?" Pulling it from under her shirt, she examined it. "Whoa!" Air rushed from her lungs. The silver needle moved from left to right, right to left, like a metronome, back and forth, back and forth, tick tock, tick tock. Startled, her fingers fumbled the compass, and it fell, the chain catching it. The ticking stopped. Silence encompassed the room. Leaning forward, the needle pointed straight at the book, dragging her towards it.

Lifting *Robin Hood*, she searched for a magnet or something else that might trigger her compass. The needle pointed with such determination toward the book, it lifted the compass away from her body. "What the heck?"

When she lowered the book, the compass moved with it, to the left, then to the right. Sitting taller in her chair, she laid the book in her lap and pulled the mysterious gift over her head. With fingers entwined in the chain, she lowered it toward the first page of *Robin Hood*.

It approached the paper. The needle spun, faster and faster. A light flashed, and the moment it touched paper, the compass fell through the pages and pulled her right along with it.

Whistling wind and words swirled past. Breathing became a challenge. Letters and paragraphs disappeared in a second. Brown branches, shiny leaves, and mossy ground took their place. She crashed into something solid. "Ooph." Groaning, gasping, confused. Checking to make sure her limbs were in working order, she wiggled her toes and rotated her wrists, then sat up and took in her surroundings.

Dark woods, rays of sunlight, thick underbrush expanded in every direction. The plaid blanket from her room tangled her legs, and she pulled it loose, hugging it. Something rustled to her right, but voices ahead snagged her attention. Deep voices, and, by their accents, British.

Chewing her lip and rubbing her head, her brain tried to sort things out. A dream? Had she fallen asleep reading? The compass hummed a few times against her skin, reminding her of its presence. She held it, studied it, scanned the woods, studied it again, gawked at the sky, and gaped at the compass.

No, no way. Impossible. Absolutely not. She pinched her arm. "Ow!" Rubbing it, she chastised herself for going full strength on the squeeze. "I thought pinches didn't hurt in dreams," she whispered, panic rising in her throat. Her hands trembled. *I have to figure out where I am.* Pushing her fear aside, she snuck toward the nearby conversation, staying hidden in the undergrowth.

The voices grew louder, and an oxcart came into view. It creaked, heavy with meat, circled by armed men in leathers. One stood taller, conversing with the plump man on the cart. Her pulse raced even more. *Robin and the Butcher!*

The details of what the man and the butcher discussed were lost in their hushed tones. She blinked, and the two men had switched places. Robin fixed a patch on one eye and gave his men the once over with the other. "Aye, lads!" he said. His bellowing voice carried all the way to her hiding spot. "Remember the plan. Be ready for us. I'm off for a bit o' fun with the ol' Sheriff of Nottingham."

He rode up the lane and his men dispersed into the woods. The soft forest floor muted her butt hitting the ground. "No way," she said, covering her mouth to hold in more words lest she be overheard.

*I am actually in a book. I'm in* my *book! That guy is Robin Hood! Those are the Merry Men! This is Sherwood Forest! Maid Marian is here somewhere!* The beauty of the moment passed in an instant. Reality sunk in. *I'm in a book. Not a very safe book. And, oh gosh, how do I get home?* Her stomach lurched. Blood pounded through her veins. The woods blurred. *Oh, sweet mercy, don't lose your mind, Jenny Fletcher.* Deep, harried breaths staved off panic. *I sound like a woman in labor.* She stood. Sweat trickled along her backbone and soaked into her leggings, but she refused to leave her blanket behind.

*Okay, what's my next move?* Leaning against a tree, she rested her head on the rough bark, thinking. If things stayed true to the story, Robin's men planned to run a herd of deer through this glen not too far into the future—part of their "fun" with the sheriff. *Not an ideal location to hide.* Her eyes darted here and there, looking for an alternative.

A rustling in the brush to her left caught her attention, and she dropped to a crouch, on high alert. Any movement? A footfall? A deer? A herd of deer? No, a bird fluttering up from the undergrowth, flying away into the sky. Merely a bird. Nothing more. *Okay, what's next? And how do I get home?*

Following Robin remained an option, but his story resolved like most of his stories did—tricking the sheriff and taking his money. It always ended with Robin taking the bad guy's money.

Following him and the Merry Men held promises of adventure. However, the possibility of the gang catching her nauseated her a little. Though Robin would not hurt her, some of his rougher men might not be so accommodating.

That left option number two: find the brave and beautiful Maid Marian, one of her own literary heroes, and see what happened.

Maid Marian made an appearance in several future chapters, but Jenny wondered if she might find her now. *I could just see what she is up to? If I am going to be stuck in* Robin Hood *for a while, I may as well make good use of my time.*

The leaves beneath her crunched when she stood, listening. Confident in her solitude, she tiptoed toward the lane. A twig snapped behind her, and she froze with a gasp, glancing to her former hiding spot. Nothing appeared amiss, and after a few seconds, she squared her shoulders, lifted her chin, and walked into plain sight.

Standing in the narrow road, glowing with dusty, golden light, she stared in the direction Robin had gone, toward Nottingham. In one motion, she whirled and headed the other way, away from Robin, the sheriff, and the Merry Men.

# Chapter Four

The Castle Fitzwalter sprawled across the horizon in the precise location Jenny expected to find it, thanks to the hours she'd spent studying the hand-drawn map in the front of her book. At the base of its walls and along the lane rose a village buzzing with life. Farmers and craftsmen sold their goods, and friends conversed in the vile, muddy streets. Unpleasant smells assaulted her nose, history lessons coming to life regarding the odiferous and unsanitary conditions medieval townspeople wallowed in.

One shabby cottage stood on the outskirts of the village, the roof thatched and drooping. She snuck behind one of its outbuildings, careful to keep her feet out of the thick sludge, a plan forming in her mind. Sauntering up to the Castle Fitzwalter and asking for Maid Marian dressed in leggings and wrapped in a dirty blanket might not get her very far. Gaining access to the Castle required some preparation.

The wind chilled her, and she pulled the blanket closer. Even with a vigorous shake, bits of leaves still clung to it, adding to her ragamuffin appearance. *New clothes must be part of my plan.* Her current clothing had helped her stay hidden in the woods, but here, in public, she stood out like a sore thumb.

"Oy, you there, girl!" A dirty woman, bent and frail, with ragged, stringy hair, had hobbled out the door of the cottage and spotted her despite what appeared to be a wandering eye. "Yes, you, wee one. I see ya back there. Come hither. Let Granny Bea have a better look at ya." Jenny shrunk into her blanket. "I ain't gonna hurt ya. I might even be willing to help ya," the woman said. "For a fee, of course." Her cackle did little to convince Jenny of her sanity or trustworthiness.

"I have no money," Jenny said in her practiced British accent. All those hours of reading *Harry Potter* aloud and doing the voices might pay off. "But I have a few things worth trading." She spun the turquoise bracelet on her wrist beneath the blanket and edged nearer to the tattered woman, stopping at a reasonable distance, prepared to run in case things went south.

*I wonder if Granny Bea knows what high ladies wear under their dresses?* Her mind raced, attempting to put together some sort of on-the-spot strategy. *Bloomers and petticoats, right? Or leggings and tank tops, perhaps? Could I convince her I'm a high lady?*

"Have you got anything I could wear? I'm standing here in my underthings after our carriage was ransacked by bandits!" Feigned emotion swelled with each word. "They stole my dress, the ruffians, and rode off in the carriage, leaving my driver and guards injured and me alone in the woods. Maid Marian is the friend of a friend, and I've come to beg her help, but I fear I will not even be allowed to see her should I arrive clad in these. Thank heavens for this blanket I managed to recover." Jenny shook it again, giving Granny Bea a glimpse of what she wore beneath it.

Holding out her arm and allowing the bracelet to glisten in the sun, she continued. "I'd be happy to trade you this silver bracelet for a simple dress and a moment to collect myself after such a terrible ordeal." With a jiggle, the bracelet rattled, and the turquoise stones reflected in the sun.

Granny Bea leaned in, eyeballing the stones. "Oh my, 'tis a pretty thing." A pensive silence followed. "Aye, I'll trade—for the bracelet *and* the blanket. I have a dress for ya, though I doubt it's as lovely as the one stolen from ya. Those scoundrels. But, 'tis a blessing they stole your dress and not your drawers too!"

Jenny forced a laugh when Granny Bea cracked herself up, hooting there on the porch. "I have salves and herbs for them cuts on your arms and face. I could repair them undergarments too."

A stinging spot swelled on her cheek, crusty beneath her touch. It hadn't hurt until that moment. A few tears in the knees of her leggings framed scrapes on the exposed skin.

"Oh aye, you're a pretty one. Your hair's a bit wild, though." Granny Bea eyeballed Jenny's tresses, disheveled from her fall and subsequent hike through Sherwood Forest. While attempting to subdue it, Jenny fished out a stick and two thin leaves lodged in her locks.

Granny Bea sniggered again, her yellow tooth glistening, one eye on Jenny and the other meandering somewhere else. "Come in, come in. Let's see what Granny Bea can conjure up today," she said, shambling into the hovel.

Jenny hesitated. *This might be the worst idea ever.* She stood on the stoop, weighing her options. The second she determined she'd better run, Granny

Bea stuck her head out the door with a grotesque grin. "Well, ya coming?"

Several windows in the larger of the two rooms let in enough light for Jenny to see the plethora of dried herbs hanging on the walls and from the rafters. It smelled earthy and calm and much more pleasant than the streets outside. Basins and baskets covered the available workspaces, overflowing with powders and petals and stems. Vials and jars in a variety of colors rested among the dry things. Several candles burned on the largest worktable, the wax dripping in long rivulets.

Shuffling into the other room where a cot sat in the corner, Granny Bea lifted the lid of a battered trunk at the foot of the bed and drew out a simple wool dress with a dark pinkish hue. "Will this do, then? 'Twas my granddaughter's afore she ran off with the miller's son."

Jenny held up her gorgeous, shiny bracelet next to the plain dress. "This bracelet is made of silver and beautiful stones called turquoise, a rarity in these parts and quite valuable. And my blanket is warm and new. Perhaps an additional shawl or cloak to ward off the cool winds could better entice me into the trade? I'm sure someone like you knows a fair trade when you see one." Granny Bea beamed at the compliment and dug a bit more. She paused before whipping a long, chocolatey brown piece of cloth from the chest with embroidered flowers and leaves along the edges in oranges, yellows, greens, and pink. "Oh, Granny Bea, how lovely." The fabric begged for her to touch it.

Granny Bea sighed. "'Twas my daughter's on her wedding day. We dyed it with walnuts. Stained our skin something fierce!" Sadness lingered on her face. "She passed many years ago, and though I'm quite fond of it, she'd be wanting it to be used, not hiding here in the wee trunk. Her daughter's the one who has run off, and she's likely married now, or dead. She has no use for it. I'll trade ya the pink dress and shawl for yer bracelet and blanket. If anyone can get that detritus gone from the blanket, 'tis old Granny Bea. And I'll throw in some salves for your injuries. Would that be to your liking? Perchance, if my granddaughter returns, she'll have something fancy awaiting her. Something from her granny. Plus, yer a gentle gal, and Granny Bea is feeling generous today."

The dress slipped over her head, fitting easily on top of her tight pajamas. The fabric warmed her in an instant. "That's a pretty necklace you're wearing there." Granny Bea pointed at the compass. "My granddaughter wore a necklace too. Said a tinker gave it to her for being gentle on the eyes. I didn't believe her. Reckon she stole it. She never was an honest one, that girl." *I reckon her necklace differed quite a bit from mine.* Jenny suppressed a giggle.

Holding the shawl in her shaky, swollen hands, Granny Bea invited her to wrap up with it. Pulling it close, Jenny rubbed her cheek against the soft cloth. The woman's timeworn face brightened, somehow sweet and almost pleasant despite the wandering eye and solitary tooth. *Wow, teeth make quite a difference. I've got to start flossing once I get home.*

Placing the bracelet in the trunk, Granny Bea faced her and held up a finger. "One more thing." Bustling about the cottage, she dug in a corner and murmured, "Perfect!" A braided leather belt appeared, and with one movement, it encircled Jenny's waist. "Now you aren't wearing a bed sheet. You'll make someone a fine wife, one day, pretty girl."

"I'm only sixteen, Granny Bea!" Jenny said with a laugh.

"Aye, you are a bit young to my mind, though people here marry off 'round your age quite often. Live a bit first, then settle," she said, sucking on her tooth. "Come on and sit for a minute and let me tend to your wounds."

The chair at the rickety table wobbled when Jenny perched on its edge, afraid it might collapse with one wrong move. Granny Bea gathered a few powders and liquids from various corners of the room. With care and confidence, she measured, weighed, and mixed them into a paste, then rolled Jenny's sleeves to her elbows. Several red, angry scratches welted on her arms, but the herby paste rubbed on smooth under Granny Bea's practiced touch. The cut slashed across her cheek smarted when the medicine touched it but subsided with some fanning. "It shouldn't scar," she said, patting Jenny's arm.

Shadows shifted on the table. "Oh, the time! I must be on my way," Jenny said. "Thank you for the dress and the doctoring. You've been most kind."

Granny Bea pressed her mouth into a grim line and gripped Jenny's wrist. "Promise me one thing, a trade for the belt. Promise Granny Bea you will come and visit me again. I'm hard up for company these days. Please." The wrinkles on her face drooped, and Jenny's heart softened even more toward this odd, elderly gal.

"I promise, Granny Bea, and, again, many thanks." Jenny hugged her, and frail arms returned the gesture.

"I'll think of you when I wear this." The shawl shifted with a gentle breeze from the open door. Jenny paused in the entry, the stench of the village hitting once again.

"Oh, another thing," Granny Bea said from the shadowy room. "Mind your tail, wee one. I thought I saw a straggler following ya. Be mindful. There's bandits about."

With a final goodbye, Jenny treaded along the dirt path leading behind the main buildings in the town. Heeding Granny Bea's advice, she avoided anyone she saw, ducking behind sheds and fences to hide, keeping careful attention for anyone following her.

Stopping behind an inn to gather her bearings, the smell of beer, stew, and bodies floated through an open window overhead along with deep voices speaking one click above a whisper.

"There's been no sign of Robin Hood today, so now would be a good time to get to Maid Marian," one of the men said. Leaning in, hoping to hear more, she quieted her breathing.

Another plotter coughed, the spoke in a wavering voice. "The sheriff reckons he can get to Robin Hood by going for Maid Marian. Me, I think it's a bit of a shame, her being such a generous and kind lady, but I dare not go against orders from the sheriff." He sounded afraid.

"What's our plan?" a third person whispered.

These awful men outlined their strategy for snatching Maid Marian, and with each minute, Jenny's ire rose at their brazen attitude toward kidnapping. Jaw clenched. Sweat trickled. She scowled until her brow ached. *I must warn the lady of her impending doom and impede the success of this ridiculous scheme.*

"Wait," she whispered, threads of reality tapping at her brain. "I know how this story ends. Maid Marian isn't kidnapped. Someone or something intervenes. So, does she even need me? Or am I the person who intervenes?" Her foot tapped against the packed dirt, and she crossed her arms, trying to sort out the compass, the story, and her role in things.

The sound of the criminals' chairs scraping backwards grabbed her attention. "Guh, I don't know how it works, but I can't just stand here and pretend it's not happening!" Single-minded and focused, she pushed off the wall and dashed through the muddy streets, skirt and shawl flapping behind her.

The men pursuing Maid Marian sounded large and dangerous and no match for an unarmed girl. But a girl with a weapon might stand a fighting chance. Step one: obtain a bow and arrows. *Dad always says to hope for the best and plan for the worst.* Thankful he had worked with her for hours on her archery technique, her body tingled and belly roiled at the thought of having to aim at a real person, or kind of real person. *This is so confusing, but here we go. Those hours shooting arrows in the backyard are about to pay off. Ugh! I hope I don't puke.*

Robin Hood and his men were busy tormenting the Sheriff of Nottingham, so she dashed to the edge of town and headed off the road, searching for landmarks and clues to their hideout's location. *The hours I spent staring at that map sure are coming in handy.* Her soft, dirt-caked slippers allowed her to glide silently through the forest. She zipped on, down a hill and beyond a rise until the trees thinned to a clearing housing a number of tents and shelters, a large fire pit at the center. The camp stood quiet, no movement, no sounds, everyone off participating in Robin's daring ruse against the sheriff.

A smaller bow and a quiver of arrows leaned forgotten against one of the larger shelters, along with other weapons, covered by a makeshift roof. *Ooh, the weapons cache!* A squeal of delight resounded in the camp. *Yikes, that was louder than I anticipated.* The bigger bows were too heavy for her, but the little one, perhaps for a child or a slight woman, ought to do.

With a few yards left before reaching the weapons, she stopped mid-step, gasping. Placing her raised foot on the ground, she squatted to eyeball the thin, almost invisible, string pulled taut at knee level, surrounding the weapons cache. *Clever Robin.* She chuckled, wiping sweat from her chin.

A long stick yanked from the brush worked to trigger the string, and she rushed behind a tree, sinking to her heels and ducking.

In the seconds following, a huge log suspended unseen in the canopy came swinging from on high, flying through her original path, a bowling ball set to drop any "pins" in its path. *Holy moly!* Though unnecessary, she shrank even lower when the trunk flew by. It swung to the shelter and reversed, back and forth, until it stopped, near where she squatted. *Well, that would've been effective.*

Scooting below the log and over the string, she grabbed the bow and arrows, slung them on her shoulder, and retraced her path to the castle. Now she wore the right clothes and carried the right weapons. Next on the list: find Maid Marian and save her life.

# Chapter Five

For a castle, Fitzwalter fell into the category of normal—neither ornate or plain, towering or squat. It appeared strong, somewhat foreboding, and defendable. A high curtain wall overlooked the village, but to the left, Jenny found the wall lowered, interspersed with several thick, barred gates allowing glimpses into a colorful garden. She'd worked up a sweat running through Sherwood Forest and tucked the shawl into her belt, adding a layer to the skirt and making it a little fancier, attempting to avoid the "muddy vagrant" vibe.

A pleasant, sing-song voice wafted by. She sidled to one of the gates and peeked past the bars. Strolling in the garden, a thin but able-bodied young woman chatted with a grayer matron with full, dimpled cheeks. The younger woman wore her thick, dark hair braided and twisted with several flowers tucked into it. Her pale blue dress flowed to the ground, adding to the beauty of the gardens. *Maid Marian!* Her friend, older by at least twenty years, with silver and copper hair wound into a bun, wore a dark green dress with cream lace, tailored to her ample proportions. Though they spoke in hushed voices, Jenny detected mentions of "Robin Hood" and "marriage" and "in danger." Arm in arm, lost in conversation, they ambled along, oblivious to anything lurking beyond the castle fortifications.

But danger approached, and Jenny followed the women from outside the ramparts, their unknown intermediary, on alert for anything dubious. Dropping the bow from her shoulder, she slid a trembling thumb along the string, her tongue sticking to the roof of her mouth. *Can I do this?*

A stick snapped to her left, and she ducked behind the nearest tree. Inching past it for a better view, she froze. A dirty, rag-tag man with a greasy beard stalked toward the wall, wielding a knife. At its base, he searched for something, peeling away a thick rope someone had slung from inside the garden. Biting the knife like a pirate, he ascended the line, awkward and unsteady.

Duty overrode uncertainty, and Jenny, far more adept at climbing than this guy, hiked her skirts and pulled herself onto the garden wall. She found holds by instinct, cursing her dress when it got in the way. One eye on her route, and one on the intruder, she raced him the top. Marian and her friend continued their promenade.

With a burst of speed and strength, Jenny hauled herself onto the top of the wall and squatted to maintain her balance. How could she warn them? Shouting might give her position away, but she must alert them of their impending doom somehow. An arrow aimed at the castle wall, well above the women's heads, clunked and tumbled to the ground at their feet.

Marian bent to investigate the clatter, then rose, alert, scanning the garden, the arrow gripped in her fist. The blood drained from her face when she saw the armed villain drop to his feet inside the garden. Marian pushed the older woman, instructing her to run for the safety of the castle, and she obliged, shouting for Marian to follow, but Marian made to take a stand against the attacker. A sword glinted in her grip, and she took cover behind a well. The intruder sauntered toward her, amused. He swung his knife in arcs, sneering.

Another arrow found its way onto Jenny's bowstring. Her aim started off shaky, adrenaline pumping through her veins. The compass hummed against her skin in slow pulses, inviting her to breathe with it. And she did—one slow inhale, one slow exhale, find her mark, take aim ... fire!

The bad guy stumbled and fell with a yelp. Her arrow quivered in his thigh, right where she'd aimed it. Air left her lungs. Muscles trembled. Nauseated, thankful she hadn't killed him, she swallowed, trying not to vomit.

Marian leered over him, her sword at his throat. "Guards!" she yelled, focused on the moaning criminal.

Soldiers marched the limping man away. Marian's friend emerged from the castle, and the two women approached the garden wall where Jenny waited. Would her shaky quads support her if she chose to jump and greet them? It wasn't the neighbor boy standing below her this time. Landing on her butt was not an option.

Maid Marian smiled at her. "And who might we thank for saving us this sunny and surprising day?"

Jenny inhaled, white-knuckled her bow, and jumped. She landed on her feet, knees bent. *That worked out better than expected!* After dusting off her dress, she stood tall and proud. "'Tis I, Jenny Fletcher." Her voice trembled but steadied at Marian's kind countenance. "I believe you may have a traitor in your midst. The intruder climbed this rope." She marched to the blameworthy item and wiggled it. "See? It's anchored here, inside the walls."

Marian nodded, troubled. "Aye, I shall speak with the groundskeeper and head guard. We don't fear for much here."

"And yet you keep a sword in the folds of your dress," Jenny said.

"Indeed. Well observed, Jenny Fletcher. An apt name for such a true shot with an arrow. You saved us today." Maid Marian bobbed a small bow. "Thank you, little Jenny, from the depths of my soul. I'm sure Lady Hildy, my wiser and surprisingly fleet-footed friend, feels the same," she goaded the other woman, whose bosom shook with silent titters.

Still tickled and wiping cheerful tears, Lady Hildy managed to speak. "Milady, old Hildy is no warrior! Oh no, I will always flee a fight. 'Tis in everyone's best interest!" She tilted forward, examining Jenny's compass. "My, what a pretty necklace you have there, Jenny Fletcher. Might I see it?"

Jenny displayed it to the ladies.

"My vision is not what it once was, and I cannot read the inscription." Lady Hildy squinted and moved the compass away, attempting to focus the words.

"If I may," Jenny said. "*Dulci distinet a domo domum.*"

The last word rolled off her tongue. An unseen force yanked her skyward. Maid Marian, Lady Hildy, and the Castle Fitzwalter disappeared. The air was sucked from her lungs. She slammed into something creaky and moaned from the impact. After a few seconds, once the jarring crash had worn off, she regained her focus. Familiar white ceilings with a skylight sloped above her, and her beloved rolltop desk perched in its rightful place. She breathed a sigh. Home.

On her bed, she reeled from the rough transition between worlds. Warm blankets welcomed her, and she squeezed the comforter. *I made it.*

# Chapter Six

The clock flipped to 9:42 p.m. Had it been a dream, those few hours in *Robin Hood?* Jenny's fingertips smoothed the pink wool dress and untied the floral shawl from her waist. Something poked her in the kidney—the quiver of arrows—and the small bow still tapped against her tricep. *It happened. I was there, in the book. Oh my gosh!* She bent forward, excitement building in her belly. Dirty fingers clenched the compass. Her heart pounded. *Best present ever!*

The bookshelf on her wall, filled from one end to the other and top to bottom, glowed with new meaning, each book an invitation into countless adventures. Warm and ticking against her sternum, the compass awaited her next choice. Maybe *The Black Stallion,* or *Alice in Wonderland,* or *Little House on the Prairie?* So many worlds to visit, villains to defeat, heroes to meet. How much did Isaac know? *Did he plan to tell me tomorrow during our tea? Or was he unaware of its capabilities?* She sprang up from the bed. "I've got to talk to him!"

Sprinting to the guest room, the clatter of arrows in the quiver echoed in the narrow corridor. *Knock, knock, knock.* "Isaac!" she said. "Isaac!" No answer.

"Isaac?" One push on the door, its hinges creaking, revealed a dark, untouched, empty room. "Hmmm. Maybe they are downstairs? Lights blazed in the kitchen and den, but no one answered her. "Mom?" she called. "Dad?" She ran upstairs to their bedroom. Also empty. Finding her phone on her bedside table, one text from Josh asking if he could stop by popped up. *I'll get back to him later.*

Next, she checked the garage. "Mom? Dad? Isaac?" Both cars remained cold in their parking spots.

The side door to the garage squeaked when she opened it, a breeze lifting her curls.

*It's a gorgeous night. Maybe they went for a walk. Or maybe they are looking for me! Yikes, I hope they aren't mad.*

Passing her truck and Isaac's little sports car parked in the driveway, something crunched beneath her slippers. "Ouch!" She lifted a foot to investigate. The conch shell from the front seat of Isaac's car lay shattered on the concrete by the car door. *Whoa, what happened here?* A modicum of dread formed in the pit of her belly, putting her on high alert.

Leaving behind the mess in the drive, she continued to the front stoop, searching the dark for anything suspicious. "Hey!" someone said. She gasped and jumped to the side, away from it, reaching for her bow.

"Whoa, don't shoot!" Someone stood in the darkness, arms lifted like a surrendered outlaw.

"Josh? Man, you scared me to death!" Pushing her hair from her forehead, she pressed her palm against it. "What are you doing here?"

"Sorry I scared you. I've been waiting here for a while." His voice sounded weird, nervous. "Um, have you seen my parents?"

"I haven't," she said, and he sagged. "Have you seen mine?"

"No. Yours are missing too? I went to the climbing gym again tonight with a friend, and when he dropped me off at my house, no one was home. No note. No text. My parents never leave without letting me know. Never ever." He paused, tapping something on his palm. "But I found this on the floor by the door. It's addressed to you. So, I came over to give it to you and ask if you knew anything. No one answered when I knocked, so I've just been waiting." He blanched beneath his tan skin. "I'm a little freaked out, Jenny."

He passed her the note. Wide-eyed and trembling, she tore into the en-velope, noting the red wax stamped with a TS sealing it. The parchment in-side contained one sentence. *Not all fairy tales have a happy ending—go to the Book.*

The compass thrummed against her chest, humming to life. Drawing it from inside her dress, she rested it flat on her palm. The needle spun and pointed to her house. "Come on." Grasping Josh's arm, she dragged him through the front door. The compass whirred as she bounced up the stairs two at a time, skirts swishing.

"What's with the outfit, Jenny?" Josh huffed behind her. "And the arrows?"

"I'll tell you in a second," she said, flying into her room. The compass pointed to the fairytale book, dead on.

"Is your necklace making that noise?" he said.

"Yes. I know, it's totally kooky-pants." *OMG, so kooky-pants.* "I'll explain ev-erything in a minute." She pushed away the rising dread, slowing her breath-ing, remaining calm. "If I disappear into this book, don't panic. I think I can get back." *Just say the magic Latin words on the compass to get home, right?*

*Fantastical Fairy Tales* rumbled. And glowed. The rolltop shook beneath it. Pencils tumbled to the floor.

Josh hauled her backward with him, pressure within the book straining against the heavy cover. With a burst of light, it blew open, blinding them. The flash lasted a second, but the afterglow remained. An envelope ejected from the book and floated onto the desk, like a leaf, quiet and still. Everything stopped when it landed. Not a sound. Nothing moved.

Josh blinked a few times and leaned in to investigate. "It says 'Jenny Fletcher and the black-haired boy' on it. Whaaaaaat is happening?" His whispery voice quavered.

Poor guy. His parents gone without a word. A strange note addressed to her on his foyer floor. Finding her dressed in a medieval costume. And now a large, leather-bound book spitting out a letter with their names scrawled on it. *Total insanity.*

"I'm not really sure." She lifted the letter with her fingertips, hesitant to even touch it. "Maybe it will have some answers. Stay nearby, please." She whispered the last part. He moved closer, the warmth of his arm on hers reassuring.

The same red wax seal, with the letters TS stamped into it, tore with little effort. Out dropped a parchment paper, thick and heavy, folded on itself several times. She peeled it apart and read the contents aloud.

*When friends and family disappear*
*It sets your heart to boiling*
*It's right for you to fret and fear*
*This Serpent's been re-coiling*
*She strikes with fury on this day*

*Her prey, the ones you love*

*You must seek the price to pay*

*You, the newest dove.*

*Gather the items laid before*

*They shan't be easy finds*

*Bring to my garden door*

*And I'll break your loved one's binds.*

*Then he can choose to stay with me*

*Or return unto his kind*

*He's blinded now, by love, you see*

*But I shall change his mind.*

*Come and find me, if you will*

*Be sure you are a good listener*

*Your four parents are stashed away*

*Your uncle, my special prisoner.*

She stopped reading, the words sinking in.

"Read that part again, Jenny."

Through tears and clenched teeth, she obliged. "Your four parents are stashed away, your uncle, my special prisoner." The paper fell from her grasp, drifting to the table.

Josh trembled, pale and panicking. "No, no. This is impossible. This person, TS, has our parents? It's a joke, right?"

"I don't think it's a joke, Josh," she said, putting the pieces together in her mind.

"We have to find them, Jenny. We have to! Where are they?" Slumped on her bed, his tears spilled onto his cheeks, fear mingled with grief and despair. He snatched the letter from the table and reread it to the end. "There's no way. I just saw them. Look, its signed 'The Sorceress.' Who is she? Jenny, who is The Sorceress? How does she know who you are? And how did a book shoot a letter to us? And why did you say you might disappear? And what's with the arrows?" Each question fired faster and with increasing volume.

The room grew close and hot. She backed away from the letter, bumping into her big chair. "Josh, I gotta ... I gotta go ... outside." And she fled, along the hall, descending the stairs, crossing the foyer, and through the front door, slamming right into someone on the stoop.

The figure seized her, eliciting a piercing scream that burned her throat. She struggled against his grip. "Jenny, Jenny dear!" A weathered, Scottish accent. "Hush Jenny, it's just me. Don't wake the neighbors."

"Mr. Neil, I'm so sorry! You scared me." He frowned at her tear stained face and wavering voice. "I'm sorry, but my parents, my parents ..." Collapsing against him, she wept, his strong arms supporting. He patted her hair, like a grandfather might, gentle and kind.

Loud thumps on the stairs interrupted them, Josh calling Jenny's name, frantic.

"I'm here," she said to him. "I'm okay."

"I heard you scream, and I thought ... I thought maybe she got you too." He dropped to the bottom step.

"I startled Jenny, though that was not my intention. I apologize if it frightened you. I mean you no harm."

Something about Mr. Neil allowed Josh's body to relax, helped him pull it together enough to ask, "What are you doing here, Mr. Neil?"

"Ah. Taking charge, my dear boy."

# Chapter Seven

"How did you know?" Josh said.

Mr. Neil sat on a bench in the Fletchers' foyer, and Jenny moved next to Josh. Moose snuck out from his hiding spot and wiggled at Mr. Neil's knees. "Of course you want some answers about what is happening. I can provide some of those answers and guidance for what should happen next." He peered at Jenny and leaned in toward her. "I know all about the Compass, Jenny. In fact, we go way back."

Her jaw dropped, and she grasped the pendant.

"That compass?" Josh said, jerking his thumb toward it. Mr. Neil nodded once.

"You know," she said, staring at Mr. Neil, both curious and suspicious. The Compass hummed and vibrated on its chain, saying hello to a long-time friend.

She gestured for Josh to confer with her in private. "If he knows about this compass, he can probably help us. Or he might kill us. I'm not sure which one."

"Fantastic," Josh said, heavy with sarcasm. "What is so special about it? Is it valuable or something?"

"It's ... maybe kind of magic," she said. "I imagine that makes it somewhat valuable."

"A magic compass? Really, Jenny?" Josh sounded incredulous, even at a whisper.

She clenched her jaw and flared her nostrils in frustration. "A book just blasted out a letter addressed to you and me saying our families have been kidnapped. Do you think I would joke about a magic compass at a time like this?"

"Oh yeah. Duh. Sorry. Okay, so, what if it's a trap? Maybe he wants it for himself, for whatever reason."

"What are our options?" she said. "We could trust this man, who appeared out of nowhere but seems like a decent, helpful fellow with some insider knowledge. Or, we could call the police and try to explain to them about the time a book vomited a letter, and someone claiming to be The Sorceress has stolen our parents and my uncle. The police would probably have us institutionalized for being insane because it sounds seriously *insane*. And then we'll never find our parents, and they'll be trapped with this horrible Sorceress forever!" She gasped, breathless.

Curtis Neil cleared his throat with a little cough. "In case you are concerned, I do not desire the Compass, not one bit, but I can tell you everything there is to know about it and train you how to use it. I can train you to do lots of things. Worthwhile things. Things to find the answers you seek and hopefully get your families home. No need to fear."

"He's our only hope to finding them," she whispered to Josh.

Josh faced the strange, neighborly man again. "Okay, Mr. Neil. What do we do next?"

"Come with me, move with intention, and bring the letter. And the dog."

They marched down the quiet lane, Mr. Neil's home looming ahead, dark and foreboding. The sturdy security gate swung toward them, and Jenny gulped. *Oh my word, we're actually doing this.* Moose trotted beside her, unconcerned. *I'll take that as a promising sign. Then again, Moose would welcome thieves with licks and bounces and lead them to Mom's jewelry after giving them the combination to the safe. Never mind! Unhelpful dog!*

"Follow me then," Curtis Neil said, leading them up a steep staircase to the front door. "Come in, come in. You too, Klaus."

"Oh, uh, my name is Josh," Josh said.

"I know, dear boy," replied Mr. Neil. "My dog is Klaus. You met earlier today." A tall, black Doberman emerged from the shadows and licked Josh's knuckles. Moose bounced with excitement at the prospect of a new friend. Klaus continued into the house, uninterested in puppies. Josh followed, fingertips resting on Klaus's steady, strong back.

Mr. Neil's impressive manse towered, dark and still. Once inside, however, soft lights and warm colors welcomed them.

He led them past a large staircase and along a well-lit hallway with greige-painted walls and expensive art. Most of the paintings depicted iconic characters from literature. The Queen of Hearts from *Alice in Wonderland,* Dickon from *The Secret Garden,* and Ishmael from *Moby Dick.* A statue of a regal lion stood on a pedestal in the corner. *Aslan?*

In the main part of the house, the kitchen, dining room, and den blended together in a classy, simple, spacious floor plan. Another staircase rose to their right, and a circular one in the corner led to a comfortable and cozy basement. There, Curtis Neil directed them to sit on one of the soft, brown leather couches. Klaus parked himself next to Josh, a living statue.

"He likes you," said Mr. Neil. "I imagine you want to know what has happened to your families and how I know about it. You see, I am the Guardian, and it's my job to be in the know."

From a cabinet, he removed a strange machine. A clouded glass sphere nestled in the middle of it, surrounded by various gears and metal arches. Dangling off the highest arch, a little bell jingled with the tiniest movement. Navigational markings etched into the dark, wooden platform smoldered with reflected light. The gears corresponded to the markings on the platform and arches themselves. He placed it on the coffee table in front of them, the bell tinkling until he stepped away.

"This is the Tracking Sphere. It illuminates and shifts gears when a particular brand of magic occurs within a certain radius, allowing someone like myself to pinpoint just where it happened." They gawked at him, and he surveyed them, little glasses perched on the end of his nose. "Pretty neat, eh? Today it notified me when an abundance of magic occurred at your house, Jenny. It happened five times, in succession, over several hours. I grew concerned, the intensity level becoming excessive, and the sphere glowed a color I've not ever seen before. A deep magenta. Quite troubling. I set off to investigate. We met on your porch, and there I saw the Compass."

The Compass purred, and he pointed to it. "Your necklace is a very special, very dangerous object. It possesses the power to change history. And I'm guessing your uncle gave it to you, though he failed to inform me of his decision. I doubt you killed him, which is the other option explaining your custody of it." She gasped, horrified at the thought. "Rest assured, I don't think you murdered your uncle," he said with all the gentleness in the world. "When you accepted it, it bound itself to you. Why Isaac passed it along is beyond me, but he has been a clever Keeper. I trust his decision."

"You know Isaac? And what did you call him? A Keeper? And what in the world is a Guardian? And how is this Compass bound to me? And what is it exactly? And that thing tracks magic? And why are my parents gone?" Her voice got louder and higher with each question, nearing hysteria by the end.

Josh's eyes got bigger and bigger with her increasing volume and pitch. Clearing his throat, he garnered their attention. "Mr. Neil, you might have to be a little more specific," he said, offering Jenny half a smile.

"Let me start at the beginning, then," replied Mr. Neil. "I will be brief."

Resting an elbow on his thigh, he launched into the story. "A century and a half ago, just after the Civil War, Arthur Abraham Neil found the Compass. It appeared on a book he had purchased from a foreign bookseller. It did not point north. You may have noticed. It did, however, lead him in a surprising direction—into stories." Mr. Neil waggled his eyebrows at them. Josh gaped, but Jenny remained still, unwavering, unsurprised. Mr. Neil noticed their different reactions, and so did Josh.

"Did you know?" Josh said in an accusatory tone, inspecting her weird outfit again, his mind obviously racing.

"I told you it was magic," she said, unmoving, waiting for Mr. Neil to continue his story.

He obliged. "Being a careful and kind man, Arthur used his toy for fun and adventure, engaging in the stories he loved. He bequeathed the Compass to his eldest daughter, who accepted it and carried on using it like her father had. She became the second Keeper."

"Whoa," Jenny said, tingles on her skin.

"Indeed. Arthur set up rules for the Compass, to protect it and the Keeper—rules to maintain order and balance. Because he loved his daughter and worried about her and the Compass, he entrusted the protection of both to his son, and he became the first Guardian. Since then, the Keeper and the Guardian have worked together, protecting the Compass and ensuring it doesn't fall into the wrong hands. The first Guardian was my great-grandfather, who passed along the Guardianship to my grandfather, then my father, and eventually to me." Josh shifted on the couch, listening to Mr. Neil's every word.

"Jenny, the second Keeper was your great-great-great grandmother, and she passed the job of Keeper down, eventually to your mom, who passed it to Isaac. And now, it has come to you."

"Wait, what? My mom? You know my mom? Wait a minute, are we related?" she said.

"I'm your great uncle."

"You're my *uncle*? But you like, run the other direction when you see me!"

"Jenny, your parents requested I not speak to you. They didn't want you involved in the dramas and dangers of the Compass until you were older and ready for it," he explained. "I guess they deemed you ready if they gave Isaac permission to gift it to you. Perhaps they were to inform me today—we had a meeting planned, your parents and I."

"Well, I can't even!" She spluttered, somewhere between anger, disappointment, and shock. "My parents knew! They knew. And they kept me away from you, my family." Shoulders slumped. "I wish they had managed this a bit differently. I'd have loved to know you better. You're so nice, Uncle Curtis. Can I call you uncle?"

"Of course, Jenny." Uncle Curtis's wrinkled face beheld her with such kindness, she almost cried again.

Josh interrupted their moment after ten seconds of silence. "Sorry, but I have a question. Honestly, I have about a hundred questions. For starters, why does the Keeper need a Guardian? Who wants the Compass?"

Uncle Curtis leaned forward to answer him. "At some point, certain powerful people got wind of the Compass's capabilities. They plotted to take it and use it selfishly, dangerously. Imagine going into a book and bringing home the bombs written into its battles or returning with murderous tyrants from a biography or some futuristic weapon with the potential to destroy the world. What about a monster or a deadly disease? They will do it if we aren't careful, if we don't stay diligent."

"Could someone bring back Napoleon? Or Genghis Khan? Or Alexander the Great?" Josh said. Both Jenny and Uncle Curtis started, surprised. "What? I like history," Josh said.

"A lovely thing to like, Josh, and to answer your question, theoretically yes, but they would be beholden to the limitations of how they were written in whatever book they came from. It wouldn't be the real McCoy, simply a literary version of him, or her. Arthur also discovered taking a person from a story, even for a short time, irrevocably changes it. Nothing else changes it permanently. A Keeper can go in and mess with everything, and the next time he or she picks up the book or decides to jump into it again, it will have returned to the original. Unless a character is pulled out. Then everything gets complicated."

"Whoa," Jenny said again. Josh just kept shaking his head.

"A Keeper must know the gravity of the weight they bear around their necks. And above all, they must not let anyone else acquire it," Uncle Curtis said, grave and sober. "This is why Arthur created the Guardian post. The Keeper needs help, a partner, someone to watch his or her back, and a friend who understands."

Josh nudged her. "I'll be with you too," he promised. "Another adventure together. No soccer to get in the way this time."

She smiled though her tears spilled, trickling to her jaw. "I'm afraid," she said.

"Yes, of course. Jenny, a Keeper must be brave, but being brave does not mean the absence of fear. Being brave means doing what needs doing even if you are afraid," Uncle Curtis said.

"My mom says that to me all the time," she said.

"Why ever use it, if it's so dangerous? Why not just hide it forever?" Josh said.

Massaging his brow, Uncle Curtis exhaled. "Oh, Josh. If only it were that easy." He pointed to the Compass. "This is not the sole magic necklace. There are more out there. We call them the Lesser Charms."

"Shut up!" Jenny said. Uncle Curtis frowned, startled at her response, and she backpedaled. "I mean, not really. Don't actually shut up. I'm just surprised. Please, please keep going."

Uncle Curtis huffed under his breath. "They aren't as powerful as this one, thankfully. That would be quite the mess."

"Where did they come from?" Jenny said.

"Ah, I wondered when you would ask. Years ago, some dubious people kidnapped Arthur Neil and forced him to take them into a book where they stole the Lesser Charms. These necklaces possess a variety of capabilities. For example, one might allow a person to travel into stories, but they can't transport anything to our world. Or they can go from story to story but not stay in our world for long, a fish out of water. And a few of them operate quite differently than yours. The Keeper and Guardians of the most powerful Charm," he nodded to the Compass, "work diligently to keep the stories intact and our world safe from people with the other ones. We also work to find them and take them out of circulation. To date, we have seventeen. We believe there are at least that many more out there still."

"Dang," Josh whispered.

Uncle Curtis reclined into the sofa and took the Sorceress's letter from his jacket pocket, crossing his legs and shaking out the parchment. "But for now, let's worry about our current quandary—this evil, conniving harpy who has entered our lives in most a dramatic fashion." He held the letter a little higher towards them. "Did you read the entirety of it?"

Jenny said no, but Josh answered, "I did. She included a ransom list, and it's a bunch of stuff from fairy tales, I think."

"Let's have a gander then." Uncle Curtis pushed his reading glasses further up his nose and scanned the letter. "Ah, here it is ..."

*Gather the chicken finger bone*

*And the sharpened spindle that's cursed*

*Bring them both before my throne*

*Or your uncle's plight will grow worse.*

*Then the dagger of the sea-maid*

*And the wicked stepsister's toe*

*Coins like the ones Jack waylaid*

*Beware his monstrous foe.*

*Bring these items all to me*

*And question not my end*

*Within my walls, waiting I'll be*

*On you I must depend.*

*Think ye hard on where I am*

*And what I do not need*

*Or no hair of me you'll see*

*And greens you shall not eat*


*You have half a year.*

*Sincerely, and with kindest regards,*


*The Sorceress*

"Wow, quite daring to call yourself 'The Sorceress'—a bit pretentious, don't you think?" Uncle Curtis chuckled. "So, the chicken finger bone? Obviously *Hansel and Gretel*, which is just the worst and most depressing story. What a place to start." He tossed the letter onto the coffee table in disgust. "This blootered boot is hell-bent on making you do her dirty work."

Josh and Jenny exchanged a confused expression. *Blootered boot?* He silently mouthed the words to her, shrugging. She shared his uncertainty.

Uncle Curtis kept on talking, either ignoring their exchange or oblivious to it. "I'm so sorry you are in this mess, Jenny. And you too, Josh. I'm not sure how your family fits into the picture, but you have a choice to make." His gaze darted to the door and then to the young man once more.

Anger burned in Josh's dark pupils. "I'm in this, sir. The Sorceress did something to our parents. I'll do whatever it takes to help save them." He gulped and choked on his words. "If they are still, I mean ... Are they still alive?"

"I don't know, Josh," Uncle Curtis said. "Until we possess more information, I'm not comfortable saying yes or no. I won't lie to you. But I will tell you to have hope. Hope will drive you on to find them. You cannot give up."

The leather couch stretched and moved when Josh slouched against it, brooding. His knee pressed into Jenny's quad, his toe tapping the floor. Cracking his knuckles, teeth grinding, rage and fear radiated off of him, hot and contagious. "I won't, sir," he told Uncle Curtis. "I'm in."

# Chapter Eight

Josh's commitment to helping find their parents allowed Jenny a reprieve from her emotions, and she leaned against him.

"Uncle Curtis, should we call the police? I mean, there will be people wondering where we have gone, what has happened. They will have questions ... so many questions," she said, her mind less jumbled and functioning with some level of clarity and logic.

"Oh! My sister!" Josh jerked forward, panicked, emotions un-reigned once more.

Pressing his palms together, Uncle Curtis peered at them. "Fear not," he said. "We already have plans in place. You must remain hidden, at least until your parents return, and I'll invite you to stay here. It's private, secure, and I have plenty of room and quite an extensive basement and property. I will see to it your houses are secured and cared for. Jenny, your family will have left the country due to unforeseen circumstances regarding your father's job. The news will travel around the climbing gym and homeschool network, so your friends don't worry, though I'm sure they will miss you. Feel free to send them postcards from your 'travels' and text them updates. We will make sure that happens. And I know enough of the neighbors to be able to spread the news of your temporary move in a way to not arouse any suspicion."

Jenny frowned. *Rae! Ugh, I can't even tell her a real goodbye.* She punched out a quick text to her, disregarding etiquette, telling Rae something had happened but not to worry.

"Josh, your family will have gone to visit your sister in England for an extended vacation. I will pull you from school, and you can send correspondence to some of your friends letting them know you are overseas. And don't worry about your sister ... I will figure something out. We may end up pulling her in. Sound good?"

They both gaped at him. Uncle Curtis clapped one time. "Okay then. It's all sorted. Now, it's time you slept. You both need rest. We must save your uncle, and soon. There is much to be done. Your rooms are upstairs on opposite halls. Tomorrow, we train. Well, you train. I just drink coffee and work on sorting this entire mess out."

"You mean, we don't start on this list right away?" Jenny asked, lifting the letter.

"Oh lass, I wish. Facing the tasks demanded by the Sorceress and dealing with her at the end will require a measure of skills neither you nor Josh currently has. But we can teach you, and we will teach you. Time is of the essence, but you do nobody any good if you die on the first mission, Keeper. Now, off to bed."

Trudging up the stairs to their respective rooms, Jenny slapped her thigh. "Shoot! I forgot to ask him what he meant by 'we' when he spoke about training. Dangit! Who else is involved? Some long-lost aunt I've never heard of?"

They found Josh's room at the top of the stairs on the hallway to the left, and Jenny's at the far end of the hall straight ahead, marked with their names and containing some of their belongings. Josh said a soft goodnight, and they parted ways.

Dropping her dress into a pile, along with dirty slippers and a bow and quiver, she climbed into bed. Moose followed her, diving deep into the fluffy comforter. Silky sheets lured her to sleep, but she took a second to run a finger along the binding of *Emma* resting on her bedside table. *One of my favorites. How did they know?* And she drifted off, too tired to be sad or to consider at length the night's events.

∞∞∞∞ ✿ ∞∞∞∞

The sounds of breakfast woke Jenny the next morning. *Ooh, is Mom making waffles?* With dark circles and a puffy face, she jolted upright in her bed. *This isn't my room.* Her throat tightened. *And it's not my mom making breakfast downstairs.*

A tear dripped onto the Compass. It hung heavy this morning. *Guh, I have to stop crying!*

The clothes she'd gotten from Granny Bea, folded with care on the big, upholstered chair by her bed, provided a needed distraction. *Did I put those there? I wasn't really in a folding mood last night. And Uncle Curtis didn't mention them, did he? I guarantee he noticed. There's not much that man misses. Gosh, does he think I'm just super weird and wear medieval stuff like it's my job? Or maybe, in his world, it's normal for people to carry weapons.* The bow and arrows leaned against the same chair, and her favorite stuffed bear lay by her pillow. *Emma* remained on her bedside table, opened to the first page.

"Wait, weren't you closed last night?" She flipped the stiff cover shut. Ignoring the sketchbook and pencils stacked beside *Emma*, she searched for something to wear to breakfast other than her pajamas.

*How did my stuff get here?* The tall wardrobe in the corner contained a mixture of her own clothes and a variety of other options, ranging from medieval lady to shabby peasant, Victorian society to black ninja. Dresses and stockings and puffy sleeves and sashes, shoes and veils and hats stuffed the antique wardrobe. Instead of serving wench, cowgirl, or superhero, she grabbed her favorite jeans and t-shirt and, once dressed, made her way downstairs.

A sweet, eggy smell wafting throughout the house beckoned her to the kitchen, and her belly growled. Josh, already at the large, farmhouse-style table, shoveled French toast into his mouth like he hadn't eaten in days. Uncle Curtis, sporting a black apron and chef's hat, flipped more French toast while scrambling eggs and sipping coffee. Klaus lounged at Josh's feet, and Moose greeted Jenny by biting at her shoe. He had slept curled next to her, warm and snug. She scratched his ears. "Oh no," she groaned. "Did someone let Moose out? Please say yes."

"And good morning to you too, Jenny," her uncle said without a pause in his cooking duties.

"Oh, uh, good morning. Of course. Sorry. It's just ... my mom usually lets him out, and she's not here." *Don't cry.*

"Don't worry about Moose. Ophelia let him out." Uncle Curtis said.

"Uh, okay, thanks. Would you mind telling us who Ophelia is?" she said, sitting on the bench opposite Josh at the table.

"No need! I'll gladly introduce myself." A smoky voice sounded from the basement stairs. Into the kitchen sauntered a petite but muscled woman, dressed in black athletic clothes, older than Jenny by ten years, and grinning from ear to ear. Her short, black hair flipped and curled, perfectly coiffed, and small touches of make-up enhanced her rich, latte-colored skin. Small, silver teardrops dangled from her earlobes, and a simple but sturdy watch graced her tiny wrist. Josh stopped chewing, gawking even. Lithe and controlled, she lowered to a chair, golden cat-eyes steadfast. "I'm Ophelia," she said. "You are both welcome to our home."

Glancing from Uncle Curtis to Ophelia, Jenny stuttered a moment. "Um, uh, are you two, uh, married?"

Ophelia slapped the table a few times, hooting with laughter. Uncle Curtis continued cooking, hiding a chuckle behind his coffee cup. Between giggles, Ophelia managed to say, "Oh no, girl ... I'm ... his daughter."

Now both Josh and Jenny swerved their attention to Uncle Curtis. "Shut up," Jenny whispered.

He beamed at Ophelia. *"Beloved* daughter. My wife hailed from North Africa, and Ophelia took after her in the way of looks. Her brother, Patrick, got more of my genes, poor, pasty fellow. Anyway, Ophelia is privy to everything I told you yesterday. In fact, she has her own special title: The Searcher. Her job is to locate the Lesser Charms and work with you to obtain them."

"Yep, that's what I do. I even get to wear one of them." She revealed a bird-shaped pendant on the chain around her neck. "It lets me travel through books to just about any location. If there is a second copy of a book I have, I can jump into my book and jump out of the other one wherever it is. I use it instead of commercial airlines. No lines. Less baggage."

"Oh! Is that how we will send postcards to our friends? You can take us places?" Jenny said. The question had niggled in her mind since Uncle Curtis mentioned sending postcards. *I'll send Rae one from a hundred destinations.*

Ophelia winked. "You're a clever one, Jenny Fletcher. So much like your uncle." Seeing Jenny grimace at the mention of Isaac, Ophelia stood and hugged her. "I know what happened to your family yesterday, Jenny. To *our* family. How overwhelmed you must be. My dad and I will do everything we can to help you get your parents and uncle back."

This sweet young woman was offering her the very things she'd lost: her home, her family, her hope. Sniffling, Jenny squeezed her ... cousin, was it?

"So, you are my ..."

"First cousin once removed. I worked it out last night when I snuck into your house to get your clothes and stuff," Ophelia said.

Jenny pointed a finger at her. "You! You were the one who brought my bear. Thank you."

"You sleep with a bear?" Josh said, surprised.

"Shut up," Jenny said, then winked at him.

Ophelia released her and moved to shake Josh's hand. "And welcome, Josh Park. We aren't sure why you are roped into this mess, but you are in it, and Dad said you are committed." She eye-balled him. "You look pretty strong, so, yay! That's helpful. I'm so sorry for what the Sorceress did to your parents. I wish we had more details." Shadows fell on Ophelia's beautiful face, now a terrifying warrior-queen. "Trust me, she will not go unpunished."

Josh bobbed a thank you, hiding a sudden sniffle. The shadows on Ophelia's face vanished, replaced by kindness and a sort of maternal understanding.

Forcing his emotions into submission, he inquired about her brother, a subject less apt to induce further crying.

"You will meet Patrick one day. He lives abroad and works in, uh, human resources. And yes, he knows about the Compass." She answered their question before they even asked it.

The kitchen door blew open and in waltzed a red-headed man about Ophelia's age with a thin, runner's build and black-rimmed glasses. "And this is Sam. He rents the guesthouse by the training room in the back." Ophelia said, introducing them each in turn.

He greeted them with a handshake and sat at the big table for breakfast, pulling up a chair next to Ophelia and digging in. They acted like familiar friends.

*How much information regarding the Compass is Sam privy to, I wonder? Surely some of it, right? Hmm, time to investigate.* Anything to keep her mind from her parents.

"Sam, mind if I ask what you do? How you're connected to the family?"

"Well, Jenny Fletcher, I work a lot for Uncle Curtis. A little bit of this and a little bit of that. I'm mostly a project manager—a *lot* of projects, a lot of deskwork. Sounds pretty thrilling, I know. I live a super exciting life, trust me." His sarcasm made Jenny giggle, a welcome change from all the crying she'd done in the last twelve hours.

"Laughing helps," Sam said. "Even when everything else hurts."

The Compass hummed beneath her shirt, and she clasped it to dampen the sound, attempting discretion, still unsure if Sam knew about it.

"Are you from here?" she said, ignoring the chatty necklace. *Maybe he'll think it's my phone.*

He shoved a final bite of French toast in his mouth and shook his head. "Nope, Texas. Don't mess with Texas." A mischievous smirk crossed his face. "And don't worry, Keeper, I know all about your little Compass. Great hair, by the way." His bony fingers ruffled her locks, and he waved to everyone, leaving by the same door he had arrived through. She raked through her hair. *What do you really do here, Sam from Texas?*

Ophelia watched him go, too. "Don't worry about Sam. He's always a bit of a mystery," she said, dabbing her mouth with a napkin. "Your training begins today. My other job, aside from Charm hunting, is to train you so you don't meet an untimely and unnecessary demise." She pointed to their clothes. "Go change. Meet me in the training room in one hour. It's that way." She pointed to the backyard. "Gear up."

∞∞∞ 🜨 ∞∞∞

In comfortable athletic wear, Jenny exited the kitchen door and scanned the large, fenced backyard. Beside what must be Sam's place, an unremarkable shed at the rear of the property appeared nowhere near large enough to contain the equipment a "training room" might require. The heavy front door creaked when she pulled it, revealing a steep staircase descending into the darkness.

Her foot lifted in midair but returned to its place next to the other one, both refusing to move.

She huffed a little to herself, at her hesitation. *How will I ever jump into another book if I can't even navigate these stairs?* Somehow, taking *this* step was bigger than just taking *a* step. If she descended these stairs, into the unknown, it meant a commitment to everything: the training, the Compass, these people. *Is this what I want? Can I do this?*

The Compass ticked, talking to her. Isaac had believed her worthy to be called Keeper. He had given it to her, with her parents' permission, which meant they had considered her ready and able too. "Being brave means doing what needs doing even if you are afraid," she whispered. "How many times did Mom repeat it? Not enough, apparently."

From the training room below, Ophelia's commands wafted up the steps, and, by the sound of it, Josh followed them. Lots of bangs and clanks and pounding. *He had found the courage to descend the stairs. He probably didn't think twice about it.* Grabbing the Compass, which whirred and pulsed, she exhaled and took the step.

ooooo 🐾 ooooo

Two hours later, Jenny collapsed to the floor, panting and sweating like a racehorse, hair spilling around her, damp and wild. "Come on, get up, Keeper. If we are sending you into stories, you have to run fast and far, defend yourself, sneak through villages and homes unseen, and do it all with grace and flair." Ophelia hovered above her, hands on her hips. "This," she perused Jenny, "is not grace and flair. This is more sad and soggy. You've got to own it, girl. Up, up." She dragged Jenny to her feet, coaxing her into ten more minutes on the treadmill, sprinting thirty seconds on, thirty seconds off. Exhausted and dripping, Jenny groaned, but the commanding drill sergeant who ruled the training room didn't take no for an answer. *This is brutal compared to five miles through the neighborhood.*

Squaring off on the mats, Ophelia and Josh glowered at each other. With his mom's height and dad's width, he loomed, but Ophelia out-maneuvered him every time with little effort. Circling her, formulating a plan, he moved fast and aimed a wicked hook to her left kidney, which she dodged, stepping in with a kick to his thigh, pushing him backwards. He stumbled, shaking his leg.

"Come on, Josh, Keepers and Guardians ignore pain," Ophelia told him.

"I'm neither of those," he reminded her through clenched teeth.

"Do you want to be?" she said, continuing to circle him. He glared at her. "That's what I thought." The taunt in her voice seemed to rattle him. He darted towards her again. "You die in the story, you die in real life, so fight. Fight hard!" she yelled, dodging his blows. They parlayed, Josh finally tapping out when Ophelia trapped him in an armbar, a tiny python going for the kill.

Though defeated, he high fived the victor. "Teach me your ways."

"Oh, I plan on it," she said.

Reclining on a stack of mats, they caught their breath, zoning out to Jenny's rhythmic pounding on the nearby treadmill. "Don't *you* want to be a Guardian?" Josh eventually said to Ophelia, stretching his hamstrings.

"I already have a job." She winked at him.

Shifting her attention to Jenny, she beckoned with a wicked grin. "Okay, gal, your turn."

Josh took up the treadmill. Jenny, pale and sweating, faced Ophelia on the mats. "Have fun, Jenny!" he said, smirking. She stuck her tongue out at him.

"Ever fought anyone?" Ophelia said. Negative. "Do you know anything about martial arts?" Another no. "Have you ever punched anyone or anything?"

"I wanted to punch *him* at one point," Jenny said, jerking her thumb to Josh.

"What?" he yelled over the droning of the treadmill.

"Nothing!" she hollered, waving him off.

Ophelia tapped the tip of her nose. "Hmmm, okay. No problem. Let's start here." She led Jenny to the heavy bag in the corner, taped her knuckles, and showed her how to punch. "Go for it. A hundred hits. Go!"

Tossing her hair and trying to focus on perfecting this skill, Jenny danced on her toes for a second, rotating her body the way Ophelia had shown her, pulled an elbow back, and punched, pivoting her core, connecting with the bag. A satisfying *thunk* rippled from her fist. She beamed at Josh who gave her a big thumbs up. Channeling her fury at the stupid Sorceress with her ugly, smug face into the bag, she struck it again and again and again.

With the one hundred required hits completed, she bounced, air boxing. "What's next?" Sweat trickled down her brow.

Ophelia grinned and pulled on headgear. "Now you hit me."

For hours, they trained. By mid-afternoon, Jenny wobbled to the house and leaned against the door. *I know nothing about fighting, self-defense, weaponry, strategy, or tactics. Absolutely nothing. Today made this totally clear.*

Deflated, she bent forward, willing herself not to cry, glimpsing the Compass dangling from her neck. It waved its needle at her. Rising to her full height, each muscle growing stiffer by the second, she wrapped the chain on her thumb, bringing the Compass closer. Ignoring protesting joints, a calm settled in her belly, the arrow ticking and tocking in her eye line.

*That's going to change. I'll work hard. I'll take some chances. I'll learn every last iota of what they can teach me. Then we are going after the Sorceress with everything we've got.*

# Chapterine

The kitchen smelled savory and wonderful. Jenny slid into a chair at the table, her legs shaky and tight. Uncle Curtis greeted her from the stove. "How was training?" he said, bringing her a glass of water.

"Hard," she replied. "Ophelia offered to begin to teach Josh about swords. They'll be in soon." She fiddled with the wood grain on the table. "You were right. We have a lot to learn." Uncle Curtis chuckled. "Do you think, while we learn, we could go ahead and study the ransom note, read up on the stories involved, and formulate tentative plans to rescue everyone?"

"Of course," he said. "Oh lass, we are going to get along splendidly. I do love a good planner."

"Oh good! I love planning. Also, I had another question. Um, last night you said it would be bad if I died on the first mission, and today, Ophelia said if we die in the story, we die in real life. Were you guys serious, or were you just trying to scare us?"

Uncle Curtis eased onto a stool, coffee cup steaming his glasses. He removed them to wiped the lenses. "Oh yes, quite serious. It's why we train you. So you can survive. Some of these stories are quite dangerous. Reading and planning are vital. I know you are anxious to get going on the list. I understand, I do. We will begin this evening. Ophelia and Josh can join us."

She sagged into the chair and gulped her water. *Now we're getting somewhere.*

∞∞∞∞ 🏛 ∞∞∞∞

Once everyone arrived and showered—goodness knows they all needed one—they gathered in the den, reading the ransom note, figuring out each fairy tale from the clues given. Jenny made a list and read it to them. "The chicken finger bone is in *Hansel and Gretel,* which, Uncle Curtis, you said was a depressing and awful story. We need to read up on it." Everyone agreed, but the disgusted grunt emitted by Uncle Curtis at the mention of it settled in their bellies. "The sharpened spindle is from *Sleeping Beauty*, and the dagger of the seamaid—*The Little Mermaid,* right?"

"I've never read it, but I saw the movie. I don't remember anything about a dagger," Josh said.

"Very helpful, Josh." Ophelia nudged his foot with her toe, and he stuck out his tongue at her.

"Get me a copy. I'll read it," he promised.

"The wicked stepsister's toe is in *Cinderella*," Jenny continued. "This task ... I mean, how gross is picking up a severed toe? What in the world does the Sorceress want a bloody toe for, anyway? Sick."

Josh guffawed at her disgust. "I'm going to make you pick it up, just you watch," he said.

"You're such a good friend," she said, heavy with sarcasm. "Okay,

95

moving on. I can't talk about grody toes any longer. Next, coins like the ones Jack waylaid will be *Jack and the Beanstalk*. And that's it. Five missions, five items, six months to do it."

"Pass me the letter?" Josh said, reaching for it and reading it again. "The first part says:

*Gather the chicken finger bone*
*And the sharpened spindle that's cursed*
*Bring them both before my throne*
*Or your uncle's plight will get worse*

So, do we take those two items to her first? Right after we get them?"

"It would seem so, to save Isaac from a worsening situation," Ophelia said. "Let's plan on *Hansel and Gretel* first, to get it over with, then *Sleeping Beauty*, and then find the Sorceress for an initial meeting. Should be an interesting one."

∞∞∞ 🝮 ∞∞∞

For the next few days, they trained. Instead of losing themselves in grief, they ran and lifted and sparred and boxed and jumped and planked until they cried. Ophelia reminded them every few minutes why. Every mile they ran, they marked the distance by yelling, "Faster than the Sorceress!" A picture of a devilish woman with a red dress appeared, taped to the punching bag, their hits directed at her. During planks and pushups, they shouted, "Planks win missions!" She even stuck a sign above the door to the training room, "To Win Them Back," reminding Jenny and Josh of their purpose when they walked in.

With mornings dedicated to training, they spent afternoons resting, oftentimes reviewing copies of *Hansel and Gretel* and *Sleeping Beauty* in the cozy den, cups of coffee or tea nearby.

Because the ransom letter had emerged from *Fantastical Fairy Tales, Fables, and Legends*, they surmised the Sorceress had stolen herself away in one of those stories and possessed a Lesser Charm or some other power allowing her access to the real world.

*Fantastical Fairy Tales* also contained all the stories on the ransom list. Her Charm must not allow travel between each autonomous narrative within the anthology. She could not leave her story for another one. Otherwise, why demand Jenny and Josh obtain the items for her?

To prevent her from repaying them a visit, Uncle Curtis had wrapped and locked the book, allowing the lock to come off with supervision while they made copies of the stories to read, study, and discuss. When the lock came off, he hovered, loitering in the corner with a coffee cup while they worked, showing his nerves by his presence.

In addition to their reading, he also schooled them in survival skills, orienteering, languages, and critical thinking—giving them scenario after scenario to analyze, forcing their minds to work in innovative ways and integrating what they learned from Ophelia into other lessons.

Each night, once the training and reading and talking ended, Jenny said goodnight to everyone, leaving them to hang out together. She proceeded alone to her room and dropped her tired body into bed. There she lay, missing her parents and Isaac and even Rae, grief leaking from the mental box she stored it in during the day. To take her mind off the pain, she read, finding solace and escape in words and pages. But when her eyelids drooped and the lines fuzzed and she put aside the book, emotions flooded in again. Every night. Always the same.

Moose stayed with her, snuggled against her leg. Downstairs, the others laughed and chatted, doing a puzzle and watching TV. A pillow covering her ears or stuffed at the bottom of the door didn't block the sound. Resentment boiled in her stomach. *How can they act so normal when everything is so obviously wrong?*

A few times, she texted Rae, sending vague messages about her whereabouts and inquiring after her friend. Rae always responded within minutes, telling Jenny about preparing for college and saying how much she missed climbing together.

Dreams assaulted her, visions of her parents and the Sorceress, of Isaac begging her for help, and of her holding her bow but unable to fire the arrow. She tossed and turned in her sleep, waking drenched in sweat. Moose licked her salty face and curled up next to her, every night her constant companion. Once, someone whispered, "You will get through this," but when she flipped on her light to investigate, nothing was amiss. *Another dream.*

One morning in the training room, Josh ran, and Jenny worked the heavy bag. With each punch, she muttered, "For Mom." And the next one, "For Dad," and the next, "For Isaac." She pummeled the bag for an hour before dropping to the floor, blinded by misty tears. Ophelia knelt beside her.

"It's okay, Jenny, to be sad. Let it drive you, but don't let it consume you."

Later in the night, she flipped through cherished family photos she had hidden between her mattresses, her teddy bear tucked in her arm. Ever since she was a child, her mom had ended each day by plopping onto her bed and sharing the same words with her: "Jenny, my lovely girl. I pray you will be strong and courageous, joyful and kind. Never stop loving, sweet child of mine." Jenny squeezed her eyelids together and shuddered. *I miss you.*

A hesitant tap sounded from her door. Eyes popped open. The pictures disappeared beneath her pillow, and she tossed her teddy bear to the foot of the bed. A quick swipe wiped away the liquid evidence of her grief, and she tossed her hair in an attempt to appear at least somewhat pulled together. "Come in."

The door creaked, and Josh peeked in. "Hey," he said with some uncertainty.

"Hey," she said, forcing volume into her voice, hiding her grief.

He shifted. "Are you okay, Jenny?" His sincerity reached deep within her, and she choked, throat tightening.

Swallowing, then coughing. "Sure. Yes, I mean, maybe?" She wilted. "No, not always." Deep inhale. "Sometimes I am okay. Sometimes I'm not. Right now, I am maybe not okay. I just really miss them, you know?" The edge of her bed protested with a loud squeak when Josh lowered himself next to her, causing him to bolt upright, flushed. "The chair doesn't squeak," she said, pointing. "Less obtrusive." He settled in with only the tiniest sound. "Josh, thank you for asking. How are *you?*"

He didn't answer right away, and his fists clenched. The weeks of training had left scrapes and cracks on his knuckles. Lean muscle corded along his forearms. "I am sad, and I am angry." *That makes two of us.* "For days, I woke up having forgotten they were gone. It would take a second for the reality to hit me, and I'd have to face the day feeling their loss again."

"That happened to me too. Man, I'm glad I'm not the only one. I feel a little less crazy," she said.

"I want to see my sister. She thinks I'm missing, along with my parents. Uncle Curtis said she can't know I'm alive or it will put her in danger from the Sorceress. She must be so confused." He studied his fingernails, eyes downcast.

"On the other hand, I love this training. It makes me forget the awful stuff for a while, and I get to hit things, real hard. One minute I'm sad, one minute I'm happy, one minute I'm yelling and punching a bag." He glanced at her with a gentle smile.

"And there's you, Jenny. I watch you run and fight and hit and kick, always driving to be stronger and faster. Sometimes you scare even *me*. You are going to be a killer Keeper. I know you are. And I ... I wanted to tell you I will do everything I can to help you, to work with you, and fight with you. Right now, you are all I have left."

She blinked. *I wonder if Josh wants to be a Guardian! But geez, that's a lot of pressure. Now's probably not the time to ask. And, I'm not all he has left!*

"Josh, you have Uncle Curtis and Ophelia, too, don't forget. They may not be your biological family, but they love you and believe in you. They must see something in you. Otherwise, they wouldn't invest all this time and energy to train you, would they? Oh, and Sam too. Sam asks you to do that dumb puzzle every night. Must mean something. And, I have a sneaking suspicion he is involved in this stuff *way* more than we know." She bridged the space between them and gripped his hand, not letting go.

"I'm so glad you are my friend, and I'm thankful we are in this together." Her mouth twitched into a mischievous smirk. "The Sorceress won't know what hit her, but it'll be you. You hit really hard."

After a silent few seconds, he tilted forward and whispered, "Can I tell you a secret?"

"Ooh, I love secrets," she whispered back.

He muttered something unintelligible, staring at the ground.

"Seriously, I have no idea what you said." She glowered at him until he chuckled and spoke more clearly.

"I want to be a Guardian."

He fidgeted, pulling his fingers away from hers, unwilling to face her while he divulged his secret. Her gasp startled him.

"I want you to be a Guardian too!" She yanked his arm, bouncing on her bed, shaking him to his toes. "So, you'll stay?"

"What do you mean? Jenny, did you think I would leave you to do this alone?"

She stopped bouncing. Curls tickled her neck, and she shifted them with a tilt to the right, lifting them away from her skin and weaving a quick, messy braid. "No, not for this part, but what about after the Sorceress? Or after we find our parents? I'll still be Keeper, and, I don't know ... I mean, you left before for soccer, which I didn't understand. This time, you'd be leaving for a safer, normal life. That I get."

"Come with me," he said, dragging her from the bed and into his room. Books on swordplay, survivalism, medicinal herbs, field medicine, fitness, even sewing, lay scattered about his floor.

She stooped to close one and see its title. "You've been studying!"

"Yep, anything and everything I can think of to be a competent Guardian."

"You need to ask Uncle Curtis about it. I'm sure he will say yes."

"I'm not ready to ask yet. What if he says no? I mean, I'm not family."

Jenny gripped his arm. "Please ask him. If you don't, I will."

"Oh, no, don't," he begged. "Let me take care of it. I know you want to help, but the best thing you can do is be an awesome Keeper and let me help you. Maybe Uncle Curtis will see what I'm capable of. He'll see I can do this."

Pressing against the corner of the book, she conceded. "Fine, but don't wait too long."

He plopped on his bed and changed the subject. "When do you think we will go into a story? I mean, it has to be soon, right?"

"I imagine we will go when Uncle Curtis and Ophelia say we are ready," she said, sitting on his floor among the twenty books littering the rug and pulling her knees to her chest. The Compass pressed into her sternum. "I want to, but I'm scared. The stories in the *Fairy Tale* book are crazy."

"They are totally crazy, but at some point, we've got to just go for it and hope we don't die."

She shifted, adjusting her seat. "Can I tell *you* a secret?" Her words were muffled with her forehead on her knees.

"Sure, of course."

Unable to face him, she confessed into her legs. "I'm afraid something else bad will happen, to you or Uncle Curtis or Ophelia ... or me. It makes me want to hide away from everyone, to keep you safe, and to keep me safe from losing you. It's why I come up here instead of hanging out with you guys, and I hate it."

Josh raked through his hair. "Jenny, instead of telling you that is a sad way to live and you ought to change it, I will share with you a little quote I picked up last year in school. "Tis better to have loved and lost than never loved at all,' or something like that. Shakespeare said it."

"Oh, uh, Tennyson, actually."

"Dangit! Seriously? I thought I had that one. Man, you are such a nerd," he said, teasing her. "Who the heck is Tennyson?"

"I'm homeschooled, remember? We read Tennyson and play the tin whistle and learn Latin." She held in a giggle at Josh's feigned disgust. "Tennyson wrote about love and loss and grief and stuff. My mom read his poems to me at night," she said. "It's a good quote."

"It is, so apply it to your life. Yes, something terrible happened to our families, and we have every right to be sad, angry, and afraid. But, in this case, we must move past the emotion and be brave. Lives depend on it. You are the Keeper. You hold us together. Our lives literally center around you and your Compass. We need you, and sorry dude, but you need us too. I'm scared, but it doesn't mean I stop being a friend or get a pass on courage. What is it your mom always said?"

Jenny rolled her eyes, sick of her mom's quote despite its pertinence. "Being brave means doing what needs doing, even if you are scared," Jenny said, gritting her teeth.

"Let me help you, to be brave, I mean," he said.

"How?"

"I'll be brave next to you," he said. "It starts with not going to bed right away. Stay with us, watch TV, do a 'dumb' puzzle. They're actually really fun."

"Talk about nerdy," she said with a wink.

They chatted for a little longer, and when she said goodnight, with one foot out the door, Josh stopped her. "Hey, when will you draw again?"

How did he know she ignored her sketchbook on a daily basis? "Maybe soon," she answered. "Real soon, I think."

# Chapter Ten

The next night, Jenny didn't trudge upstairs once dinner concluded. She lingered in the kitchen, helped with the dishes, and, with a nudge from Josh, plopped next to Sam on the couch. "Want to help with a puzzle? It's hard. No edges," Sam said.

"I sure do, Sam," she said. Josh gave her a discreet thumbs up and joined them at the puzzle table.

With him on one side and Sam on the other, it took less than a minute for the fart talk to commence. Unaccustomed to guys being so *honest*, Jenny blushed and pressed her lips together, focusing on the puzzle and ignoring them. But they continued, the laughter building, and her giggles rose to the surface.

"It's so hard, sometimes, to keep them in while running," Josh said with feigned seriousness.

"Right?" Sam said. "I don't know which is worse—the pain of holding them in or the consequences of failing to do so, especially after Curtis's homemade macaroni and cheese. And, I have to ask, why do we feel the need to hold them in in the first place, hmm? It just makes things worse ... for everyone."

Josh glanced at Jenny and Ophelia, the two girls he trained with on a daily basis. "Because most of our training is done in a small, cozy, sweaty underground bunker. Not a lot of ventilation. It's a lot of pressure, literally," Josh said, cracking himself, and Sam, up. Jenny put her temple on the puzzle table, unable to remain upright due to her belly aching from laughter.

Even Ophelia chortled and thanked Josh for his consideration from her quiet corner, nose in a magazine. "Maybe I'll buy us a fan," she said.

"For real," Josh replied, and Jenny agreed with vigorous nodding, still unable to speak. Listening to them go on and on about the dire consequences of Uncle Curtis's broccoli quiche kept it going until she wept.

Once the laughter subsided, she directed her attention to Sam, still wiping her eyes. "Whew, that was so funny. Oh, my word." She fanned herself. "Okay, Sam, I have a question for you."

"I'll answer if I feel like it," he said, elbowing her in an already aching side and chuckling at his own sarcasm.

"Thank you for your condescension. So, how did you end up here? Everyone else involved with the Compass is related, other than Josh, but his situation is unique, right? Are you some long lost cousin I haven't heard about?"

Sam placed a puzzle piece, clicking it into place. "Ah, good one. I love puzzles. The little hit of dopamine when a piece fits perfectly ... there's nothing like it. And, no, no relation. It's actually a pretty cool story. Do you have time for the extended version?"

Jenny stuck another piece in the puzzle and leaned against the back of her chair, folding her arms. "Go for it," she said.

∞∞∞ ❁ ∞∞∞

Sam McGregor told them how he'd lived in a small town outside a bigger one in southwest Texas. One of three children whose dad valued athletic achievement rather than academic prowess, Sam never lived up to his dad's expectations despite excelling at swimming and biking. If it wasn't football, basketball, or baseball, it did not count in Mr. McGregor's mind. He failed to praise his son for the straight A's or skipped grade levels or the college credits he earned in high school. In fact, he berated him daily and allowed his two older brothers to do the same.

His mom, meek and mild and fearful, refused to stand up for her youngest boy, even though the torment from his father and brothers sometimes resulted in a broken nose or bruised ribs. It always ended in a broken heart and damaged soul. Her unwillingness to intervene wounded Sam deeper than anything incurred from the men in his family. By the time he graduated high school at the age of sixteen, he had set his sights on moving as far away from them as possible, forever.

Several prestigious universities accepted him, offering full scholarships and allowing him to enter three semesters ahead due to the advanced credits he had earned in high school. He chose the one farthest from home where he studied both Religion and Chemistry, an odd combination, yes, but both worthy of further study, in Sam's mind at least.

Though he thrived in his university environment and enjoyed a number of accolades, Sam grew restless. A lot of intelligent people talked and argued and did little else. He longed for purpose and adventure and excitement and life, learning from living, not just from a book or lecture.

However, he still loved the libraries, and one night in the Divinity School library, beside some dusty, forgotten stacks, he thumbed through a book about Karl Barth. Another book crashed to the floor nearby, tumbling from the shelf by some unseen force. *That's odd.* He rose to return it to its rightful spot. But the book began to tremble and shake. It blew open and spat out a girl. IT SPAT OUT A GIRL. A petite girl with short, black hair and golden eyes staring at him surprised and on the verge of panic.

Sam's extraordinary brain attempted to process what he had seen. At the same time, he tried to not just stand there gaping, staring at the pretty—and very real—girl in front of him dressed like a spy or an assassin or some kind of modern ninja with a katana strapped to her back.

When she tensed, ready to flee, he reached toward her. "Please don't go."

"I should." But she wavered. "I have to be somewhere."

Sam refused to allow this moment, this most exciting, strange moment, to end. His future hinged on it. He knew it. "Take me with you," he blurted, shocked at his own words. "Take me wherever you are going."

"I don't know you," she said. "And you don't know where I'm going, or where I came from."

"I'm Sam. Sam McGregor. I'm a genius who likes cycling and longs for adventure, and I don't care where you are going as long as it's not here. What's your name?"

"If you let me do one thing, Sam, I'll tell you my name."

He eyeballed her katana, certain of other weapons hidden on her person. "Does that 'one thing' mean killing me?"

"You'll have to trust me." Closing the gap between them, she stood on her tiptoes. He flinched but remained unmoving. One of her tiny palms pressed against his chest, and another on his brow. Staring deep into his soul, she searched, and he shuddered. Surely she felt his pulse racing and his skin warming under her touch.

With a little push, she backed away and bent to retrieve the fallen book and return it to the shelf. Rising to her full, unimpressive height, she reached for a handshake. "Ophelia. My name is Ophelia."

A moment later, she whisked them away from the Divinity Library and into another, smaller one. A man spoke with a soft, Scottish brogue. "Ophelia, I didn't expect you so soon. Oh, and I see you've brought a guest."

ooooo 🐾 ooooo

"And that was the start of it, how I ended up here six years ago. Ophelia eventually took me back to school where I finished my semester with the promise to return to work with her and her dad and Isaac. Once the school year ended, I packed my stuff and wrote a letter to my parents telling them I had found a new job and would not visit them much, or ever. Ophelia brought me here, along with my bags. Isaac took me into stories, and Curtis put me in charge of ... something I can't tell you about yet." He almost let it slip.

Jenny groaned. "Oh man! Come on! Put you in charge of what? I'm so curious now."

Sam apologized with a shrug. "They trained me and trusted me, but mostly, they taught me how a family loves and lives in honesty and generosity. The night in the library changed everything. Best night of my life," Sam concluded.

"Hold up," Josh said, turning to Ophelia. "What were you doing when you touched him?"

Ophelia tittered, her attention still on her magazine. "Wouldn't you like to know," she said, teasing Josh.

"I do! I want to know all about it!" Jenny said. "And I want to know what Sam 'manages' that he can't talk about just yet." Her air quotes were ferocious, her frustration unquestionable.

"Yeah," Josh said. "What she said."

"In due time," Uncle Curtis said. "And don't worry, due time won't be long."

Josh threw the puzzle piece he held into the pile on the table. Sharing in his frustration but unwilling to let the night end on a low note, Jenny took a massive swig of Sam's seltzer water and burped an A, another swig, and a B, and so on through the alphabet. Sam hooted, folding forward in his chair. Ophelia began shaking and dropped her magazine. Uncle Curtis guffawed behind his book, and when she got to "L, M, N, O, P" and said it fast in one big burp, Josh relented and cracked up, his frustration dissipating. "That's it, I'm done."

They continued to giggle on their way to bed, and Jenny leaned against Josh's door frame, blowing a curl away from her face. Books still covered the available surfaces of his room. "Thought any more about asking him?"

"About being a Guardian? Jenny, it's on my mind every second, along with trying to decipher the secrets they are keeping. But I need to ask about being a Guardian in my own time, when I'm ready." He rubbed his face. "It's a huge question!"

"I know it is. I just ... don't like unanswered questions," she said. "And I realize this is about you, not me, so I will shut up about it, for now. Goodnight, Josh."

"Goodnight, Jenny."

She eased into her bed and slept a still, dreamless sleep, the photographs beneath her pillow untouched.

# Chapter Eleven

A week later, the morning sun poured in the window, warming Jenny. She rolled from the bed, her alarm still beeping on the desk. Her feet curled when they hit the cold floor, and she had to hold her hair off her face to find the snooze button. Sleepy and dazed, she sat at her desk and rested her cheek on her hand, yawning. The alarm blared a second time, and she slapped it with a groan. "Ugh, stupid clock."

In the kitchen, Uncle Curtis plated breakfast, chatting with Josh. This morning's menu, eggs on English muffins with hollandaise sauce and sautéed asparagus on top and fruit on the side smelled divine. He insisted on always having fruit. "It keeps you moving, if you catch my meaning," he said in his typical, jovial way.

Jenny slouched in her seat, attempting to like asparagus for breakfast, and Josh ladled more hollandaise onto his plate. Uncle Curtis's chatter got a little more interesting. "So, you guys have been training so hard, and Ophelia says you're doing quite well."

"She might be overstating," Jenny said, studying the melon on her fork. "Where is Ophelia anyway?"

"Ophelia is off hunting a Charm with some of her, uh, contacts. She left last night. Someone unleashed a significant amount of magic in a library in Valencia, Spain. I don't know when to expect her to return. However, just because she's gone, your training does not end. You will still go to the training room every day and practice with each other while she is away. I can supervise if you require it, but Ophelia assured me you were both motivated and disciplined. After training, we will also pick up on some classroom learning we have let slide these last seven weeks. Things like literature, Latin, science, social studies—all these will help you be more prepared as you use the Compass."

A knife clanked on Josh's plate, and he whispered, "Yes!"

Before the Compass, school was a means to play soccer for him, but now, he consumed information like his life depended on it. Jenny studied him, inwardly smiling at his enthusiasm. *The more knowledge he can retain, the better Guardian he will be, and he knows it.*

"Oh man, that's sounds great, Uncle Curtis." Josh beamed. "Seriously, I have so much to learn."

"That is good of you to say, Josh. If you want to become the Guardian I think you desire to be ..."

Josh's mouth dropped open, and he spluttered, choking on his muffin. "How did you know?"

Uncle Curtis placed his cup on the table. "Oh, a Guardian can always spot his own. Ophelia and I talked about it the night you got here, and every day, you confirm how much you deserve it."

He jumped up and hugged a surprised and pleased Uncle Curtis, then grabbed Jenny, jostling her, melon falling to the floor. "Did you hear that, Jenny? I get to be a Guardian. A *Guardian*, with you!"

She stared at him, pushing her chair away from the table and standing. A curl fell against her cheek. "It would be an honor, Josh." And then she smiled.

He embraced her and whispered, "I'll stay with you ... and the Compass."

"Should we make it official, then?" Uncle Curtis said. He offered something to Josh—a silver cylinder, intricately carved, a hand's width in length.

"Whoa, is that an emerald?" She gaped at the large gemstone embedded into the cylinder. "Dang, dude."

"If you take this, you are bound to the Compass, and its Keeper, as Guardian. Magically bound," Uncle Curtis said. "Don't ask how it works because I really don't know. You must protect the Keeper and Compass, even to the point of death. So, Joshua Kwan Park, I leave it up to you."

Without hesitation, he took the cylinder from Uncle Curtis and held it with a firm grip. A wave of goosebumps prickled on his skin and a silver light flashed in his eyes. "Whoa," he said, voice raspy.

"And so you are bound to it. When you are ready, push the emerald, but step back a wee bit first, for our sakes," Uncle Curtis said.

Josh followed his advice and pressed the blazing green stone. A sword burst forth from his hand, shimmering, magic tendrils swirling off of it, mist in the morning sun. "Whoa," he managed to say again. Solid, thick metal shone with fine etched markings pointing north, south, east, and west, a sunburst reminiscent of the Compass it protected. It balanced on his palm, sturdy and strong.

He cocked his head to one side. "Is that the Compass?" A thrumming buzzed in their ears.

Jenny nodded. "They must know each other," she said, holding the Compass close to the sword.

"The Guardian Sword. Another gift given to Arthur for his son, the first Guardian. They *do* know each other."

Brandishing it this way and that, his strong arms never faltered under its weight.

"Josh, you're like Aragorn. So cool!" Jenny said.

"Who made this, Uncle Curtis? And the Compass? Do you know?" he said.

"Put it away, and I'll tell you what I can," Uncle Curtis said, getting comfortable in his chair.

With a zip, the Sword returned to its cylinder, and Josh dropped next to Jenny to listen. The older man took a sip of his coffee and cleared his throat.

"I should've explained before. There's just so much to teach you. I can't always keep up." He sighed, adjusting his seat. "Now, what I'm about to tell you is what has been passed down from Keeper to Guardian through the years. The Compass, Guardian Sword, and Lesser Charms all came from a mysterious book called *The Gilded Coffer*—the book Arthur Neil bought from a savvy book merchant on one of his travels. I think I mentioned it the first night you arrived here."

They nodded. Who could forget the night when everything changed?

Uncle Curtis sipped again. "From what I understand, he found the Compass sitting on the book in his library, picked it up, and was pulled in before he even knew what was happening. He returned several days later to his worried wife, a changed man. He whisked her into his arms and danced her around the house, fully alive for the first time since his son, William, had died eight years before. He laughed again, played with his other children, became the friend and husband he was before losing his boy." He smiled, identifying with the love, loss, and joy Arthur Neil experienced.

"He returned to *The Gilded Coffer* multiple times and learned he could also travel into other books, which he made a habit of doing, with care, of course. He did all things with careful consideration, always." He eyeballed them, firmly driving this point home.

"But then, tragedy. A handful of evil men captured him. They wanted the Compass and anything else they could get their hands on, and they forced him to take them into *The Gilded Coffer*. There, they found and took the Lesser Charms. Once they were in the real world again, they tried to kill him for the Compass. He escaped, but the damage was done. The Compass was now a liability. He brought the Guardian Sword from *The Gilded Coffer* for his son and the Tracking Orbs to help find the stolen Charms. Then he hid the book. It has not been seen since."

"Whoa," Jenny breathed.

"Mmm hmm," Uncle Curtis said. "Quite a story."

"Wait, did you say *orbs*, as in more than one?" Josh said.

"Ha, indeed I did. Good catch. That's a subject for another day."

Josh rubbed his face, growing accustomed to waiting for information, though still frustrated by it. "So, does this mean the Compass is beholden to the magic written in *The Gilded Coffer*?"

"We think so, but because only Arthur read it, we don't know everything written about the Compass. Maybe it can do even more than we know."

Jenny pressed her lips together. *So much to consider! I gotta find that book.*

"We do know the Compass, Guardian Sword, and Lesser Charms do a bit more than just their surface ability," Uncle Curtis continued.

Two sets of eyebrows shot up.

Dimples appeared in the old Guardian's cheeks. "Oh yes. I love this part." He cracked his knuckles, letting the suspense build.

"Well, go on!" Jenny said.

"Patience, Keeper."

"Seriously, Uncle Curtis. Our entire world demands patience. Throw us a bone now and again!" She huffed, glaring at her uncle, curiosity and frustration piqued.

He leaned forward, closer to them, watching them. "These items possess a second power, another benefit to the bearer. They can impart a talent to the person bound to them—a supernatural skill to keep the Compass safe and to be a help to the bearer. We call them gifts, a simple way to label a precious thing. I have a gift. Ophelia has a gift. Sam mentioned hers when he told you some of his backstory, and he has one as well."

"Wait, Sam has a Charm?" Jenny said. *Guh! What is his deal? What does he do?*

Uncle Curtis nodded. "Isaac has a gift too. And your mom, Jenny. Even though their time with the Compass is finished, their gifts remain. All the gifts I know of are good, noble things given to the bearers."

*Whoa., I wonder if I will get a gift. I bet Josh is wondering the same thing. Hmm, what is Uncle Curtis's gift? And Isaac's? So many mysteries!*

Uncle Curtis tapped his chin. "A few other things must be said. Our magical objects give us access to other types of magic—the magic authors imagine and write into their stories. The number of magical stories is staggering. Within a story, we might encounter other magical powers or objects, like a flying broom or a magic wand or a unicorn. Usually, these imagined, literary brands of magic do not translate to the real world. They dissipate once a person returns from a book. Like, if you bring a magic wand back here, it would just be a stick. A flying broom would be stashed away for the next dirty floor. A crystal ball would be a garden decoration."

"Like the one in the flowers out back?" Jenny asked.

"Like the one in the flowers out back," Uncle Curtis answered. "In some cases, like the Compass and Guardian Sword, the magic remains, but this rarely happens. When it does, we heavily guard those objects." His voice dropped. "Heed my warning—be very wary of magic in books. It is almost never as manageable as the magic you have. Sometimes, it can be deadly. Don't touch it. Don't use it. Run from it."

A shiver shook Jenny's spine.

Uncle Curtis clapped his hands together. "So, going back to my original point, we will add more lessons to your day. You both will need to learn fast. Isaac and your parents cannot wait for us forever. And yet we cannot rush into things, else you may end up in worse shape than them."

*Like, dead.* Her foot tapped the floor. "Let's get going. Meet you in the training room in thirty minutes," she said to Josh, dashing to her room to change.

∞∞∞∞ 🐾 ∞∞∞∞

Josh bounded in, bouncing on his toes.

"You are always so happy to be here," Jenny said, lowering a set of dumbbells. "I wish I had some of your enthusiasm."

He grabbed a jump rope in the corner. "You like running, I like training. We could both use some encouragement from the other." After one hundred skips, the rope dropped to the ground, and he handed her headgear. "Hey, want to spar?"

Hesitant, she crossed her arms. "I don't know."

"Don't worry, I grabbed the biggest one we've got, to hold all your hair," he said, chuckling, hitting a nerve.

"You're hilarious. Really, you should do stand-up. I'm not worried about my hair," she said, rolling her eyes. "In case you haven't noticed, you've got several inches on me and a tad more muscle. I feel like my chances are slim."

"It's the only way we are going to get better."

"I guess it'll be good practice in case I have to go head to head with an ogre," she said.

"Ha! More like a handsome prince," he said, running his fingers through his hair and sliding the headgear on.

She choked, coughing and spluttering at his lame joke. "Oh, I see how it is. This'll be good practice for *me* in case I have to fight a flamingo," he said.

With flared nostrils, she snatched the headgear, slammed it on her head, and squared off with him on the mats. "An awesome flamingo," she huffed. "Ever seen a flamingo fight? Terrifying." She muttered under her breath, shifting from foot to foot. Calling on everything Ophelia had taught her, she launched herself at him.

Despite the size and weight differential, she managed to hold him off for some time, her quickness and skill making up for what she lacked in strength and size. It wasn't enough, and he pinned her to the mat, breathless from the effort required. She pushed him off and stood, fighting wounded pride from losing. He fiddled with his shoe, watching her pace. "Again," she said and faced him once more.

Over and over they fought. Over and over he won, until, she snuck in a move Ophelia had shown her the week before. Through the fog of exhaustion, she tried it on him, and he landed on his back. With ankles locked and one leg pressed against his neck, the other on his chest, she grabbed his arm from between her calves and flung herself backward, squeezing his elbow with her knees. He conceded with a groan, and she rolled to the mat beside him. They lay side by side, both shaky from the exertion.

"You wore me down, Jenny. That's what did it in the end." He high fived her. "You never stopped."

# Chapter Twelve

An hour later, with lunch wrapping up, Uncle Curtis appeared wearing a colonial-type suit with short pants and coat tails, white socks, black shoes, and a triangular black hat. A traditional sword hung at his side like a fancy revolutionary. "Ready to go?" he said with a tip of his hat.

"Go where?" Josh sat forward. They hadn't left the house for weeks.

"London, 1790," said Uncle Curtis. He glanced at their athletic wear. "You may need to change first. And Josh, don't forget the Sword."

Jenny bolted upstairs, hair flying. *We are going into a book, and I know just what I'm going to wear!* One particular dress in her wardrobe begged to be showcased, and this was the perfect occasion. The Compass ticked and tocked. It knew where they were headed.

When she reappeared forty-five minutes later, both men stopped their conversation, watching her descend the stairs on slippered feet. "Ah, Jenny, you put us to shame." Uncle Curtis gave her a small bow.

The long, chocolate brown dress with a square neckline and fitted bodice cinched her slim waist. The skirt spilled to the floor and gathered at her low back. A brown hat wrapped with white lace and dainty flowers adorned her head, the majority of her hair tucked beneath it with bits of curls trickling down her neck. It had taken her thirty minutes just to do her hair.

"Are you wearing makeup?" Josh said.

"Don't sound so shocked." She batted her darkened lashes. "Ophelia showed me some tricks. What do you think?"

"You will fit right in," he replied after clearing his throat and tucking a rogue strand of hair by his ear.

He wore something similar to Uncle Curtis's suit. When she pointed to his white stocking socks with a bit too much enthusiasm, he reddened. "I might die if anyone outside this house ever saw me with knee socks, a black hat, and buckles on my shoes."

"I don't know," she said. "The tails and big buttons on your jacket are quite dashing." He donned his hat, owning the look and giving her a dramatic bow.

"You are debonair, good sir. Though your darker skin and hair might garner a few stares. They will think you quite exotic—an Asian in their midst. Extraordinary!" Uncle Curtis said before passing him a small dagger. "Here, add this to your arsenal. Consider it a birthday present, in addition to the promotion to Guardian. Be careful. It's sharp," he added.

"Josh! Your birthday, I forgot! I can't believe it. Happy birthday!"

"Thanks, Jenny. And don't worry about it. I almost forgot too. Uncle Curtis, how did you know about my birthday?"

"Oh, I know a lot of things."

"It would seem." Josh strapped the dagger to his belt. "This is great."

"With pleasantries out of the way, let's move on to our lesson for today. We shall jump into a story together. You must practice blending in, observing, interacting with the story, and staying away from trouble." He laid a book on the table: *A Tale of Two Cities.*

With a few excited bounces, she hid her face in her hands, muffling a squeal. "Sorry, but this is one of my favorite books. You said London, right? Because I think Paris might be a little ... violent. I mean, I think I'd prefer London, if that's okay?" She rushed her words and apologized a second time.

"No worries, Jenny, and quite right," said Uncle Curtis. "We will jump into London, hang about a bit, and return home. I'd love to have a cuppa while we are there. Jenny, you need to hold our hands to form the link, lean over the desired page, and let the Compass do the rest of the work. The jump is quick, and if you don't watch for it, the ground will meet you faster than you expect. Ready?"

"Wait! I have questions," Josh said, throwing a hand in the air.

"Oh, of course, dear boy. I'm sorry if I'm getting ahead of myself. Please, ask away."

"Well, I'd like to know how we can do this. How can we just hang out in a book and not be swept up in the plot?"

Uncle Curtis nodded, resting his chin on his fingertips. "I'll explain. When a person jumps into a story, the world within the story, created in the mind of the writer, exists around the plot. Writers call it the setting. I imagine you've heard this word before, maybe in your English class at school?"

*I hope Josh has heard of setting before! He doesn't appear confused. That's reassuring.*

"The characters interact within the setting, driving the plot forward, but once they move on, the setting remains, working and functioning as it did when the writer created it. For example, today we are jumping into the 1790 London that Dickens envisioned and created in his book. While Lucie and her father and Charles and Sidney move about the story, the setting stays the same, with shops and homes and streets and people and carriages and ox carts. When we jump into the story, we temporarily become another character in the setting.

"Through trial and error, Arthur Neil discovered that we, the Keepers and Guardians, can interact with the plot and even the characters, and, short of taking a character from the story, the plot returns to its original story once we're gone. We're not written into the story, and no one will read about us or our interactions in the book. That being said, we try to stay away from the plot and main characters as much as possible. It can get messy if we get ... attached to any of them."

"Because we might want to pull them out?" Josh said. "Has that happened recently?"

"It has," Uncle Curtis said, confirming their suspicions and eliciting a "whoa" from both Josh and Jenny.

"Anyone we know?" she said. Uncle Curtis bit the inside of his lip, something he did when he pondered a difficult topic. He did not want to continue this line of inquiry. "Maybe we could talk about it later," she offered, and he relaxed.

Josh raised his hand again. "So, we can walk around and mill about and even investigate things without a care in the world?"

"In some ways, yes. But some stories pose their own threats, like thieves, illness, weather, wild animals. We must stay alert," said Uncle Curtis. "Any further questions? No? Good. I'm sure more will come up as we go, so please feel free to ask away while we stroll about. Now, Keeper, you're up."

She reached for Josh, and he took her arm without hesitation. Opening the book, she selected a page allowing them a private landing in London. Uncle Curtis nodded his approval when she pointed to their destination. Taking his arm with her empty one, the Compass ramped up, pulsing with her heartbeat. By instinct, she focused on the words where they wanted to land, and leaned forward, holding onto her companions for dear life. Warm light illumined her skin, and they fell.

A cobblestone street appeared beneath them, and Jenny couldn't get her feet under her quickly enough. She slammed into it with a loud thunk, followed by a moan.

Josh fared a little better, landing on his feet, though stumbling and unbalanced. He steadied himself using her head. "Josh, my hair!" She pushed him away and stood, adjusting her hat and ensuring everything went back to where it had been. "It took a massive effort to get it to stay like this!" She huffed, twirling a lock on her finger and placing it against her neck. "I have to look good."

Dusting off her dress and smoothing her skirt, she straightened to her full height. "Is it okay?" she said. He stepped in close to fix a curl trapped under her hat. She jerked away from his hand.

He froze. "It's just me," he whispered.

"I know, you just ... startled me." Her cheeks warmed when he tugged the ringlet loose.

"Thanks," she said with a curtsy.

"Indeed," he answered with a bow, heels clicking together.

Uncle Curtis, no worse for wear, surveyed their surroundings, motioning for Josh and Jenny to join him.

They stood in a vacant alley next door to a plain building with a shabby exterior and few windows. A busy street crossed in front of them and the building bustled with people of varying stations entering and exiting through the squeaky doors. Creak, THUNK. Creak, THUNK. Again and again. Some were finely dressed, in knickers with white stockings and tailored jackets or bustled dresses layered with petticoats and lace. Others wore plainer, more modest clothing, simple but still in good condition. Uncle Curtis explained these were likely merchants, doctors, possibly bankers—moneyed individuals but not the upper class.

Still, most of the people on the street itself dragged their feet, ragged, tired, and ill. Dirt and age clung to their clothing and hardship hung on their skin. The upper-class folks avoided the paths of the urchins, doing their best to pretend they did not exist despite the overwhelming smell of bodies and excrement assaulting anyone who dared inhale.

Horse droppings littered the streets. Puddles of sewage and the bloated bodies of dead rats steamed in the cool air. *Lovely.* Jenny breathed through her mouth, unable to not stare at the swollen rodent carcass to her left.

The building next to them, dark and dank, was none other than Tellson's Bank near the Temple Bar. Jenny had landed them exactly where she had chosen. Its initial impression was even more depressing than Dickens' description, yet it remained a steady landmark and rendezvous point should they get separated.

Uncle Curtis indicated right. "Let's go this way." He led them down the street, careful to avoid foul pools and fresh piles. Their finery, though not the fanciest, stood out among the poor city dwellers. Each dirty, partially-clothed child they passed stared at them, weathered and broken.

"Eighteenth-century London sucks," Josh said. She agreed. Holding her purse close, she wondered how many pickpockets would target them along their way.

After a few blocks and turns, they emerged onto a more upscale street lined with larger homes, posh dress shops, and haberdasheries. "Ah, a café!" Uncle Curtis clapped once, sighting a small tea shop on the corner. "When tea first became popular in England, you could only get it in coffee shops. But at this point in British history, tea shops were a thing as well. This is splendid!"

They sat and sipped, taking in all the hustle and bustle of the city. Every young man Jenny saw could have been Sidney Carton or Charles Darnay walking by, and she said as much to Josh and Uncle Curtis.

"I've not read this one, so I have no idea who Sidney Carton or Charles Darnay are," Josh said, sinking into his chair.

"Well, Guardian, it's your lucky day because I know this story inside and out. I'd love to fill you in." Resting her elbows on the table, she coughed with a bit of dramatic flair to ready her voice.

"Dr. Manette was a prisoner in the Bastille in Paris. Once freed, he is a little bit crazy. But he is rescued by his daughter and a friend and sets up a new life in England. There, his daughter, Lucie, grows into a lovely girl, and she wins the hearts of both Sidney Carton, a troubled lawyer too fond of the bottle," she pretended to take a swig of wine, "and Charles Darnay, a French aristocrat who has renounced his title and desires a quiet life in England. The two men look similar, almost like twins, but Lucie falls in love with Charles, and they marry and have two children. Sidney remains close to the family, which has got to be hard since he lost the love of his life to his fake twin and has to see them happily together all the time." Her frown betrayed the soft spot she had for Sidney.

"Eventually, Charles must return to France to save a former servant of his family, and there he is arrested for crimes his aristocratic family members committed. This takes place during the French Revolution—a dangerous time to be gentry in France. Anyway, Sidney Carton, the alcoholic Charles Darnay look-alike, works out a plan to save Charles by trading places with him on his way to the guillotine and sacrificing himself instead. Charles is reunited with the family he loves. Poor Sidney dies in the end, a redeemed and honorable man."

"Why in the world did Sidney Carton do that?" Josh said, flabbergasted.

Jenny sighed. "Because he still loved Lucie, and he would do anything for her happiness, even die so she could be with the man she loves, the father of her little girl. Sidney is the opposite of heroic until the very end, and then, he's epic."

"You can see why Jenny would want to see some of these characters. They are all quite interesting." Uncle Curtis added. "In fact," he dipped forward and whispered, "Very carefully, look to my two o'clock. You will see a nicely-dressed couple strolling arm in arm down the street."

She managed to peek over her shoulder with some measure of discretion in the direction indicated by Uncle Curtis, and there she saw them, their foreheads inclined towards one another, talking with sweet smiles. It was them! Lucie Manette and Charles Darnay, there, right in front of her. Lucie glowed, meek and demure, glancing at Charles through her long lashes. Charles, sturdy and ever the gentleman, guided her down the street, avoiding the occasional puddle.

They disappeared around the corner, and she reclined in her chair, her mug clunking to the table. "I cannot believe it," she said.

Josh tried not to laugh. "Wow, total fan-girl."

Her eyes narrowed. "At least I have the emotional capacity and maturity to be moved by the almost tragic love story of two decent people swept up in circumstances beyond their control," she said, daring Josh to comment again. "And anyway, I *like* being a girl *and* a fan."

Uncle Curtis stood and drained his cup. "Okay, time to go home, you two, before you bite each other's heads off. Josh, can you lead us back to the alley?"

"Wait! We didn't do anything!" Jenny said, knocking her cup by accident, sending it skidding across the table. She steadied it, trying to not create a scene, blushing and holding in a few, lingering fan-girl giggles.

"We had tea," Uncle Curtis said. "Listen, I know you want adventure and excitement, but sometimes just being in a place, getting a feel for it, experiencing a bit of what is has to offer, is enough. It should be enough. I also have another surprise for you back at the house, so we need to get home."

"Ooh, I do love surprises," she said, conceding with reluctance.

"I'm ready when you are," Josh added. "Also, I think I like tea!"

# Chapter Thirteen

Josh led them through the dirty streets back towards the Temple Bar to Tellson's Bank. He moved closer to Jenny. "Don't look now, but I think we're being followed." Uncle Curtis heard and agreed, holding up three fingers, then slowed, pretending to peruse some street vendor wares. Taking Jenny by the elbow, Josh continued walking, pushing her along at an ever-increasing pace. "Keep going," he said. "To the alley. Go!" They were almost running. Tellson's drooped ahead.

He flung Jenny into the empty alley then faced the thugs following them. Three men closed in, fanning into a line, grimy, sneering, and armed.

"Oy," one said to the others, "What do ye call two young nobles trapped in an alley?" They chuckled. "Dead," he said, licking his lips. He got a better view of Josh. "Oh, not a noble. A Chinaman!" he said, redoubling his aggressive stance.

Pulling himself to his full height, calm and haughty, Josh sniggered. "Korean, actually, on my father's side." He took a step toward the vagrant, unafraid. With a quick flick of his wrist, a throwing knife slid into his hand.

He launched it towards the man, hitting him in the shoulder. It sent him staggering backward, collapsing with a moan.

Jenny gasped. *Whoa, that was fast! Oh man, is that dude pulling the knife out of his body? Oh, I think I'm gonna barf.* But, instead of averting her eyes, she swallowed her disgust and stayed focused. The bloodied knife clattered to the cobblestones.

A second later, Uncle Curtis materialized behind the aggressors. With a single move, he hamstrung the man to Josh's right, who tumbled, screaming in pain and unable to stand. Uncle Curtis strode toward Jenny and gave a shout. "Jenny, behind you!"

Her hat flew off when she whirled a one-eighty, clutching her purse, white-knuckled. A wraith rose from the heaps of garbage in the alley. He lurched toward her, reaching for her bag, her dress, anything he might seize with filthy fingers.

Ophelia's training kicked in, and Jenny dropped low, trapped between the wall of Tellson's and the hooligan coming for her. Another shout from the street distracted him, and, taking the opportunity, she crunched down on his instep with a vicious stomp. He screeched in pain, doubling over. His neck snapped back when she caught his chin with a hard uppercut. He stumbled away, but recovered and came for her again, limping but still persistent. When he lunged, she threw her purse at him, catching him off guard, spun, and clocked him in the gut with a kick. He crumpled into a heap.

Josh appeared at her right, his Guardian Sword at the ready. "Nice, Keeper," he said, impressed. Uncle Curtis was at her left. Before anyone else got hurt, Jenny linked with them and whispered, *"Dulci distinet a domo domum!"* And they were gone.

A moment after their feet left the ground, they jolted sideways, an unseen force jerking their bodies. They landed on cobblestone streets filled with shouting, gunshots, and chaos. It only took a second to know this was not home.

Uncle Curtis lowered into a defensive position, trying to determine where they were and what was happening. He scanned the crowds of people running past them. "Jenny, what was the last thing that went through your mind as you spoke the words? Think fast, Keeper."

She blanched. "No, no, no, it can't be." The words filling the streets were unfamiliar, but she knew the language. French.

"This is Paris. I brought us to Paris, and the revolution has begun." She swallowed, frozen, the city of love on fire. "We are dressed too fine for this. They will think we are nobles!" Her voice shook.

"Take us home, Jenny. Take us home now!" Uncle Curtis said with a firmness she'd not yet heard. But before she could utter a word, a Frenchman, dressed in rags and dirt, burst through their small circle and, in his revolutionary fervor, snatched Jenny and slung her over his shoulder. He continued down the street, yelling in French.

"Josh!" she screamed, crowds closing in. She pounded on him and kicked her legs. The Frenchman shook her and barked an order for her to shut it. They took one street and then another. People crowded everywhere, their fury at the aristocracy boiling, shouting, *"Vive la révolution!"* Windows shattered, muskets barked, and carts overturned. Everyone ran in one direction, to the Bastille.

She shouted Josh's name again. "Please ..." she whispered. And then he was there, emerging from the throngs of people, sword drawn and coming for her. He moved through the crowd, eyes only on Jenny.

*Oh! My knife! Oh, how did I forget?* Reaching into her dress while bouncing upside down was difficult, but the knife pulled free with some wrangling. Using all her strength, she drove it into the soft spot behind the Frenchman's knee. It buckled, and he fell, flinging Jenny forward. She slammed into the stone street, her head whipping back and striking the ground. Groaning and dizzy, she crawled away from the trampling feet threatening to crush her, curling into a ball against the wall.

Shielding herself with her arms, her head spun from the fall, and she felt nauseated and shaky.

A body loomed by her, casting a dark shadow into the corner where she hid. Her heart pounded and body tensed, gripping the knife even harder. She prepared to fight or run. Someone touched her forearm. "Are you all right?" Josh said, pulling her to her feet, holding her against himself when she swayed. The knife in her hand clanked to the ground, and she clutched her temples.

"Gimme a minute," she said. "I'm okay. Thank you for coming."

"You're welcome." He retrieved the knife, shoving it in his belt.

His attention returned to the chaos and crowds. "We have to find Uncle Curtis. He yelled to meet him at the Bastille if we got separated." He surveyed their surroundings. "I think we got separated."

"Follow them," Jenny said, pointing to the mass of people moving along the street in unison, an angry and hungry hive. "The Bastille will be rough." His palm against hers stopped it from trembling.

The pair joined the mob. Just as the Bastille came into view, casting long shadows over the revolutionaries, Uncle Curtis materialized, pushing his tall, thin frame through some rowdy protestors, elbowing one of them in the face when he refused to move. Uncle Curtis said something to the guy's friends in French, and they slunked away.

"Ah! Jenny and Josh. Glad to see you. Jenny dear, would you please get us home? All this racket is giving me a headache."

A second later, they touched down in the kitchen. Uncle Curtis leaned against the island and muttered with relief. "Well, that ended differently than I had planned. Is everyone all right?"

Jenny's dress rustled as she threw herself into a chair, drooping. "I obviously did something wrong when we tried to leave London. I'm so sorry, you guys. That was scary." The bump on the back of her head stung under her fingertips, and she winced.

"I believe your mind wandered during your attempt to get us home, taking us to another part of the story. Now you know. You must concentrate lest you prompt an unexpected turn of events," Uncle Curtis said, and he passed her an ice pack from the freezer.

"Now I know," she said. Despite the ice pack, she was sweating and fanned herself with her other hand. "I've got to get this dress off. It's unbearably stuffy. I don't know how those women did it."

Halfway up the stairs, she stopped. "Uncle Curtis, I see why we train. Those were just French revolutionaries and street thugs. The Sorceress will probably be much worse. As much as my heart is ready to go find our families, I get why we can't just saunter in there all willy nilly."

Uncle Curtis agreed. "We have one more jump before your first mission. It won't be long now."

After a shower and in normal clothes, Jenny ran her fingers through her curls. Rebelling against their earlier prison of braids and pins, they poofed even more than usual while drying. "Why do you have to be so big?" she moaned. Flipping over and shaking them out made them even bigger, so she conceded, tying on a headband. "Still big, but at least not so annoying," she said to herself in the mirror.

She ran into Josh at the top of the stairs. "Hey, are you okay after, you know, everything?" she said. He wasn't smiling.

"Yeah, I'm okay." He rubbed his forehead. "It's weird, hurting people that are characters in a book. They aren't real people. But they seem so real, and in the moment, they are so real. Honestly, it's weird fighting in general." He grimaced. "Soccer isn't quite so intense. And if you do hit someone, it's an automatic red card. Today was more like, if you *don't* hit someone, you get a red card. But it also felt so natural to react, to protect. It felt normal. Is that bad? I don't know how I feel about it being so easy."

"I guess it's why you're a Guardian. But if it ever gets to be easy *and* enjoyable, we might have a problem."

"You're right. Periodically ask me about that, would you? Just to check in." He gave her half a smile. "Are you okay after being temporarily kidnapped by an overzealous French revolutionary?"

"I'm fine. It was crazy, but you were right there, fighting to get me back. If anything, today proved just how much the Compass and I need a Guardian and how perfect you are for the job." She peered at him through her lashes, like she had seen Lucie Manette do to Charles earlier in London. "Oh my, Josh, are you blushing?" she goaded him, his cheeks reddening.

"No! You're blushing!" he said, chuckling. "But, seriously, I was terrified when I lost sight of you. One second you were there, and then you were gone, and I could hear you screaming my name. If anything bad had happened ..." his voice trailed off.

"All I got was a bump on the head. I'm fine, and I have you to thank for that." Fishing around in her pocket, she said, "I got you something, in London. Straight from the cafe where we stopped. I might have, uh, borrowed it." She whispered the last part.

"Keeper *and* procurer of small utensils, otherwise known as the Spoon Thief." He examined the little spoon she had passed to him.

"They had loads of them. So, there you go. Happy Birthday!"

"A stolen spoon from a 1790s work of fiction. Best gift ever." He nudged her with his elbow. "Look, it has CD engraved in the handle. What do you think that stands for? Coffee Depot? Compact Disc?"

"Probably Charles Dickens," she said with a wink.

"Oh of course. Ha! I didn't even think of that! Thanks for the wee spoon, Jenny," Josh said, mimicking Uncle Curtis's accent.

"Sure thing, Guardian. Anytime."

# Chapter Thirteen

They met Uncle Curtis in the den. "Ah, there you are!" He held a large, jingling key ring. "You ready to go?"

Josh, with dark circles already under his eyes, sighed. "I'm not sure we're up for much more excitement. This has been a great birthday already."

"Our next destination is close and requires little energy, and there are no Frenchmen, though maybe a stray Texan," said Uncle Curtis.

"Sam?" Jenny said, brightening.

"Come, come. You will find out soon." Uncle Curtis led them to the spiral stairs, into the basement, and along a narrow hall opening to a wood-paneled study. A few soft leather chairs, a large desk, and vintage lamps added to its rich, cozy vibe. In a corner stood a tall bookshelf built into the wall. On the shelf, at eye level, sat a small gargoyle lion.

"I've never seen a gargoyle this close before," Josh whispered. "Or one so small."

"Me either!" she said. "He's so cute."

The stone shimmered for a moment, and the lion shook his mane with a yawn and stretched. "Well, I've seen *humans* this close before and have never enjoyed such proximity." Gasping, Josh and Jenny jumped back, bumping into each other.

"Whoa," Josh said.

"My nap was just getting good." The lion stretched and growled, voice deep, with a posh, English accent. The old man scratched the lion's mane.

"Good day, Fang. Sorry to disturb you." He sounded only a little sarcastic.

"It would appear you've brought visitors."

Jenny, fascinated and slightly freaked, edged closer. "I'm Jenny Fletcher, and this is my friend Josh Park. Guardian Josh Park."

Josh bowed, which for some reason seemed appropriate. "At your service," he said, which also seemed appropriate, though he surprised himself saying it.

"Guardian, eh?" Fang's stony eyebrows lifted. "Last name of Park. Korean, then?" he said.

"Yes, sir," Josh answered, raising his chin.

Fang returned his attention to Jenny. "And what can I do for you, Miss Jenny Fletcher and Guardian Park?"

"Um, well, I don't actually know, Fang. What can you do for me? And, if you don't mind me asking, what are you? And where did you come from?" she said, powering through her uncertainty.

"By what authority do you question me, little Jenny?"

"I guess by the authority of the Compass? Ahem. I mean, by the authority of the Compass." Feigning confidence, she lifted the Compass from inside her shirt and held it toward the stone lion. Fang stretched forward, getting even closer to the Keeper from his post. She stood, resolute. The creature sniffed, searching for any trace of falsehood.

With one last snuffle, he returned to his original position. "You and I have something in common." He ran a claw through his mane. "Substantial hair. And since you asked, *Keeper*, I will gladly answer your questions." Sitting tall on the shelf, he licked a paw. "I came from a book, one with living gargoyles. My author had a vivid imagination, but my part in the story was small and inconsequential, though I, obviously, am neither of those things."

Jenny and Josh glanced at each other, confused at the gargoyle's opinion regarding his own size. "I was procured to guard this ..." The bookshelf creaked open. "Welcome to the Collection," he purred. Jenny took a chance and patted his nose with a hesitant finger before venturing into the room beyond the bookshelf.

"Good job," Josh whispered in her ear. She smiled.

Cold concrete walls enclosed the small space, and another door stood opposite the bookshelf. Her smile faded. *This can't be right.*

"Well, this is anticlimactic," Josh said.

From a dark corner emerged a familiar face, unsmiling and grim.

"Sam!" Jenny said. "Yikes, why do you look so weird?"

"Jenny. Josh, or should I say, Guardian. Welcome. Behind this door," he gestured to the one that wasn't the bookshelf, "is what we in this family call the Collection. I am its curator, another kind of Keeper, if you will."

Jenny shifted her weight from foot to foot. Josh crossed his arms.

"But before we enter, I have news. It's not good." He turned to Uncle Curtis. "A Charm is missing."

139

Uncle Curtis pulled himself to full height. "Oh my. Which one?" he asked, biting the inside of his lip.

"It's one of the less powerful ones, which is weird. I mean, if you are going to steal a Charm, why not go for a big one?" Sam said, leaning against the gray wall. "The one stolen lets a person jump into a story, but they need a second Charm to jump out, to sort of boost them back to the real world. It's the one shaped like a star. Pretty unremarkable as far as Charms go."

"Who could have broken in? No one knows about this place except the Keeper, Guardian, Searcher, and me," Sam said. "Hey Fang, who has been here in the last eight weeks? That's about the last time I checked on the Charms."

Fang's shaggy brows knitted together. "How long have you been Keeper, Mistress Jenny?"

She shrugged. "Uh, I have no idea. I'll have to count back. Does anyone have a calendar on them?"

"Fifty-two days," Josh said.

"That's pretty specific," she said.

"I, uh, keep count of how long since everyone disappeared. It helps somehow. It was the same day Jenny became Keeper." She leaned against his arm, reassuring him.

"Hmm, fifty-two days ... Oh heavens, oh my. No, that's not possible," Fang muttered more to himself than the others. "I think I know who stole the Charm. It was Isaac." Jenny gasped, Josh gaped, and Sam huffed.

Fang went on to explain how fifty-two days ago, Isaac had shown up at the door. He had seemed nervous and smelled a bit different, but seeing as he was a Keeper, Fang had no reason to question his presence and allowed him in. Isaac had stayed for just a few minutes, then left with a sad goodbye.

"I should have stopped him." Fang drooped. "Or at least told you about it sooner. It never occurred to me that he might do something devious."

Jenny patted his cheek. Fang thanked her and rested his head on her forearm.

Sam pushed off the wall and started pacing. "Maybe he *had* to get *this* Charm, for some reason. Maybe the Sorceress forced him to. I mean, why else? I was gone; Ophelia was with the ... gone." *What did he nearly let slip?* Jenny watched him carefully, but Sam plowed ahead. "No one was here that night. The binding was passed to Jenny earlier in the day, so when the Sorceress came into our world, Isaac had nothing. Maybe she needed him to have a Charm for some reason?"

"But wouldn't that give him a means to escape?" Josh said.

"Well, this particular Charm isn't strong, like I said earlier. He couldn't use it to escape. It could, however, be used to boost another Charm if someone needed some help moving a group of people like Isaac and y'all's parents. Only the Compass can move a group that large on its own. Perhaps the Charm the Sorceress wears needed a booster to move the whole group. Could that be it?" Sam's pacing speed increased.

"Move them where?" Josh wondered, his mind moving as fast as Sam's. "They aren't with Isaac, as far as we know."

Sam stopped. "Because ... maybe, instead of a booster, she used the stolen Charm to dump them into a book, like a literary prison." He snapped his fingers. "The stolen Charm can get them in, but not out. And only she knows where they are."

"But why would she do that?" Jenny said, the lightbulb casting shadows on her face.

"Insurance," Uncle Curtis said with a grunt. "And leverage, to ensure you finish the task, put you off rescuing Isaac, and to give you a reason to keep her alive. If she has information you want, she knows you won't just kill her. She's smart." He chewed the inside of his lip.

"Josh, when you first arrived, you asked if I thought the Sorceress might've killed your parents. Based on this new information, chances are higher now than ever that she's kept them alive," Uncle Curtis said. "Have hope, but hold it loosely."

*But we need to know for sure.* "If they are trapped in a book, we have to find out which one and get them, and it has to be soon," Jenny said.

The only way to get this information was to ask the Sorceress. And the only way to get the Sorceress to talk was with a chicken bone from *Hansel and Gretel* and the spindle from *Sleeping Beauty*.

"We can't waste any more time," she said, hands on hips. "Sam, show us the Collection, please."

"Yes ma'am," said Sam, cracking the door. "Get ready!" Light shone in from the space beyond it, and faint tinkles and clinks echoed off the concrete walls.

"Have fun!" called Fang, then yawned. He returned to his previous nap, lounging on the shelf, a snoozing stone monster cat.

# Chapter Fourteen

Walking into the Collection smelled like climbing the stairs into her grandmother's attic, but on a grander scale and with fewer mothballs or clouds of dust. Machines, chandeliers, netting, ropes, and a myriad of other things hung from the ceiling. Various items chimed and ticked and hummed, a gentle cacophony echoing off the walls and along the aisles. Lights flickered, blinked, and dazzled from every aisle.

Painted signs hung from the ceiling and shelves, indicating the various sections within the room. Flying Objects. Traditional Weapons. Unique Weapons. Armor: Regular, Elvish, and Otherwise. Doo-dads. Wild West Clothing. Treasures. Fictional Artifacts and Souvenirs. Jewelry. Jewels. Trick Furniture. Antique Furniture. Unknowns, Miscellaneous, and Downright Confusing. Ninja. Possibly Dangerous. Explosive (Please Be Careful and Don't Blow Yourself Up), Mundane. Medicinal. These were just the ones Jenny could read from the door.

"Feel free to close your mouths," Uncle Curtis said. "Though it *is* fantastic, isn't it? Here is 150 years' worth of invention, discovery, and procurement, started by my great-great-grandfather and continued through all the Keepers and Guardians. Their other job, aside from guarding the Compass and finding the other Charms, is to add to it. I didn't mention that part before." He gestured around the room. "It's our arsenal, treasure box, bank, and closet. We need all the help we can get to defeat the Sorceress. This is where we will find it."

Jenny tried to orient herself. "So, where are we, exactly?"

"The basement," Uncle Curtis said. She raised an eyebrow at him, and he chuckled. "The basement extending past the house all the way to the fence in the backyard. It's encased in concrete and steel and guarded by motion sensors and Fang, lest anyone tries to dig in."

"And where did this all come from? Stories?" Josh said

"Think back to how, earlier today, we walked around the 1790s London Charles Dickens created for his book. Because that world continues to exist even after the plot has moved on, so does all the stuff in it. If the jumper, that's the Keeper and anyone else she's brought into the story, sees something that might be helpful or interesting or valuable within the story, it is safe to take it or, in some cases, buy it, without consequence or compromising the story." Uncle Curtis grinned then sobered and raised a finger.

"We do, as an unwritten rule, stay away from major magical objects like the Ring from *Lord of the Rings* or the lamp from *Aladdin*. Though their magic probably would not translate into the real world, we cannot be sure. Anything else is basically up for grabs, and the story will regenerate the item when it is read again. These are the types of items comprising the Collection. Fascinating, useful, and valuable things procured responsibly by the past Keepers and Guardians from the books they jump into."

"I did that when I was in *Robin Hood*!" Jenny said. "I met a village woman named Granny Bea, and she gave me clothes to wear in exchange for my bracelet." She rubbed her empty wrist. "It's what I was wearing when I first came here, along with my bow and arrows, courtesy of Robin Hood and his Merry Men."

"Hmm," Uncle Curtis said. "I wondered why you were armed when we first met. In all the excitement, I forgot to ask you about it. And you will need to tell me a bit more about this trip into *Robin Hood*. I am surprised you kept this to yourself for so long."

With so much else happening the same night, *Robin Hood* had been placed on the back burner of her mind.

"Yes, I know. I'm sorry I haven't said anything. I kind of forgot, honestly. I'd be happy to tell you."

"I'd love to hear all about it," replied her great-uncle.

Josh nudged a shelf with the edge of his shoe. "So, with all the books ever written, the possibilities for exploration and procurement are basically endless."

"Yes and no," Sam said. "Most of the items here are either helpful or valuable. Certain magical items brought from stories, like Fang, for example, continue to work here in the real world. Their magic is somehow compatible with our environment. Other items are magical in their stories but don't work here once they leave, which puts a limit on possibilities. But outside of magical objects, yes, the literary world is your oyster."

Jenny stared at the shelves. "Yes, Uncle Curtis mentioned that about certain magical objects." She gestured to everything around her. "So, Sam, this is the job that keeps you so busy. The project you 'manage'?"

"Yes indeed. I am Sam McGregor, manager of all things magical, fantastical, extraordinary, and mundane. And we've got ourselves a doozy of a situation with this Sorceress, but fear not. I can outfit you with everything you need to beat her so bad, she'll be begging for her mama." He rubbed his palms together. "Go ahead, have a look around. See what you can see."

*Did I detect a hint of his Texas accent just now?* She grinned.

"Thank you, Sam. Jenny, Josh, I'm sorry we weren't forthcoming about Sam's role," Uncle Curtis said. "He likes to keep a low profile, and guarding the Collection is as important as guarding the Compass itself."

Josh's arms crossed, and he studied the ground. "Sam, I can't believe you didn't tell us. I mean, we've sat with each other every night at dinner, and you never said a word."

Sam pulled up a chair and plopped into it. "I'm sorry, Josh. We couldn't tell you until you were made Guardian, for security reasons. I didn't like keeping secrets from you. But now that you bear the Sword, I don't have to. I hope you can understand. If you knew about the Collection but had refused the Sword, it would be a liability for us."

The hardness on Josh's face softened, the reason for withholding the information sinking in. "No, I get it. I mean, it stinks, but I get it. You had to know I was committed. I wish I'd asked to be a Guardian sooner. Then we could have known about you, and all this, earlier."

Sam stood and hugged his buddy, clapping him on the back. "We wanted it to be on your birthday."

"Oh, well, in that case, that's pretty cool, actually," Josh said.

"So, happy birthday, Josh, and welcome to the family, officially." Sam spoke with such sincerity, Jenny swallowed back a few tears and refocused on the overstuffed shelves to keep from crying.

It didn't take long to sense the beauty and mystery of the Collection. Various sections of clothing ranging from medieval to Madison Avenue hung in neat, long rows, a massive stage closet full of real live costumes. Another immense shelf held all sorts of ropes: twisted rope, braided rope, and climbing rope, which Jenny noticed straight away and showed to Josh.

"We should go climbing in a book sometime," he said. "Maybe after we get everything sorted out. Ooh, look, they even have Elvish rope."

"Whoa," Jenny said, running her thumb along rope she'd read about in several of her favorite books. "I wonder if this came from Tolkien's imagination."

"What didn't come from his imagination?" Josh said.

Jenny laughed, conceding his point, but her laughter came to an abrupt stop. "Wait, do you hear barking?"

Klaus and Moose barreled through the concrete room, Fang peering down his nose at them from the bookshelf. Klaus dared to return the glare. The lion growled. "Off with you, dog."

But Klaus, fearless and haughty, refused to be bossed by a mere stone kitty cat. He marched to Josh with his chest lifted and rested on his haunches as if to say, "Make me."

Josh stroked the dog's wiry coat while he continued to peruse the aisles and shelves. Klaus slept in Josh's room by night and parked himself outside the training room by day. The Guardian's guardian.

Moose bounced in behind him, wagging and panting and sniffing here and there. "Don't pee in here, Moose!" Jenny warned her little guy, bending to scratch under his collar, giggling at his enthusiasm. "You're a good boy. Come on, follow me! Heel, or something."

She meandered to a section labeled Jewelry. *Ophelia would approve.* A pair of braided leather pieces, some kind of bracelet type thingies, caught her attention. "Sam, what are these?" Her voice was echoey and big, and it startled Moose. "Oh, sorry, buddy. It's okay! I'm not a monster," she whispered to him.

Sam met her in the Jewelry section and examined the bracelets. "Oh, those we call Flanklets. They go on your ankles and allow you to walk up walls and on the ceiling, like a fly. Fun little trinkets and quite useful in certain situations. They are one of my favorite magical objects that actually work here. We aren't sure what book they came from. Someone procured them a long time ago. And, I'm don't know what they are doing here, with Jewelry."

He strode to a set of large, heavy doors, input codes into several keypads, scanned his palm, eye, and thumb, and removed a key ring to disengage the remaining, old-fashioned locks securing it. The doors swung forward. "These Flanklets should be in here. Let me show you."

The small room he invited her into, an impressive walk-in closet with rows of shelves lining every wall, held various items, some quiet and still, some glowing or pulsing with faint light.

The hair on her arms stood on end, a tingle in the air tickling her skin. Josh joined them and shivered with the same tingle.

"This is where we keep the magical objects, the ones that work here.

They are our treasures among treasures, thus requiring a bit more security," Sam said, tapping the thick doors with multiple locks. "By the way, these Flanklets work, so if you're up for it, give them a try, once you are done in here, of course. Not a lot of space to climb the walls."

Though she wanted to see all of the magical objects, the thought of running up a wall intrigued her enough to put off the magical closet for a second. "If I'm up for it?" Jenny said, cracking her knuckles. "Gimme those." Outside the closet doors, she knelt and tied the bands on her ankles. Josh offered her an encouraging smile while she stretched her quads.

"Might I suggest starting at a bit of a run," Sam said.

"I got this," she said, tucking in her shirt. "I think." She traced a path to the ceiling with her eyes and went for it. Within seconds, she dangled like a bat from the rafters. "Eek!" she said. "Shut UP!" She moved with care, avoiding low-hanging obstacles and the many procured items stored where she now traveled. "This is awesome! Can I keep them? Please?" She danced a little jig, tentative at first but then with increasing vigor.

"Of course, Jenny. You are the Keeper. Everything in this room is at your disposal." Uncle Curtis gestured in all directions, then rested his chin on his fingers. "Let's think about the story of *Hansel and Gretel*. What do you reckon you will need to accomplish your goal of obtaining the bone from the story? What would help you most?"

"I'm a little rusty on this one, guys. Would you mind filling me in on it? Fairy tales are not my usual literary wheelhouse. I'm more of a sci-fi and fantasy type guy," Sam confessed.

*No surprise there.* She continued to view the world from a new perspective while they chatted. *This is crazy awesome! I'm never coming down.*

Rifling through a pile of coins and buttons, Josh said, "I've read the story so many times now, I think I can recite it in my sleep."

"Would you like to recount it for us, then?" Uncle Curtis asked. "For Sam's sake."

Leaving the buttons, Josh got comfortable in a chair, elbows on his knees. "I'd be happy to. Sam, you listening?"

"Yep!" he said, putting down a weird, spiky leather ball he was fidgeting with. "Sorry, this place always fascinates me, and I basically live here. Please, carry on."

"Okay, so, once upon a time there were two little kids named Hansel and Gretel who had a terrible, awful stepmother. She convinced their despondent dad to leave them in the woods to die because there wasn't enough food for all four of them. Hansel and Gretel try to find their way home and end up at an amazing, Candyland-type gingerbread house and start eating it because they are starving because their parents abandoned them in the woods." He flared his nostrils in disgust.

"An evil witch, who had built the house to lure unsuspecting children into her grasp, captures Hansel and Gretel and puts them in cages, feeding them lots of yummy things to fatten them up so she can eat them."

Jenny feigned gagging sounds overhead. "Gross, what is wrong with people?" she muttered, then shushed, allowing Josh to continue.

"Every day, the witch checks Hansel's finger to see how chubby he's getting. Hansel, wise to her plan as well as her poor eyesight, sticks out a chicken bone instead of his finger for the witch to feel. So, she thinks he isn't eating enough and continues to bring him plate after plate of food. Eventually, she tries to cook Gretel instead, but Gretel pushes her into the oven, frees Hansel, and they escape, back to their father."

A long silence followed Josh's recap—the reality of having to interact with this story sinking in. "Yeah, pretty messed up," Sam said, breaking the silence with a disgusted tone. "What happened to the stepmother? Kind of a loose end."

"The story just says she died," Jenny said.

"Convenient timing, don't you think? She dies the same time the evil witch does? Maybe the stepmother was the witch the whole time? And if not, how did the author miss an opportunity like that? Shame." He shook his head in disappointment. "Anyway, you need to get that bone without being caught by the witch, right?"

"Got anything in mind that will help us?" Josh said.

Sam held up a spray can. "How about some witch repellent?"

Conveniently and creatively labeled "Witch Repellent," it also had a warning. **DO NOT INGEST. WILL CAUSE VIOLENT VOMITING.**

"Ew," Jenny said with a groan.

"What story did *that* come from?" Josh said, wary of the can.

"I make it with my own tried and true recipe from a mixture of essential oils, deer urine, dirt, and Ipecac syrup. I've faced a lot of witches, and it works," Uncle Curtis said. "But heed the warning. I would suggest just putting some on your shoes and pants. Hold your breath while spraying it. Keep your mouth shut and run far, far away before breathing again. It works well. She won't be able to smell you. This witch is basically blind which means ..."

"Her other senses, like smell, will likely be heightened." Josh finished Uncle Curtis's thought.

"We'll take it," Jenny said. "What else could we use? Oh, and how do I get down from here? I'm starting to get a headache."

Uncle Curtis sniggered behind his coffee cup. "Either run back down or click your heels together three times."

Jenny rolled her eyes. "Seriously? Like Dorothy?" But she clicked three times anyway and flipped onto her feet, upright and dizzy. "Whoa."

"I've got to try those," Josh said, steadying her before disappearing into the Magical Objects Closet.

"How about these?" He reappeared in the doorway a minute later, holding two shimmery coats. "Watch!" With the cloak on and the hood over his head, he disappeared.

"No way!" She scooted in closer, examining the place where he had stood. "Oh, you moved! I saw you, kind of. And now you're gone again!" Searching once more. "There you are! You're camouflaged!" She gasped, poking his shoulder once she determined how it worked. "That's amazing."

"You found the Chameleon Cloaks!" Sam said. "Ooh, those are perfect for the mission. They are made from dragon skin that camouflages itself. If you need to stay hidden, pull the hood up. Then you basically disappear. If the hood is down, you reappear. If you move too quickly, less camouflage. They tend to get lost easily, as you can imagine. Here, turn them round, inside out in the meantime, to keep up with them. These will help you stay out of sight while sneaking into the old witch's cottage."

"Yes, this is a story where you will be in proximity to a particularly dangerous character," Uncle Curtis added. "Staying hidden is a good idea."

"Wow, I love this fabric!" Jenny said, admiring the inside of the cloaks, bright with a blue and green tartan. "These are, hands down, the coolest reversible cloaks ever."

They browsed for a while longer, and Uncle Curtis showed them a small dagger with a golden hilt. "This is an interesting little thing." He weighed it in his palm. "If you're hurt, hold this blade on the wound, and it will heal. However, you must be touching something else alive. It sucks the life from whatever you are touching and puts it into the injury. So, hold on to a plant or tree or an enemy, not a friend, lest you wish them pain and faintness, or even death. Tricky little tool, this one. I'm not sure how it will help in *Hansel and Gretel*, but does anyone feel drawn to it?"

"Ooh, me, me!" Jenny bounced on her toes. Uncle Curtis tossed it to her, and she slipped it into her belt. "This sounds like something from a video game instead of a book."

Sam started laughing. "Isaac actually got it from a book inspired by a video game. Good call, Jenny."

"I think I read it," Josh said. "It was a long time ago. Another lifetime ago." He stared off into space for a moment before Uncle Curtis interrupted his thoughts.

"So, Jenny, you've reached your rule of three." Her confusion made him smile, and he explained, "A Keeper or Guardian can carry no more than three magical objects into a story, in addition to the Compass and Sword. You've got your three: the Flanklets, the Chameleon Cloak, and the Healing Dagger. Any more, and you run the risk of magical overload or, more likely, losing one or all of them should you get caught by an antagonist. We can't risk losing more than three."

"What is magical overload?" Jenny said, blanching.

"It's kind of like when a fuse blows. When too much magic is involved, it can shut other magical things down, and if the Compass gets canceled out, well, you can imagine the trouble that might cause," Sam said, raising an eyebrow.

"But three is okay, no chance of overload?" she said, still worried.

"Highly unlikely," he answered, and Uncle Curtis confirmed with a nod.

She gave them a thumbs up. "I like my three," she said.

"I only have one," Josh said, holding up the Chameleon Cloak. "Well, two if you count the Sword. The Witch Repellent doesn't count. It's not magic, right?"

"Sit tight with the one for now and the Sword," Uncle Curtis told him. "Sometimes less is more for a Guardian."

Josh agreed, and then, before he could ask why, his stomach rumbled so loud it echoed throughout the Collection.

Uncle Curtis checked his watch. "It's no wonder you are hungry, Josh. It's far past dinner time, and we've had a long day. We can return here anytime. For now, give the items you'd like to keep to Sam. He'll store them for you. Will you come home for dinner, Sam?"

"For sure. I had a message earlier that Ophelia is coming back tonight. She's got another Charm!" Sam's countenance was pure joy. "And she has some information to pass along from the Netwo ..."

Uncle Curtis cleared his throat, and Sam stopped talking. This drew questioning, curious looks from both Jenny and Josh. The older man sighed, his shoulders slumping forward. "There's so much to tell you." Rubbing his face, his considered some things, sighing before he straightened up. "Okay. There is more to Ophelia's job as Searcher than we have disclosed. With your parents and Isaac gone, I feel we should focus your efforts on finding them. Once that situation is resolved, everything will come to light. Can you, *will* you, trust me with this? I promise to bring you up to date on every part of our world, but I fear if we do it all at once, it might prove a tad overwhelming. There is already so much to overwhelm you with."

Were it not for Uncle Curtis's sincere tone, Jenny knew Josh would've pushed back, demanding more information. He even took a breath like he had something to say. But the older Guardian's words were offered with such conviction and kindness, Josh's rising frustration dampened.

Uncle Curtis had not yet steered them wrong, and Jenny trusted his judgment. Plus, everything else they had to do regarding the Sorceress *was* overwhelming, and she could do without her brain exploding from an information onslaught. *I don't love not knowing, but I can live in it, at least for now. I hope Josh can do the same. He hates being in the dark.*

"You promise to tell us everything soon?" Josh said

Uncle Curtis offered him a handshake. "Aye," he said. "Of course." It took a full thirty seconds before Josh shook it, but he did.

"I'll hold you to it," he said.

"You'd better," Uncle Curtis replied.

# Chapter Fifteen

The main level of the house was dark, and Uncle Curtis pulled dinner together while everyone else washed up. Josh stepped from his room and paused,
alert, even bristling. "Hello?" he said. "Is someone there?" He stalked toward
Jenny's room, listening, prowling, and threw several doors open along the way.
Sweat beaded on his forehead. Investigating each room on the hall, he tilted
his head, listening for anything out of the ordinary. "I guess it was nothing," he
said, muttering to himself when the last room, which happened to be Jenny's,
showed no signs of trouble. "I must be really hungry or tired or something.
Thank God Jenny wasn't here to witness this."

Satisfied, he headed to the stairs. Muted giggling ricocheted off the
high hallway ceilings, followed by a shuffle. Josh groaned. "I knew it. I knew
something was off." He crossed his arms, refusing to glance up. "Come on
down, Keeper. You got me." His attempt to sound annoyed caused her
more giggles and made it impossible for him to stay angry.

With three clicks, she flipped down from the ceiling, this time landing
balanced and with panache. "Pretty stealthy," she said, laughing. "I asked

Sam if I could keep these for a while."

"I gotta try those," he said, admiring the Flanklets she revealed by lifting her baggy pajama pant legs to mid-calf.

"By the way, great room clearing skills. Seriously. Really good. Next time, check the ceilings too."

He flared his nostrils at her. "Thanks, Keeper."

∞∞∞ 🙉 ∞∞∞

Sam joined them for dinner, and just before they sang "Happy Birthday" to Josh, Ophelia strode in, swinging a Charm on her finger. Sam brightened when she tossed it to him. "You did it. Go Philly!" he said with a big high five.

*Philly?* The smiling Ophelia parked herself between Sam and Josh, all confidence and sass, but she failed to hide the tear in her sleeve, scuffed pants, and bandaged arm. Jenny raised an eyebrow.

"Rough day?" she asked her mentor.

"I'm just glad I made it in time to say, officially, Happy Birthday *Guardian*." Ophelia mussed Josh's hair then gave him a big hug. He brushed off the attention and returned to his post-dinner tea, hiding a blush beneath his loose locks.

Ophelia and Sam both passed him wrapped gifts and cards. "You guys, you didn't have to get me anything! This day has been one giant birthday gift literally wrapped in magic. What more could a guy want?" But, with some cajoling, he mustered enough energy to tear the paper. A shiny new pair of running shoes. He groaned. "This means lots of running in my future, doesn't it?"

"Oh yeah," Ophelia said.

"I love them, and I hate them," he said with a grin. "Honestly, thank you. Maybe they will help me like running more."

"New shoes always help me," Ophelia said.

"For sure," Jenny added. "Those look awesome."

Sam's gift, a vintage shaving kit in a beautiful brown leather bag, received several oohs and ahhs.

"Whoa, Josh, you shave?" Jenny said.

"Uh yeah, every day. Why are you so surprised?"

Heat crept into her cheeks. "I ... just never thought about it before."

"You shave your legs, right?" he asked. She answered with a mortified nod. "So what's the difference?"

"I guess your dad doesn't seem very, you know, hairy."

"You should see my mom's dad. He's a bear. Maybe that's where I got it from."

"Uh, maybe?" she said, refusing to make eye contact, uncomfortable discussing bathroom habits at the dinner table.

Uncle Curtis saved her any further embarrassment by bringing over the double chocolate ooey gooey cake he'd made earlier in the day. While they licked chocolate from their forks, he asked Jenny to expound on her adventure into *Robin Hood*.

"Okay, well, I sort of fell into a book by accident when I first got the Compass from Isaac." Uncle Curtis's eyebrows lifted, surprised. "I met this kooky old lady and traded her my favorite bracelet for a dress and shawl so I could fit in better. And I stole a bow and quiver of arrows from Robin's camp. And I shot an assassin in the leg with it. I still have them, actually, the bow and arrows. In my room. And the clothes."

"Oh my. Is that all?" the Guardian asked. Jenny couldn't tell if he was angry or joking.

"I think so. I got home because one of the characters, Maid Marian's lady in waiting, asked me to read the inscription on the Compass for her. When I did, I returned before I could get into any more trouble."

Josh watched her, savoring every crumb of his cake. "Were you scared?" he said, scraping chocolate icing from his plate.

Jenny rolled her eyes. "No, I wasn't scared ... much."

Uncle Curtis put down his fork and reclined in his chair. "In light of your story, perhaps now would be the time to go over the Rules Arthur Neil established to help maintain order, literary integrity, and safety. Breaking them could lead to dire consequences." His eyes darkened for a second, something Jenny had not witnessed yet. A chill ran up her spine. But the cloud passed, and Uncle Curtis returned to his normal self. "Have a gander at these."

He passed a framed document to Sam, who passed it to Jenny, whispering, "Good luck, little Keeper. Especially with Rule Number 1."

Calligraphed on fancy, hand-pressed paper, straight from an ancient library, was a list of seven short rules. Sitting straight and tall, she read them aloud.

**"Rule 1: Do not die in the story because you will also die in real life.** This is a rule I can get behind," she said with great seriousness. Josh concurred.

"**Rule 2: Do not remove characters from the story.**" She lingered on this one, then said to Uncle Curtis, "You've mentioned this before. Could you elaborate?"

"Sure. So, pulling someone out, whether permanently or temporarily, has irrevocable literary consequences. It will change the story. It has happened in the past, and we do all we can to keep it from happening again, like avoiding the plots of stories as much as possible and not getting attached to any characters, especially plot heavy characters. Removing a character that exists solely in the setting, like, for example, the old lady you met in *Robin Hood* ..."

"Granny Bea," Jenny chimed in.

"Yes, Granny Bea. Taking her from the story would have no bearing on the plot so she would be somewhat safe to remove, but as a rule, we just don't do it, ever."

Josh and Jenny nodded, trying to wrap their heads around it all.

"Have you ever read *The Final Problem* by Arthur Conan Doyle?" Uncle Curtis asked. Jenny nodded and, to everyone's surprise, so did Josh.

"What?" he said. "I like Sherlock Holmes."

"How does it end? Do you remember?" Uncle Curtis asked him.

"Well, Moriarty and Sherlock both fall to their deaths over a cliff by a waterfall, right? Though the only physical evidence is some footprints indicating a fight between the two men at the cliff's edge," he said.

"Quite right, in the version you read. However, that is not the original ending." He waggled his eyebrows. "In the original version, Dr. Watson sees Sherlock's broken body at the bottom of the cliff, obviously dead, and goes to him, confirming his death. Yes, it was overly dramatic and emotional. The public was outraged at Sherlock's death. They wanted more Sherlock, demanded more books, and Mr. Doyle was pressured to oblige them. Now, how does an author, even of his caliber, resurrect the 'obviously dead' for another Sherlock Holmes mystery? No trick or sleight of hand would do. He needed to change the ending of the story to allow Sherlock to come back. But how?"

Jenny clapped a hand over her mouth. "He used the Keeper!" Her voice croaked between her fingers. Uncle Curtis nodded.

"No way!" Josh said. "How? How did Arthur Conan Doyle even know?"

"Ah, very good. He had met Arthur Neil on a transatlantic voyage. They shared a love of literature and knowledge, and they had the same name, which they both thought was fortuitous. After building a measure of trust in their friendship, Arthur Neil confided in Mr. Doyle his secret, trusting his friend's discretion. An unwise move, in hindsight." Everyone sat stock still, enraptured by the story, anticipating the ending.

"Mr. Doyle agreed, though he eventually called upon Arthur to help him change the ending of *The Final Problem*. Arthur balked at the idea, but when Mr. Doyle pleaded with him, begging for his help, even threatening to make knowledge of the Compass public, the Keeper quelled. He jumped into the story at just the right moment for he was quite good at it by then. In the nick of time, he grabbed Sherlock Holmes and saved him from falling by whisking him to the real world for a few minutes, during which time they were said to have had a lively conversation. Arthur then returned Sherlock to the story where he would hide in a cave through the ending and be available for future narratives."

"Whoa," Josh said, leaning on his elbows. "He actually got to meet Sherlock Holmes. Amazing."

Uncle Curtis continued, "When Arthur pulled Sherlock out, it changed the ending of the story. There was only one edition, thankfully, printed in a magazine. People remembered reading how Dr. Watson saw Sherlock's body, held him, cried over him, but when they went back to read it again, it was different. It caused some frustration among readers. Confusion. Even panic in some cases. People rummaging through stacks of magazines, pulling their hair, thinking they were crazy. Can you imagine?"

They shook their heads, picturing people sweating, frantically flipping pages, consumed by confusion. "When the book finally went to print, it ended the way you remember, with no bodies in sight, and it's been like that ever since."

"Whoa," Josh breathed.

"Knowledge of the Compass, in part, also led Mr. Doyle down a strange and unexpected path into Spiritualism, a movement he helped popularize right before the turn of the century. Unfortunately, it succeeded in duping a great deal of people, giving them false hopes and needlessly emptying their pockets.

"Arthur Neil was dismayed. He was a careful, cautious man by nature, and he took a chance sharing the secret of the Compass with a trusted friend who later threatened him, used him, and caused literary chaos. It's even been suggested that Arthur Conan Doyle possibly leaked the knowledge of the Compass to the very people who eventually forced the Keeper back into *The Gilded Coffer* and stole the Lesser Charms. *This* is why we have the rules."

The others stared at Uncle Curtis. The power of the Compass and the consequences of misusing it shook Jenny to her core. She exhaled a heavy breath. Josh met her eyes with a pained expression on his face, attempting a half smile, letting her know he was with her.

"You've never told me this story, Dad," Ophelia said.

"Now you know why we are so careful," Uncle Curtis said. "With this in mind, shall we continue?" He crossed his legs and sipped from his cup. "Jenny?"

She shook her curls, an unsettled feeling lingering in her stomach from Uncle Curtis's story.

**"Rule 3: If you do take a person out of the story permanently, you must give up your role as Keeper.** Seems reasonable," Jenny said. "Knowing there are consequences to doing something so drastic would be a deterrent."

"Huh. Maybe that is why Isaac gave the Compass to you. Maybe he broke rule 3," Josh surmised.

"Whoa, Josh, what if you are right? I mean, why else would he give this up?"

"I wonder who, and why." Josh directed his glare at Uncle Curtis, who shrugged.

"I've had the same thought, and to be honest, I have no idea. Honestly. This is not information I will tell you later. I truly don't know. Isaac has some secrets, it would seem," Uncle Curtis said, more to himself than the others.

Jenny waited for Uncle Curtis to continue talking, and when he didn't, she kept reading, but not before a niggling thought wiggled into her head: *Why had her mom given the Compass to Isaac? Could she have pulled someone out? Guh, I can't even go there right now.* She read on.

"**Rule 4: Keep the Compass a secret**. No problem." She nudged Josh. "Don't tell anyone."

"Who am I going to tell?"

"We've seen how even telling one person, like Mr. Doyle, complicates things. It's better for everyone if we keep our cards close," Uncle Curtis said.

Jenny continued reading. "**Rule 5: Travel with the Guardian as often as possible.** Ha, good thing I like you guys." Uncle Curtis remained quiet. Josh beamed.

"**Rule 6: Guard the Compass at any cost**. Ooh, like, even killing people?" Jenny asked, shifting in her seat.

"Yes," said the older Guardian, "but only as a last resort, of course. We have so many other ways to deal with people who want to take the Compass."

"Such as?" Josh asked.

"Well, we can threaten them. We can move them. We can imprison them in a particular book we have called *The Long, Long Road to Nowhere*, which one of the Guardians wrote for this purpose. There are only a few people there. Really bad people. The last resort is ending them, but we only do that if they are especially violent toward us." He didn't elaborate any more on the topic. Jenny stared at her great uncle, agape, shocked at the extremes of these methods.

"These are terrible people, Jenny," Ophelia explained. "They would kill for the Compass. They would do even worse if we gave them the chance. This is our world. It's not always pretty."

Jenny swallowed, forcing down the yuckiness in her throat and read the last rule. "**Rule 7: Collect the Lesser Charms as if your life depended on it**. Ophelia, isn't that your job, mostly?"

"Yes and no. Primarily, I am the Searcher, but I often need your help, and when you aren't doing missions like the ones you are about to embark on, finding Charms becomes more of a priority."

Josh cracked his knuckles. "I could be into that. And we've been promised more information regarding this part of things once our Sorceress missions are completed." He jerked his head toward Uncle Curtis. "Just don't want you to forget."

"Indeed," Ophelia responded with a wicked grin. "There's a lot to teach you, young Guardian."

"Are we all Charm hunters then? Traveling the world in search of them?" Jenny asked.

"Actually, no," said Uncle Curtis. "No Uncle Curtis unless absolutely necessary. I'm getting older, and the traveling hurts my joints. I start to miss my bed a great deal. Even the jump into *A Tale of Two Cities* has left me pretty achy. No, I'll stay on as Guardian-in-Situ and offer advice and direction on both Keeper and Searcher missions. Josh, you will be the sole Guardian on jumps unless absolutely necessary."

Josh sat taller a little taller. "I've got some work to do then," he said.

"A Guardian must be humble, and brave, and wise, and able. You are growing in all these areas, Josh. I see it every day," Uncle Curtis said. "So tonight, I have something for you, from one Guardian to another. One more birthday present, and another magical item to add to your arsenal." Uncle Curtis placed a small ring in front of Josh. "This is the Keeper Ring, a little something Arthur obtained when he created the Guardianship. Since we've met, I've worn it, but from now on, it is yours. It will alert you if the Keeper and Compass are in danger, even if she doesn't know it."

The Ring fit snug on Josh's pinkie, and he sucked in a breath once it was in place. His eyes widened, and he almost said something to Uncle Curtis, who shook his head one time to stop him from speaking. *Curious.* Jenny observed their silent interaction. *What was Josh going to say?* But, seeing as it was a thing between the Guardians and likely none of her business, no matter how curious she was, she studied the Ring instead. It was small and delicate, unassuming and simple. The thin, silver band became thicker at the top where a stone might be inset. Instead of a stone, flat, darker metal was inlaid within the silver and etched with an intricate K. *K for Keeper, I guess?*

"Does it fit?" she asked. He nodded, lifting his hand, and she high fived it. "It's like a Keeper alarm. Pretty cool. Be sure to tell me if I'm in danger, okay?"

"No problem."

"Josh, how's it going with the Sword?" Uncle Curtis inquired.

"It's good, I think?"

"Very good," Ophelia said.

"Then continue to practice it. The first mission must be soon. The Sorceress only gave us six months, and we've used the first two for training," Uncle Curtis said.

*He'll be up early, training tomorrow. I guarantee it. Thankfully Ophelia is here to practice with. I'm no match for him with the sword. I bet he would go practice right now if he could.*

"Hey, if you want to go, I'll clear your dishes. I mean, it *is* your birthday." She stacked his plate on hers and shooed him toward the training room. He whispered a thank you and was gone, his earlier exhaustion forgotten.

∞∞∞∞ 🕸 ∞∞∞∞

After cleaning up from dinner, with her mind mulling over the Rules, Jenny slouched onto the couch, eyes heavy after a more than full day. Uncle Curtis reclined in his reading chair. Moose had charmed Ophelia into playing with him on the floor. Sam, book in hand, sunk into the couch beside Jenny. He had barely read one page before Klaus barked, interrupting his reverie. "Was that a knock on the door?" he asked. A faint rapping sounded again, and Klaus growled. "That's odd. I'll go. Jenny, stay hidden. Klaus, come on."

Jenny's heart pounded, and she ducked behind the staircase. *Who would visit here? And how did they get past the gate?* Uncle Curtis leaned forward, alert, and Ophelia stood.

Moments later, Sam returned with a smirk. "Uncle Curtis, it's someone for you."

A pale, perfect face emerged from behind Sam, with long, white blond hair shimmering in the lamplight. Big, bright, blue-green eyes blinked. A pretty, aqua scarf accented her high cheekbones. "Hello." She stepped forward, her British-accented voice sounded like a soft current running over river rocks. "You must be Curtis Neil. We've never met, though I believe you know my parents." He returned her gaze somewhat bewildered, his spectacles resting at the end of his nose.

"Liddy!" Jenny dashed from her hiding spot and embraced the surprised guest.

"Jenny? Is it you?" They separated, Liddy's palm moving to Jenny's cheek. All the strength the lovely young woman possessed melted. Tears formed in her eyes. "I've been searching for you and Josh." It took her a moment to compose herself again. "I'm sorry to intrude on you, Mr. Neil. I'm Liddy Park, Josh's sister. Adopted sister. But I expect you might know me by my other name. In the world of books, I was once known as the Little Mermaid."

# Chapter Sixteen

After staring at the young woman for what seemed like an eternity, Jenny closed her mouth. *Where is your fishtail?! How did you get your voice back?! How could you possibly want to trade the sea for land!?* The questions screamed in her head. "How?" she asked instead.

Liddy extended her left hand, which sparkled under the lights. A sapphire, bookended by diamonds, glittered on her finger. "I'm engaged to your Uncle Isaac." After these words floated from her mouth, her emotions overcame her, and she began to cry. Jenny led her to the couch, mouthing "HELP ME!" to Sam. Sam silently pleaded with Uncle Curtis. Uncle Curtis leapt into action.

"Dear, oh dear, my darling girl. Let us help you in any way we can." He sat beside her, bringing tissues.

Through her tears, Liddy tried to speak, but before she could say a word, Josh came jogging into the house, sweaty and on a mission, unaware of their guest. "I'm just going to grab something from my room," he called, dashing through the den.

"Josh?" Liddy whispered as he started up the stairs. "Josh? Joshua Park, stop!" She shouted at him, scaring Jenny half to death.

Josh indeed halted, spun to face them, and froze.

"Liddy? Liddy, what on Earth are you doing here?" he spluttered. "How did you find me?"

He ran to her, mission forgotten, and embraced her, his voice breaking. "Liddy, I'm so sorry. I'm so sorry about Mom and Dad. I wasn't there. I couldn't protect them. And I'm sorry you thought I was dead or missing or whatever story they told you. It had to be a secret, to keep you safe." His broadening shoulders, trying so hard to be grown up, shook—the grief held off by weeks of training pouring out.

The other four exchanged glances. *What has Isaac done?*

When the tears slowed, Uncle Curtis took charge. "So, you are Josh's sister." Liddy and Josh both nodded. "And you are engaged to Isaac?" She nodded again, but Josh jumped in his seat.

"You're engaged? To Jenny's uncle? What? Wait, when did that happen? How do you even know him?"

Her ring shone in the lamplight. "I'd love to tell you the story." She addressed everyone else. "I'd love to tell you *all* the story."

"Oooh, I know!" Jenny said, squealing. "Pick me!"

Liddy grinned, her cheeks still damp with tears. "Jenny, I've missed your enthusiasm. What have you figured out?"

"Isaac pulled you from a story, didn't he? Eek, oh my gosh! I can't believe it. That's so perfect and romantic." Uncle Curtis frowned, causing Jenny to backtrack. "Uh, I mean, that was totally against the rules, and he should be so ashamed. Bad Isaac. Very, very bad." She leaned in to whisper, "But OH MY GOSH!"

"Hold up. You are from a story?" The shock on Josh's face induced a giggle in Jenny, but she suppressed it with great effort, pressing her lips together, waiting for Liddy to break the news.

"Please don't freak out," his sister said.

"I mean, I'll try not to," he answered.

She took a deep breath. "What Jenny deduced is correct. Smart girl. Isaac did indeed pull me out of a story six years ago, just before I joined your family."

"No way," he whispered. "No way! Are you serious?" He seemed almost angry, but then he started laughing. "I can't believe this," he chortled, rubbing his forehead. "Can my life get any weirder? Are you gonna tell me what story, Liddy? Wait, let me guess. *Cinderella*? No, a Jane Austen novel? No ... *Buffy the Vampire Slayer*? No way, are you Buffy?"

Liddy guffawed and shook her head, her hair like a silver waterfall at dawn. "I wish. Buffy is way cooler than me."

Jenny rustled her fingers through her own curls, resisting familiar jealousy, waiting for Liddy to stun Josh with her confession. *Wait for it. Wait for it.*

"I was the Little Mermaid, Josh," she said.

He gaped. "No! No way. She has red hair."

"Ha! Oh, cinema. The power it has. The *original* Little Mermaid is pretty different from the movie," Liddy explained. "But I am her. I ... I'm sorry I didn't tell you. You can see how complicating that would've been before this happened. Before you knew about the Compass."

"This is crazy, but I guess I'm kind of used to crazy at this point," Josh said.

Uncle Curtis shifted next to her, moving to his reading chair, making more space for everyone. "We'd love to hear the story, Liddy. I think I speak for all of us when I say we are intrigued," he said, easing into a comfortable position. His joints did seem more creaky than usual.

So, Liddy settled into the couch. "Josh's parents adopted me six years ago when I was eighteen, one year after Isaac saved me from my story." She glanced at Uncle Curtis. "He ... he kept it a secret because he wasn't prepared to give up his role as Keeper. He never told you, and it gnawed at him. He asked Josh's parents to let me live with them for a while, to help me adjust and to maintain our secret. Isaac knew Amelia from the library, where he spent quite a bit of time. They were good friends. He knew she had a younger son and no daughter and was a gracious, kind, resourceful person." Josh smiled at the mention of his mother.

"What began as a short-term solution became long term. I grew to love my parents and brother in a way I never experienced in my first family. My mer-sisters were more into their hair and marrying a respectable merman, and my father was cold, consumed with maintaining his power rather than raising his daughters. My new family returned the love I had for them, and they offered to adopt me. They somehow legalized me as a citizen and their adopted daughter. I'm not completely sure how they accomplished it. I fear it might not all be quite above board."

She spoke to Uncle Curtis once more. "I'm sorry Isaac broke the rules. He was in love and not thinking right, and he wanted to give the Compass to Jenny, but she was too young. Just after he asked me to marry him, he came here, to celebrate your birthday, Jenny, and pass along the Keeper binding to you. He knew it wasn't his to keep once our secret was out, and he felt you were old enough." Jenny rested her cheekbone against her fingers, remembering her last interactions with her uncle the day he had relinquished the Compass.

"I'd hoped he'd told you, Curtis, about us, but it seems he never made it this far. That was two months ago. A few days after he left, I was not able to get ahold of him. He was not responding to anything. I tried calling him, over and over, for days, but nothing. The same with my parents. No one was answering. I knew it had something to do with the Compass. " Liddy's voice broke again.

"So how did you get here?" Jenny asked.

"Since I couldn't reach my family or Isaac, I knew I needed to find you all. But Isaac had said if anything happened to him to sit tight, to wait for him, that he would return. He had seemed especially distracted and busy lately. And banged up. Always a new injury. I realize now he probably was trying to keep me safe, especially in light of what happened to my parents. Even he couldn't have seen that coming."

Jenny squeezed her eyelids together. *Oh, Isaac, I wish you were here too. Then you could explain all the gaps in this crazy thing we are living in.* He had known something bad might happen to him, which accounted for his strange, intense words on her birthday. They made a lot more sense in light of Liddy's story.

"Anyway, after a while with no word from Isaac, I got tired of waiting.

I was too worried. I had nearly worn a hole in my rug, pacing. So I flew home and arrived at my parents' empty house. Jenny's house was empty too. And Isaac's flat. That's where I've been staying. I knew better than to go to the police. How can they help when it's Compass-related?"

"Liddy, you are a clever girl. And a brave one. We know what happened to Isaac. We are working on what happened to your parents, and Jenny's as well. They are gone too. I'd be happy to fill you in, but first, if you don't mind, let me ask you ... how did you find us?" Uncle Curtis said.

Liddy smiled, though it did not fully erase the grief etched into her skin. "This morning, as I trudged through Isaac's house, I heard a thud. A book had fallen. It had the name *Curtis Neil* inside the cover. You must have given it to him at some point. I was never so thankful for your family's weird obsession with literature." She almost laughed, and the rest of them exchanged a few chuckles. "I didn't know your name until then. Isaac always just called you Uncle C, for security, I guess. My parents had mentioned your name before, so I put the pieces together and came knocking. I wish I'd come sooner."

She nudged Josh with her shoulder. "I should've been here for my brother. But I am here now, and I want to help. And Josh, I'm sorry I never told you. I have few secrets, but the ones I bear are ... significant. I hope you can forgive me."

"Of course, Liddy. I have secrets now too. I get it. And, as cheesy as it sounds, this is the best birthday present ever."

Ophelia, who had been silent since Liddy's arrival, playing with Moose on the floor, scrutinized the latest addition to the room. "Well, that was one heck of a story." She stood to her feet and sauntered closer, offering their guest a hand. Liddy took it, allowing herself to be pulled to her feet.

The two young women, polar opposites in the looks department, faced each other. Liddy, with flowing blond locks and piercing blue-green eyes, was tall and lithe. Ophelia, petite and muscled, her dark hair cut short, narrowed her golden cat-eyes, daring Liddy to meet them. Liddy dared.

"I'm Ophelia. Searcher. Seeker. Finder. I also have a knack for seeing into people's hearts, figuring out their story, their motivations, the good and the bad. Those of us bound to a Charm receive a gift from it, and this is mine."

*Well, Ophelia doesn't beat around the bush, does she?* Jenny leaned forward, anxious to see one of these gifts in action. Josh did the same thing.

"It's a gift I don't use often, but when strangers show up here, it comes in handy. We tend to be a little suspicious in this house, as you can imagine," Ophelia said.

Josh huffed. "Ophelia! Liddy is my sister. How could you even … ?"

"It's all right, Josh. I understand her apprehension. And I happen to know a thing or two about these gifts." She winked at him before facing Ophelia once more. "I'm Liddy, former mermaid princess. If you look into my heart, I fear it will not be a cheerful place. If you are not afraid, then I'm an open book." Ophelia did not hesitate to pull Liddy closer, pressing one palm on her chest and one on her brow. They stayed that way for a minute. A long, quiet, tense minute.

Exhaling, Ophelia let go. "You ARE her. You are the Little Mermaid. Oh, you poor dear. You poor, sweet darling." Ophelia embraced Liddy, a tear trickling to her jaw.

ᐤᐤᐤᐤᐤ 🝔 ᐤᐤᐤᐤᐤ

They stayed up late. Josh didn't leave Liddy's side, and Ophelia squeezed in beside her.

When Jenny inquired how Liddy had gotten her voice back, how she could walk without pain, and how she'd managed to escape being turned into seafoam since she didn't hold up her part of the bargain with the Sea Witch, Liddy smiled softly. "So, you've read my story before." She went on to explain how those things had been a concern for her and Isaac before she left the story. There was even a chance leaving the story could have killed her. But she was fated to become seafoam anyway, so it was a risk she felt was worth taking.

"Remember when I said I knew a thing or two about the gifts?" Liddy said. "It's because Isaac's gift saved me. In fact, it's the impetus for a lot of this mess."

She went on to explain how the Compass had bestowed on Isaac the gift of curse-breaking. His gift drew him to Liddy from the start for he was able to see that she was riddled with curses from the Sea Witch and suffering because of them. He broke the curse binding her voice so she could speak, and the one causing her legs such pain when she walked. The biggest curse, the one condemning her to 300 years as seafoam, was complicated and difficult. Isaac wasn't sure he had done enough.

"And it worked, obviously," Liddy said, flipping her hair over her shoulder with a little shrug. "Thankfully."

Jenny told her and Josh's side of the story again, hating to break the news to Liddy regarding Isaac's kidnapping. She took it bravely, tearful yet hopeful that they were working to rescue him. The news of her parents hit a bit harder, the ambiguity of their whereabouts and situation such a hard pill to swallow.

"Don't worry, Liddy. We are training hard and preparing to get them all back, or at least get some answers," Josh assured her. "It'll be soon. I promise."

ooooo &#x1F46A; ooooo

Exhausted by the intensity and emotion of the evening, they soon decided to turn in for the night for some much needed rest. Jenny flopped into bed, savoring the soft mattress and feather pillows. A gentle tapping sounded on her door. *Ugh, I just want to be alone!* But she sat up anyway. "Come in," she called, trying to not appear quite so sleepy or irritated.

Josh peeked in. "Were you asleep?" She shook her head no. Leaving the door cracked about six inches, he plopped into the chair by her bed.

With her knees drawn into her chest, she waited for him to start talking. He sat still, his elbows on his thighs, staring straight ahead at the floor, then meeting her gaze. "Liddy is here, Jenny. My Liddy, my sister—and now I find out she's the freakin' Little Mermaid! What the heck? This is all just ... insane." He rubbed his eyes. "But you know what? I'm so happy about it."

Jenny's heart squeezed. If Isaac walked through the door just then, she would feel the same delight. *I could be so jealous right now.* But, she shared in her friend's joy instead. They needed any smidgeon of joy available.

"Josh, I want to ask her about her tail. And how things work underwater, like talking. Have you ever talked underwater? I mean, it's impossible. How do mer-people do it? Do you think she would mind if I asked?"

177

"I don't think she would mind. She's easy to talk to and far stronger than she appears. I want to know why you asked her how she can walk without limping?"

"Oh, sure, I'm happy to explain! So, in the story of the Little Mermaid, after she gets her legs, it's really painful to walk, like she's stepping on daggers. It's part of the curse of the Sea Witch. But Liddy walks just fine. I wanted to know why."

"Speaking of daggers, we go into her story to get a dagger for the Sorceress," he said, remembering what was written in the letter.

"I did consider that, and I hope Liddy will help."

"It sounds like she wants to help with as much as she can. Getting Isaac back is her primary concern, and Uncle Curtis said she could stay here until then, but he doesn't want her jumping into stories. I guess she will be support, like him and Sam. Jenny, I still can't believe she's here. Part of my real family is meeting my found family!"

Jenny wilted, despite her best intentions.

"Did I say something wrong?" he said, concerned.

"No, it just makes me wish my uncle was here, for me, for Liddy. You would love him too. He is so fun." Jenny rested her cheek on her knee.

"I liked him the few times we met before all this. We'll get him back, Jenny. I promise."

Though his words warmed and encouraged her, she balked at his promise. "Can we do something for each other, because we are friends? Could we avoid making promises we might not be able to keep?" He bristled for a moment.

"Don't be offended!" she said. "I don't doubt your ability or the heart behind your promise. It's just that some promises shouldn't be made. Not everything can be controlled or manipulated or predicted. We won't always succeed despite our best efforts."

He mulled over her words. "Can I rephrase then? How about, I'll do everything in my power to get him back, Jenny, and I know you will too. If anyone can do this, it's us, and Ophelia. She's pretty amazing, and terrifying, and usually gets what she wants." They both smiled, then snickered, and then buried their faces in pillows for fear of waking the others with their increasing volume, which made them laugh even harder.

# Chapter Seventeen

Once the hilarity subsided, Jenny bounced with new energy despite a long and eventful day. She tapped her chin. "Hey, want to jump into a book?" Then she hid behind her pillow again, waiting for him to poo-poo the idea.

Josh frowned. "Seriously? Do you think it's safe?"

"Wait, you'd even consider it?" She peeked from behind the pillow.

"Sure, why not! We've been training a ton. Let's put it to work."

Tossing the pillow to him, she grabbed a few books from the shelf. "Nothing scary, just somewhere beautiful, and outside. I miss being outside. I want to climb a tree." She sighed, then tossed a book on the bed in front of him titled *Hills and Coves of the Blue Ridge Mountains: 100 years of Photographs in Middle Appalachia.* Josh flipped through the book. Pictures of rolling mountains and silver cascading streams begged to be explored. "As long as we avoid these random cabins in some of the pictures, the biggest dangers will probably be bears or falling off a cliff," he said.

"Always thinking like a Guardian," Jenny goaded him. "I think we can avoid all of those fairly easily."

"Okay, let's do it, but wait just a second." He dashed to his room, and when he returned a few minutes later, he wore hiking boots and a jacket and held a small spray bottle. "Bear spray, just in case." It tucked perfectly in a small pack slung on his shoulder. "I have a few other things, too."

"Just in case?" Jenny asked.

"Just in case," he said.

She shoved her feet into her boots and pulled a jacket over her sweats and t-shirt.

The Compass sensed their intention, and it hummed to life against Jenny's chest, her heart beating faster with anticipation. "This is so exciting!" she whispered.

He flipped through the book. "What page do we want to jump into?"

"Oh, I don't know. Surprise me!" She closed her eyes.

He studied her for a moment, thinking, then flipped to a particular page. "Perfect," he said. "Okay, don't look." She reached for his hand, and he led her to the book. "Now lean in closer, a little more ..."

And they were gone.

Strong arms drew her close, and she relaxed into them. His longer legs hit first, taking the impact of the landing, and he lowered her onto the soft grass. "You can look now." His voice was gentle.

She lifted her face to the warm sun, letting it splash across her skin. A smile followed. One eyelid slid open, and then the other.

They stood in a large field, part of an even larger cove crisscrossed with old fencing, enclosed by towering green mountains reaching skyward. A creek rushed through the field, swelled to its banks. One big, lonely tree perched on the bank. A narrow path led to the tree, well worn by those seeking shade and a place to rest. Jenny gave Josh a high five and, with a whoop, took off running toward the tree, her arms extended like an airplane and hair flying free.

Swinging onto the lowest branch and letting her feet dangle, she waved. The breeze rustled the leaves and her tresses.

"Come on!" Jenny said. "Come play!"

He jogged to her, examining the creek, then removed his boots, rolled up his pants, and tiptoed into the cold mountain water. From her roost, she spotted minnows darting about his toes, curious of this big stranger in their midst.

He waded through the stream, slow and careful, searching for something. When he stopped, the Guardian Sword, sleeping in its silver cylinder, came to life with nary a whisper. When he raised it overhead, the world stilled and grew silent, save Jenny's pounding pulse. She gasped. He was so fast. One second he stood frozen, a perfect statue, and the next, his sword swooped out of the water, a large bass harpooned by the blade. He threw the fish on the bank. "Hungry?" he said.

Within a few minutes, he had a fire blazing, placed two potatoes wrapped in tinfoil on it, and passed her a bottle of water. A stick of butter, salt, and a citronella candle were set on a small, cloth napkin.

"When did you get butter?" Jenny asked, surprised. "And everything else?"

Josh got a little red. "You know how hungry I get, especially when I'm training a lot. I asked Uncle Curtis if I could keep a small fridge in my room for snacks and drinks. I *might* keep some extra butter in there, because can you really ever have too much butter? And the foil stays on top of my fridge. I kept needing it to wrap up leftovers and got tired of walking downstairs." She giggled, picturing Josh cramming bread and butter into his face at midnight in his room while poring over some book on using a crossbow or herbal medicine. "The potatoes—those are from the kitchen. I doubt Uncle Curtis will notice. There are like, fifty in the pantry. You'd think he was Irish or something."

"Ha, don't let him hear you say that!" she said.

The fire popped and crackled while Josh cleaned the fish, and Jenny busied herself by twirling a curl on her finger and taking in the scenery, trying not to think about fish guts. Once it was clean, he patted it with butter, wrapped it loosely in foil, and set it on the coals along with the potatoes. Then he walked through the field, searching for something. He returned with a handful of little green leaves and long stems. "Chickweed," he explained. "It's edible, and I think it might be good sprinkled over the fish. I'm just guessing, though. I'm not a good cook." Jenny rolled her eyes at his humility and took a few stems of chickweed to chew on while they waited.

The sun started to sink behind the mountains, and the moon hinted at making an appearance with a silhouette in the sky. Savory fish flaked in their fingers, and they shoved potatoes slathered in butter into their mouths. Jenny didn't talk much. She didn't need to. All thoughts of the Compass and her parents and Isaac and the Sorceress floated away with the smoke and ashes from the fire. Breathing came easy.

Josh was just as peaceful, staring into the fire and sighing occasionally.

"Want to explore?" she asked him once the bones were discarded and plates licked clean.

"Sure, but we need to get back pretty soon. It's getting late at home, and we don't have much daylight left here." He always kept up with the time, which meant she didn't have to. She never wore a watch, but Josh checked his often. Somebody had to.

They doused their fire and tidied their makeshift camp.

"Okay, which way?" Jenny asked.

"I wonder if your Compass can tell direction here. Like, could it point north?" He gestured to the North Star, already shining bright despite the twilight sky. Sure enough, when Jenny held the Compass flat in her hand, it spun right to the North Star, which was stationed above one of the higher peaks. "How about north, then?" he said. "At least we would know to return straight south should we get lost."

"Or just ask the Compass to take us home," Jenny reminded him.

"Oh yeah, I forgot that was an option." He chuckled. "It feels so real here."

"It is, in a way," she said.

He took the lead, marching toward the base of the mountain, the grass rustling at their feet.

Just when twilight gave way to nighttime, they spotted a cabin nestled in a small field, the mountain rising behind it, thick with hardwoods. A few out-buildings dotted the periphery. A small copse of trees near the cabin provided a safe place to observe.

The house drooped, with a hand-shingled roof and cluttered front porch. Dried plants hung upside down, tied to the rafters. Buckets and bowls and pans lined the railings and floor. A lone rocking chair managed to fit there, among the things. No decoration, no beauty. "Should we take a quick peek inside?" she whispered. Curiosity urged her on, and the cabin was quiet. No one was home. "I think it's empty."

Scanning the holler, Josh balked. "I think we should leave well enough alone. People in places like this can be jumpy. And I'm pretty sure that's a shotgun leaning up against the wall on the porch."

She pressed forward. "I'm going. Just to look in the windows. I've never seen a real live log cabin like this."

He grabbed her hand. "Jenny, I don't have a good feeling about this. Please, please let's just go home."

Shaking off his hand, she darted for the cabin. "Just for a minute! It'll be fine!" Thirty seconds later, her nose pressed against the old, cloudy glass. "You've got to come see this," she called to him.

"Jenny! The Ring! It's hot!" And he disappeared into the shadows.

A pack of young men stepped from the woods behind the house, a mongrel growling in the lead and a long-gun on more than one shoulder.

They halted, surprised to find a girl standing at the window. "Hello," she said and took off running, straight toward Josh, still hidden, she hoped, in the trees. The dog sprinted after her, the men yelling in accents she could barely understand. A rock launched from the copse of trees kicked up dirt near the dog, and another, and another, slowing it enough for Jenny to gain a few extra yards before it continued its pursuit.

The men followed the mutt. A gunshot sounded, and she grimaced, ducking. Something swiped at her ear. The darkness consumed her, and she blindly reached for Josh. Her fingers found nothing but air. Panic rose in her throat. "Josh!" she cried. The dog grew ever closer, covering ground at twice her speed. Frantic, she searched the dark for a tree or a rock or a stump to climb. Anything to help her escape the hound pursuing her.

A crash and a yelp. A ragged, angry voice shouted, "Go on, get outta here! Git!"

Clouds broke, and the moon greeted the night, oblivious to the chaos below, kindly illuminating the forest and casting long shadows along the uneven ground. Men marched through the trees, surefooted, familiar with the landscape. Glimpses of gun barrels glinted in the moonlight. Jenny pressed herself flat against a wide trunk. *Where can I go?* The Compass hummed, urging her home. *I can't leave without Josh! Where are you? Please!*

Her head ached from searching the blackness for any sign of him. Crunching leaves underfoot disclosed the pack of perturbed hillbillies' proximity to her. Trying to slow her breathing and remain hidden, she scolded herself for coming without any weapons. *How could I be so stupid? And why does my ear hurt?* She rubbed her earlobe, which felt wet and sticky.

"Fan out, boys!" someone commanded in a loud whisper from the other side of the tree. "They can't have got far."

The Compass was cold against her skin. Every sound garnered her full attention. A stick snapped to her left. She whipped her head around.

A dirty, sweat streak face grinned maniacally not six inches from hers. "Boo!" he said, laughing at her, grabbing her hair at the nape of her neck and yanking back. She cried out, slamming her body into the tree, trapping the man's fingers between her shoulder blades and the bark. With a gasp, he released her, shaking his bloody knuckles. "Owwww!" he hissed through clenched teeth.

Before he could utter one more word, she rammed her fist into his hateful mouth. Several teeth loosened on contact. Grabbing a low hanging branch, she drew her knees into her chest and kicked, shooting the man backward, leaving two muddy footprints on his chest. He crashed into a boulder and moaned before slinking away, holding his flank.

A shot sounded nearby. Everything grew quiet. *Josh!* Words wouldn't form on her tongue. *Please be okay.* A silent prayer drifted up through the branches overhead.

Breathing hard and holding in her tears, she slumped against the tree, reminding herself to stay alert, aware. Wiping the bark from her damp hands, she let her arms drop to her sides.

In that instant, calloused fingers found hers. She gasped. "Let's go home," a familiar voice rasped. The clouds shifted again, and moonlight illumined Josh's damp black hair and scratched face. Relief flooded her chest. Stepping in close, ensuring a firm grip on him, she whispered the Latin words to take them home.

They landed on her floor with a thump, the photography book sitting undisturbed on the table.

"Welcome back," said a sweet voice from the direction of Jenny's bed. Startled, they found Liddy in the bedside chair. She smiled and leaned forward. "I went down to Josh's room earlier to tell him goodnight one last time, and he was gone. So I knocked here, and you were gone too. And then I saw the book open on your bed. Since I'm no dummy, I figured you went for an adventure. Want to tell me where you've been or why your ear is bleeding, Jenny?"

Jenny touched her ear once more. "Ouch!" Blood stained her fingertips.

Josh handed her a tissue without a word. Obviously angry, he paced in front of her door. "Why didn't you leave when I said we should, Jenny?" Sweat beaded on his brow. A red welt raised on his cheek. "You wouldn't listen, and you end up grazed in the ear by shot, Jenny. Bullets. Do you see how close that was?"

"Hey, I'm the one who's bleeding!" Jenny sputtered.

"I had to fight a massive dog!" Josh shouted. "And two men with guns! All because you took too big a risk. Your curiosity got the better of you." He slumped against the wall. "Just to see a cabin. A dumb old cabin." Deflated and tired, his voice withered.

"You are the one always telling me to be brave," she said, blood dripping off her earlobe. She wiped it with another tissue.

"There is a difference between bravery and stupidity." He stared at her, then slid to the floor, his head in his hands. There he stayed, silent and still. A muffled sob caught in his throat. His shoulders shook for a second time that day. So many tears on his birthday.

*Oh heavens, what have I done?*

Liddy, being the oldest and most mature, let her brother work through his emotions on his own. Once he wiped his nose and stemmed the flow of tears, she took both of their wrists, creating a bridge between them. "You both have a job. One as Keeper, one as Guardian. I happen to know a little about this. Because of Isaac, I know how this all works." She gave them both a little shake.

"You are a team, and you must listen to one another and understand where the other person is coming from. Jenny, trust your Guardian. He is your friend and co-protector of the Compass. He will always have your safety and security, and the safety of the Compass, as a priority. You cannot do *your* job if you are hurt or dead." Jenny, downcast and contrite, nodded.

"Josh, understand that your Keeper has goals that might put her in harm's way. Help her achieve them as best you can while keeping you both alive. You need to trust one another and appreciate that you are different people. Perhaps one is weak where the other is strong. You make each other stronger together. Now kiss and make up."

"What?!" Jenny's shock was too much for Liddy, who snorted with laughter.

"Just kidding, you guys. Seriously, don't do that. It might be disastrous. Shake hands or hug or something. Talk to each other. Be *friends*, and apologize." She strutted to the door. "I expect a normal morning tomorrow. No weirdness between you two. And if you can pull it off, no one else will know about your little escapade tonight. Okay then, sleep well." And she left. She had not wasted any time making herself quite at home.

The door clicked shut.

"I'm sorry ..." they said simultaneously, breaking the iciness between them.

"You go," Jenny said.

Josh let out a breath. "I'm sorry I got so angry. It's just that ... I knew it was a bad situation and you kept pressing. My job is to protect the Com-

189

pass, and that means protecting *you*, and I'd rather avoid needless encounters with gun-toting mountain men if possible, as part of my job. Our first two jumps together have culminated in fighting, and this one ended in *us* fighting. I don't like that."

Jenny frowned, ashamed that her curiosity and willfulness had put them in a tricky situation. They had gone there for fun. They had no mission, no plan, no goal except to have a little side adventure. "I'm sorry too. I was stubborn and stupid. In the future, feel free to remind me if I'm being dumb."

"I'll be happy to!" His enthusiasm elicited a smile from Jenny. "Just don't get mad when I do."

"I won't. I promise," she said, shaking off the discomfort between them. The comment Liddy had made about them not kissing, however, was not so easy to shake. It had weaseled its way into Jenny's mind and ruminated. *I mean, it would be a terrible idea. Not that I even want to. It'd be like kissing my brother. Ew. Don't even think about it, Jenny. But I wonder what it'd be like to …*

"Jenny? Hey, are you there?" His voice broke through her internal dialogue.

"Huh? I mean, yeah, I'm here. Don't worry, I won't."

ooooo 🜨 ooooo

When Jenny got into bed, she saw her clock—1:12 am. *Longest day of my life.* She lay there, visions of campfires, fish, shotguns, and Josh's face drifting through her mind. Just before drifting off, a small shuffle and thump sounded from her bookshelf, but her heavy eyelids drooped shut before she had the inclination to investigate.

∞∞∞ 🕸 ∞∞∞

The next morning, Jenny lingered in bed, stretching, replaying the events of the day before. They had visited *A Tale of Two Cities*, explored the Collection, met the Little Mermaid, and kind of gotten shot by Appalachian homesteaders. She and Josh had also had their first argument since he had started soccer all those months ago. Though they'd made up last night, her stomach still had a knot in it. *Why didn't I listen to him and at least consider his concerns?* She reprimanded herself. The wound on her ear, now scabbed over, was an obvious reminder of her mistake. *Never again. We've got to be a team. Not just Jenny and her handsome Guardian. Oh no. Not handsome. Why did I say handsome? Faithful. Faithful Guardian. That's better. And no kissing. As if he'd want to anyway.*

With a sigh, she buried her face in a pillow, anything to shut off the stream of consciousness rattling in her head.

"Oh! That's what I'll do!" She threw the pillow off and hopped out of bed. Her sketchbook and pencils, long ignored, waiting patiently on her desk. "What's this?" she wondered, picking up an unfamiliar box of colored pencils, ones she had never bought. "Huh." A little note fell from the box, which she unfolded and read. "Oh Josh," she whispered, putting down the note and dropping into her chair. "I don't deserve a friend like you." Selecting several pencils and pulling the sketchbook into her lap, she drew for the first time since her family had disappeared.

# Chapter Eighteen

The kitchen table was empty, save for a gorgeous breakfast, when Jenny sauntered downstairs. Uncle Curtis greeted her, coffee cup in hand and chef's hat in place, starting her waffle without a word. "Could I have two?" she said.

"Hungry after yesterday's jump?" he wondered, and she nodded, shoving a handful of blueberries into her mouth like she hadn't eaten in days. *More like jumps. Man, I could eat a horse.* She reached for bacon.

Josh crept into the kitchen a few minutes later, hair sticking in several directions, dragging his feet. He fell into a chair at the table, eyeballing Jenny, loading his plate with bacon and blueberries and toast. His stomach growled. She passed him the butter. "It's for your bacon," she whispered, giggling, and he stuck his tongue out at her in a good-natured way. *I guess he's not mad.*

While Uncle Curtis placed waffles on the table, he noticed Josh's injury. "Oh dear, what happened to your face, Josh?"

"Training accident," he half-confessed, stealing a glance at Jenny. She kept her lips sealed.

"I see," Uncle Curtis said. "Can't be too careful, eh? Now, your studies this afternoon begin at 1:00 p.m. sharp. It'll be something a bit different today."

"The usual spot?" she said, hoping to spend more time in the well-stocked library that smelled of old books and knowledge.

"No, near the Collection," Uncle Curtis answered.

"Something different? Can you give us a hint?" Josh said. He did not like surprises.

"Your hint will come at 1:00. Don't be late."

Jenny grinned. "Eek! I love hints!"

Ophelia arrived, dressed in cold weather gear with a thick pullover slung on her arm, and told them to dress warmly for training. "Wear your new running shoes, Josh."

"Great," he muttered, rubbing his forehead, still trying to wake up. "Any more coffee in there, Uncle Curtis?"

Jenny shoveled her breakfast and dashed upstairs, stopping in Josh's room to drop off his gift then heading to her own to change for training. Minutes later, he tramped up the stairs, his heavy clomps ringing along the hall. *I hope he finds it soon and doesn't hate it.* Waiting for him to knock with something sweet to say, she pulled on running tights and thick socks and a fleece jacket. But no knock came. She delayed an extra few minutes, milling about her room, straightening some scattered books and pages. "Hmm." She sighed and headed to the kitchen, stealing a glance at his closed door. On the table in the kitchen was a note from Ophelia: MEET ME IN THE TRAINING ROOM.

She waited at the kitchen table for Josh, who soon arrived. He wore sweats and gloves and a winter hat for added warmth, per Ophelia's instructions. If Ophelia said dress for the cold, they anticipated a blustery training session.

"Hey," he said to Jenny.

"You ready? Ophelia wants to meet us in the training room," Jenny said, holding up the note.

"I am," he said. "At least I think I am. I hope I survive today."

Jenny adjusted her ear warmer. The curls bloomed around her face, and she'd added little braids to the wilder parts, like an untamed savage Celtic fitness princess.

"You'll be fine," she said, rolling her eyes. "You are the fittest person I know, except for Ophelia. Sometimes I think she's like, part machine. Ophelia—the most beautiful cyborg ever." When Josh didn't respond, Jenny swallowed. "I realize cyborgs probably aren't part of your purview. They aren't generally popular topics in the soccer locker room. Just a guess."

"You guessed right. But I like the idea, and cyborg is a cool word. Maybe we can meet one in a book sometime."

They walked together, shoulder to shoulder. "I found a little something on my pillow this morning," Josh said halfway across the yard.

"Oh yeah? Was it a cyborg?" she asked, feigning ignorance.

"A drawing, actually, of a campfire by a stream, near a big tree."

"Well, how nice. Did you like it?"

"It was okay. Kind of amateur." Now it was her turn to stick her tongue out, and she punched him in the arm.

"Honestly, I love it."

"Really?"

"Really." There was a quiet moment between them before they descended into the training room. Jenny held the shed door shut for a moment blocking his entrance.

"Do I really bring more color to your life?" she asked him with an unusual amount of sincerity, her fingers squeezing his note from the pencil box she'd tucked in her jacket pocket.

"Yes," he said. "I wouldn't have said it if it weren't true." Her hands fell to her sides, and he held the door for her, extending the invitation for her lead the way to their doom.

Ophelia stood in the training room in her coat, holding a book. The Compass sprang to life, anticipating the next few moments. Jenny jumped, startled by the vibrations.

"Okay, Keeper, time for you to show us your stuff. We're doing our training elsewhere today, and I need you to take us there."

"Oh! Okay, sure. Where, exactly, are we going?"

Ophelia showed them the cover.

"Wales?" Jenny squealed and bounced on her toes.

"Good, you know it. And not Wales exactly, but the Wales represented in this book. There will be no people there since the book is about the mountains in Snowdonia and has no people in the pictures, so that's a win for us. We will run and work there for a few hours and return in time for you to make your 1:00 lesson with my dad."

"Wales? For real? Like, for real?" Josh asked. "But ... why?" Jenny couldn't tell if he was excited, nervous, or confused.

"Well, it's cold, it's rocky, it's pretty barren, and Mount Snowdon is a great, big hill. If you are going to face the Sorceress and finish all her tasks, at some point, you will probably have to run hard and fast. Just trust me on this. Being a Keeper or Guardian involves a lot of running."

"Yeah, I've gathered that already." He pointed to his new shoes. "But don't we …" he slapped his forehead. "I almost asked if we needed our passports before I realized that was a stupid question."

"No passport necessary," Ophelia said with a snort.

Gripping Jenny's elbow, Josh stretched his quads, using her for balance. "Even though I don't love running, this is starting to sound awesome," he said. "You will both totally school me on the mountain, but you know what, I don't even care, because it's WALES." He shook her arm with excitement. "Wales, Jenny! I've always wanted to go!"

"I've actually been there before, and it is just as awesome as you think it'll be. And I wouldn't count on us beating you. You've gotten good at running. It'll be close."

"It's not a race, it's a run. Don't forget that. Let's go." Ophelia took Jenny's other hand, and they approached the book. The Compass pointed straight to it, pulling them in, and then they were gone, the rocky ground of Snowdonia fast approaching. Josh landed with ease, steadying Jenny when she stumbled.

"Thanks," she said. "I have a hard time sticking these landings."

Ophelia touched down without issue, of course. "Everyone good?" She had to yell above the whipping wind tugging at them, begging them to run with it. With two affirmatives, she pointed to the top of the mountain looming overhead, obscured by clouds. "Let's roll."

Rocks crunched under their feet as they took off, ascending Mount Snowdon. Light rain, threatening to turn to snow, pelted their faces. Despite the rain, the beauty of the place was undeniable. Patchy green and brown meadows stretched between the peaks, dotted with huge boulders and miles of stone fences breaking up the landscape. These were not the biggest mountains, but they were breathtaking. Treeless, rocky, desolate, and gorgeous.

Jenny soaked it in. Each step carried her closer to the summit, closer to the sky. Her breath drove her on. The air and the landscape and Uncle Curtis's waffles fueled her. The Compass pulsed with her heartbeat, quickening with every new vista or steep hill. Her vision blurred from both the rain and the overwhelming impression of being truly alive.

"You love this, don't you?" Josh said, breathless next to her.

"Oh yes!" she said. Strong legs carried her swiftly through the crags and past ruins of old stone cottages, so still and lifeless, completely opposed to how she felt. A quick glance at Josh proved he felt the same, brimming with life, pressing, pushing, reaching for the top. Their lungs were almost to bursting when Ophelia slowed, stopping by the gutted skeleton of an old church. The ceiling was long gone, but the remaining stone walls reached from the ground to the heavens. Remnants of arched windows framed the vistas beyond. Snow clung to existence in the shady corners of the church walls.

"Could you climb this?" Ophelia asked Jenny, gesturing to the tops of the roofless walls.

Jenny hesitated. "I think so. My friend Rae could, easily. She's really good." With a few quick movements, Jenny made her way ten feet off the ground before dropping to her feet. "It's tough. The holds are really shallow, and I'm rusty."

Ophelia's eyebrows raised. "But Rae could do it? All the way?"

"For sure."

"Cool. Okay, we're done here." They hit the trail, up and up, always up. The air thinned, their breath came faster, more desperate. Now the wind attempted to stop them, pushing them, slowing their progress. Jenny fought against it with all her might, refusing to let this invisible force to defeat her. "Come on Jenny!" Josh called to her. "Keep going!" With each ragged breath, he encouraged her.

She dropped back to follow him, using his big frame as a windbreak. He glanced at her, smiling and then refocusing on his task. The cold seeped in, first her nose, then ears, then fingers and toes. *I hate being cold.*

Drafting behind him offered her a break from the freezing gusts, and he seemed to never tire despite them.

The summit loomed ahead, and she dashed next to him. "Want me to take the lead for a few minutes?"

"I'm fine!" he said. "Let's finish together!"

Nearing the top, the incline became steeper. They scrambled over rocks and rises. The ground changed to gravel and snow, and the rain turned to tiny snowflakes dancing on the airstreams. Breathless and exhausted, they scaled the final stone staircase to the top of the British Isles.

Hands on hips, Jenny paced, sucking air in an attempt to not faint. Josh collapsed to the ground, panting and laughing. "That was so hard!"

he said. Ophelia high fived them both. With rosy cheeks and snow on her lashes, she sat on a step to rest, a picture of athletic perfection, not one hair out of place.

Jealousy panged in Jenny's chest, and she raked her fingers through her half-curly, half-wet, totally chaotic mane. *I'll never be as beautiful as Ophelia. Never ever.*

Josh, now recovered from his exertion, grabbed her into a big hug, jostling the jealous thoughts rampant in her mind. "Great run, Jen!" He had to shout over the wind to be heard. "And we tied! The best way to end a race, I mean run." His exuberance pushed the cold and insecurities away, returning her to the moment and allowing her to find joy despite jealousy.

He twirled her there at the top of the mountain, their laughter lost to the wind. Clouds blew in, the world around them disappearing into white. "That was the best, Jenny." His voice tickled her ear, and even when her toes touched the ground again, he didn't let go. Damp fog closed tightly, but the warmth of him blocked the cold. He stepped back to brush away a snowflake that had landed on her nose, pushing a few rogue curls from her cheek.

Another gust and the fog thinned. Snowdonia returned, and there was Ophelia, leaning against a stone, surveying the view.

Josh pushed Jenny away gently and shoved his hands in his pockets, shrugging off the cold, hiding a grin.

"Good run," Jenny said. "Really good." *Ugh, please let me find something else to say that doesn't involve the word "good" because, seriously, I can do better.* "Great work," she said. "That was great." *Really? That's the best you could do, Jenny?*

Just in time, something nearby caught her attention—a man-made pedestal capping the mountain. Flat metal overlaid the pedestal. "Hey, look at this!" Thankful for an excuse to gracefully exit their mountaintop moment, she darted to the plinth to investigate. The metal, spanning the entire pedestal, was a map. Like a sundial, it pointed to all the surrounding peaks, naming each one. An envelope, weighted by a rock, waited at the center of it with Jenny and Josh's names scrawled on the front.

"This is your reward for summiting Snowdon," Ophelia said. "Go ahead."

Jenny passed the envelope to Josh. "You deserve to open it. You kept me going. You used to hate running, but now you are better than me, some days."

He nudged her with his elbow then tore open the letter.

*What's the place you own but rarely go*
*And sometimes is only just for show*
*Where guests can rest and enjoy their stay*
*And a little faun said in his own special way?*

"I think 'faun' is misspelled," he said, passing her the note. "I'm not good at riddles. I'll leave it up to you, Keeper-who-loves-hints-and-mysteries."

"Faun can be spelled with a 'u' if it refers to a mythical creature who is half human, half goat." She reread the poem then stuffed the paper into her pocket. "Honestly, I'm too cold to solve riddles," she said through chattering teeth. "I'm not too cold to venture there, however." With a trembling finger, she pointed to the large building sitting just off to the side of the summit. "I'll be back shortly," she said and ran off.

"There's an entire restaurant, pub, and shop in there! It's empty today, but at least it took the chill off," she said upon returning. "And a bathroom, in case anyone else might require one."

"Jenny, I'm a guy. Nature is my bathroom."

She groaned. "Did you …?" He chortled and shook his head. "Oh thank goodness. I'd hate to step in a frozen puddle of … not water."

"Did you warm up enough to solve the riddle?" he asked.

"If you want it solved now, go for it. Otherwise, be patient!"

"You know this isn't my forte. Clever things are your wheelhouse. I just punch stuff." His compliment wasn't missed, and warmth spread in her chest at his words.

"That is not true. Your mind is always going, so don't even say you aren't good at riddles. But since I'm the one who likes puzzles, I'll think on it when we get home and warm. I promise." She rubbed her arms and legs, which were starting to stiffen.

"So, are we heading home from here or running back down?" he asked, hopping from foot to foot, eager to go again.

Ophelia sighed. "We'll take the trail. I can't believe you want to run more. This is a pleasant change of pace."

"It's downhill all the way!" he said. "That's the best kind of running!"

"We are only doing this because we love you," Ophelia impressed on him. "It's about four miles to where we began. We'll go fast. I'm freezing, and I asked Sam to have fresh coffee ready. I want some now, so let's go."

And off she went, the other two close on her heels.

As the valleys and rocks blurred past them, Josh called to Jenny, "Hey, how do you think the letter was there? Ophelia couldn't do it, she doesn't have a Charm with that power. You didn't do it, did you?"

"Of course not," she said. This question intrigued her. "Maybe ask Sam. He might be more willing to divulge information than Uncle Curtis or our crazy freak-show trainer up there," she yelled above the wind, gesturing towards Ophelia.

They got home just after noon, cold, wet, and starving. The downhill run had cured Jenny of her grouchiness from the chill. It was too fun to fly past mountain lakes and stone walls at breakneck speed to stay perturbed.

Sam, true to his word, had coffee and hot chocolate waiting for them, and Uncle Curtis had left tomato soup and grilled cheese sandwiches on the stove. Liddy sat at the table across from Sam, sipping coffee.

Without bothering to change, Jenny perched with her sandwich by the fire, letting it dry and warm her. Josh and Sam were deep in hushed conversation, and Ophelia stood at the kitchen island, her hands wrapped around a mug, observing everyone else. Ophelia often watched people, studying them, learning them.

Unhappy to leave the fire, Jenny dragged herself away to get more coffee for herself and hot chocolate for Josh. When she handed him his cup, he thanked her and, mid-sip, noticed the spoon in it. It had "Mount Snowdon" etched into the handle. She grinned when he glanced her way. Another souvenir for his spoon collection, lifted from the unoccupied gift shop on the mountain.

Back at the hearth, mesmerized by the fire, Jenny mulled over the riddle. *Where guests go without pay, and a little faun said in his own way.* A little faun? If this riddle came from Uncle Curtis, it had to be something from literature. And it had to be something she had read. *He would not be so cruel and obtuse as to reference a book she had never heard of, right?*

She decided to write down the riddle since Josh had asked for the paper earlier. He examined it now at the table, Sam biting his lip. Without a doubt, Sam knew the answer. *So much for being willing to divulge information.*

"Does anyone have a spare pen I could ..." Jenny paused. Why? Why did she pause? Her brain reached to retrieve something, but she couldn't quite lay hold of it.

"Are you okay?" Josh asked.

"Spare!" she whispered. "Spare!" This time it was more like a bark. *Guh! What is wrong with me?* "Spare pen? Spare, spare, spare. Spare Oom!" It clicked, and even the Compass knew she'd solved it. It whirred around, celebrating her mental victory.

"I got it!" she said.

"You got it? I knew you would!" Josh came and high fived her. "So, what is it?"

"I'll tell you later," she answered, enjoying the frustration on his face.

Just then, the clock struck one. Moose came trotting in and stood in front of the pair. He barked and trotted away, then turned back to them again.

"Okay Lassie," Josh joked. "You think he wants us to follow him?"

"Heck yes he does!"

# Chapter Nineteen

Moose led them to the spiral staircase, into the basement, along the hallway to Fang's room, and stopped in front of the stone lion, wagging his tail. Klaus followed, marching in, nonchalant and bored, glancing at Fang before plunking to the floor in front of the bookshelf and falling asleep.

"Should we wake him up?" Josh wondered. "Maybe he knows the answer to the riddle."

"Who? Fang or Klaus?" She suppressed the urge to chuckle at her own joke.

Josh rolled his eyes. "The one who can talk, Keeper."

She rolled hers too. "I know, *Guardian.*"

The stone lion's pelt roughed her skin, but at her touch, he shimmered, shook his head, and yawned. The Compass hummed at him.

"Well, if it isn't the Keeper and Guardian," he said in his deep, rocky voice. "What can old Fang do for you today?

"We have a riddle, presumably from Uncle Curtis, and I think I know the answer. I hope you know what to do with it." Fang waited, so she continued. "The riddle says,

*What's the place you own but rarely go*

*And sometimes is only just for show*

*Where guests can rest and enjoy their stay*

*And a little faun said in his own special way*

"The faun, Tumnus in *The Lion, the Witch, and the Wardrobe,* thinks Lucy says she is from 'Spare Oom,' though what she actually said was 'Spare Room,' where the Wardrobe she entered through was kept. It's the place you rarely go and is nicely decorated for guests to stay when they visit. So that answer is ... Spare Room." She squeezed her eyelids shut. "Please say I'm right."

Fang continued to stare, first at Jenny, then to Josh, drawing out his response. "Very good, Jenny. Behind this bookcase is a room you have already been in, though it's a bit different now. Uncle Curtis told me he left you a little puzzle to get here. Why he didn't just tell you to come back to the Collection is beyond me. The man likes to make things more difficult sometimes. I'm sure he had his reasons. Let me be the first to welcome you to the Spare Room." With a slow creak, he opened the bookcase again, giving them access to the concrete room beyond it.

But when they walked into the room this time, they both gasped. It was no longer just an empty room with dark corners and cold walls. Now, it glowed with soft lamplight reflecting off the polished concrete floor. The walls around them were a deep aqua except for one painted black.

Several small, mid-century modern desks lined the walls, each with a brown leather office chair of the same era. Pretty lamps lit the desks, which contained a stack of books, a compact laptop, and office supplies. Miniature chandeliers hung from the white ceiling, warmly illuminating every inch of the room and the one black wall in particular. It was divided into five sections, each labeled with the title of a fairy tale book: *Hansel and Gretel, Sleeping Beauty, Cinderella, The Little Mermaid,* and *Jack and the Beanstalk.*

Two of the desks were occupied by a proud Sam and a pensive Uncle Curtis, who monitored the Keeper and Guardian over his glasses, coffee cup in hand.

"Welcome to the Spare Room, your new headquarters," Sam said. Then he leaned in and whispered, "It turned out great, didn't it? Liddy and I worked on it all morning while you guys were away with Ophelia. She, however, selected all the decor weeks ago, when we planned this little surprise for you."

Jenny gaped at them. "You did all this for us?"

"Well," Uncle Curtis said, "Not just for you. We'll be using it a bit as well, but it's mostly for you to plan your missions into the fairy tales."

"Ophelia thought you needed your own space, and she wanted it to be amenable to deep thinking and productive planning. I think she nailed it," Sam said.

"I'd love to thank her myself, and Liddy, and you, Sam. Thank you so much," Josh said with such sincerity, Jenny looked twice to make sure he wasn't crying.

"You can tell her in about five minutes. Ophelia, I mean. She should be here soon," Uncle Curtis said. "Today, you plan your mission into *Hansel and Gretel*. Tomorrow, you jump into it to get the chicken bone. It's time."

The pounding of Jenny's heart deafened her, and her palms sweated thinking of venturing into *Hansel and Gretel* in less than twenty-four hours.

"We still have a lot to learn. Do you think we're ready?" Josh said, his voice steady and quite matter-of-fact, without the nerves Jenny felt.

"Aye, it's true—you *do* have a lot to learn, and it will remain true your entire life. But for now, you have what you need, and you are ready."

"He's right," Ophelia said, leaning against the doorjamb next to Fang. "You're ready enough. I watched your sword practice last night, and I ran with you both this morning. You are fit, tough, and skilled, more skilled than I expected at this point. So, we go, tomorrow. And don't worry, I'll be there with you."

"And I'll be monitoring you from here," Sam said. He sat straight and tall at his new desk, fingertips pressing into it, all business. "Tomorrow, you will be given a sort of walkie-talkie that lets you communicate with someone outside the book. In this case, and in most cases, me. One of my rather cooler inventions, I must say."

He revealed a pendant hidden beneath his shirt, letting it dangle between his fingers. "We haven't told you yet, but I have a Charm, one of the first ones ever hunted down. It isn't strong enough to move a person into a book, but it will let the wearer move objects in or out of stories as long as they aren't too big. I can kind of 'ghost' down into the story and leave you things that you need, like food or water or clothing or anything else to help you achieve your goal. You just have to tell me what you need, and I'll deliver it as fast as I can. I can also pick up things and remove them from stories when the need arises, as long as it isn't a person. There's just not enough power for something so substantial. What I do, we call it ghosting."

"Sounds pretty awesome," Josh said. "Hey! Were you responsible for the letter on Mount Snowdon?"

Sam chuckled. "Maybe."

Jenny's heartrate stabilized with this new information. She and Josh would not be alone on the first mission. Next to her, he rotated the Guardian Ring on his pinkie. *He does that sometimes—a nervous habit maybe? Or a tell? Or maybe he's getting used to a ring. Not real popular among seventeen-year-old guys. Or* maybe *it's letting him know we are in danger, and he isn't sure how to break the news to me.* Swallowing, not lingering on her final thought, she marched to the *Hansel and Gretel* section of the black wall, snatched a piece of chalk from a small, wooden cup holder, and faced the room. "Okay then, where do we begin?"

Because they had read and talked about this fairy tale for weeks during their afternoon sessions with Uncle Curtis, the plan fell into place with little effort. Jenny outlined it on the black wall while the others lounged in their office chairs.


*Needs*

*Compass*

*Guardian Sword/Ring*

*Chameleon Cloaks*

*Witch Repellant*

*Healing Dagger*

*Flanklets*

*Replacement Chicken Bone*

*Must not*

*Be seen by the witch*

*Be seen by Hansel or Gretel*

*Forget to leave a replacement chicken bone*

*Eat any of the gingerbread house*

*Be captured by the witch*

*Obstacles*

*The witch's sense of smell*

*The witch's potential magic*

*Interacting with the plot too closely*

*Hansel and Gretel's desperation*

*Plan*

*Jump in*

*Use Witch Repellant*

*Don Chameleon Cloaks and Flanklets (for Jenny)*

*Cause a diversion for witch (Ophelia)*

*Sneak into house unseen*

*Josh stand guard*

*Jenny find chicken bone and replace*

*Sneak out of house*

*Regroup at landing point*

*Leave, mission accomplished*

"Tell me again why we need to leave a replacement chicken bone?" Josh said, twirling in his chair.

"Mostly to keep Hansel from panicking if he wakes up and can't find his bone. It would be a safety hazard for you if that happens. He could alert the witch," Ophelia said. "Now, let's just hope it goes according to plan," she added as they all stood to head inside. Sam just started laughing.

∞∞∞ 🐙 ∞∞∞

Later on, Jenny paced in her room, mulling over tomorrow's jump. The million potential mishaps flooded her thoughts. Her breath came faster. Sweat beaded on her brow. The room blurred.

Cold water on her face helped snap her back to reality. Exiting the bathroom, toweling off, she heard Liddy call her down for dinner. *Maybe human interaction will help me feel not so crazy.* Pinching her cheeks and throwing on some lip gloss didn't hurt either.

Sliding into her seat, she sat with folded hands, staring at nothing. Uncle Curtis must have noticed her quiet entrance, for he put down a bowl of rice and squeezed her shoulder. "Jenny dear, is something on your mind?"

She glanced at him and to the others, who all now focused on her. *Deep breath. Don't fidget. Be honest.* "Well, to tell you the truth, I'm scared. I thought I'd be ready, but I don't know. What if I mess it all up? I mean, I know we have to do this, but there is also a lot to consider and so much that could go wrong. It's freaking me out!" Once she made her confession, she lowered her forehead to the table, embarrassed for her outburst and hiding from their responses.

A gentle palm rested on her shoulder blade. "I remember your mother's first jump as Keeper," Uncle Curtis said. "My father wanted her to retrieve some treasure from a book he'd jumped into years before. Three men guarded the treasure, men known for their mental prowess and skill with a sword. The treasure itself was a footnote in the story. However, getting past the guards—well, that troubled me. You see, I was to go with her as Guardian, a job I had already had for many years. I'd faced these men before. I knew about their riddles and mind games, and I nearly lost my head when they drew their swords the first time we had met. Now, I would have to face them again, this time with a young, inexperienced Keeper to boot." Jenny stared at him, picturing a younger version of her mom with the Compass, preparing for this, her first jump.

"But your mother, Jenny, she bested them. She solved their riddles, and when the mental games gave way to physical ones, she and I held our own against those three exceptional fighters. We completed our mission and returned home, tired, injured, and elated. Your mother later told me that she'd been terrified the entire time. But she never wavered, never showed her hand. I think that's when she coined her phrase, 'Being brave means doing what needs doing even if you are afraid.'"

Jenny groaned and scowled. *How many times would that phrase come up? How many times must I hear it repeated before I'm just naturally brave? Probably many, many times.*

"Ophelia tells me you are prepared enough physically to start jumping. Based on our lessons, I think you are as mentally ready as a new Keeper can be. You won't be alone. Josh will be with you, and Ophelia too." Ophelia flashed her an eager, almost wicked, grin. "Sam and I will be waiting for you here, listening in on the walkie-talkies. And if worst comes to worst, you can always jump out to return another time. Remember, however, that jumping in and out of stories becomes exhausting if done too often in one day, especially for someone as inexperienced as you. We try to avoid it unless things are going quite poorly."

Josh stuck his hand up, waiting for her to high five him. "We've got this, Jenny," he said, full of confidence, perhaps enough for both of them. She stared at him, letting everyone's encouraging, optimistic words sink in. "Don't leave me hangin'," he whispered. She relented, and the clap echoed through the house. Everybody cheered.

After dinner, Ophelia offered to work with Josh more on swords, and he dashed to the training shed without another word.

While the two warriors battled one another in the underground bunker beneath flickering lights, Jenny cozied up in a chair with a copy of the original *Hansel and Gretel* story, yet again, hoping to glean anything else helpful from rereading it.

She only got through it once before her eyelids grew heavy. She said goodnight to Liddy and Uncle Curtis, trudged to her room, and pulled on the soft, silky pajamas Ophelia had bought for her. The edge of her bed creaked when she leaned against it, holding the picture from her bedside table and tracing the outline of the Compass with her finger.

"You did this loads of times, Mom," she said to the picture—a family portrait taken last year. "And you never told me about it. Did you want to? Did you think you would fill me in on everything after Isaac gave me this thing? Would you have told me it was how you knew so much about bravery?" A rogue tear escaped and dripped onto the picture.

Swiping it away, she returned the picture to its place, deciding right then and there she *would* be brave, no matter the cost, no matter the chance of failure. She would be brave for her mother and, like Sam had been when he said "yes" to Ophelia, be brave for herself. "I want to live—really live, and not just exist," she said.

There was a familiar knock on the door, and she smiled, nearly caught talking to herself. "Come in," she said.

Josh stuck his head in her room, sweaty and smiling. "Ready for tomorrow?"

"Yep. Yes. I think I am."

# Chapter Twenty

An insistent alarm woke Jenny early the next day, the day of her first mission. She flew from the bed, adrenaline pumping through her veins. Shaky and sweating, she pulled on the clothes Ophelia had suggested for the jump, pushed her hair into a messy knot, and sighed, calming her nerves.

Just because it was a big and busy day didn't stop Uncle Curtis from doing a grand breakfast with some help from Liddy. Cinnamon rolls, quiche, fruit, and coffee graced the table. "You need to fill up. The jumps drain you, especially the first few times," he advised. "Ophelia ate earlier and will meet us in the Spare Room."

"These cinnamon rolls are amazing, Uncle Curtis," Josh said while chewing one and loading his plate with two more.

"Don't thank me, Josh. Those were Liddy's doing," said Uncle Curtis, nodding towards a blushing Liddy.

Josh raised his eyebrows. "I didn't know you could bake, Liddy!"

"I dabble. I've been working on more than just history in England."

Uncle Curtis chuckled. "Liddy, you do know how to keep a secret. I'm thankful this one is out." He popped a big bite of cinnamon roll into his mouth and chased it with a swig of coffee.

Once plates were licked clean, they left Liddy, who generously offered to clean up, to head to the Spare Room. "Great outfit," Josh said, tugging the end of the belt cinching the deep red, flowing tunic Ophelia had found for her in the Collection. Brown leggings and soft leather boots laced to mid-calf completed her medieval guise.

She tied a bandana across her brow to the nape of her neck. "How about now?"

Josh snickered. "It's a bit pirate-y. You just need a few gold teeth and dreadlocks,

and you'll have nailed it."

"Arrrgh, I do love a good pirate. I'll have to thank Ophelia, that saucy wench, for doing me up so pretty, me hearty!" Her pirate accent made them both giggle.

"Thank me for what?" asked a voice behind them. They spun to see the Searcher striding toward them. Their mouths dropped. While Jenny was dressed in medieval, swords-and-sorcery type clothes, and Josh much the same, Ophelia, *ninja warrior*, sauntered down the hall. Slim black pants concealed several weapons, no doubt, in addition to the short sword strapped to her waist over a long, tight black shirt. Soft-soled, black boots allowed her to move silently across the floor.

Mascara darkened her lashes, and her lips glistened with a touch of gloss. She never failed to put on the finishing touches.

*Man, I wish I'd remembered to wear makeup. At least tinted lip balm or something.*

Jenny sidled further from Ophelia in an attempt to avoid any comparison. But she stopped, chastising her insecurity. *Ugh, why do I even care! Get your mind in the game, Keeper, and off how ridiculously freaking gorgeous and terrifying your cousin is.* "Um, we wanted to thank you for dressing us like pirates," she said to Ophelia, then licked her lips and pinched her cheeks to encourage some natural color in them.

Swaggering past, Ophelia pressed something small into Jenny's palm. "Anytime, Keeper. Pirates always spice things up a bit."

While she and Josh continued to the Spare Room, Jenny took a second to investigate the tiny, mysterious gift. "Oh! Wait, how did you ...?" but Ophelia was at the end of the hall, waking Fang, unable to hear her question. That didn't stop Jenny from applying the tube of plum-colored balm to her lips then sticking it in her pocket to future reapplication.

"Good morning, Keeper," Fang said with a kind growl when Jenny greeted him. "Ready for the big day?" Unsure what to say, Jenny hugged the stone lion in an attempt to hide her nervous countenance. "You'll be fine," he whispered in her ear.

The Spare Room welcomed them with the smell of coffee, more cinnamon rolls, and warm lamplight. Sam sat at one of the desks, awake and alert, jittery with excitement. "Welcome to home base, y'all," he drawled. His southern accent came out when his adrenaline was pumping, and he rubbed his hands together. "I've got everything ready in your packs." The compact bags on the table in front of them bulged with supplies. "I've put everything from our list in there except your Flanklets, Jenny, which I am assuming you already have on?"

"Check!" Jenny said, lifting a boot to display the band she'd placed there earlier.

"Well then, step right up and grab your pack," Sam instructed. "But no climbing walls yet, little Keeper."

"Ha ha," she replied. "I'll try to restrain myself."

They each shouldered a bag, adjusting for various weapons. Jenny had her bow and arrows, healing dagger, and a short sword. The only weapon visible on Josh was the dagger Uncle Curtis had given him, but the Guardian Sword was certainly within quick reach along with several throwing knives and maybe other things she didn't even know about.

Uncle Curtis cleared his throat. "I will be here, monitoring the book and making sure the Sorceress doesn't try to make an entrance once we take the lock off. I'll also be helping Sam keep tabs on you guys." He laid the book on the middle desk.

"Oh, the walkie-talkies. I nearly forgot." Sam slapped his forehead then dug into his own bag of supplies. "Here you go, little Keeper." He handed her a thin piece of metal tipped with a forged rosebud. It shone and shimmered with each movement. Jenny handled it as if it might easily break. Sam reassured her it would not.

"Oh my," she said, rubbing her thumb on the ruby-encrusted bud glimmering red. The metal bent in a way to loop around her ear and the rosebud rested on her cheek, like a fancy headset or pop-star microphone. "This feels more like jewelry than a walkie-talkie," she sighed. "I love it."

Ophelia laughed. "That's my girl."

Sam handed one to Ophelia. "I saved you your favorite one, Philly."

Brightening, she tucked it over her own ear. It was identical to Jenny's but with a golden yellow bud glittering with peridot instead of rubies. Ophelia smoothed her hair back. "It complements the gold in my eyes," she explained.

"Philly?" Jenny whispered to her, eyebrows raised.

"That's what Sam calls me," Ophelia whispered in return.

"It's cute."

"I know." She winked and dropped into a chair.

"Is there one that's less, uh, pretty?" Josh asked, deepening his voice a tad. Sam held up a black one, etched with feathers and tipped with an eagle's head, a simple emerald for its eye. "That's what I'm talking about." Josh tucked it around his ear, and Jenny giggled. "What?" he asked. "Does it look dumb?"

"You look like a pirate-warrior-telephone operator. It's pretty awesome."

"We're dressed the same, Keeper," Josh said.

"I know. That's what makes it so awesome."

"And you can hear me, right?" Jenny's walkie-talkie hummed, Sam's whisper coming through. All three gave him a thumbs up. "Okay, to talk to me, all you have to do is touch this little guy, here." He demonstrated pressing a small button on the metal, just in front of their ears and shaped like a leaf—or, in Josh's case, a feather. "You can also talk to each other, but just know that we can all hear you." Sam glared with a grin at Ophelia, who blushed. He winked at her. "Sometimes, people forget their conversations are not private. Consider yourselves warned. And also, remember, these are not magic. They are technology, amazing technology only someone with my brain could invent. So be careful with them. They are one of a kind. And now, you are prepared to go."

Uncle Curtis unlocked the *Fairy Tales* book, and Jenny's heart rate increased, adrenaline surging through her veins. "Remember the plan?" he said. They did. It was simple enough and completely terrifying.

Jenny linked arms with Josh and Ophelia. The Compass whirred to life, ramping up its magic or whatever it did.

"And so it begins," Josh whispered. She glanced at him, too focused on the task to smile. Emotions bubbled in her chest. It took a few deep breaths to keep them from overflowing.

"Let's do this, for our parents, and for Isaac," she said, her voice catching.

With great care and little drama, Uncle Curtis laid the book on the center desk, opened to a particular page in *Hansel and Gretel*. The Compass arrow stopped spinning, locked onto the book, lifting off Jenny's chest and pulling her toward the story. *It knows.* Tightening her grip on the other two, she leaned forward, allowing the Compass to drift over the pages. When it touched the paper, light illumined their faces, and in a second, they were gone.

She stumbled but recovered faster than before when her feet hit. The ground almost cracked when Josh landed next to her, one knee down, steadying himself with his fist on the ground, full-on warrior-mode. Ophelia touched down like a cat, an eager, dangerous cat. "First things first—everyone okay?" the Searcher asked, giving them a quick scan.

"Couldn't be better," Josh said, studying the glen surrounding them. His eyes were focused and bright with no hint of fear. Life drummed through his body, which was tense and alert. "Let's find them," he said, taking lead.

"Hold on a second, Guardian. I appreciate your eagerness, but let's gather our bearings, figure out where we need to go. There's no rush." Ophelia raised an eyebrow at her trainee, and he acquiesced to her request.

"Training never ends, does it?" he said. Ophelia chuckled.

They had dropped in near the witch's candy cottage, where she already held Hansel and Gretel prisoner, but they didn't know how to get there from their current location. It required a bit of detective work.

The three fanned into a line, searching for any clues to lead them in the right direction. Soft grass dampened their footfalls, and tiny buttercups lifted their heads toward the sun. Leafy green trees circled the glen, and a narrow path cut through it, disappearing into a shadowy forest.

Jenny squatted to examine a tiny piece of potential evidence along the path. "Hey guys, look at this!" The other two rushed to her. On her fingertip, a small, white something demanded their attention.

"Is that what I think it is?" Josh said.

"Maybe?" Ophelia said.

Without thinking, Jenny popped it in her mouth. "Yep, it's a breadcrumb! I guess the birds failed to find this one. The children must've passed through here at some point on their way *into* the woods, which is when they dropped breadcrumbs to find their way home again."

"I can't believe you ate that," Josh said, disgust written across his face. Jenny shrugged. "I mean, what if it was, I don't know, bird poop or bat droppings or just a clump of mud?"

"I think I can tell scat from bread," she said. "But it was a little gritty. Probably just dirt."

"I really hope it was just dirt," he muttered, a breeze tugging at his tunic. Sniffing the air, he smiled. "Hey, smell that? Sugar and cinnamon, peppermint and vanilla. We're close." Like an excited bloodhound, he zig-zagged along the path, sniffing this way and that. "Here," he said, pointing to the path into the woods.

The trail wound through the trees, and the scent of sugar permeated the air. The forest thinned to another grassy glen below the crest of a hill. Unsure of what could be lurking on the other side of the hill, they stopped.

"Whoa, look at that!" Jenny pointed to flowers growing along the path that were, upon further investigation, small lollipops sprouting from the ground. The lollipops continued past the hill, luring unsuspecting children into the clutches of the witch.

"Let's get ready," Ophelia suggested, moving to the edge of the glen, just into the trees, and plunking down her backpack.

Josh fished the witch repellent from his bag. "Remember, hold your breath and then run away before breathing or you might throw up, with great violence apparently. That is not part of our plan. Jenny already ate bat poop, so no more gross stuff, okay?" She punched him, stifling a giggle, and told him to shut it.

He tossed the witch repellant to Ophelia. "Maybe you should show us how you do it."

Ophelia stepped away from the others, covered her mouth and nose, and sprayed her clothes and shoes with the repellent. She ran a few yards from where she'd been standing before allowing herself to breathe again. The other two followed suit, and no one puked.

"This stuff should be called something different, like 'Scent Remover or 'Avoid-a-Hag' or 'The Great Neutralizer.' It doesn't actually repel witches, does it? It just removes your scent so they can't smell you, right?" Josh said, after the recommended amount of time keeping his mouth shut, of course.

"Deep thoughts with Josh Park," Jenny said, elbowing him. "Avoid-a-hag," she muttered. "I hope it works." They sobered, considering what lay at the end of the lollipop path.

Instead of following the path directly, they skirted the glen through the woods and soon found the cottage, tucked away in a small cove surrounded by tall, dense forest. Even from their hiding spot behind a brush pile in the trees, the house appeared even more delicious, and more ridiculous, than they'd imagined.

White, buttery icing spilled from the roof. Jenny's mouth watered, the smell of gingerbread walls enticing her. A candy cane fence emitted a gentle peppermint scent, and within the fence, a number of gingerbread dogs with frosting coats and red-hot eyes stood frozen, keeping watch. "This is making me hungry," she whispered to Josh, but his focus was so single-minded at that point, the edible delights did not faze him. *Wow, I think for the first time ever I'm hungrier than he is.* She fought against her desire to grab a handful of something tasty. That could be deadly. The power of the candy cottage had attempted to overtake her, and she was fully aware of its dangers. What chance had Hansel and Gretel had?

Ophelia lingered in the woods as planned while the other two donned their Chameleon Cloaks, which allowed them to sneak closer to the cottage without being seen. Because they were interfering with a dangerous, cannibalistic witch, it behooved them to stay hidden.

They followed the candy cane fence, treading with care through the witch's garden. A loud creak echoed through the holler. The back door of the cottage squeaked again. The old hag, heavy and haggard and horrible, appeared. She shuffled along the path, mumbling to herself. Jenny, watching their foe and not her footing, stumbled on a broken piece of icing. The witch whirled, alert, sniffing the air. She moved much quicker than either of them had expected.

They froze, sinking their faces deep into their hoods and their hands into their sleeves, praying the witch repellent hid their scent. The witch sniffed and moved now with catlike agility, weaving her way through her garden. They slowed their breathing, still and quiet. "My turn to play," Ophelia's voice whispered through the walkie-talkie in Jenny's ear.

A rustling across the garden in the woods caught the hag's attention. She sprinted toward it, leapt the candy cane fence, and disappearing into the woods. "J and J, go now!" Ophelia hissed.

"Come on," Jenny said. "You first." Josh led the way to the house, and she bumped into him when he stopped at the door to peruse the house. "Drat!" she murmured. "It's like, impossible to see you." But before he could respond, her attention turned to the room before them. Little Hansel and Gretel lay on the ground in cramped cages, dirty and glistening with sweat. A bowl of water sat in the corner of each cage, and old straw littered the floor. By some miracle, Jenny found Josh's arm and squeezed it.

"They escape, Jenny, don't forget that," he said. He knew she wanted to save them, to spare them any further damage, but that wasn't the story. She couldn't free them. They had to do it themselves. And Josh and Jenny had to get the chicken bone.

"I know. But they are so little ..."

"They get out," he said again. "Without our help. Let's get in and finish this."

He posted himself by the door, keeping watch while she crept deeper into the cottage, through the heat of the fire, past the table, closer to Hansel's cage, searching for the chicken bone. She felt for its replacement in her pocket. The little boy lay in his cage, facing his sister. Both slept, not far from the fire blazing in the hearth. How the candy in this cottage didn't melt was a mystery, but Jenny didn't have time to dwell on it. She found the bone, held tight in Hansel's tiny hand.

Pushing off her hood to get a better view of things and not die from heat stroke, Jenny reappeared, visible again. She maneuvered between the two cages and stooped near Hansel, her shoulder blades pressed against Gretel's prison. With careful and gentle fingers, she pried opened the boy's fist and collected the chicken bone, replacing it with the counterfeit one. It wouldn't matter to Hansel that this was a different bone, but it would certainly matter to the Sorceress.

"Who are you?" A timid voice spoke from behind her. Jenny whipped around to see Gretel's curious and frightened face staring at her through the bars. "Please don't hurt him." The love the little girl had for her brother poured out along with her words. *Oh, my heart!* It ached in Jenny's chest. *I could save you and take you home and you'd have a family and food and no more cages!*

*And ... I'd have to give up being Keeper and never see my parents again, and you aren't real. You aren't! Are you?*

A gentle warmth replaced the heartache, swirling and edging its way through her arms and to her hands and up her neck and through her eyes and mouth. A faint glow sparkled off of Jenny's skin, and fascination replaced Gretel's fear.

"Jenny, what is happening?" Josh's concern rang in her ear, but she shook it off. *Not now, dude!*

"Gretel, you are strong. You are quick. You are smarter than this awful creature. You will save your brother. You will escape. Your father is waiting for you, desperate for your return. It's safe to go home now." The words flowed from her mouth and rolled into a small ball of golden light, floating to Gretel and settling into her ribs, like a seed planted in rich soil, taking root and glowing for a moment before fading under her skin. Gretel nodded, sitting straighter with a determined brow.

Josh's voice sounded in Jenny's ear. "Witch! Witch coming! Hide!"

The old hag shuffled nearer, her footsteps clunking through the garden.

"Where?" Jenny whispered, unable to move or make a decision.

"Hood! Flanklets!" Josh hissed through the walkie-talkie. *Oh! Right!* In two steps, she dashed up the wall and onto the ceiling, upside down, her hood falling over her head, rendering her invisible. The Flanklets held her cloak tight around her ankles so it didn't succumb to gravity and reveal her position. *Glad I tucked the cloak into them earlier.* Only her brown shoes showed on the slanted ceiling, and the witch couldn't see that far, hopefully.

The walkie-talkie hummed again in Jenny's ear. "I'm right outside if you need me," Ophelia said as the bloated, disgusting crone tromped in, her breathing hot and audible. The smell of her wafted to the ceiling, burning Jenny's nose.

The witch puttered about the cottage, no longer suspicious, and Jenny crept towards the door. From her vantage point on the ceiling, she spotted a hole in the roof towards its peak, some sort of ventilation situation. *That would be a safer exit than the door at this point. Less attention, and less chance of drawing the witch towards Josh. Also, OMG it's so hot.* Sweat dripped from her chin to her nose and from her forehead to the Chameleon Cloak. Her clothes clung to her, drenched and sticky.

She inched toward the escape window and eased through the opening. "I'm on the roof," she whispered into the walkie-talkie. "Be there in a sec." Gretel crouched in her cage below, eyes trained on her captor. Jenny knelt to take one last peek into the cottage, giving Gretel a silent, "Go girl!" Sleeping Hansel still clutched the chicken bone like it was his job. The witch tended her fire, humming to herself directly below Jenny.

Heat rose through the vent framing Jenny, and a bead of sweat dangled off the tip of her nose, then before she had a chance to swipe it away, it dropped right onto the hag's head.

The humming stopped, and two glassy eyes jerked skyward. The witch inhaled and snarled. "I can smell you now, little thief."

Scrambling away from the vent, Jenny pressed the button on her walkie-talkie. "RUN TO THE RENDEZVOUS POINT!" She took off, plunging through thick, white frosting, flew off the eaves with a flip, and hit the ground running. Her speed left her less camouflaged, the Chameleon

Cloak couldn't adjust fast enough to the rapidly-changing surroundings. Josh must have seen her because an invisible hand grabbed hers. Side by side they ran, their cloak hoods trailing behind them, unable to keep up with their mad pace, rendering them visible once more. "You gonna tell me about that golden ball?" Josh asked her, breathing hard.

"It'll have to be later!" she said, huffing beside him, listening for a pursuit.

Barking erupted behind them, the gingerbread dogs in the yard springing to life and tearing after them. Hardened sugar filed into razor-sharp points lined their gaping mouths. "We've got company," she said, grabbing her bow from her back and nocking an arrow. Still running, she fired, dropping the lead dog. It flipped into a pile of crumbs flying everywhere.

"Nice!" Josh said, palming the hilt of the Guardian Sword and bringing it to life. The next dog dodged her arrow and leapt long and high, landing right on Josh, pummeling him to the ground with a ferocious growl. Jenny swung her bow like a bat and knocked its head off, screaming, "Don't you even!" The dog swayed and fell off Josh, who jumped up and kept running, Jenny at his side.

"Thanks," he said. They neared the rendezvous point when he turned and slung his throwing knives at two of the hounds hot on their heels, shearing one's leg clean off and slicing through the other one from chest to tail. The last pursuing canine, in a burst of speed, bit at Josh's hand, trying to yank him off his feet. One arc of the Guardian Sword separated its front half from its rear.

With the dogs all managed, only the old witch screeched in pursuit, her swollen feet pounding the forest floor. They saw Ophelia ahead, her hands stretching, ready to link with them. The witch lurched for the Keeper, her claws bared and razor sharp, just inches from slicing Jenny's skin. Josh jerked away from her, the Guardian Sword swinging. In one fluid motion, he struck, cutting off the offending hand, leaving the hag shrieking in anger and stumbling in pain.

Jenny grabbed for Josh. At the same moment, the witch clawed at him with her remaining appendage before dropping to the dirt, holding her bleeding stump. Josh surged forward and linked with Ophelia. Jenny yelled, *"DULCI DISTINET A DOMO DOMUM!"* The world below them disappeared in a swirl of wind, and the rustle of flipping pages sounded in their ears. The old crone's curses echoed in the cacophony, and her hot breath lingered on Jenny's neck. They landed in a pile in the Spare Room.

"We need to work on your arrivals," Uncle Curtis said as the three jumpers untangled their limbs and packs.

"Well, did you get it?" asked Sam from his desk chair.

"Wait, what? Was I supposed to get something?" Jenny patted her pockets in mock dismay. "Oh, you mean this?" Smiling, and with great drama, she brandished the chicken bone.

"Oh yeah!" Sam said, taking it from her for safekeeping and giving her a high five.

Ophelia embraced her. "You did great, Jen-bug." Jenny blushed at Ophelia's affirmation. "And Josh! You guys, he cut off the witch's hand before she could claw Jenny to shreds. It was epic," Ophelia told Sam and Uncle Curtis with pride. "He was amazing." Her words brought a little heat to the Guardian's cheeks, and he ducked his head, swaying a little where he stood.

"That was crazy and scary and awesome," Jenny conceded.

Uncle Curtis patted her arm. "It always is. Well done. Your mother would be proud."

*Now only four more.* Jenny laughed to herself at the thought.

She finally got around to hugging Josh, whispering a soft "thank you" in his ear. He shuddered at her touch, and the back of his shirt was wet. Pulling away, Jenny studied him, concerned. "What's wrong?" Her palms were bloody where she'd embraced him. "You're hurt," she said, stepping behind him. His shirt was shredded and deep, angry gouges from neck to sacrum oozed dark red blood.

"She might have made contact at the last minute," he confessed just before his knees gave way.

# Chapter Twenty-One

"Help me!" Jenny yelled, bearing Josh's weight best she could, and the others jumped in. "Lie down here," she commanded him. Jerking the healing dagger from her belt, she laid it on Josh's wounds. The cold hilt chilled her fingers but glowed warm at the blade. Beneath it, the bleeding slowed and Josh's skin, little by little, knitted itself together.

The coolness of the hilt crept into Jenny's wrist, then up her arm and across her chest, stealing the life from her to heal Josh. She shivered, each gash closing with increasing speed. Uncle Curtis, Ophelia, and Sam put a hand on Jenny's shoulders, offering some of themselves to Josh and keeping her from giving too much.

When the last wound closed, Jenny returned the dagger to her belt, shaking at the effort. "Josh? How do you feel?" He stirred, then pushed up from the floor, stretching his torso. Long scars still told the story of the witch's attack, but his skin was intact and healthy. "It's tight, but it doesn't hurt at all. That's amazing. Thank you," he said to Jenny, dropping beside her on the floor. "You okay?" he asked. "You're really pale, yikes, and shaking."

She laid her temple on his shoulder. "That was a close one," she said, mumbling and closing her eyes. "I'm really cold, and also really hungry."

"Want to order a pizza? Jenny? Uh-oh." Everything faded to black.

ooooo 🦋 ooooo

She woke in the middle of the night, tucked into her bed, sweating beneath a slew of blankets and comforters. Pressing herself to sitting, her muscles barked with each movement. *What time is it? And how did I get here?* Blips of memories floated through her mind: Josh, shivering, someone carrying her, the *clunk, clunk* of boots dropping to the floor, and then, not much else. With a gasp, she felt her clothes. *How did I get into my pajamas?* Falling against her pillow, the bed creaking beneath her, she rubbed her eyes. *Surely Liddy or Ophelia had done that part and not Josh. Please say it wasn't Josh.* Her cheeks burned at the thought.

A heavy sigh and rustling sound startled her, and she propped herself onto her elbow. Sore muscles growled again, and she groaned in pain. Peering into the darkness, nothing was amiss. She leaned a little further, peeking to the floor beside her bed. "Oh!" she said, then clamped a hand on her mouth.

Under a heavy quilt and snuggled on his side with his pillow, Josh looked less like a warrior and more like the nice, normal neighbor boy she'd known for years *asleep on her floor*! *What is he doing here?* She crossed her arms and hunched forward, ensuring the covers hid her entire body. *What is my problem? He's seen me in pajamas before. Yeah, but not IN BED with nothing on beneath them. Thankfully, he's asleep and can currently see nothing but the back of his eyelids.*

But then he shifted again, and his eyes popped wide.

231

In less than a second, Jenny lowered herself to the mattress before he could register her staring at him, and feigned sleep. He sat forward and scratched his arm, then adjusted his covers.

"Jenny?" he whispered, waiting to see if she responded. "Are you awake?" She remained still. He stood, and a calloused palm rested on her brow, checking to see if she was still cold. "I would've killed her," he said. "If she'd laid a claw on you. I was ready to." And a few moments later, he settled into his pallet once more, easing into sleep.

She squeezed her eyes together. "Thank you," she whispered when she heard the slow, deep breaths of sleep.

Liddy's far-off words, from the night they were nearly killed by mountain men, regarding her and Josh "not kissing" and "being friends" rattled in her head. For the next hour, she tossed and turned, trying to push them aside.

∞∞∞ 🙊 ∞∞∞

Sunlight flooded in the windows, warming Jenny awake the next morning. She stretched, not ready to leave the bed except for the gnawing hunger in her belly. *I think my stomach is trying to eat my heart.* Dishes and pans clanked in the kitchen, which meant Uncle Curtis was cooking. Careful to not step on Josh, she tip-toed across the room, avoiding the creaky spots in the floor. Before leaving, she faced him once more, her eyes closing with gratitude.

The smells of bacon and eggs and toast beckoned her to the kitchen, but she made a quick detour into Josh's room before heading there.

"I need bacon," were the first words she said when she saw Uncle Curtis. "And good morning!" She kissed his cheek and stole bacon off the plate on the counter at the same time.

"Good morning to you, Jenny. You seem no worse for wear after healing Josh, though I'm sure you are starving." He scrutinized her over his glasses, sipping coffee. "All in all, how do you think yesterday went?"

Munching on her bacon, Jenny took her spot at the table and pulled her knees to her chest. "I don't have a lot to compare it to, but I think overall, it was okay. I mean, we got the bone, and no one died. So that's a win, right? But Josh got hurt pretty badly, which puts a big strike on the mission despite completing it."

"It happens a lot. Stories are more dangerous than you think." Uncle Curtis's stool creaked as he shifted on it. "You healed him, though, Jenny, to your own detriment. A generous move."

"He's my best friend, Uncle Curtis. Wouldn't you have done the same?"

"Oh quite right. I'm not faulting you for it. Not one bit. He carried you upstairs afterward and stayed with you all night, making sure you were all right. You two have a bond, brokered, oddly enough, by the Sorceress. When she meddled in your lives, she didn't know you would band together, fight together." He held up a long, bony finger. "I am of the opinion this oversight will be her undoing." His gaze intensified, and then he stood and continued about the kitchen.

He placed a plate brimming with eggs in front of her, and she dug into them without hesitation.

"I'm starving," she said between bites, nearly inhaling everything on her plate. "And sore."

"That's to be expected with the jump and the healing. I've already set aside eight eggs and half a loaf of bread for Josh. What else can I get *you*?"

"More bacon?"

With her plate half empty, she reclined in the chair and sipped orange juice. "Something happened yesterday, Uncle Curtis. Something unexpected," she said, then briefly explained her conversation with Gretel, the golden ball that had floated from her mouth to Gretel's heart, and the effect it had on the poor, caged girl.

But instead of being shocked, flabbergasted, or even irritated, which Jenny kind of expected, Uncle Curtis continued cooking, taking in her story and nodding every so often. Once she finished it, he placed a spatula on the counter and suppressed a smile.

"What do you think it was, Jenny? You're a smart girl. I reckon you have an idea."

"Was it my gift? The one given to me by the Compass?"

"Aye! I wondered when it would happen for you and what it might be. Tis a gift you always carry and can always use, but the story ... the story somehow lets you see it." He wiped his hands on his apron and carried more food to the table. "Ophelia can see truth in a person, as she demonstrated with Liddy. Had you been in a story with her and she used her gift, you might have seen trickles of soft blue mist leak from her eyes. It's quite a thing to witness. It would appear *you* can speak encouragement to those who need it, like poor Gretel. Perhaps your words girded her up, allowing her to believe that she could change her circumstances."

"So, I have the gift of encouragement?" Jenny asked. "Wow. That's pretty cool. What's your gift, Uncle Curtis? Oh, wait, let me guess!"

"Please." He responded with a small bow.

Jenny pondered several different options while licking grease from her fingertips. "Ooh, I think I know. Peace. You bring peace. Your words are peace." Every time things got hard and complicated in her life, Uncle Curtis was there, unflappable, speaking to her in a way that allowed her to rest. He was a peacemaker.

"See, I knew you were a smart girl," he said, sipping his coffee. "Would you like to know your mother's gift?"

"Yes, I would!"

"She brings out the goodness in people."

Jenny sighed. Of course that was her mother's gift. It made complete sense. Knowing it was a small, valuable heirloom she would never grow tired of holding.

"Does she still have it after giving up the Compass to Isaac?"

He nodded. "'Tis a gift, not a loan. It remains though the binding does not."

"That is so cool." She paused and bit her lip. "Uncle Curtis, um, I've wondered ... why did my mother give up the Compass? Surely you know."

His coffee cup clinked on the counter, and he folded his long fingers together. "Your mother took someone out when she was Keeper."

Jenny's eyebrows arched. "I suspected as much. Someone I know?"

"Oh lass, it is a story that is not mine to tell. Ask her about it when you are reunited."

She huffed. "Well, now I'm curious. It wasn't my dad—he was born in Montana, and I know my grandparents really well. Maybe her best friend, Madeline? I could totally see her being an entitled princess. She 'requires' a biweekly mani/pedi, which Mom thinks is ridiculous, of course. Hmm, who else could it have been?" She pondered away at the table, staring over her own cup of coffee into nothing.

"Your mind will go a number of directions, I'm sure. Your mother has a big heart, as you well know. It could have been anyone. Don't jump to conclusions just yet."

It almost made her angry, not knowing something so important about her own mom. In an attempt to follow Uncle Curtis's advice, Jenny opted to eat more instead of play a frustrating game of *Who Doesn't Belong Here.*

She was halfway through her second pastry when Josh scooted into a chair at the table, still in pajamas with major bedhead.

"Is there coffee?" he asked with a scratchy, morning voice, and Jenny volunteered to get him some. By the time she returned, he had loaded his plate and was working his way through several slices of toast, multiple pieces of bacon, and all the eggs Uncle Curtis had promised him.

"Dang, Josh," she observed, trying to hold in her giggles. "Maybe we should invest in some chickens." The butter dish slid toward him. "Just in case you need more."

"Yeah, yeah, thanks. Man, I'm so hungry," he said, shaking off his sleepies and trying to sound halfway human. He chuckled too. "That *is* a lot of food, isn't it?

"It was a crazy day yesterday. You deserve all the bacon. Did you sleep okay?"

"Your floor is hard," was his only response. A big bite of eggs made more talking impossible.

After cleaning his plate, he made plans to train with Ophelia, who had joined them at the table, then headed to his room to digest and get dressed. Ophelia extended the same offer to Jenny, who declined. She wanted to talk to Uncle Curtis about the next mission and reread the story.

"There is something we need to do today, Jenny, so keep your afternoon a little free," Ophelia said.

"Uh, okay. Sure. Why?" Jenny waited for more of an explanation but only received a shrug. She stuck out tongue at Ophelia, who smirked and jetted from the kitchen. Liddy took her place at the table, listening intently while Uncle Curtis and Jenny chatted.

"So, the next mission is to get the cursed spindle from *Sleeping Beauty*," Jenny said, "and then we must take it, and the chicken bone, to the Sorceress."

"*Sleeping Beauty* shouldn't be too hard. Everyone is sleeping after the spindle prick," Liddy said. "No one will see you, right?"

Uncle Curtis nodded. "Yes, Liddy, you are right, in one respect. Everyone will be asleep. But remember, in the story, thick and terrible vines surround the castle, shutting everyone in and everyone else out, except the prince who comes to break the spell. And since none of you is a prince, it may not be as easy as you think."

Jenny's toes tapped the floor. "I might join Josh in the training room," she said, shooting to her feet, the chair tipping with the force of her movement. "Yesterday was too close. We needed to be faster, more careful." The old witch's screams echoed in her ears, and putrid, hot breath stung her nose. A shiver tingled along her spine, images of Josh's torn and bleeding flesh flashing through her mind. A knot formed in her gut.

"Maybe ..." She paused, sighed, and tried again. "Maybe I should go alone this time, into *Sleeping Beauty*." Gripping the back of her chair, knuckles white, she waited for a response.

"It's against the rules, Jenny dear. You know it. I know it. Josh knows it. And why wouldn't you want him with you? Or Ophelia?"

Jenny shifted from foot to foot. "Josh—what if he had died? What if the witch had run just a tad bit faster yesterday? Or what if he asks me to choose between my life or his? To leave him behind in a story to spare myself? He would do something like that. His selfless heart would do all it could to save me, even stop beating."

"Oh, love. To ask Josh to stay behind on the missions robs him of his purpose, Jenny. He needs purpose, especially now. Don't take it away," Liddy said with kindness and understanding. "Lingering on the 'what ifs' will consume you. Trust me, I know."

Uncle Curtis agreed. "It's normal to feel afraid, Jenny, of losing someone else after Isaac and your parents, but past losses cannot dictate future friendships. When you allow other people in, you always run the risk of losing them, and with them, a piece of your heart—a painful thing, to be sure. However, being brave sometimes means taking the risk, because a life without friends is mighty lonely. Your heart is too big and loving to play it safe. You'd shrivel up and die without others. I think you tried that once, when you first came here ..." He raised an eyebrow at her. "It didn't work out so well, did it?"

A few tears dripped onto Jenny's cheek, and she shook her head, remembering the sad nights she'd spent alone in her room with nothing but pictures and Moose for company. Her heart warmed with Uncle Curtis's peaceable words.

"Uncle Curtis," she said, wiping her face, "Did you just use your gift on me?"

He smiled. "Perhaps."

She smiled a little bit. "Thank you."

Once in her room, she leaned against her desk, pressing her palms into her chest. The pain of her parents' kidnapping still cut deep, though it had been mitigated somewhat by the love she had found in Uncle Curtis's home. Still, she did not relish the thought of another gaping wound in her soul. Losing Josh to a stupid story might be unrecoverable—an injury unending. However, going about these missions alone, or the pain on Josh's face if she ever asked him to stay behind, left a terrible taste in her mouth. She couldn't wound his heart to protect her own.

She paced her floor, mind racing with the "what if" questions Liddy warned her about. *What if Josh dies? What if I die? What if we can't beat the Sorceress? What if we never find our parents?* Then, one monumental question broke through the mental roundabout. *What if we face this together, and win?* The pacing stopped. "What if that is the only way?" she said.

Sunlight flooded through the window, and she sank to the floor, letting it warm her face. "Then that's how we do it, no matter the risk," she whispered. A little laugh huffed out her nose. "Another chance to be brave, I guess. Man, I would love an opportunity to not be brave, just for a second."

Jenny stayed there in her room for a while, resting in the sunlight, shifting across her floor with its movement. She needed to send a quick hello to

Rae, something she tried to do every few weeks, and pulled her phone from the drawer by her bed. She'd stuck it in there after they had arrived and only periodically turned it on. It hurt to know there would be no missed call or texts from her parents, and she was afraid she'd blow her cover if she chatted too much with Rae. However, she missed her friend and needed to maintain the ruse of traveling. *Just left Wales,* she sent. *It was gorgeous—lots of climbing opportunities. Come with me next time! Miss you XOXO.* She flipped it onto her bed where it immediately buzzed with a reply.

*Wales sounds awesome! I might be heading to Scotland soon for an exchange program. Any chance you'll be up there? OXOX*

Rae always reversed Jenny's closing.

*Really? Scotland! Sounds dreamy. Not sure our next stop. Let's keep in touch. Would love to see you. Everything ok? XOXO*

*Everything is fine. College is fun—lots of climbing, reading, and hanging out, in that order, of course. Are you still considering a gap year? OXOX*

Jenny giggled. She had no idea if she'd even go to college at this point. *Remains up in the air. Let me know about Scotland! Talk to you soon XOXO*

A familiar rapping on the door startled her. "Come in," she called, powering off the phone and returning it to its drawer.

A sweaty and grinning Josh poked his head in. "You okay?" Jenny nodded from where she sat on the floor, leaning against her bed. "Good, because Uncle Curtis just told me we jump again tomorrow. We're heading to the Spare Room this afternoon to prepare."

"What? So soon?"

"Is there a problem?"

She chewed her lip. "Josh, aren't you afraid you might get hurt again? Or like, you know, die?"

The slight wince he tried to hide brought another round of tears to Jenny's eyes. He crossed her room and slid next to her on the floor, joining her against the bed. "I'm a little afraid, maybe," he said. "But what we are doing makes me feel so alive, like I have a purpose that's more than just scoring a goal or passing a math test. I can't let that purpose go. And anyway, you have the healing dagger," he added with a grin. "But don't worry, I don't place all my faith in that little thing. It's just nice to have around."

"Josh, what if we get this all wrong, or we are too late? What if we don't ever get them back?"

He scooted a few inches closer to her, their arms touching. "Then we are wrong together, too late together, and we deal with it together." She leaned against him, but he jostled her, pulling something from his pocket. "Oh, and thanks for this." A modest wooden spoon lay square in his hand. "I assumed you stole it off the witch's table."

Jenny started laughing. "Oh, you found it! Yes, I confess, I stole it. I might have a problem. Oh, Josh! I almost forgot to tell you. Remember the golden ball that floated out of my mouth and, like, into Gretel?"

"Seriously, how could I forget?"

"I asked Uncle Curtis about it. Josh, it's my gift! It's the gift of encouragement. That's what he called it, at least."

"Jenny, what a great gift! It's perfect for you. The Compass knows." It hummed at him from beneath Jenny's shirt, making him laugh.

"You have one too, I know it. We just don't know what it is yet. We'll find it, though. I'm sure."

He relaxed against her shoulder. "I'd love to find it. This is a crazy little world we live in, isn't it?"

Before she could respond, Uncle Curtis called for them to come eat lunch.

"Okay, let's go," Josh said, hopping up. "We've got a lot to do."

# Chapter Twenty-Two

The Spare Room invited them in, Fang growling a deep "hello" to everyone. They chatted and laughed, well rested and well fed. All were there except Liddy, who had offered to stay in the kitchen and work on dinner. Feeding everyone was a full-time job.

Sam posted himself at what was now his preferred desk, and Ophelia leaned against it. Josh pulled up one office chair, and Uncle Curtis occupied another.

"So, let's review the story first," he said, sipping his coffee. The steam fogged his glasses.

"I'll go," offered Josh. "A princess is born, and all the kingdom is invited to celebrate her. Fairies come to bless her with gifts. Just before the last fairy gives her blessing, a new fairy arrives, angry she was not invited. She curses the baby: on her seventeenth birthday, she will prick her finger on a spindle and die. Of course, the kingdom is horrified and dismayed, especially the king and queen."

"I hate that fairy," Jenny said. "She's so vindictive. So she didn't get an

243

invite the party—is that really worth killing a kid over?"

"These fairy tales are sometimes a little ... excessive," Ophelia said. "If you hadn't noticed."

"Oh we've noticed," Josh said. "Mind if I keep going? Okay, so the last fairy approaches the little girl, and while she cannot undo the curse, she can lighten it. The girl will not die but only sleep until she receives true love's kiss. In some versions, it says she will sleep 100 years and then a prince will come, but in this one, it's the kiss that matters." His gaze darted to Jenny, and she smiled, encouraging him to continue.

"When the princess is seventeen, she pricks her finger and falls asleep, along with everyone in the castle, and giant, thorny vines create a hedge around it, only allowing in the one prince who could break the spell. He arrives at some point, kisses her, everyone wakes up, and they live happily ever after."

"The obstacles in this story are different than the last," Jenny said, standing at the black wall with chalk in her hand. "Thorns, mainly." She nodded to Uncle Curtis, remembering his earlier comments about them.

"Avoiding the thorns might be tricky. Princes died on those thorns," Ophelia said.

"So, we jump into the castle, avoid the thorns, find the spindle, and leave. Sounds pretty straight-forward, but I doubt it will be that easy," Josh said, arms crossed. "We need to jump in well before the prince arrives, else we risk running into him. He might be confused and defensive. I imagine medieval princes aren't really into competition." He cracked his knuckles. "And let's be honest, I'm pretty serious competition." Jenny rolled her eyes, the room dissolving into giggles.

"Is there anything you need from the Collection?" Sam asked, sitting forward.

"What about something we could wear to keep us from getting snagged on the thorns, just in case?" Ophelia asked him.

"Hmm, I think there is some chainmail Isaac got from a *Lord of the Rings* fan fiction novel. Elvish-made with tiny links, not easily snagged. Would that be helpful?"

They all resounded a hearty yes, and Sam went to go find it with a big, happy smile. A little squeal escaped Jenny's mouth. *Elvish chainmail!* "This is so exciting!"

"Want some help finding something to wear over the chainmail?" Ophelia asked, and they excused themselves from the Spare Room to venture into the Collection's medieval costume section in search of the perfect outfit.

"You need to be streamlined and nimble but also fit in if you happen to run across someone," Ophelia explained.

"Like the prince?" Jenny giggled and pretended to curtsy in an imaginary ball gown.

"I'd love to meet a prince," Ophelia said, glancing at Sam who was several rows down in the "Armor" section.

"Maybe you already have, eh? Prince of the Collection?" Jenny said in a hushed tone. Ophelia redden, which made her even prettier. *How is that possible?*

"You noticed?" The Searcher spoke with an unfamiliar uncertainty, almost on the verge of tears.

"Oh my, I've hit a sore spot. Uh, yeah, I've noticed you look at him like my mom looks at my dad," Jenny said. This wasn't the first time she had observed how Ophelia snuck glances at Sam, or how she always ended up sitting next to him at meals, or how she let him call her Philly. *No one else could get away with that.*

Ophelia laughed, a little sad. "I may as well be invisible to him. Sam seems to only have eyes for all this." She gazed at the Collection.

"When he told me about the day you guys met, I specifically remember him mentioning how pretty you were. And exciting."

Flipping through more clothes and costumes, Ophelia softened. "I remember him saying that during his story. I think he was just being nice. And it probably wore off after he got to know me, the real me, not the Searcher me. He sees me as a friend. Just a friend." Her shoulders drooped, and her hanger-flipping slowed to a stop as she rested her forehead against the rack.

"Hey, maybe he will see with new eyes one day, Ophelia. Maybe he will look up." Jenny tried to encourage her.

"Maybe," she replied with a shy but disbelieving smile, wiping off her cheeks and resuming flipping through clothes. "Enough about that." Her smile returned. "There's something else I wanted to talk to you about, if that's okay."

"Sure," Jenny said, curious.

"Obviously, your mom isn't currently around, and I know I'm not even close to being her, but I wanted to let you know that I'm here for you, Jenny, anytime you need to talk about girl stuff or *boy* stuff, or anything. I'd love to be available to you." Ophelia squeezed her arm.

"I know what's it like to not have a mom around. The other girls and I stick together. There aren't a lot of us. And I want to take you traveling. That's what I call it when I move through a book to another place. I know, super creative name for it." She grinned. "Anyway, I'd like to take you today, just real quick. Would you ... I mean, what do you think?" Ophelia asked so sweetly, Jenny could do nothing but embrace her cousin.

Once she pulled back, Jenny kept a grip on Ophelia's elbows. "Yes, of course I'd love to go, and I'll come to you if I need to talk."

"I'm so glad!"

"Also, Ophelia, what other girls? And please, please don't say we can talk about it later."

Ophelia pressed her lips together, realizing her mistake. "Woops." A small chuckle escaped with her breath. "You don't miss a beat, do you, Keeper?"

Jenny shook her head and tapped her foot, hands on her hips, sassy enough to get some answers.

"Okay, I'll tell you some, to hopefully tide you over to a time we can chat more." Jenny leaned in, eager to hear more. "Yes, there are other girls in this game. They do not live here. They are not involved in the day to day of the Compass. They are, however, involved with me and my day to day as Searcher. And before you ask, yes, there are more guys too." With each revelation, Jenny's mouth dropped further and further. "That's all I will tell you for now. We need you focused on *this* mission, not *my* missions, okay?"

Inwardly, Jenny wanted to splutter and stamp her foot and demand the rest of the information about these guys and girls, but instead, she returned to sliding hangers. All would be revealed in time. *Patience is a virtue, right? Guh, but I'm already so freaking virtuous, kind of!*

"Hey, what happened to your mom?" Jenny asked, changing the subject.

Ophelia kept perusing the long dresses and tunics. "She died when I was eleven. Her name was Amina, and she was as beautiful as her name. I still miss her, but she left quite a legacy. Like my great fashion sense." She patted a flip of her hair with a grin then pulled something from the rack. "How about this?" The narrow red tunic sported a silver wolf embroidered on the front and gold trim reflecting the Collection lights.

"Ooh, perfect!" Jenny said, hold it to her lithe frame. "Think it'll fit?"

"You will be so gorgeous!"

"What'd you guys find? Oh, wow, red tunic! With a wolf. Man, even better. Where'd this come from?" Sam, who had appeared out of nowhere, pondered Jenny's costume. He threw his hands in the air. "I can't keep up with this place, and I'm borderline savant."

"Just another mystery of the Collection," Ophelia said with a wink.

"Well, I found the chainmail. Want to come see?" He enticed them away from the racks into the Spare Room where Josh stood, smiling like a kid in a candy store, head to toe in metal.

Jenny squealed again. "Oh my gosh, you look amazing! How does it feel?"

"It's so light," he told her. "And I can move easily. It's awesome."

*I think Josh secretly wants to be a knight.* His goofy grin did nothing to dissuade her opinion.

"Where was this on our last mission?" she said with a hint of sarcasm, thinking of Josh's flayed skin.

Sam shrugged. "I can't win 'em all," he said.

"I would've died from heat stroke, I think," Josh said. "That cottage was so hot. I don't think even Elvish mail comes with air-conditioning. And, I'm still alive, so it's all good."

"See? It worked out." Sam winked at Jenny. "Okay, I also grabbed this to put the spindle in so none of you gets poked," Sam said, holding up a thin wooden box. "DO NOT get poked by the spindle. Do not. Don't do it. Comprende?" No one missed the intensity of his warning.

Grabbing chalk at her position by the black wall, Jenny proceeded to record all they discussed, just like last time.

*Needs*

*Compass*

*Guardian Sword*

*Guardian Ring*

*Chainmail*

*Healing Dagger*

*Spindle holder*

*Fabulous red tunic (for Jenny)*


*Must Not*

*Get poked by the spindle*

*Get poked by the thorns*

*Get stuck in the thorns*

*Interact with the prince*

*Kiss the princess, okay Josh? (ha-ha!)*

Josh scrunched his face. "Are you seriously concerned about that?"

"I hear she is irresistibly beautiful," Jenny said with a little more snark than she intended.

He glared at her. "I think I can control myself."

"We'll see, won't we," and she returned to her notes with a smirk.

*Obstacles*

*Thorns*

*Not knowing exactly what tower the spindle is in*


*Plan*

*Jump into the courtyard of the castle*

*Avoid the thorns*

*Find the spindle*

*Don't kiss the princess*


"So, the spindle is in a tall tower, right?" Jenny said.

"That narrows it down some, I hope. I mean, how many towers can a castle have?" Josh ran his fingers across the chainmail while he talked.

"You'd be surprised," Uncle Curtis chimed in. "Okay, I think we have what we need for tomorrow. I smell something garlicky and amazing coming from upstairs. Let's go eat."

ooooo 🙢🙠 ooooo

Liddy buzzed around the kitchen putting the finishing touches on the meal. Josh and Sam helped her get the table set. During dinner, everyone chatted, forks and knives clinking on plates, finding every last delicious bite. Ophelia sat next to Sam, quieter than usual. His elbow grazed hers, and she jerked it away, glancing at Jenny, who rolled her eyes. Ophelia narrowed hers, but then chuckled and shoved a forkful of spaghetti into her mouth.

Over dessert, Uncle Curtis lifted his coffee cup. "To tomorrow's jump. May you accomplish your mission and all return home alive." Each of them cheered a "Hear, hear!" But Jenny's came out a whisper.

A small box of fear was creeping open in her mind once again. She sipped her water, thinking about the plan, ruminating on it. Everything else blurred. Voices muffled. The fear threatened to overrun the box's edges, infiltrate every fiber of her mind, control her, send her running for the hills. It would be so much easier. Hiding required far less energy. No one would ask anything of her. She'd be free.

And alone.

Gritting her teeth, she stuffed the fear inside the box where it belonged and slammed the lid shut. *Free indeed! That's the most insane thing I've ever tried to tell myself. Hiding under my covers would get me nothing but bedsores and bad dreams. NONE. OF. THAT.* With a huff, she clunked her cup to the table. *I DON'T WANT ALONE.*

The box remained in her mind. It was part of the job, but it did not control her.

With a quick shift in her seat, she clinked Josh's glass and made eye contact. "Cheers! Please don't die tomorrow."

∞∞∞ 𝆕 ∞∞∞

After dinner, Ophelia corralled her and Josh and whisked them off to

251

the Spare Room without explanation. A copy of *Tess of the D'Urbervilles* rested on Sam's desk. The lights were dim with just one lamp glowing.

Ophelia instructed them to grab a pen each and stick them in their pockets. Then she moved the book to the floor and flipped the pages to somewhere near the middle. Taking their hands, she warned them, "Whatever you do, don't let go." Her grip emphasized the warning, and without further ado, she stepped right into the pages of *Tess*.

They fell in together, the wind pummeling them as they plummeted, trying to tear them apart from one another. Unlike with the Compass, where the ground appeared faster than it should, there was no ground this time. Instead, things blurred by. Voices and forest sounds and the hum of a town swirled past. Jenny's limbs kept trying to be part of this story—they wanted to somehow meld together with the words and keep her there. She resisted, squeezing Ophelia's fingers harder while searching for Josh with her other hand. A firm grip found her wrist, and she linked arms with him like her life depended on it. The Compass, knowing it wasn't needed, remained quiet and still against her skin, the world of *Tess* flying by while they continued to fall.

A light materialized far beneath their feet, growing bigger and brighter by the second until it enveloped them. A second later, everything jolted to a stop.

They stood in a small apartment with honey-colored wood floors and simple, white furniture. A copy of *Tess of the D'Urbervilles* lay on the floor in front of a wall to wall bookshelf packed with books. Three small, tidy bedrooms stood off the main room, and a spotless kitchen flowed into the main living space.

"Welcome to my other home," Ophelia said, applying a dab of lip-gloss in the mirror by the front door.

"Where are we?" Josh inquired, stepping to the big, arched windows overlooking a sprawling city.

"London!" Ophelia answered with a grin. "Ready to go find some postcards?" The questioning looks she received from the other two made her laugh. "Remember how your friends at home think you have moved or are traveling? We've got to keep up the ruse. Time to send some mail and check in with them. Oh, and be sure to apologize for taking so long to write."

They hit the fast-moving streets of London and soon found a small tourist shop peddling a plethora of postcards. After selecting a few each and addressing them with the pens Ophelia insisted they bring, they stuck them in the British postboxes and returned to the flat.

"That was easy enough," Josh said, dropping onto the couch.

"Don't get too comfortable," Ophelia said, placing another book on the ground.

Within the next hour, she jumped them to Marrakesh, Milan, Cheng Mai, and Buenos Aires where they bought postcards and wrote quick notes. Ophelia promised to post them at various times in the coming weeks and months to sell the story of their absence.

ooooo 🐱 ooooo

By the time Jenny finally sat on the side of her bed, she smiled a peaceful smile. The travel from city to city had allowed her to forget, for a few minutes, the weight of the Compass. The foreign chatter in each destination had

253

filled her heart, and she enjoyed being in the middle of things in so many beautiful places. And Rae would love getting a postcard from her, which made things even more perfect. Ophelia had inquired who she was sending postcards to, and it'd been fun telling her more about Rae. *I miss you, friend.*

Tracing the Compass with her finger and watching the door, she waited for a knock. She checked her watch, and waited a little more, twirling a curl on her finger.

Just when she decided to turn in, the knock came, a soft rapping. "Hey," she said, knowing who stood in the hall.

"Hey," Josh said, coming in, leaving the door cracked, per the usual. "Did you know it was me?" he asked, sitting in the chair by her bed. She nodded. Without warning, the images of his shredded back slammed through her head. Stuffing those in the fear box, along with everything else, she rammed the lid shut once more and smiled.

For the next hour, they talked. Conversation with Josh was always easy. He laughed more now than when they had first arrived, and he expounded on the things Ophelia had taught him during their training sessions. Reading between the lines, she figured he was killing it with the Sword and other weapons. After their encounter with the witch in *Hansel and Gretel*, the importance of these skills was non-negotiable.

"I need to train more," she said. "I'm good with a bow, but I need to know more."

"I'll work with you," he said. "I'm just learning, you know, but I'd be happy to show you what I know."

"Ooh, I'd love that!"

The hour grew late, and their conversation mellowed. Jenny curled up in the middle of her bed, lying wrapped in covers while they talked. Sometime, when Josh was pontificating on how much he didn't miss school, she fell asleep.

∞∞∞ ✿ ∞∞∞

When she woke in the morning, a quilt covered her, and she savored its warmth. A note lay propped against her pillow with her name scrawled on it.

*I so enjoy our chats. Good night, Keeper. J*

Liddy's words rattled around her brain again. *Seriously, don't do that. It might be disastrous. Shake hands or hug or something. Talk to each other. Be friends.*

"I get it, Liddy!" she hissed, then laughed to herself. Liddy wasn't anywhere near her room.

Tucking the note in her bedside table drawer, she eyeballed the chainmail she had to wear today along with the beautiful tunic Ophelia had found for her. Thoughts of yesterday's conversation regarding the other people involved with the Searcher and Charms niggled at her brain. *Guh, I'm so curious!* She clenched a fist, then released it. No, she couldn't think about it right now. Today she had to focus. Today was *Sleeping Beauty.*

# Chapter Twenty-Three

Everyone filed into the Spare Room, chatting and laughing, trying to keep it light despite the upcoming mission. The chainmail Jenny, Josh, and Ophelia wore tinkled with each step. Jenny's red and silver tunic glimmered under the lights. Josh wore a simple, dark brown tunic over his mail, and Ophelia had donned a purple one, regal as ever. Sam divvied out their walkie-talkies, and Ophelia hid a smile when she got her favorite yellow one again. Sam had moved on by the time she glanced at him with her happy, golden eyes, and she slumped in disappointment. Jenny touched her arm.

"You're gorgeous," she whispered to her cousin as they adjusted the walkie-talkies over their ears. "The purple is perfect. He noticed, I'm sure."

"Thanks Jenny. You're sweet to say it," Ophelia replied. Squaring her shoulders and lifting her chest, she initiated her "general" voice. "Okay, I'm ready. You guys?" Josh and Jenny gave her a thumbs up.

Uncle Curtis unlocked the book and placed it on Sam's desk. The three jumpers linked arms, and the Compass hummed to life, pulsing and whirring. Once off-putting to Jenny, it now felt natural, like she was right where she needed to be. With a bit of grace, she leaned over the book, and they were gone.

Uncle Curtis's far away words echoed through the rustling pages of the book. "How about some coffee?"

The ground approached quickly, but Jenny managed to not let out an "oomph" when she landed. Josh dropped next to her, solid, balanced, hard as nails. His stance was strong and alert. He held an ax in one hand and his sword in the other, magic misting off the blade. "Where'd you get the ax?" Jenny whispered.

"Sam, just before we left. And in case you were wondering, it's a plain old ax. Nothing magical."

They took in their surroundings, shivers traveling the length of Jenny's spine. Weapons lowered and stilled.

"Whoa." Jenny's voice fell flat in the stillness of the courtyard.

High, sturdy walls, built for strength and protection, removed any hint of the world outside, protecting the castle from invaders, no doubt. They could not, however, protect the courtiers from the curse, and those unlucky enough to be there the fateful day the princess pricked her finger now lay scattered about, asleep, dusty, frozen in time. White flowers had sprung up around them, between their fingers and ankles and by their ears, entwining in their hair. Tiny green vines crept along the arms and legs of the slumberers. Jenny stooped and picked a flower, twisting it between her fingers, continuing to peruse the scene.

People appeared to have fallen asleep in the midst of their normal daily activities. They slumped against the lifeless fountains or under the flowering trees scattered about the enclosure. Several couples held hands, locked in timeless, unconscious affection. Their chests rose and fell, keeping them alive while they dreamed with slow, rhythmic breaths. But other than that, there was no movement. The eerie stillness left the jumpers unsettled and ill at ease. They drew nearer to each other, finding comfort in living, breathing, *moving* bodies.

More concerning than the nearly lifeless bodies in the courtyard were the massive, woody vines coiled about the walls of the castle, thick with long thorns capable of impaling even the most careful person.

"Don't touch those," warned Ophelia. She didn't have to say it twice.

"Pretty freaky," said Jenny. "I don't like this."

"Let's go." Josh took the lead. They followed, avoiding the thorns like they were the plague.

Four tall towers, one at each corner of the keep, rose above the thick walls, all wrapped in thorny vines. One of them housed the spindle. And somewhere in the castle lay a lovely girl on a bed fit for a queen, waiting for her prince to come and break the spell with a gentle kiss. Jenny blushed just thinking about it. *Who will be my first kiss?* She glanced at Josh marching on ahead. *Absolutely not.* "Focus," she whispered to herself. Josh must have heard her, for he gave her a questioning look. "I'm good," she said.

"You sure?"

"I'm sure."

They picked their way through the courtyard, avoiding the thorns and the random bodies draped on benches, walls, and the dry fountains that had once undoubtedly brought such life to this place. Ducking into an open doorway not completely blocked with thorns, Jenny stepped ahead and directed them into the Keep, Josh and Ophelia ever vigilant, weapons drawn and ready.

Jenny released her breath. "Those bodies were ... I don't know. They made me feel gross. But now, since we know they are definitely asleep, you guys can chill a little, don't you think?" she said. Josh shook his head no, and Ophelia didn't answer, nor did she alter her movements. They continued moving in the direction of the first tower at a decent pace.

Josh stopped. "Did you hear something?" Jenny and Ophelia both nodded. A far-off hum broke the unnatural quiet, and it grew louder and louder, along with tiny, female voices speaking at normal volume.

"This place gets more overgrown every time we are here," one voice said.

"Yes, but I doubt we will have to wait much longer. I received word of a prince headed this way, intent on finding the castle," another added.

"Oh goodie!" said a third. The humming continued to fill the halls. No other voices were heard.

'Quick," said Josh, putting away the Guardian Sword. "Go to sleep. If they try anything, we each grab one." They dropped to the floor, pretending to be asleep, careful to not touch any vines. Jenny let her hair fall in front of her face so she could spy on the incoming visitors.

Around the corner flitted three little fairies, presumably heading toward the princess. Jenny watched them from beneath a curl. They were petite and fragile, the size of small children. Translucent wings created the humming sound and a soft breeze that tickled her cheek.

Tiny flowers decorated the first fairy's dark bun. She wore a dress made of leather and wool, which complemented her freckles, with tight leggings beneath it. Leather boots reached mid-thigh.

The next was pale and fair, with big blue eyes and pink cheeks. Her hair hung loose. A yellow, woolen tunic stopped at her knees over dark leather leggings and short boots.

The last fairy's black hair and tanned skin glistened in the lantern light, her loose braid slung over one shoulder. The dark orange dress and black boots she wore enhanced her rich coloring.

*These do not look like fairies from any movie I've ever seen.*

Jenny tried breath normally while they passed by. She needed to act natural, asleep, still but alive. *Can they hear my heart pounding?*

The third, darker fairy paused, examining the three sleeping humans a little closer. "Have we seen these three before?" she said to her companions. "They feel new."

"I don't know. It's been a while since we've been here. Maybe they came to visit the princess and were pricked by the thorns? Are they dead or just asleep?" The brown-haired one said. "I see them breathing. Maybe they've been here the entire time and we just never noticed."

Feet now on the floor, they edged toward the trio, alert for anything off, any movement other than breathing. Jenny waited for Josh to tense, but he kept still and calm. *Of course. He does everything well.*

The pale fairy even poked him—still nothing. *Oh, he's good.*

"Let's bind them up and try to wake them with magic," said the brown-haired one. "If they truly are part of the curse, they will remain asleep. But if they are not, they will be forced awake, and we can know what we are dealing with." Before the fairy could utter another word, a large hand clamped over her mouth, and an arm reached around her waist, rendering her helpless. Her fairy friends found themselves in the same position before they could blink.

"We don't want to hurt you," Jenny said. The calm command in her voice surprised her, but she didn't show it. Instead, she stood a bit taller. "Nor do we want to hurt Briar Rose. We need to acquire something from the castle. The cursed spindle. Surely you don't need to have it here. If we release you, will you let us complete our mission? We just need the spindle, and we will leave." She let go of the brown-haired fairy's mouth with a warning. "No magic, or *he* will slice you in half. I am *not* kidding." The fairies quelled under Josh's scrutiny, and jumped when he ignited the Guardian Sword once more.

"You have attempted to fool us and taken us hostage. Why should we believe you?" The fairy in Jenny's custody squirmed as she spoke.

"I'll prove it to you." Jenny radioed to Sam, and within seconds, a wind brushed past her hair as he ghosted in with her request. A quick blur, and then he was gone. The letter from the Sorceress materialized, and Jenny passed it to the fairies to read, taking care to highlight the part about the spindle. "This Sorceress has taken our parents and my uncle. We need the spindle to secure his release."

The pale fairy mumbled beneath Josh's palm, and he released it so she could speak. "What magic is this?" she asked, jerking her head toward the letter and its abrupt arrival.

"Compass magic," Jenny said. "My magic. It is very different from yours. Will you allow us to complete our task peacefully, or must we detain you further?"

The three fairies communicated silently. "Release us, and you may have the spindle. We should be rid of the thing anyway. However, we will accompany you," the freckled one said.

Josh released his fairy. "You lead the way. Even one hint of magic, and you will regret it. Let's go," he ordered, his voice gruff. Ophelia looked impressed.

The fairies led them further into the cold, stark beauty of the Keep, the sound of their wings humming through the corridors once again.

All stone and wood, the Keep's main level was simply, but richly, decorated. Iron lanterns lined each hallway along with the occasional mosaic or tapestry, telling the history of the kingdom, tile by tile and stitch by stitch. The woody vines stretched along the walls and through every doorway, putting the Keeper, Guardian, and Searcher on an even more precarious edge.

When the stairs opened into the top floor of the Keep, Jenny sucked in her breath. This floor oozed luxury, a proper home fit for a king, or a princess. Red and gold rugs warmed the floors, and crystal-tipped chandeliers hung from the ceiling, the candles long melted away. A hallway, thick with thorns, extended from the foyer where they stood to a golden bedroom—a beacon for princes and spindle thieves alike. The canopied bed, lavender and green and gold, enshrined the sleeping princess, Briar Rose.

"Should we go see her?" Jenny whispered to Ophelia.

"Unwritten rule number eight of being in a story: always take a gander at royalty if the opportunity arises," Ophelia answered, grinning. "Fairies, please take us to see the princess."

"No touching, no magic," the pale one said.

"No problem," Josh replied. "Same goes for you."

They fanned out on either side of the bed and examined its occupant. Golden hair framed her heart-shaped face and slipped onto a silken pillow. She wore a soft pink and white nightgown, placed there by the fairies who attended her after the curse. Briar Rose ticked all the boxes a princess ought. She even slept perfectly, on her back, hands folded on her chest, rising and falling with each breath. On one finger glimmered a small, garnet ring.

"Well, there she is, waiting for her true love's kiss," Ophelia said, arms crossed.

Jenny nudged Josh. "Feeling any urge to plant one on her, oh great Guardian?"

"I'm good," he replied, clearing his throat, cheeks red. He took a quick step back to prove his point.

"In one version of the *Sleeping Beauty* story, she gets pregnant while she is sleeping and giving birth to twins before waking. How crazy is that?" Jenny said.

"I don't even want to know the details." Josh cringed. "This story is better. Love at first sight ... that's the way to go."

Ophelia laughed with a hint of bitterness, shaking her head. "This love at first sight thing that happens in fairy tales is ridiculous. I mean, what if pretty Briar Rose is also a grade A snob or snorts when she laughs or eats like a horse? What if she is hateful and horrible to live with? The poor prince wouldn't know. All he knows is she is lovely to behold. For his sake,

I hope her character matches her appearance. But in real life, love takes a while." Her cheeks heated as she spoke.

The freckled fairy grunted. "She is a fair girl, kind and generous, with perfect manners and a pleasant laugh. And why do you speak of other stories about our Briar Rose? We do not understand."

Jenny sighed. "It's a long story." She laughed at the irony of her words. "Trust us, this one ends well. You have nothing to fear."

The same fairy watched her, then asked, "It wouldn't have anything to do with your necklace, would it?" And with those words, she launched herself at Jenny, reaching and clawing for the Compass. Her pretty face was contorted into an ugly mask, her mouth full of pointed teeth bared in effort.

"Whoa!' Jenny shouted, taking the full brunt of the petite but determined fairy.

The other two turned on Josh and Ophelia in the same moment, catching them unaware but not unprepared. As the other two fended for themselves, Jenny fell back on her training. She spun, full speed, flinging her nemesis off, then dropped into a defensive stance, the vicious fairy coming at her again. In one movement, she flipped the imp over her head and heaved with all her strength, hurling her toward the wall. The fairy hit the stones like a bird on a window but recovered in a breath and redoubled her efforts, eyes focused on the Compass as if its magic called to her. "This is not how you act in the movies!" Jenny said through gritted teeth.

Despite the fairy's small size, she was relentless, and even with all her training and endurance work, Jenny began to tire. When the fairy managed to wrap her legs round Jenny's waist, Jenny held her off with every bit of her strength, her muscles shaking. The fairy reached and pushed, her delicate hands almost slipping past Jenny's grip to the Compass.

"No!" Jenny yelled. "You may not have it!" And with a surge of power, Jenny grabbed a spindly fairy arm and ripped the creature off before hurling her to meet her friends in a heap by the corner.

Ophelia's dark-haired fairy was pinned to the wall by Josh's ax, having caught her by the tunic against a wooden beam. Josh's pale fairy lay in a heap, her wings drooping, at the feet of the one who was pinned. When Jenny's attacker came hurtling toward them, she toppled the pale one and terrified the other. With no attempt to hide his irritation, Josh bound them together with a rope from his pack. They struggled against it.

"It will not give," he assured them. He then laid his ax on a table by the window. "This will free you given enough time and if you work together. We don't want you dead, but we can't have you bothering us anymore either. Make no mistake, you will not impede our plans again. Do not be stupid and try to come after us. And don't even try your magic. We will meet you with our own." He swung the Sword to life with a whoosh to emphasize his point and completely freak them out.

They quelled at his words, and even Jenny's eyes widened at his intensity. *Josh is super scary when he wants to be.*

On a whim, she stuck her tongue out at the fairies, turned to her friends, asked if they were ready, and walked away from Briar Rose. Josh followed, and then Ophelia, who tripped on the corner of a thick rug and steadied herself against the wall. Her hand barely grazed the edge of a vine before she jerked it away, pausing to see if anything would happen.

For a few seconds, all was quiet. A popping sound echoed through the castle. Then creaking. Louder and louder. Pop, creak, POP! CREAK! The hallway trembled. Jenny, Josh, and Ophelia reached for each other. The sound of the angry vines mixed with the cackling of the bound fairies.

"Oh, now you've done it," one of them howled.

With the next pop, the vines started to grow, filling the hall, reaching for the trio, thorns razor sharp, splitting their bark as they expanded. "Run!" shouted Jenny, and run they did, heading for the staircase leading to the tower they hoped housed the spindle. They took the stairs two at a time, the floor rumbling beneath their feet. Fairy laughter followed them through the hallways.

Thorns stretched, reaching, trying to cut and grab arms and legs, but the chainmail repelled them, even snapping the pointed tips off. Up and up and up they raced, around and around the tower.

A door! *Please be unlocked!* The handle turned, and she threw it open and held it for Ophelia and Josh, who slammed it closed and flung his weight against it. Jenny helped him, the vines, pushing, pressing, striving to enter the room.

A spinning wheel stood in the middle of the tower, oblivious to the chaos behind the door. It appeared harmless, covered in dust and cobwebs. Even with the rumbling of vines outside, Ophelia approached it with care and reverence. She grasped the spindle, examining it as if she could see the curse coating the wood. It mesmerized her for a moment, but when the door to the chamber bowed against its hinges, creaking and groaning under pressure, she snapped back to reality. "I can't hold it!" Josh yelled, he and Jenny leaping away, toward Ophelia.

Before Ophelia could tuck the spindle safely in the wooden box, the door to the room splintered and thorny vines clawed their way in.

The entire tower shook, and the old walls shuttered and cracked, daylight streaming through the fissures. When the floor lurched, it pulled Jenny away from Ophelia and Josh. With a shout, she tried to lunge for them, grazing Josh's fingers before the collapsing tower pulled them further apart.

"Jenny!" Josh bellowed. Panic contorted his face. She tried to keep her balance, the walls crumbling in every direction. Ophelia screamed her name too, over the sound of the crashing rocks plummeting to the ground. "Jump!" Josh roared. "Jump now!" He stretched for her, screaming for her to jump as the floor gave way. Plumes of dust clouded her vision, but she jumped anyway, with all her might, towards their voices, slamming into them midair. Josh held onto her with one arm, and Ophelia with the other. Coughing and choking, she spluttered the words to get them home, shattering rocks and fairy laughter reverberating behind them.

Uncle Curtis and Sam jumped to their feet when the trio rushed from the book, dust flying everywhere and pebbles clattering to the ground. Jenny landed on her feet, staggering, but Josh fell, bearing the full weight of Ophelia, who slumped against him, unconscious.

"Oh dear," Uncle Curtis said as Josh lowered the tiny woman to the floor. Her head fell to one side. The spindle clattered to the ground when her hand fell open, blood trickling from a small wound in her palm.

"Oh no!" Josh said. "The spindle. The spindle got her. She's asleep."

# Chapter Twenty-Four

They knelt on either side of Ophelia, watching her breathe, just as they'd done with Briar Rose. Ophelia, with her purple tunic and sweet face, looked just as regal.

"Someone has to kiss her. On the lips," Jenny said. "Someone who loves her. This version of the story says only true love's kiss can break the spell. Apparently, this magic works here in the real world." She steadied her trembling voice.

"Well, I love her, but she's my daughter. I don't think I qualify," Uncle Curtis said.

"I'm only seventeen. And I love Ophelia too, but I don't, you know, *love* love Ophelia. She's like my cool aunt or something."

Jenny knew it pained Josh to feel this helpless.

They all stared at Sam, who swallowed audibly. "Well, no pressure or anything," he managed to say before he stood and stalked away.

The other three watched him go. "Do you think he loves her enough?" Josh whispered to Jenny. "Like, love loves her?"

"Ophelia doesn't think so. Ooooh, but what if he does? Josh, this could be it!" Jenny said, excitement rising.

Josh frowned. "I'm more concerned with *what if he doesn't?* Then what do we do?" Jenny's eyes got big, realizing the weight of his words. They returned their attention to Ophelia, and to Uncle Curtis, who was holding her hand but watching Sam.

And then Sam was standing by them again, his eyes only on Ophelia. He knelt by her, and Uncle Curtis placed her fingers in his before moving to observe with the others, giving him space. With his other hand, Sam pushed her short hair from her face, his fingers caressing her cheek, his thumb brushing over her mouth. Ever so slowly, he leaned in and paused, inches from her lips.

Jenny drew in a sharp breath when he paused. *Why? Why not just go for it, Sam?* Then it dawned on her. For Sam, everything would change in this moment. This kiss would tell all. His true feelings, feelings he kept hidden away behind charm and smiles and an intense dedication to the work. They would be laid bare for everyone to see. Everyone, including Ophelia, once she woke up. *If* she woke up. She would know. What would she do? How would she react? He would never know unless he tried. *Be brave, Sam! Take a chance like you did when you first met her.*

Before he had time to reconsider, Sam closed the gap between them, softly kissing her. Then he retreated, waiting for what would happen next, scanning her face for any sign of life.

Nothing happened. Jenny held her breath. Did he love her enough to break the spell? Surely he did. Surely. The way he held her, touched her, gazed at her just then ... only a man in love could be so tender. Next to her, Josh's breathing slowed too, waiting, wondering.

A finger moved. And a foot twitched. Ophelia inhaled a full breath, then blinked her eyes. Josh exhaled and nudged Jenny, relieved. She sagged against his arm.

"What happened to me, Sam?" Ophelia asked, lifting herself onto her elbows, closer to him. "All I remember is the tower collapsing. Then blackness. Oh my, such blackness." She shuddered. "But then, a ray of light pierced it. What a strange dream."

Sam tried to smile. "The spindle pricked your palm." He got quiet again. "You fell asleep."

"Oh! And, um, how did I wake up?" she asked.

"You woke up when I, uh, when I, uh, uh, uh ... when I kissed you." He ducked his head, his last few words nearly inaudible, but then he looked at her again, nervous and apprehensive.

"But only true love's kiss would work, according to the story," she replied, her voice gentle, knowing.

"Yep."

Shifting forward, she pressed herself to sit up, facing him. He watched, unsure what was happening. Still weak, she leaned her forehead against his chest and whispered, "I always hoped I'd be awake for our first kiss."

He pushed her back, holding her head in his hands so he could study her face. "Say that again, Ophelia?" he asked, a catch in his voice Jenny had never heard before.

"I said, 'I always hoped I'd be awake for our first kiss.'"

270

"You—you wanted to kiss me? I mean, you thought about it?" Sam sounded dumbstruck.

"Yes, Sam, so many times." Sam brushed away the tears trickling down her cheeks with his thumbs. "I've loved you for years, Sam." She smiled behind the tears.

"You never said, or even hinted!" He was somewhere between tears and laughter. "I mean, sure, I'm lovable and handsome in kind of a nerdy way. I didn't really think you were into nerdy. Maybe more like, oh, I don't know, ninja or cowboy or international spy."

Ophelia wiped her eyes with her fingertip. "Cowboy? Really?" Her shoulders shook with silent laughter. "I don't mind nerdy," she confessed once the giggles stopped. "As long as there's not too much talk of D&D."

"What about *Settlers of Catan*?" he wondered, half-serious.

"Sorry, what's *Settlers of Catan*?" she asked, feigning ignorance before dissolving into laughter once more.

With a hearty guffaw, Sam leaned in to kiss her again amid cheers from the peanut gallery behind him. They had held it in until they could hold it no longer. Jenny cried, Josh clapped, and Uncle Curtis smiled, whispering, "Finally."

Concerned for everyone's safety, Josh snatched up the spindle and tucked it away in the wooden box while Sam helped Ophelia to her feet.

Jenny hugged her with all her might. "He looked up!" she said, just for Ophelia to hear.

"Oh Jenny. Oh, he did. He did." Ophelia had a quiet, contented air about her despite the close call with some rabid fairies and a cursed spindle.

"So, what happens now?" Jenny said.

Uncle Curtis stepped in and put his arms around Jenny and Josh's shoulders. "Now we rest and plan the next mission. And before I forget to tell you, great work on the one today. Only three more to go."

He led them from the Spare Room and marched ahead to the stairs. Jenny glanced over her shoulder to see Sam and Ophelia slow dancing together as Fang swung the bookshelf door closed. "Did you hear any music?" Josh whispered to her.

"I don't think they need any."

ooooo 🎭 ooooo

Jenny woke the next morning, her stomach growling. She trudged to the kitchen, her legs heavy and body tired. When she slumped into her chair at the table, Uncle Curtis raised an eyebrow and poured her an extra-large mug of coffee. "Feeling weary today?" he asked, sliding it towards her. Her hair fell over one eye when she lifted her head and grunted, swigging the hot liquid energy in front of her.

"New Keepers often tire after jumps, especially if they are stressful ones. But fear not, over time, your stamina will increase until you can make multiple jumps a day with no issues." He patted her on the arm. "But until then, you must rest and eat. I believe I can help with the eating part."

"You haven't failed me yet," she said, her voice scratchy and still half-asleep.

The smell of her favorite French toast soon filled the kitchen, along with the sound of Irish music, which Uncle Curtis was sometimes partial to when cooking. When he brought her a full plate, she croaked a "thank you" and dug in. She ate and ate, debating on whether to return to bed right after breakfast or wait an hour or two to see if she perked up.

Halfway through her meal, Josh slid into the chair next to her. "Can I have a bite?' he asked, staring at her food with tired but hungry eyes.

"No need," Uncle Curtis said, setting a plate piled high in front of him. "Go for it."

"Uh, how many pieces of French toast did you get?" Jenny asked Josh, staggered at the height of his food.

He quickly counted them. "I think there's seven."

"Eight!" Uncle Curtis said from the stove where he pan-fried a few more.

*Wow,* Jenny mouthed to Josh before returning to her own measly three.

They ate in silence, elbows on the table. Ophelia soon floated into the kitchen. "Good morning!" she beamed, resting her cheek on her knuckles, staring past them with a peaceful smile. Jenny and Josh exchanged a glance, trying not to giggle.

"Good morning," Josh said, sounding too tired to put much effort into talking.

"Oy, are you okay?" she said, leaving her dreamland long enough to consider someone else for a moment, though her eyes were still glazed a tad.

"Ophelia, do you mind if I take the day off? I'm exhausted," he said. "I need sleep more than punching."

When she failed to answer, he threw a wadded-up napkin at her, startling her back to reality once more. "Earth to Ophelia!" he teased her.

"She's just thinking about me, aren't you?" Sam said, walking in from his apartment in the backyard, kissing her cheek. "Good morning, Philly."

Jenny had never seen Ophelia blush so deeply before. Sam sat next to her and scooted his chair closer.

"Hi," she managed to chirp.

"Why Ophelia, have I rendered you speechless? My, you must be quite infatuated." Sam's eyes twinkled behind his glasses as he goaded her. "It's my dashing good looks and irresistible charm," he explained to Josh and Jenny.

"Oh, of course!" Jenny said.

Ophelia punched him in the shoulder. "You do think highly of yourself," she said, linking her arm through his before turning her attention to Josh, asking him to repeat the question and agreeing to a day off. "I have plenty to do anyway," she told them. "Searcher business."

"Oh good, you can spend your day with me, or rather, I can spend it with you, going about your 'business', whatever that means," Sam said to her, the genuine smile on his face making her blush again. Jenny watched them throughout the rest of breakfast. It was both cute and nauseating to see them together. How Uncle Curtis managed to eat his eggs with all the flirting and canoodling was a mystery.

Weariness finally winning, Jenny excused herself for a mid-morning nap, thinking about the Sorceress and their next move while she walked to her room. "Oh shoot, my water," she said, realizing she had left it in the kitchen.

Retracing her steps, she found Josh at his door attempting to turn the handle with a glass of milk in one hand and plate piled with toast in the other. "Hey," he said, glancing at the top piece threatening to slide off. "Everything okay?"

She leaned against the wall. "Yeah, I'm just thirsty. Hey, I was thinking, we need to figure out where the Sorceress is as soon as possible. We got so into mission planning we kind of forgot about that part. I'd need to read the ransom letter again and have access to the *Fairy Tale* book. I'm sure Uncle Curtis and Ophelia wouldn't mind being with us to unlock it."

Josh stuck his plate toward her. "Take a piece of toast. That top one if you would. You need it. And go take a nap. You look so tired, Jenny. This morning, we rest, and later, let's talk to Uncle Curtis about when and where to unlock the book. We can start this afternoon. I know you want to start now, but if you get sick from exhaustion, you won't be any good to anyone, especially Isaac."

Unable to resist the toast, she took a bite and closed her eyes. Bread and butter tasted so good, and the swig of milk he shared hit her just right. Swaying on her feet, Jenny agreed to rest and promptly fell asleep as soon as her head hit the pillow, dreaming of toast with a great deal of butter on it.

Hours later, she emerged from her room and wandered to the den. Uncle Curtis sat in his reading chair, nose in a book. When she entered, he closed it and took off his glasses.

"Good nap?" Uncle Curtis asked.

"Affirmative," she answered with a still sleepy voice, making Uncle Curtis chuckle.

"Josh was telling me how anxious you are to find the Sorceress and take her the first two items," he said.

"Is Josh awake?" Jenny asked.

"I am!" he called from the kitchen, closing the refrigerator door and holding an apple and jar of peanut butter. "Still hungry," he confessed.

"Shocking," she said with a grin. "And yes, Uncle Curtis, I think we need to figure out where she is and take her these items as soon as we can," Jenny said, dropping onto the couch.

Uncle Curtis pulled the letter from his pocket. "I agree," he said and reread the clues aloud, emphasizing the last part:

*"Think ye hard on where I be*
*And what I do not need*
*Or no hair of me you'll see*
*And greens you shall not eat."*

"And there is also something about 'garden walls' earlier in the letter," he added. "It has to be something in this book." Uncle Curtis lifted the locked *Fairy Tales* book with his bony hand. "She's in here somewhere."

"Can we unlock it and have a peek?" Jenny said. "There are a lot of stories in there."

"Are you rested enough?" Josh asked, giving her a hard stare.

"I'm fine. I'm good. I promise. Are you?" He nodded, shoving more apple into his mouth with a crunch.

They called for Ophelia to join them—an added layer of backup just in case the Sorceress decided to reemerge. As unlikely as that would be, it couldn't hurt to have their top warrior nearby. Sam and Liddy came too, surrounding Josh and Jenny, who held the book in her fingertips. The Compass rested against her skin, quiet and unmoving. It seemed to sense this was not the time for a jump. It knew Jenny was too tired.

"How about we make copies of all the stories you haven't read through yet? Then we can divide and conquer?" Liddy suggested. Jenny brightened at this idea and headed to the office.

Twenty minutes later, she handed stories to everyone. "We need to find any story with a wall, a garden, maybe greens? And think about what she does not need from us. It has to be something she could get on her own because she is there."

The room grew quiet as they each read their assigned stories. Many were unfamiliar and required more than a quick perusal. Jenny flipped to a page with a title she recognized. As she read, it dawned on her—the answer was right in front of them the whole time, only in different terms. "This is the one!" she said. The couch shook as she bounced with excitement. "Look, here is the part about the garden, and here is the wall. And the part about the greens, but the writer of this story doesn't say *greens*, he says *Rapunzel.* Rapunzel is a type of lettuce! Greens!"

"Seriously? Who knows that?" Josh asked her, both impressed and annoyed. "I need to learn more," he huffed.

"Poor Rapunzel was named after a lettuce?" Sam said. "Good thing it wasn't radishes growing in the garden. Or turnips. Those names just wouldn't do. I guess Rapunzel is much prettier than Arugula or Butterhead." Ophelia giggled at him.

"And she must have access to Rapunzel's hair, so she would not need us to get it. The letter says *hair*—that must be a clue. This is where she is. This is where we go. Are you guys ready?" Jenny yanked the Compass from inside her shirt.

They stared at her and then started laughing. Jenny shrank a little, uncertain what to do. Josh noticed and contained his chuckles. "Sorry, Jenny. Don't you think we should plan a little first? I mean, this means us facing the Sorceress. She was cunning enough to kidnap five people at once. Five very capable people." He raised a brow.

Her cheeks hot, Jenny replied, "I know. I just want my family back. And now I know where at least one of them is." The pages of *Rapunzel* felt smooth when she skimmed her fingers on them. "I need to know he is all right. Liddy needs to know. And we all need more information about our parents, to see if our theory of them being dumped in a book is correct." Jenny snuck a glance at Liddy. Liddy kept it together most of the time but being this close to knowing more about Isaac affected her too.

Josh addressed Uncle Curtis. "Can we try and go tomorrow?"

"We will need to plan tonight, but if you guys are rested enough and we have a solid plan, then yes." He took Jenny's hand. "I want to know too. I get it, Jenny."

Liddy brought snacks, and they settled in to plan their first encounter with the Sorceress. Sam had some ideas for Collection items that might come in handy, and Ophelia reminded them of various training scenarios they had perfected over the last few months.

Their meeting moved to the table for dinner, and there, Jenny started to fade. First, her cheek rested on her palm, then lowered to her arm, her eyes growing heavy. Soon her forehead was on the table, and she slept.

# Chapter Twenty-Five

She woke the next morning, still in her lounge clothes from the day before, unsure of how she had gotten to bed, her stomach rumbling. She didn't worry, however, hearing Uncle Curtis in the kitchen and smelling something amazing wafting up the stairs, down the long hall, and into her room. She stepped into the hall at the exact same time Josh and Ophelia did, called by flour and butter and the other sweet scents swirling about the house. Jenny practically ran to the kitchen, beating the other two who took a minute to get dressed and make their beds like normal people.

She shoved a strawberry muffin in her mouth while simultaneously pouring a glass of milk. "So, what'd I miss?" she asked Uncle Curtis, who had stopped cooking to watch her attack the muffin.

"Hungry, Jenny?"

"If I don't eat this muffin right now, I might die."

He chuckled and then filled her in on the parts of the meeting she had slept through. "We figured the Sorceress is either in Rapunzel's empty tower, or she is in the house of the original woman who took Rapunzel in the first place. Both are empty by the end of the story, so she must be living there, in the setting. We thought you guys would jump in at either of those two places and see. What do you think?"

Jenny considered the story. "I think we should jump in at the tower, mostly because I want to see it, and there will probably be a trail between the tower and the house, since the old woman walked to see Rapunzel every morning in the story. I'd bet my curly hair she wore down a good trail."

"Aye, good thinking, Jenny. And will you just hand the two items over to her, then?"

"Well, it depends, I guess. It depends on the state Isaac is in, and it depends on how difficult the Sorceress is."

"I agree. It might be prudent to give her what she needs up front and hope she is generous with information. Or, it could be worth bargaining with her. You will have to see how it goes when you get there."

When Josh and Ophelia walked in, Jenny gawked at their clothing: all black, tight-fitting, scary-looking items, the ones Ophelia donned when she needed to be a ninja. Josh had some now too. Glancing at her own clothes, rumpled and slouchy, Jenny grimaced. Her co-jumpers were scary, brave warriors that could make even the fiercest general wilt. She was a tired psychology student who'd been up all night studying for a final and fallen asleep on her book, only to wake up just with enough time to rush to class and take her test without a glance in the mirror. "Do I get some too?" she asked, hopeful.

Ophelia grinned. "On your bed, Keeper." Jenny jumped to her feet, but Ophelia caught her before she could bolt upstairs and whispered in her ear, "And a little surprise from me on your dresser."

Grabbing another muffin, Jenny flew to her room. A matching ninja outfit lay on her bed, but instead of black, hers was deep gray, setting her apart from the other two. *Maybe gray is the Keeper color?* The clothes fit perfectly, hugging her long arms and legs, tapering at the ankles and wrists. Soft but sturdy black boots laced to mid-calf. She strapped her quiver of arrows and bow on one shoulder and her short sword on the other. The healing dagger fit in her belt, and the Compass rested beneath her shirt against her skin. On her dresser, she found Ophelia's gift—a pair of silver earrings in the shape of arrows and a black and gray headband to hold her hair off her face.

When she turned to check herself in the mirror, she noticed another gift, sitting on top of *Emma*, which had stayed by her bedside since her arrival. Her heart gave a squeeze as she picked up the small ring with a pretty garnet setting. It was familiar. "No way," she said aloud, remembering it on Briar Rose's pinkie, rising and falling with each breath. *Josh? Did you ... no. You couldn't have. But I guess you DID!* She slipped it on her finger, admiring how it sparkled in the lamplight.

Then, adjusting the arrow earrings and pushing her hair back with the headband, she added a touch of lip-gloss and mascara, trying to bring some color to her face. Sometimes she wished she was built more like Ophelia and Liddy, striking or gorgeous. Instead, she was ... nice. Maybe cute? But not beautiful. *Not with this hair!* She tugged at a curl. A little wave of sadness settled on her shoulders, allowing thoughts of the Sorceress and their task today to slip into her mind.

But her mom's words rang in her ear, fighting against the fear. "Being brave means doing what needs doing, even if you are afraid." *I can be brave.*

*I will be brave! After all, I am the Keeper. I don't have a choice.* She squared her shoulders and lifted her chest. *I got this.* We *got this.*

Walking with purpose, like her mom would, she marched downstairs and strutted into the kitchen. Both hands hit the table, and she leaned on them, glaring at her people. They all stopped what they were doing to stare back. "So, what are we waiting for?" she said.

Within twenty minutes, they were in the Spare Room, their packs on the table and walkie-talkies in their ears. Jenny's Flanklets were strapped to her ankles, and a small picture of Liddy she hoped to slip to Isaac was stowed away in her pocket.

"Remind me again why we aren't just rescuing Isaac?" she asked, tapping her foot, irritated and impatient.

"Because the Sorceress knows about our parents, and she won't give that up if we take Isaac. She wants every item on the list, and she wants Isaac, for some reason," Josh explained. Knowing he was right and hating the truth, Jenny sighed.

"Oh yeah. Ugh, I hate leaving him there any longer! Stupid Sorceress."

Always on the hunt for the other Lesser Charms, Ophelia reminded them to try and get information on whatever necklace the Sorceress had that allowed her access to the real world. "I've got to get it at some point," she had said the night before. "But this isn't the right time." Now, Jenny could almost see Ophelia's adrenaline pumping, and she prowled back and forth in the Spare Room.

Someone squeezed Jenny's arm. "You look ready," Josh said, standing close to her.

"I'm ready. You?" He nodded and linked his arm through hers, but she pulled away, holding up a finger. "Give me just a second." She ran to give Liddy a big hug, and tears sprang into the former mermaid's eyes.

Jenny took Ophelia's hand, and then Josh's. "We'll be home soon," she said to the remaining three. The Compass hummed to life, and Jenny let it lead her along, right into the book. Pages ruffled and swirling words floated about their heads, disappearing before the ground approached.

This time, she was ready and landed on her feet, in a deep squat. Next to her, Josh hit the ground with one knee bent and a fist into the dirt, solid and strong. Ophelia stepped from the air onto the ground. *How does she do that?*

They peered up and up and up at the fantastical tower rising above their heads. Tall and thin, built with stone and mortar, it reached to the sky, the top balanced on the ivy-laden walls of the pillar. Pointed roofs and turrets stabbed the sky. It seemed too pretty to have such a sordid history, its exterior masking the ugliness that had happened within.

But they weren't here to ogle the tower for long or discuss the ins and outs of Rapunzel's tragic childhood. They were here to find the Sorceress.

"Think they're up there?" Josh asked, jerking his head toward the tower.

"Only one way to find out," Jenny said. Squaring her stance, she called up in a loud voice, "Sorceress, Sorceress, let down your hair!" She smiled at the other two, basking in her cleverness.

When nothing happened after a minute, Jenny dropped her hands from her hips and declared, "Nope, not up there."

Just past the tower, leading into the woods, they found a lone trail.

"I knew it!" Jenny said, beaming. "I love when I'm right."

After an hour of walking, the woods thinned, and they came into a large clearing. A stone and iron fence loomed ahead. The barred gates were closed and guarded. Through them, a large home sprawled within the fence, a castle and a cottage merged into something in between, both grand and quaint. Great stone walls with iron cross windows, alcoves, and balconies supported a thick, thatched roof. The grounds dripped with a lush garden. Roses climbed the walls, flowering bushes grew green and colorful every which way, and an abundance of flowers filled in the empty space with paths cut throughout, allowing access to every part of the immense property. To one side, a vegetable garden, still thick with greens of every sort, also sprouted beans and root vegetables and tomatoes and squashes. It could have fed scores of people, or Josh.

The menacing gates towered even higher as they approached, and the guards called for them to halt. Josh, bigger than Jenny remembered, sauntered toward the guards and declared, "We've come to see the Sorceress. Tell her the Keeper, Guardian, and Searcher bring what she requires." The gates unfastened, and the guards allowed them entrance, instructing them to go straight ahead to the front door.

The three marched to the house, their noses filled with the fragrant smells of the garden. A large, wooden front door creaked, and a well-dressed young man with long, blond hair tied into a low pony-tail emerged. Though his clothes were tailored and his hair perfectly coiffed, his face was smug and haughty, a smirk plastered on his smooth skin. "Good day," he crooned. "Welcome to Middlegate Manor. I am Julian, friend and assistant to the loveliest of women and witches alike." Eyeing the trio with distaste, he reluctantly invited them in, no doubt acting under orders and not on his own accord. Given his prerogative, Julian would surely have turned them away at the gate without a second glance and had their footprints raked from the path.

He led them in a circuitous route through the castle cottage. Josh surely memorized it as they went in case they needed a speedy exit, eyes darting this way and that, standing as tall as possible. He spun the Guardian Ring with his thumb, a tell regarding his level of anxiety. Catching Jenny watching him from the corner of her eye, he stopped spinning the ring and gave her a quick wink. "Nice ring," she whispered, attempting to help him relax.

"You too," he answered, glancing at the garnet on her finger.

They both refocused. A staircase appeared before them, descending into a dark basement.

Jenny had faced a dark basement before, standing at the top of a staircase her second day as Keeper, having to decide then if she could face everything that came with taking a step into the unknown. She had done it then, and she would do it again. *I've got this one.* Without hesitation, she moved ahead of Josh and followed Julian into the darkness. But she did reach behind her to find Josh's hand, which he squeezed with each step.

The stairs ended at a long, narrow hallway, dark, cold, and damp. Julian worked to ensure none of his clothing touched the dank stones. After one turn to the right, they emerged into a large room with a high ceiling and massive fireplace. A ten by ten-foot cage was opposite the fireplace. Inside sat Isaac, slumped on a cot, his long hair dirty, obscuring his face. He'd lost several pounds and had bruising on his wrists. Jenny resisted the urge to run to him, hug him, tell him over and over how much she loved him. But this was a time for strength, not a show of emotion.

"Danger lurks here," Josh whispered, placing his palm between Jenny's shoulder blades. The heat of the Guardian Ring seeped through her shirt, hot against her skin. *Lots of danger.* The Ring pulsed with adrenaline.

The danger in the room rose from a large, ornately carved chair—a tall, striking, and terrible woman. She wore an exquisite red dress, trimmed with black, fitted in the bodice and flowing to the floor. Long, ebony hair streaked with red hung thick and free, and dark brows framed her stunning face. She was a queen.

Jenny slumped, small and inadequate. The thoughts she'd had while standing in front of the mirror earlier in the day returned like a torrent in the presence of such terrifying beauty. Somehow sensing her wavering confidence, Josh bent and whispered, "You are more than her equal." He then stood straight but stayed by her side, Ophelia next to him.

With a deep breath and hardened face, girded by his words, Jenny took a step forward. "I am the Keeper," she managed to say with some measurable volume. "You have asked me to bring you two items, and I have done so." She dug the spindle and the bone from her pack and offered them to the Sorceress who nodded to Julian. He snatched them from Jenny and laid them before his mistress before bowing back into a corner. "I intend to bring you the remaining four in exchange for my uncle's freedom in the time allotted. Until then, are these enough to ensure his continued safety? I trust I am interpreting your letter correctly." Jenny never broke eye contact, her voice never faltered.

The Sorceress considered Jenny, walked closer to her, studied her up and down with a hint of disdain. "You are a child, and yet you bear such a weight around your neck." Her voice lilted with an old English brogue, deep and demanding respect. She sneered. "You looked older in the mirror."

*Mirror?*

"Sorry?" Jenny said. "What mirror?"

Surprised crossed the Sorceress's face, and she guffawed. "Oh! Did Isaac never tell you?"

"Tell me what?"

A small looking-glass appeared from some hidden pocket in the Sorceress's dress. She held it for Jenny to peer into, and there was Isaac, hunkered in his cage but from an odd perspective. Jenny swooped her gaze to his confines and saw *her* wall mirror, the one Isaac had reclaimed, hanging from the bars.

"That was mine! How did you ... how could it ...?"

"Ma-gic," the Sorceress crooned. "And I stole it back during my last jaunt in your world. It's a useful little thing—my second-most-treasured possession." She eyeballed Isaac. "Well, perhaps now third-most-treasured. Or maybe it's a draw." The little mirror in her grasp disappeared into the folds of her skirt once more. "Your uncle introduced me to you long ago, unwittingly, through the mirror. I knew about him as well—the dark-haired Park boy. I didn't intend to see you today looking so ... capable." She jerked a thumb at Josh who growled through gritted teeth. "Isaac also introduced me to your little trinket, though it was his at the time."

Jenny stiffened as the Sorceress traced a finger along the Compass.

Josh and Ophelia took a step closer, ready to defend their Keeper in a moment. The Sorceress noticed. "Fear not," she reassured them. "I do not intend her harm today. She must complete my list, and she will, driven by love for her uncle, just as I am." The Sorceress gazed at Isaac, her commanding voice more wistful. Julian drooped and pressed his lips together.

"I will complete your list. You can rest assured. I want my family returned," Jenny said. The Sorceress reclined in her magnificent chair, listening. Emboldened, Jenny continued. "Why are you doing this? Why do this to him? To *them?*" A warmth in her chest, like in *Hansel and Gretel*, began to build, rising to her arms and neck. For the first time, her voice wobbled with emotion.

The Sorceress stared at Isaac for a long time, then turned to Jenny, doe-eyed. "For love. Why else go to all this trouble?"

*You've gotta be kidding me.* Jenny fought rolling her eyes. *The Sorceress fancies herself in love with Isaac?*

She cleared her throat. "And our parents?" Her voice regained its original composure, and she worked to hide her disgust at the Sorceress's confession.

This question hardened the Sorceress's face in an instant. "Do you speak for the mermaid as well?" she snapped. "I took them to punish her, and him." A long, angry finger jabbed toward Isaac. "That mermaid stole him from me, and now she is paying for it."

*Liddy? She took their parents to punish Liddy?*

"Please, where are they?" The warmth in her chest spread, and a faint glow glistened from her skin. "In taking them, you are punishing more than just Isaac and the mermaid. We are all suffering. We don't even know what has happened to them. You are beautiful and powerful and incredibly clever—all the things I am not." Josh shifted at her words, disapproving of her self-deprecation.

"You have masterminded this entire plan, and we are impressed. Could you find it in your heart, somehow, somewhere in the part that is obviously capable of loving to at least tell us where they are? Tell us they are all right?" The golden ball floated from her mouth, and, as she breathed into it, it drifted toward the Sorceress, who watched it, mesmerized. It enraptured her, captured her, and sank into her chest.

Then she screamed.

# Chapter Twenty-Six

Heaving, the Sorceress clawed at her chest, blood blooming beneath her fingernails. She arched against the high back of her throne. "Take it back! Take it back!" Her head shook, tossing her hair in front of her eyes, and she screamed again, half sobbing. Then she stopped, still and statuesque. Her eyeballs glared at Jenny through her hair, hands balled into fists at her chest. And she lunged, straight for Jenny, no longer composed or elegant, but angry, frantic, and frenzied.

Josh seized the Sorceress from behind and held his sword to her neck. "Touch her and you die," he hissed so harshly it almost frightened Jenny, and she glanced at him before returning her focus to her foe. Ophelia pulled her sword on Julian, who made to rush the scene, warning him to back off. He quelled like a hurt puppy but never took his attention off his mistress.

"Answer the Keeper's question, and I let you live," Josh spat. Anger roiled beneath his skin.

"Remove this magic, and I will," the Sorceress said, begging, drops of blood dripping down her chest and crusting on her fingernails.

"You first," Jenny said, unsure if she could remove it, but not willing to let her nemesis know that.

"They are alive, at least they were when I left them."

"Where?" Josh pulled his sword tighter.

"Kill me, and you will never know," she warned him, sucking in air, the blade pressing into her throat.

"She can always leave the magic burning in your veins," Josh said.

The Sorceress's eyes were wild, and she stomped her foot and screeched in frustration. "In a book! They are in one of my books. That is all I will say. Now take it out, Keeper, soon, or it will kill me and take with it all knowledge of your parents' whereabouts. No one else knows, not even Julian. They will be lost forever." She wheezed the final words, her perfect and hateful face pale, sweat beading on her upper lip. Her legs faltered, and she staggered against Josh, breath coming in gasps. Fear clouded her eyes.

"Help her!" Julian cried, tears on his cheeks.

Jenny placed her fingertips on the Sorceress's bloody chest and filled her lungs, drawing the magic into her own body. The Sorceress's skin felt so hot under her touch, she almost snatched her hand away. The Compass warmed and hummed, and the glow on Jenny's skin grew brighter and hotter. Her breath came fast, and her heart thundered. Josh grew concerned and took a quick look at her, frowning. *Can he hear my heartbeat? How loud is it?* The Sorceress relaxed in his arms. But just for a moment.

One second, she was there, and the next she was across the room, fuming, her magic revving up now that the Compass magic wasn't neutralizing it. Black smoke billowed, surrounding her with darkness, her face contorted into a monstrous snarl, fire blazing in her eyes. The Compass warned Jenny, humming against her skin. Josh shook his hand with the Ring.

The Sorceress hurled something at Jenny, which she side-stepped, but not before another something, a flaming knife, flew right for her face. Josh knocked it aside with the sword—*wham!*—just inches from her nose. Jenny stood there, stunned.

"Go!" Josh yelled, stepping in front of her, Ophelia appearing at his shoulder. Another flame blade clanked against the stone wall, stopped by a fierce line of defense. Another one came at them, and another, and another. Josh and Ophelia battled the Sorceress while Jenny ran to Isaac, examining the lock, trying to figure a way to help him escape. "You can't stay here a minute longer!" Tears blurred her vision. "Hold on, Isaac. Surely there is a way out!" The lock wouldn't budge. She slammed her hands into the bars.

"No, Jenny dear. Leave me here for now." Jenny acted like she didn't hear him, "Leave me!" he said, this time with force, and she stopped. "Otherwise, we'll never find Connie and the others. She's got them in a book, somewhere. I can find out where. I just need time." Isaac, worn and weak, still on mission, willing to stay for his sister. Jenny started to cry, rattling the cage door in frustration, the clang of flaming knives clattering behind her.

"No!" she sobbed. "I want you home. You should be home."

Her uncle touched her cheek through the bars. "I couldn't live knowing I'd left them behind."

"Like you are asking me to do? Leave you behind. What about Liddy?"

Isaac blinked at her words, then refocused. "You know about Liddy? She's alright? Oh, thank heavens." He paused. "Trust me, please. I'll make it, and then we will find the others. It's my choice. Tell Liddy I'll be home soon. Tell her ... I love her." He choked on his words. "Find the other items, Jenny. Find them soon. Now go!"

"Jenny!" Josh called. "We need to go!" Ophelia had several burns on her clothes and one on her forearm. Josh coughed, choking on the rising, black fumes.

"Lie down, Isaac, under your cot, and watch out for the knives," Jenny whispered.

"This way!" she yelled to the others, running behind Isaac's cage, dodging a few flames that got past Josh and Ophelia.

Smoke filled the room, limiting their vision, and the Sorceress's too. She dared not throw burning knives in Isaac's direction. So instead, she shrieked, "You will pay for this, Keeper! You have one week to get the rest or he dies, and your parents remain trapped forever! One week! And come alone! If I see that Guardian, Isaac will suffer!"

She parted the smoke with a wave of her hand, fuming, eyes as wild as her flaming red-streaked hair and locked on Jenny. "Come alone or I kill you on the spot!" Her words echoed as the trio linked and left the story.

Jenny crumpled to the floor when they landed. Uncle Curtis and Sam rushed in, but Josh held her while she wept.

"We have one week, one week to get the rest," Jenny said once she had stopped crying. She remained slumped on the floor, leaned against Josh's shoulder.

Uncle Curtis knelt beside her. Sam and Ophelia perched on a desk, and Liddy sat in Sam's chair, waiting for any information Jenny had to give. "Isaac is alive, or he was when we left him, but he is suffering. I used my gift on the Sorceress, kind of accidentally, and it hurt her, maybe even almost killed her. She got angry, and once I removed it, it got ugly. Isaac ... he chose to stay so we can eventually find our parents. I wanted to bring him back. I know it wasn't part of the plan, but he just looked so miserable, and the Sorceress, she's like, insane, Liddy. She loves him, but in a bad way. He told me to leave him so he could find out where our parents are. Liddy, he told me to tell you he'll be home soon. And that he loves you."

She nodded, dabbing the tears threatening to spill onto her cheeks. Sad, but also understanding. "He's always so generous," she said. "I just want him home, though."

"With only one week to get the remaining four items, it will be soon, Liddy," Josh said.

"It'll be the longest week of my life," she replied.

"Our parents are trapped in a book, just like we thought, but we don't know which one. The Sorceress also promised to kill Jenny unless she came alone the next time, and make Isaac suffer as well," Josh said.

"Fabulous," said Sam, slumped next to Ophelia, who was singed and covered with soot.

"I saw her Charm. It was an hourglass. Do we have a description of that one in the book?" Ophelia said.

"What book?" Jenny asked, sitting taller, curious.

Uncle Curtis walked away and returned holding a small book. "This is a book recorded by Arthur of the various stolen Lesser Charms—some of them, at least. We don't think it's complete." He flipped through the pages. "Ah, here we go. Something like this?" He displayed a hand-drawn picture of a pendant shaped like an hourglass.

"Ooh, that's it!" Ophelia said.

"It says this Charm has the power to move a person from a book to the real world, but only for a short time, the time allowed by the hourglass. And it does not allow them to make that jump often—again, the time allowed by the hourglass. It is not a powerful one, but she has it and has made the most of it. The question is, how did she get it? And when can she use it again?"

No one answered. There were no answers to give.

"Another question for another day. I think it's time for a well-deserved rest." Uncle Curtis held a wizened hand to Jenny, pulled her to her feet and into a hug. "You did well, little Keeper," he whispered.

They trudged upstairs where Jenny and Josh ate a quick but hearty lunch and then fell asleep. By mid-afternoon, they awoke ready to plan their next mission, the one Liddy could help them on. Tomorrow, they were going after the Little Mermaid's dagger.

ooooo 🌿 ooooo

With everyone gathered at the big table in the kitchen, Liddy, her hair cascading over one shoulder, offered to share her story, though it pained her to do so.

"It's not always pleasant to recount memories," she said. "But should it help Isaac, I will gladly do so." She shifted in her seat, then folded her hands on the table and cleared her throat. "When I was really young, I fell in love—or what I thought was love—with a prince. As you already know, I was what you all call a 'mermaid.' We called ourselves 'sea people.' I made the fatal mistake of traveling to the shallows, longing to see the land people, and spent hours watching how they lived, what I could see of it, anyway. There I saw, and became infatuated with, the prince of that land." Liddy's eyes clouded, remembering those days. Jenny gave her wrist a squeeze and urged her on with a smile.

"I saved him from drowning when he fell overboard during a windstorm. I laid him on the beach, unable to leave the water. Another girl came by as he woke. He thought she had saved him. He had no idea *I* had pulled him from certain death in the depths of the sea."

"Is that when you sought out the Sea Witch?" Jenny said, jumping in. She checked herself and clamped her lips shut. "Oops, sorry!" she said with a touch of embarrassment.

"Yes, Jenny, you're right," Liddy said. "I wanted to be with him, and I wanted legs to run and jump and dance like the land people. My life in the sea wasn't as joyous as Sebastian implies in the movie." She chuckled a little. "It's not always better down where it's wetter, though I do love that song."

"I like that song too," Josh said. "What? It's so fun!" he said, defending himself against a few surprised reactions. "Okay, I'll be quiet now. Liddy, please continue."

"Anyway, I visited the Sea Witch and asked her to make me human." She grimaced. "It cost me my voice and caused me great pain."

Liddy went on to explain how walking on her new legs was terribly painful, like treading on glass with every step. She also revealed the evil

Sea Witch's nearly impossible stipulation: Liddy had to somehow win the prince's heart, or she would turn into seafoam, dissolving into nothing. Young, foolish, and in love, Liddy willingly took the risk.

"It was a reckless wish, and it didn't pay off," she said. "When I finally met him on land, he was kind enough, but he had given his heart to the other girl, the one he thought had saved him. And I had no voice to tell him otherwise."

She lifted her shoulders and smiled, making eye contact with each person in the circle. "But that's not the end of the story. There was an intervention—a beautiful, wonderful interruption in my story. A traveler came along, a visitor to the prince's court. He treated me with far more kindness than anyone ever had before, even the prince. I soon realized that what I had thought was love for the prince was merely a girlish infatuation." She smiled at the memory of how true love had taken root and blossomed.

"This traveler won my heart and gave me his. Though we could not speak at first, we found ways to communicate, and we grew to respect, trust, and admire each other. And we kept our love a secret."

"Isaac!" Jenny breathed.

"Yes, he came into my story to explore and observe. He hadn't expected to fall in love with anyone, let alone the main character. One day he told me, through tears, that he would have to leave. I was heartbroken. I wondered, *Was I not enough for him? Did he want someone who could speak?* I managed to make him understand how I felt—and he told me everything: about the Compass, about the real world, and how he knew a way to rescue me from my fate."

297

Everyone leaned in, spellbound and anxious for more. They knew how the original story ended. By dictate of the author's pen, the little mermaid would spend 300 years as seafoam, once her prince married another, before rising up to heaven. The heaven part didn't sound so bad, but the seafoam part—less than ideal.

Liddy explained how Isaac's eyes had brightened when he told her the next part. "He said to me, 'If it had been anyone else who stumbled into your story, they could not have saved you. But this is my gift. I am the Cursebreaker, and I *can* save you.'"

"Oh my word!" Jenny said, swooning. "This just gets better and better. Oh, sorry Liddy, sorry to interrupt. Keep going!"

The first curse he broke was the one on her voice—her beautiful, melodic voice. "Hello, Isaac. I'm Liddy," she had said. "It's a pleasure to speak to you." He embraced her, laughing and crying together in their initial victory.

Then they hatched a plan. Isaac knew Liddy's sisters would offer her a dagger obtained from the Sea Witch, one that would turn Liddy back into a mermaid if she used it to kill the prince. Liddy would hide the dagger on the ship and leave with Isaac, effectively changing the end of the story. "He knew there were not a lot of editions of the *Fantastical Fairy Tales* book, so it wouldn't affect many, and he could not see a way around changing the plot," Liddy explained. "And frankly, he didn't care about changing it." Her eyes darted to Uncle Curtis, who hinted at a frown. "I know, not very 'Keeper' of him," she said, "But he was in a bit of a desperate place."

Isaac broke all the curses, she went on to tell them, except the final one, the death one. It was powerful, and though he worked with diligence to break it, he wasn't sure what would happen when they left the story. They both had held their breaths when he pulled her out. The moment her feet landed on real-world ground with Isaac's arms around her, she had breathed again, and again, and again.

"Welcome home," he had said.

ooooo 🕱 ooooo

After a long, silent pause, Liddy pressed on the table. "So, all you have to do is jump in at the right time, just after I hide the dagger, get it, and come home."

"Wait a second, how does your story end now?" Jenny said. Already familiar with *The Little Mermaid*, she hadn't read through the entire version in the *Fairy Tales* book. *Minor oversight.* She silently chastised herself.

Liddy threw an apologetic glance at Uncle Curtis, then turned back to Jenny. "I read it right after I arrived, from the same book you now have, just to see how it changed. Now it says that on the prince's wedding day, the Little Mermaid receives a dagger from her sisters, something they bought from the Sea Witch in exchange for their beautiful hair. She hides the dagger and is never seen again.

"The prince marries the other girl, and they live happily ever after. The Little Mermaid's sisters wait and wait for her until sunset, then return home, saddened to have lost both their sister and their hair. I checked other editions, just to be sure, and they are unchanged."

They sat in silence for a few moments, taking in what Liddy had told them.

Josh raised a hand. "Is there a risk in returning to a story that is already altered?"

Uncle Curtis didn't respond right away, rolling Josh's question around in his mind. "This is a bit unprecedented. I believe there is some risk," he finally answered. "When Isaac decided to take Liddy out, he wrote himself into the story, seizing the role of author, changing the very essence of it. There is a chance you could run into the character Isaac 'wrote' for himself, and he could recognize you and completely panic. But it wouldn't be him, just who he was while in the story. A character. And Liddy would be the same as she was, preparing to leave with Isaac." Uncle Curtis pushed his glasses further onto his nose. "Do you understand? Am I explaining this well?"

"It's a little hard to get your mind around," Jenny said.

"Running into an Isaac exactly like Isaac but not actually Isaac would be really weird, and I hardly know either of them well," Josh added. "But we've got to take the chance of seeing the fake Isaac in order to save the real Isaac."

"This is one of the reasons we don't pull people out. Unforeseen complications always arise. That said, I am grateful to have you here, Liddy dear. I never did like the ending of your story. You are far better off here than seafoam, and we are all the better for having you with us." She smiled at his kind words and bit her lip, holding in her emotions with unseen strength.

"I have more questions," Josh said, interrupting the moment and allowing Liddy to compose herself. "Could we go in and pull Liddy out again? Like, could there be two Liddys in the world?"

"No! It could never happen. I guess perhaps it could work, but it would be a nightmare. Oh, this pulling out characters becomes so convoluted. This is why we have the rules. To prevent such occurrences!" He pounded on the table with a fist.

"Don't worry, Uncle Curtis, we won't be pulling anyone out anytime soon," Jenny said to reassure him. "The last thing we want to do is cause more trouble."

The old guardian sighed. "Aye, I know. Forgive me. It's just—so many things can go wrong, and we need things to go *right*. So, for now, avoid Isaac, avoid everyone. The less we cause him or anyone else to panic, the better. This will be a nuanced jump, Jenny. Are you up for it?" Uncle Curtis asked.

"I am," she said, though she wondered if Josh heard her heart thundering in her chest again. It rang in her own ears so loud, it distracted her from the continuing situation. Josh simply spun the Guardian Ring on his finger again, just like the last time. Jenny shook her head, trying to refocus. "Now, Liddy, please, tell us about this dagger."

# Chapter Twenty-Seven

Sam had their packs prepared right after breakfast the next morning. Because they needed to remain hidden, Josh and Jenny had their Chameleon Cloaks, and Sam handed them each a walkie-talkie. It would be just the two of them today. The ship was tight quarters, and two people could stay hidden more easily than three. Also, with only two Chameleon Cloaks, Ophelia was the odd one out—her choice, not theirs. "You two are strong and capable, and this will be a good test for your partnership. But, if you need me, you can always jump back and get me."

Once they were ready, Jenny selected the right page of the book. Concentrating on the specific words with all her might, she linked with Josh, and they were gone. They landed with a thump in a small, dark room on the bottom level of the ship carrying the prince, his new bride, and everyone else in the story. They hoped Liddy and Isaac were already gone, but it was hard to get the timing perfect, so they would take no chances.

Dressing for the occasion, Josh wore sailor's clothing, complete with puffy white sleeves and a bandana tied over his hair. Jenny had opted for a serving-wench ensemble, the bodice cinched tight over a pale blouse. This, she hoped, would enable her to move unnoticed among the others on the large ship if she had the need to remove her Chameleon Cloak.

The bilge smelled damp and stale, with empty barrels scattered about and an inch of water on the floor. "It's kind of gross down here," she whispered to Josh, searching for a dry spot to step. Skittering feet and a few squeaks echoed from the corner behind them, and Jenny grabbed Josh's arm. "I hate rats," she said. "Vile creatures."

"Okay, Indiana Jones. They are unpleasant, I agree, but they are our only company down here, so that's a win," he said with a wink. "Good job getting us here. Now, based on what she told me, I think I can get us to Liddy's room."

They made their way through the bottom of the ship, scaling old boxes and barrels. The side-to-side rocking threw Jenny off balance. She gripped a low beam overhead to keep from falling. Josh helped steady her with a hand on her lower back. The garnet ring on her finger caught a glimmer of light.

"Hey, nice ring. You like it?" Josh asked.

"I do."

"I didn't think Sleeping Beauty would mind," he said.

The boat heaved again, forcing Josh to tighten his grip on her.

"Thanks," she breathed. "For the ring and for helping me not fall. I have terrible sea legs. My stomach is already angry about it."

He smiled. "Happy to help." Her heart beat a little faster when he moved an inch closer. A matching beat pulsed in the Guardian Ring on the hand steadying her. Her mouth dropped for a moment before she snapped it shut again.

"You good to go?" he said.

"I think so," she answered, eyeballing him with suspicion.

They ascended a set of steep stairs, then another and another. She stepped into a dark hallway, squinting, trying to determine if this was the right level or not. The ship was massive and not well-marked. Josh trailed behind her, close enough for his breath to tickle her hair.

"This isn't it," he said. They turned to head up another set of stairs when two people appeared at the other end of the hallway. A tall man with a well-trimmed beard and glasses, and a beautiful blond woman with piercing blue eyes.

Josh spun Jenny and dashed the other way. "Walk fast but don't run," he whispered, and they scooted away from the couple.

"Excuse me!" the man called out. "Hello? Pardon!" His quickening footsteps followed them. They took one corner, then another, and Jenny yanked Josh into an empty cabin, both flipping on their hoods and sinking into their cloaks. Pressed against the wall behind the door, they quieted their breathing, hoping Isaac would pass them. His footsteps neared, and they heard him muttering, "I could've sworn that was Jenny ... but that would be impossible!"

Josh and Jenny exhaled when he disappeared in Liddy's direction.

"That was close," Josh said.

"Should we continue searching for the dagger? What if she hasn't hidden it yet?" Jenny said.

"I think we wait a little while, just to be safe." They barred the door to enjoy a few moments of relative safety while Liddy and Isaac exited the story. Jenny rolled onto the bed, trying not to vomit.

In an attempt to take her mind off her bubbling belly, she dared to ask a probing question. "So, uh, Josh, uh, what *exactly* do you feel in the Guardian Ring? I know it can get hot to warn you of danger ... anything else?" He spun the ring on his finger with his thumb, something he did when he was nervous or thinking.

"Do you really want to know?" he asked her, leaning in from his seat by the bed. His eyes searched deep into hers, never wavering, with a seriousness she hadn't seen before.

"Yes, I do."

"I feel your heartbeat."

"I knew it!" she said, gasping then laughing. "I thought you could sometimes hear my heart beating, when it was pounding ... that it was like, super loud or something. But it was the Ring. It was the Ring the whole time."

"I don't notice it most of the time, but when things are intense, it's hard to ignore."

"Do you mind it?"

"No, not at all. I like it."

They locked eyes. Jenny groaned inwardly when her pulse increased, knowing he felt it. He half-grinned but didn't look away. *Guh! I won't, Liddy!* Jenny shouted in her head. *Josh, stop being so cute!* A static sound crackled in their walkie-talkies, and the muffled voice of Ophelia broke through, interrupting their moment. Jenny scrunched her face and pressed the device harder against her head. "Did you catch that?" she asked Josh.

"Something about a Network, maybe? And the Book Snorters? Or

Book Turners?" he answered.

"I think it was Book Burners. What are they talking about?" With a quick push of the button on her walkie-talkie, she asked them to repeat what they'd said.

"Oh!" sputtered Ophelia, sounding surprised and confused and clear as day. "Uh, sorry guys. That was just us chatting here. Nothing to do with you. Carry on!" Then, radio silence.

"Well, okay," Josh said. "Now I really want to know. There's a lot they don't tell us."

"Yeah, but I think they will. I think—I think it would feel very overwhelming otherwise."

"I know, but I'm just so curious. There's so much more involved in the Compass than just us. I know it. And we've got to step into that once we're done with this stuff."

"It won't be too long," Jenny said, trying to encourage him. "Once they start talking, you'll probably want them to stop. I think there's more than we think there is."

"I think you're right." He smiled, pushed off the wall, and rubbed his hands together. "Okay, want to try and find the dagger?"

She stood and straightened her cloak, swallowing hard against another wave of nausea. "Let's do it. And let's hurry please, before I get to revisit breakfast."

After checking to see if the coast was clear, they determined to find the empty room of the woman who had once been the Little Mermaid. With everyone from the boat on the main deck, and Liddy and Isaac hopefully gone, they kept their Chameleon Cloaks on but with hoods lowered. That way, they could see each other but disappear at a moment's notice.

The wedding reception was in full swing on deck. Partygoers danced overhead, their footsteps clunking on the ceiling above them. Jenny ducked, then realized what she had done and giggled. Josh smiled and whispered, "It's weird with such a low ceiling. It feels like they are stomping on our heads." The narrow hallway allowed Jenny to remain upright and not fall over every time the ship tilted a little left or right, but the movement left her feeling several shades greener.

"I think this is it," Josh announced, pushing into an empty room that fit Liddy's description to a T. Though small, it was comfortable, a final gift from the prince. Two small windows let in the dwindling sunlight, illuminating the dark wood of the bed frame, table, and wardrobe, which were all secured to the floor. A chamber pot was stowed politely beneath a bench, and Jenny thought she might need it if the boat stayed on the water. A few candle holders with stumps of wax sat scattered about the room, and Josh found matches to light them in his pack. Jenny watched him for a moment. "Always the boy scout, eh?"

He shrugged. "I do like being prepared."

Jenny shook her head with a chuckle, thankful for his ability to think ahead and plan accordingly. "Okay, Liddy said she put the dagger under a floorboard near the bed."

Josh pressed on each floorboard with his toe, listening and feeling for any plank looser than the others. After a few attempts, one creaked louder than the rest, and their eyes met with excited expressions. He knelt and used one of his throwing knives to pry up the board. There, just under it, lay the dagger, shiny and new. Josh lifted it with care and handed it to Jenny. She slipped it into a sheath fitted on her belt.

Footsteps approached from the long, dark hallway just on the other side of their door. In a second, both hoods went up, and Josh and Jenny shrank beneath the table. "Should I take us home?" Jenny whispered.

"Let's see what happens."

The door creaked. Two menacing guards with leather jerkins and swords overwhelmed the small room with their hulking presence. One wore an eyepatch. The other had a striped kerchief. His hair was disheveled, his coat askew, and he rubbed his eyes. His voice was rough and scratchy. "Oy, why'd ye wake me up from me nap and drag me up here?"

"The prince wanted us to find his guest, the one who calls himself a traveler, and the mute girl. This is her room. She's a pretty one, that girl," the one with the eyepatch said.

"Mmm hmm," Stripes croaked. "Any sign of her?" They searched under the pillows and in the wardrobe.

"They're talking about Liddy," Josh said, barely audible. "I want to hear what they say."

"Looks like she's done a runner, or a swimmer. We should check the dingy, or could be a gal overboard situation," Eyepatch said, closing the wardrobe door. "The prince worries about her, he does, being so quiet and all. He cares for her despite marrying another. Not sure why he's marrying this other lass, but we just do his bidding, don't we?"

"So, what do we tell him?" Stripes asked, leaning against the table, his legs just an inch from Josh's shoulder. Josh leaned away from the guard, forgetting his size. He bumped the table, enough for the guard to jump as if he'd been bitten by a snake.

"What was that?" Eyepatch asked, startled by his friend's sudden movement.

"The table moved," Stripes said, hand on his sword.

Eyepatch chuckled. "Mate, we are on a boat."

"No, no, no—this wasn't a sea movement. This was different." And without warning, he swept his foot under the table where it collided with Josh, knocking him sideways, sending Jenny scrambling backwards to avoid him, and giving the guards a glimpse at his shape before the Chameleon Cloak readjusted.

"Did you see that?' Stripes asked, dancing on his toes. "Where'd he go? Where'd he go?"

Eyepatch searched the space with calculating eyes. Jenny made herself as small as possible, not daring to move, and kept her focus on Eyepatch. He was the leader between these two, and the scars on his face and hands hinted at a history of violence.

"Come on, face us like a man," Stripes taunted.

*No! Just reach back here and take my hand so we can leave!*

In one swift motion, Josh stood and threw off his cloak, the Guardian Sword singing to life. "Gladly," he said with a grin.

*Seriously?* Jenny flared her nostrils, both annoyed and slightly impressed at his dramatic flair. The guards shifted into fighting mode, drawing their swords. Stripes and Eyepatch circled him, and despite the confidence on her friend's face, Jenny's heart was in her throat.

And then they were upon him, swords slashing, feet shuffling, eyes on fire. First Stripes moved in, arcing his weapon, which Josh parlayed easily with his exceptional strength, throwing his opponent off balance. While Stripes recovered, Eyepatch tried to sneak in from the other side, but Josh was ready. He responded with a smirk, forcing Eyepatch to retreat several times and angering him in the process. Eyepatch lunged at him, but Josh sidestepped and sent him careening into the wardrobe, breaking one of the doors in the process.

By that time, Stripes was ready to re-enter the fray, and he came at Josh with renewed ferocity. Thinking fast, Josh grabbed a candleholder, now full of melted wax, and flung it at Stripes' face. The giant screamed when the hot wax hit him in the eyes, temporarily blinding him. "You may need an eyepatch too!" Josh muttered through clenched teeth as he grabbed Stripes by the collar and threw him into the hall, slamming the door and bolting it. Now, just Eyepatch to deal with.

Josh faced the guard who had pulled himself free of the wardrobe, shaking with rage.

"Come here, you little brute!" Eyepatch yelled.

Jenny scrambled to the other side of the table, her hand gripping the dagger they had just pulled from the floorboards, her attention never leaving the remaining guard. The two warriors circled one another again, sizing each other up, wondering who would make the first move. Eyepatch dared, driving toward Josh with slashes and stabs, making him work. He caught Josh square in the kidney with his fist, eliciting a grunt from his opponent. Josh staggered, but he recovered and again met Eyepatch with relish, forcing him backwards toward the table. The cabin door flew off its hinges after Stripes threw himself against it and careened onto the floor. It surprised the other two, and Josh took the opportunity to leap over Stripes and exit the room, drawing Eyepatch away from Jenny.

Her grip on the dagger tightened as Stripes groaned, still sprawled on the floor. *Don't get up, don't get up,* Jenny repeated in her mind as she kept one eye on the guard and dug in Josh's discarded pack for some rope. "Surely the guy who has matches also has some rope. Surely! Ah hah! Yes, I knew it. Thank you, Josh," she whispered. "Now I can just tie this guy up instead of bashing him over the head with a candlestick." She snuck behind the incapacitated guard and bound his wrists, then grabbed Josh's pack and Cloak. Beneath the cover of her own, she went in search of her friend and his pursuer, following the sounds of a ruckus.

Gasps and shouts met her before she saw what was happening. And when she reached the reception, she screeched to a halt, along with the rest of the partygoers who seemed to think this sword fight was part of the entertainment for the evening. Some people cheered for the guard, big and brutish as he was. Most of the ladies backed Josh, whispering about his exotic appearance and wondering where on Earth the prince had been hiding him.

The two "entertainers" volleyed across the deck, weaving in and out of tents and guests, occasionally knocking a drink from someone's grasp and, at one point, crashing into a table. Eyepatch's sword slashed Josh's cheek, and Josh wiped it, staining his sleeve deep red.

Despite his strength, skill, and passion for a good fight, Josh was tiring. So was the guard. Things were getting sloppy, and sloppiness caused injuries. Jenny needed to end this. Sneaking near them, keeping to the periphery of the crowd, she dropped and crawled on all fours, dagger in her mouth like the assassin in *Robin Hood*, under the long row of tables, laden with food. There she waited, watching for her in. Their feet shuffled nearer, Josh panting, unwittingly pushing Eyepatch right toward her. When he was within reach, she struck, like a viper, plunging the dagger through his boot and deep into his Achilles tendon until it struck bone. She wrenched it free and secured it once more in its sheath.

Eyepatch screamed, his leg buckling, and he fell to the ground writhing in pain, his weapon and the fight forgotten. The crowd gasped and retreated.

Josh, sweating and exhausted, held him at sword point. "Yield!" he demanded. Eyepatch continued screeching, blood now pooling on the deck. "I'll take that as a yes," Josh said. He rotated toward the murmuring crowd. It dawned on Jenny that this was not solely for their entertainment.

More guards appeared, and a handsome, well-dressed man with a ringlet on his brow marched to the forefront. *The prince!* Jenny sprinted toward Josh, a spooky blur in the evening sun.

The head guard, who stood next to the prince, raised his arm and barked the order, "Seize him." The others drew their swords.

Jenny clutched Josh's hand, still invisible, and they ran. The wind yanked at her Cloak, the hood blowing off so everyone could see her, and an audible gasp rang when she appeared. Several guards deflected their route to one side of the boat, and more came at them from the other.

With guards moving in from both flanks and the prince at their rear, they stopped. Josh pulled Jenny close, his sword brandished, the dagger in her hand once more, their cloaks whipping around them in the wind.

"Give up," said the prince. "You have nowhere to go."

"Should we leave?" Jenny said under her breath.

"Bow!" Josh whispered.

"I'm not gonna bow to him!" she hissed.

"No, *bow*! Of the boat. Let's go out with a bang." He tilted his head to the front of the boat, a long way off, dipping up and down in the waves. "NOW!" he cried, and they dashed toward it.

*Man, what happened to super cautious Josh?* She couldn't help but notice his scheming grin from her peripheral vision.

The guards followed, along with all the wedding guests who attempted to run in their heels and dresses without spilling their drinks. Josh and Jenny covered the entirety of the boat in seconds, and without hesitation, leapt onto the railing and off the bow. Several people dropped their drinks, a collective gasp issuing from the crowd.

The guards and partygoers sprinted to the front of the boat, listening for a splash, scanning the water for bodies, but all they saw were blue swells and white foam, the calls of passing gulls in the air.

# Chapter Twenty-Eight

In the Spare Room, they landed with a hard thud, crumpled on the floor. Josh was holding Jenny tight, and she could feel his heart pounding, even without a magic ring. "Ow," he groaned and then started laughing. Shaking, not letting her go. "Bow…" he managed to say between chuckles. "She thought I meant literally bow, to the prince, as if that would get us somewhere." His giggles were infectious, but she felt silly for missing his meaning, so she kept trying not to smile. It was not easy.

"Can you let go of me?" she asked in a muffled voice, her face squeezed into his chest. "You're sweaty. And how was I supposed to know what 'bow' you were referring to?" He released her, and she rolled onto her back.

"We were on a boat!" Josh howled, still shaking.

"In front of royalty!" Jenny retorted, eyes rolling.

Then she noticed Uncle Curtis, Liddy, Ophelia, and Sam all staring at them, hovering closer with confused and questioning faces.

They both rolled to a seated position, Josh's cheek bloody and his hair soaked with sweat.

"Oh Josh, your face!" she said.

"I'm fine," he said, touching the gash. "This is the worst of it." He still had the giggles but tried to get it under control and be serious for a minute.

"It'll be a dashing scar," Ophelia said.

"You were too pretty anyway, Josh," Sam added with a wink. "Now you are terrifyingly handsome, like me."

"So, care to elaborate on what happened?" Uncle Curtis said, lifting an eyebrow.

Jenny, still sitting on the floor, pulled the bloodied dagger from its sheath on her belt and threw it on the floor. "This stupid dagger was almost more trouble than it was worth." She flashed them a wicked grin. "But it is quite sharp. No doubt about that."

Ophelia's eyes bugged out of their sockets. "You used it?"

Jenny nodded, both elated and disgusted, and recounted to them the story of Josh's insane duel with not one, but two guards, sparing no details of his amazing performance throughout the entire thing.

"You got to use the Sword, like, for real?" Ophelia asked.

"I think that's what I did," Josh said, laughing again. "All the training paid off, Ophelia. I did everything you said, and it worked perfectly." With a quick swipe, he wiped the blood from his sole injury once more. "Well, almost perfectly."

"It was, like, a movie, Ophelia—and he was the star. All the ladies at the reception were cheering for him, and he'd just smile and toss his hair and continue on fighting," Jenny said. "Seriously, I was super impressed." She nudged him with her elbow.

"Yeah, but I'm pretty sure I had some help at the end there, Jenny. What exactly did you do?"

"Oh yeah, that was me. Well, I snuck under a table, and when Eye-patch was close enough, I cut his Achilles tendon," she said, her mouth dropping open, the realization of what she'd done hitting her full on.

"Girlfriend!" Ophelia said, giving Jenny a high five and pulling her to her feet, then offering a hand to Josh.

"He dropped like a sack of grain," Josh told them. "Crying like a baby. That fight could have gone on for a long time. You saved me some further cuts and bruises." He elbowed Jenny in the arm.

"You're not mad I interfered? I know you were having fun, but that guard was getting madder and meaner with each passing moment. And you were, maybe, getting tired?"

Josh chuckled. "I was tired, and you did the right thing, Jenny." He gave her a quick squeeze, letting her know he was the opposite of mad.

"Here, Sam," Jenny said, passing the dagger to him to keep until they returned to the Sorceress's house.

"And no sign of Isaac?" Uncle Curtis asked, still a little worried about that part.

"We did see him, and Liddy, but only for a moment. We promptly went the other way, and Isaac followed us, but he didn't find us. I'm not even sure he knew for sure it was me. After that, we only saw the two guards and all the wedding guests, and the prince. No one else." Jenny turned to her almost aunt. "Liddy, the dagger was right where you said it'd be. You were a great help." Liddy beamed, her shoulders sagging with relief.

"So, what happens to Isaac and Liddy when they leave the story now that the ending is rewritten?" Josh asked.

"I'm not totally sure. I think they just cease to exist in the world of the story, or go to the world character Isaac has in his head, since he hijacked the authorship of the story. It's a bit of a mystery." Uncle Curtis said. "They certainly don't come here, so don't let that keep you up at night."

Josh's stomach growled so loudly it almost sounded fake, and he blushed. "I'm starving," he said.

Uncle Curtis clapped him on the shoulder. "Let's get you and Jenny some food and a rest. We have six more days to get two more items. I may need to make an extra run to the grocery store."

Then her own stomach gurgled, and Jenny laughed. "You might need to, Uncle Curtis."

"I'll have plenty ready for after tomorrow's jump into *Cinderella*. You'll likely be famished."

∞∞∞ ✿ ∞∞∞

The next day, Jenny blinked awake to a quiet room, rested and refreshed. *I love bed!* She stretched in the warm sun coming through a cold window. The chilly glass stung her fingers when she touched it. Winter had snuck in. *What day is it? We've got to be close to Christmas. Not that it matters this year.* Her shoulders drooped. *We can't celebrate Christmas with them gone.* The sadness lasted only a moment, and she sat tall and determined and rolled from her bed. *There are items to hunt.*

Breakfast was filling but quick, and Josh slurped the remaining syrup from his plate. "Man, I love syrup," he said with a grin. "Ready for some planning? I think the others are already in the Spare Room." She grabbed an apple, and they headed to meet their people to formulate how in the world they would get the wicked stepsister's toe demanded by the Sorceress.

Ophelia, Sam, and Uncle Curtis each had a seat and a cup of coffee in the Spare Room. The coffee scent hit her before she entered, and she went first to the coffee maker to pour some before assuming her role at the black wall. Josh stood near Sam. "I think better standing," he told them, then crossed his arms.

"Where's Liddy?" Ophelia said

"She volunteered to go grocery shopping this morning," Uncle Curtis answered with a smile. "We are running low on everything." He eyed Josh who offered a half-hearted apology.

"I think most of us know the story of *Cinderella* fairly well," Uncle Curtis said, "But the original one, the one in this particular fairy tale book, involves one wicked stepsister cutting off her heel to fit in the glass slipper, and the other one cutting off her toe."

Ophelia pulled a disgusted face. "Desperate times," she muttered.

Jenny agreed. *I know it's going to be me who has to get this toe.* The very idea made her spine shiver and her tongue feel too big for her mouth. It escaped her lips with a "gyeuck" sound. All eyes swiveled to her. "Sorry," she said, "but it's totally gross. And ol' Prince Charming better be the most amazing guy ever for two grown women to chop off body parts so they can marry him. They have lost their minds."

Josh grinned. "Tell us how you really feel, Jenny."

She straightened, hands on hips, ready to do just that.

318

Uncle Curtis lifted a finger. "As much as we'd love to hear you expound on your opinion of the lengths the stepsisters will go to become queen, we ought to stay on task. We have a lot to accomplish today. Let's think about what we need to do to get this mission done."

"I have an idea," Josh said. "What if I go in as a peasant but procure an outfit from one of Prince Charming's guards and pose as one of them. Then I can be in and out of Cinderella's house without issue and keep an eye on Jenny and the Compass."

"By 'procure,' you mean take from an unsuspecting and unlucky guard you will gently render unconscious, right?" Ophelia asked.

"Basically, yes," Josh said.

"Good. Just making sure." His trainer winked at him.

"And what's your plan for me?" Jenny said.

"I thought you could go into the house in the Chameleon Cloak and wait for the right moment to grab the toe and make your exit," he said, like it was no big deal.

*I knew it! I knew it'd be me getting the toe.* Her throat bobbed, swallowing her disgust. Staring at Josh to convey her grouchiness until he fully understood that she did not want to do it at all, she snatched some chalk to begin their lists, writing with a touch more aggression than normal.

*Needs*

*Compass*

*Chameleon Cloak for Jenny*

Peasant clothing for Josh (as scratchy as possible)

Guardian Sword

Guardian Ring

Something to put a toe in (how about Josh's armpit?)

Gloves for Jenny so she doesn't have to touch the toe

Healing Dagger, as always, just in case


Must Not

Be seen stealing toe (Jenny)

Be seen taking out a guard and stealing his clothes (Josh)


Obstacles

Can't find the toe

Discovered as an imposter guard

Discovered under Chameleon Cloak

Evil stepmother


Plan

Jump in when Prince Charming first arrives at Cinderella's house

Josh kidnaps a guard, ties him up, takes his clothes

*Josh poses as a guard in Prince's regiment*

*Jenny hides, finds toe, gets toe, doesn't vomit, gets out, finds Josh (if he's lucky) and returns home*


"Pretty straightforward for me on this one," Jenny said. "I still don't want to touch the toe."

"We got that," Uncle Curtis said.

"You love to torture me, don't you?" Jenny grinned, her good humor returning.

"*Challenge*, Jenny. I love to *challenge* you." Uncle Curtis raised his cup to her in a tiny salute.

Josh and Sam headed to the Collection to get him some peasant clothes, and when they returned a few minutes later, he wore brown pants, a loose-fitting, faded green shirt, and worn leather shoes.

"Remind me why you aren't just using your Chameleon Cloak too?" Jenny asked, taking in his new duds.

"Because of the relatively tight quarters at Cinderella's home, we thought it would be better if only one of us remained hidden. Two mostly invisible people might cause more problems than it's worth, like it did in *The Little Mermaid*. I hope it works the way I imagine it."

"We will make it work," she said.

Sam got their packs and walkie-talkies ready. He showed Jenny a small wooden box to stash the toe in once she retrieved it, and he also handed her some gloves. "I didn't forget," he said.

"Perfect! Thank you, Sam. This is the grossest thing I've ever done, ever." She paled against her black shirt. "Except for the time I assisted in a cow birth."

"What?!" Josh stared at her, gaping.

"Don't you remember? I told you about it, I'm sure."

"How on Earth did you get to …?" Sam began.

"Homeschooled, remember? We do weird stuff in the name of learning.

And trust me, I learned a ton that day. Like, I never want to birth a cow again."

Sam guffawed. "Yeah, for real." With a clap of his hands, he lifted a tiny container. "Okay, I have something for Josh too." He displayed a pair of contact lenses. "These, I made specially for you, buddy. They will allow you to see Jenny when she is using the Chameleon Cloak. I thought it might help on this one."

Josh slipped the contacts in, which took some coaching from Uncle Curtis. Once they were in place, Jenny donned her cloak and disappeared. She snuck behind Ophelia and pinched her, Josh chuckling when the Searcher jumped. He snagged Jenny and knocked her hood off. "Quit that, Keeper," he said, laughing. "These things are great. Thanks, Sam. Jenny, don't go picking your nose beneath that cloak. I will see all." She met his jovial warning with an eye roll and pretended to shove her finger in her nostril.

When she went to hold his hand before the jump into *Cinderella*, Josh feigned revulsion. "I'm not holding your boogery hand," he said, snatching his fingers away.

"Better boogers than bloody toes, don't you think?" She leaned in, grabbed his hand again and whispered, "I didn't really pick my nose."

"I know," he whispered back, squeezing her fingers.

She paused, hovering over the book, peering at the others. "We'll be back soon."

"All the best in there," Uncle Curtis said.

"Be awesome," were Ophelia's words of encouragement.

"Think fast," Sam said.

The Compass ticked and whirred, revving its engines, pointing to the book, and pulling the duo in with the usual flash.

They landed in the wood surrounding Cinderella's large but weathered home, the peaks of the roof jutting beyond the trees ahead. To their left, the clop-clop-clop of tired, trudging horses echoed through the trees along with shuffling human feet dragging on the gravel road. They caught glimpses of a colorful banner at the front of the line of horses—the prince and his retinue.

Sneaking in for a closer view, Jenny and Josh saw the prince at the front, flanked by several guards on horseback and more on foot following him. Dust had settled on their faces and clothes, accentuating their weariness, including the prince. Despite his road-worn appearance, he was tall and handsome, and he seemed kind rather than spoiled or hateful. Based on appearances, Cinderella had chosen well. Apparently, the stepsisters agreed, if they were willing to lop off body parts to win his favor.

Jenny swallowed down her rising disgust a second time and brandished the Chameleon Cloak. "Ready?" she asked Josh, who was already watching the guards, choosing which one was about to have a bad day. "Never mind," she said with a smile. "I can tell you are ready."

He glanced at her and whispered, "Once I get my guy, head inside. Be careful. I won't be there for a few minutes." She nodded and disappeared, camouflaged to the tree she leaned against.

Josh hid behind another large trunk, and when the last of the guards passed by, he grabbed him from behind and within minutes had him stripped, bound, gagged, and tied to a tree farther into the forest where no one could hear him. "I'll come back to release you soon, I promise," he told the angry guard. "I'm not here to hurt the prince. You probably don't believe me, but rest assured, I am no threat to him." The guard's eyes narrowed, and he continued to fight against his bonds. "Don't tire yourself. They will hold," Josh said, trying to not make this the worst day of the guard's life. "Please just be still. I'll release you soon if you don't cause any trouble."

Jenny, hidden in her Cloak, turned away and stifled a giggle. She glanced around as Josh stepped past where she crouched.

The uniform, which involved some white fabric and lots of leather, as well as a helmet, fit well enough, and Josh stalked to his place in the line of other guards. The guy next to him asked, "Where have you been?"

"Call of nature," Josh said, and resumed his duty, not giving the guard another chance to question him.

Since he was fine and settled into his new role, Jenny sighed, and with some reluctance, embraced her own role of Toe Hunter and headed for the large house.

# Chapter Twenty-Nine

Skirting the prince's party, which was now parked in front of the house, Jenny made her way to the front door. With one boot on the stoop, a cheer resounded inside the house. She retreated several steps, and a young woman burst from the door wearing a golden slipper on her foot. The woman gave a small, triumphant kick and the prince waved to his retinue from her side. But when her foot contacted the ground again, she stumbled and cringed. The prince caught her and swept her onto his horse to ride with him. The horse started off. Little birds in the trees keeping watch sang their song for all to hear as the horse passed by:

*Rook di goo, Rook di goo*
*There's blood in the shoe*
*The shoe is too tight*
*This bride is not right!*

Jenny craned her neck to see the birds. This was the first story she'd been in where animals talked. *CRAZY!* Her heart jumped at the sound, though she had read about the talking birds earlier. It didn't seem to surprise the prince one bit, to hear birds talking. Maybe this was a normal thing in the world of *Cinderella*. He did, however, consider his bride, concerned and suspicious.

The prince dismounted and investigated the girl's shoe, and indeed, the birds were right. He took the shoe, cast her to the ground, and she limped home to her mother. Josh, who now stood near Prince Charming, offered to escort her inside the house. *Always the gentleman.* When he glanced her way, Jenny gave him an approving nod from beneath the Chameleon Cloak. *I love that he can see me!* She feigned picking her nose again, suppressing a giggle when he returned his attention to the stepsister, clenching his jaw to keep from laughing.

Jenny followed Josh and the stepsister inside the house. There the imposter flung herself on the couch and cried, whether from her broken foot or broken heart, Jenny could not tell. Josh stood nearby, not consoling the silly girl whose life of ease consisted primarily of eating, dressing up, and giving Cinderella orders day and night. Instead, Josh surveyed the foyer, searching for any evidence of a foot injury. When he caught sight of a blood smear, he cleared his throat and made sure Jenny saw it.

Catching his meaning, she followed a little trail of blood leading from the foyer to the parlor, she went in search of a bloody, dismembered toe. *Not behind the couch. Not under the table. Ooh!* She peered beneath a small upholstered chair in the corner, finding several blood-soaked rags on the floor, hidden behind a coal bucket. Suppressing her displeasure, she tugged on the gloves Sam had given her. More confident with their protection, she unwrapped the rags, taking care not to drop their contents, eventually discovering a small, blood-smeared toe. *Ew, ew, ew!* Holding in the gags, she attempted to stuff the toe into the wooden box. To her dismay, it slipped and bounced across the floor, catching the eye of a large cat basking in the sun on a tufted chair.

Jenny gasped and dashed for the toe. So did the cat. He beat her to it. The cat lapped up the toe into its mouth, only to receive a stern swat on the backside. It dropped its snack, screeching and jumping a mile high. Jenny dove beneath the flying cat, straight for the bouncing toe, forgetting her previous disdain for touching it. The cat landed square on her back, claws bared, latching on to Jenny's Chameleon Cloak. She reared, one hand palming the toe, the other swatting for the cat. With a firm grip on the scruff of its neck, she wrenched it off.

Lifting the offending animal in front of her face, she scolded it. "Bad kitty!" she growled, then tossed it onto the couch. It sniffed and pawed at her fingers, smelling for the toe. "No!" she said again. "That is gross. Don't eat toes, stupid cat!"

The toe clunked into the box, and Jenny shoved it into her bag along with the soiled gloves.

She considered what the last fifteen seconds must've looked like, her invisible self fighting a clearly visible cat. Glancing to the foyer to ensure her cover was not blown, she groaned.

To her dismay, Josh stood in the doorway, blocking anyone's view but his own and laughing so hard, tears streamed and the tassels on his guard uniform trembled.

He took a step toward her, but then spun on his heels when the prince entered the foyer and asked, "Is there another young woman in the house?" He gestured to Josh, implying he should have already investigated this possibility.

Josh left Jenny to her own devices and approached the now nine-toed girl who still sat there crying and demanded, "Where is your sister?"

"She's right here!" sang a voice from behind them. The stern stepmother, with her high collar and gray-streaked hair, entered the room, followed by a downcast and homely girl who limped along. Josh dared not glance in Jenny's direction when she pressed past him, watching from the safety of her cloak.

"Greetings, your highness. May I present my other daughter, who is more than happy to try on the slipper. Here darling, sit, sit," she instructed her daughter, who carefully and painfully slid the shoe onto her foot, half hidden beneath her dress. It fit, and she stood, wobbling. The prince studied her.

"Are you sure you are her, the one I danced with through the night?" he questioned her, not so tired to be beyond suspicion.

"Oh indeed, your highness. I was a bit more made up then, of course." The stepsister batted her eyelashes at him and curtsied. He was either stupid, exhausted, or over his search, and he took the bait. Thinking this woman was his bride, he carried her to his horse and led the royal party along the lane yet again. Josh and Jenny followed, one doing his duty and the other invisible to everyone but him. The birds sang their dubious song once more, giving the prince pause.

*Rook di goo, Rook di goo*

*There's blood in the shoe*

*The shoe is too tight*

*This bride is not right!*


The prince dismounted with a sigh and checked the golden shoe, just like the last time. And, just like last time, he pulled the girl off his horse and sent her to the house, bleeding and limping all the way, this time from her heel, which she'd cut off at her mother's behest. *What kind of mother is this woman?*

The prince did not follow her, exhausted and forlorn, too tired to even be angry. He dropped to the nearest step.

Josh stepped forward and bowed. "Sir, there is a maid here. Cinderella, they call her."

From the doorway, the stepmother silently raged. "Surely she could not possibly be the one you are searching for? She is a scullery maid, covered in dirt." The woman spat the words and tapped the floor with her walking stick.

The prince huffed and dusted off his jacket. "Much like me?" He demanded she be allowed to try on the shoe, at this point more for duty than desire. The stepmother acquiesced and summoned Cinderella.

After several minutes, a petite young woman, just a couple of years older than Jenny, made her way into the foyer where they had gathered. Even dirty and in rags, Cinderella's gentle beauty shone through. Jenny's heart thumped in her chest when Cinderella slid her tiny foot from a clunky wooden clog and slipped the dainty shoe on. A perfect fit.

The tired Prince beamed, and he invited a smiling Cinderella to her feet, finally recognizing the girl he loved smiling at him through dirt and ashes. "You haven't had to remove any parts of your feet, have you?" he inquired. She shook her head, pulling her foot free from the shoe and inspecting it for any damage.

"All parts accounted for," she confirmed with a chuckle. The stepmother and sisters watched the drama unfold, first breathless, then paling. Paying them no mind, the prince lifted his true bride onto his horse, certain this would be the last time he had to do this. The birds sang a new song:

*Rook di goo, rook di goo!*
*No blood's in the shoe.*
*The shoe's not too tight,*
*This bride is right!*

Holding her close, the prince took his bride towards the palace, away from her misery and into a loving home where she would live happily ever after. The remaining stepsisters and stepmother stood there with their mouths agape, shocked. The punishment these terrible women ought to receive would come at Cinderella's wedding. Perhaps the singing birds were already planning their retribution. Perhaps they already intended to fly in and peck out the eyes of the stepsisters for their mistreatment of Cinderella and for their lies to the prince. Josh must have remembered this detail too, for when he strode past the stepsisters, he said to them, "Mind the birds."

Jenny followed him into the woods. There, Josh freed the guard and helped him into his uniform. She averted her gaze, not wanting to see the guard in his underwear. Josh said to him, "Thanks for the help. Trust that I wished you, your Prince, or the new Princess no harm."

The guard bowed a thank you, and Jenny, still invisible, grabbed Josh's elbow and whispered the magic words. They disappeared before the guard's eyes. The last thing they saw was him falling backwards, fainting from fright. Jenny and Josh landed in the Spare Room, chuckling at the guard's shock when they disappeared.

Uncle Curtis eyeballed them, wondering what was so funny. "That was your best landing yet. And I assume you have the, uh, the, uh, the thing?"

Jenny dug the box from her pack, shaking it so they could hear the faint "thunk thunk thunk" of the toe inside. "If by 'thing' you mean severed, bloody, mangled toe, then yes, yes I do."

Ophelia feigned gagging sounds.

"I sure am glad you got it before some cat or rat got ahold of it," Uncle Curtis mused.

With a gasp, and trying to hold in her giggles, Jenny spluttered and managed to say, "Uncle Curtis! How did you know? Believe it or not, a ridiculous cat almost did eat it. There was a short but epic battle for the toe. Do I have any claw marks on my cloak?" She leaned back, peering over her shoulder, searching for evidence of the cat's handiwork. Several tears dotted it, which made her laugh even more, and Josh too.

He wiped his eyes. "Guys, it was so funny." He tried to retell the story, but the hilarity of it prevented him for uttering even a word more.

"That's two jumps ending in laughter," Uncle Curtis said.

"Well, better than bleeding, right?" Josh said.

"Aye, 'tis indeed."

They made their way to the kitchen together, chatting easily.

"That was our easiest mission yet," Josh said, shoulder to shoulder with Jenny.

"And grossest, from my perspective," she said. "But also fun. We got to see Cinderella! Like, up close. She was so pretty, and so young. I can't believe she was getting married at her age."

"I know! That would be like you falling in love and getting married in the next year or two. Whaaaaaat? And the singing birds! That was so cool," Josh said. "But my favorite part—the cat fight." He gave Jenny a wink.

"Ha ha," she said with a smirk. "Glad I could be part of your favorite moment." She kept her gaze forward, cheeks red.

"You always are, Jenny," he said. When she faced him to say *something* in return, he was already ahead, reaching the stairs and striking up conversation with Sam.

⚬⚬⚬⚬⚬ ✴ ⚬⚬⚬⚬⚬

Their afternoon was spent reading and discussing *Jack and the Beanstalk*, which was their final jump. "This one could be easy or awfully hard, depending on where we jump in," Josh said.

"I say we avoid ogres at all cost," Jenny suggested.

"Only one more fairy tale, Jenny. And then, the Sorceress again." Josh lounged into the soft couch, but his concern wasn't missed.

She sighed, moving pages off her lap and leaning forward. "I know.

And I have to go to her alone."

"I can feel your heart pounding," Josh said, spinning the Ring on his finger. "I'd be afraid too. Don't worry about it yet. We will figure something out."

Trusting him with every fiber of her being, she offered him a reluctant smile. "I know."

ooooo �ంంం ooooo

Dinner was quiet, person after person refusing to meet Jenny's eyes while they ate. Clinking her fork to the plate, she finally asked them what was wrong. "Is there some awful secret I'm not in on?" she said, taking a gulp of water.

Swirling his wine, Uncle Curtis sighed. "Tomorrow is Christmas, Jenny. It snuck up on me, and I'm sorry we ... we are not prepared. Isaac told me how much you love Christmas. We've been so focused on what is happening within this circle, we've forgotten about the world going on beyond our walls. Did you know it's snowing outside?"

Jenny's chair scooted on the floor, and she darted to the window, staring into the night sky. White flakes danced from the heavens, sinking to the freezing ground. Flinging the door open, she stepped into the soft darkness. Everything was quiet except the sound of snow falling. She stood still for a moment, just hearing it. The yard was covered, and she sank to her ankles, not caring when snow seeped over the tops of her low boots.

Facing the sky and sticking out her tongue, she squealed when the cold flakes melted on it. With arms wide, she ran in figure eights, the chill on her face, laughing, forgetting about all the things that had happened and might happen. Much like climbing the tree in the picture with Josh so long ago, she escaped the Compass's requirements for just a moment, enjoying a bit of freedom.

She glanced to the house. Observing from the door, Josh stood with his arms crossed, witnessing her joy in his own quiet way. The cold must be biting into his skin, but, just like her, he didn't let it bother him.

"Come play!" she called to him. *Come be in the moment with me, like my parents used to.* The realization that they weren't there hit her, and she stopped and turned away from him, hiding her sudden sadness. *Why must grief strike at the most joyous times?*

Josh only had on a t-shirt and jeans, but he jogged to her. "Jenny?" he said. Tears ran, dripping off her chin. Josh took a deep breath and hugged her, one hand about her waist, the other entwining in her hair. He pressed her cheek into his chest. It was warm and solid.

Once she had composed herself, she pulled away from him, muttering a soft thank you. Whenever she cried, he would stare at her, deep into her eyes.

"Why are you staring?" she asked, sniffling and wiping her nose.

"Your eyes are so green when you cry, with gold around the center. It's so pretty," he said before he had time to consider his words. She blushed, and he blushed once he realized what he said.

"Thanks," she managed to say.

"Want to tell me why you are crying?" he asked her, rubbing his arms, snowflakes tickling his bare skin.

She squatted and drew a heart in the snow with her finger. "This is my first Christmas without them, without my parents. You know how it is always a huge deal in our house. Lights, decorations, a big tree, so many cookies and always hot chocolate, every night. And on Christmas morning, this breakfast casserole with sausage and cheese and eggs in it, and some fancy pastry thing my mom would make, all braided together with raisins and cinnamon. We would open presents together by the fire, in our pajamas, and go about our day just enjoying each other and our gifts and being a family. And I forgot them this year. I forgot Christmas. I feel so awful about it." Tears trickled, cold on her cheeks.

He helped her to stand and gripped her shoulders tight, with intensity. "You're doing all you can to get them back, Jenny. More than anyone could ever ask or expect of you. If they were here, they would be so proud of you. I will not let you think you have let them down. If anything, it is the opposite." He smiled. Gently, he shook her, and a small grin appeared on her face, trying to break through the grief. "Once, for Christmas, Liddy got me a fart machine. She left it on my pillow all wrapped in dark brown paper, which was, you know, ingenious. I went around making clandestine farting sounds all day, and everyone thought everyone else had some serious issues, too much sweet potato casserole or something. It was totally awesome." Jenny cracked at his story and started laughing. "That's better," Josh said. "Now can we please go inside? I can't feel my toes."

He let her lead the way, deciding at the last minute to hit her with a snowball, square in the butt. She spun so fast, the fire in her countenance startling him, and he sprinted, trying to avoid the onslaught of snowballs she hurled his way, laughing when one hit its mark. He turned to offense, and they volleyed for a few minutes until a rogue snowball slammed the glass door into the kitchen. Liddy stuck her head out. "I think it's time to come in. You guys need some rest after today's jump, and all this ruckus is, well, frankly, it's annoying," she said with her best mom voice. Josh aimed a snowball for her head and missed. She stuck out her tongue at him before ducking inside.

But she was right. They needed rest, and Jenny could ignore the cold no longer.

She ran in and shucked off her boots, which were now soaked through. "Cold cold cold!" she yelled, dashing upstairs to take a hot shower and defrost.

Reemerging sometime later, Jenny returned to the kitchen, wrapped in a bathrobe with her jammies on underneath. She sat at the table with the rest, only to be disappointed that no one wanted to talk.

Sam and Ophelia excused themselves and went off somewhere together. Liddy was cleaning up with Uncle Curtis, and they talked in hushed voices to each other as they moved about the kitchen. Moose and Klaus lay side by side by the fire, both completely zonked. Only Josh stayed at the table. Together, they indulged in some of the amazing carrot cake Liddy had made. He ate half of it.

"Are you going to bed early?" she said, licking cream cheese frosting off her fork, wanting to lick her plate as well.

"I think so. I'm not so tired with the last few jumps, but if we have two more this week, we'll probably need some good sleep, don't you think?"

She nodded and put her head on her arm. "I'm pretty sleepy, and this cake isn't helping."

Soon, she was in her bed, in the dark, and fading fast. It might be hard to sleep, having felt so sad about Christmas and her parents, but Josh's words about them being proud of her encouraged her heart. They stayed in her mind, and she drifted off.

# Chapter Thirty

In the morning, Jenny lay in bed, savoring the warm blankets and anticipating the cold air of her room once she emerged from them. And, anyway, it was Christmas, and she wanted to remember it for a few minutes before everything went crazy with their jump.

The snow still fell outside her window. Families everywhere would be enjoying Christmas together. Mounds of discarded wrapping paper, screaming children jumping with excitement because they'd received the one thing they had always wanted, parents curled on the couch with coffee, watching the mayhem. A single tear trickled to her nose. None of that would happen today for her and her family. "Merry Christmas, Mom and Dad," she whispered. "And Isaac."

She slipped from her bed and into her robe and slippers, ran fingers through her hair, and stepped into the hall. It glowed brighter than usual, almost like ... "Christmas lights!" she squealed, seeing them twinkling on the stair railings. "And the doors!" She spun in the hallway to see how each door was decorated with wrapping paper and bows.

Not sure what awaited her at the bottom of the stairs, Jenny hurried down, heart starting to pound. There stood Josh and Ophelia and Sam and Uncle Curtis and Liddy, all in their pajamas. "Merry Christmas!" they shouted together. A happy Josh stepped forward and took Jenny's hand. Her other one covered her mouth, and she took in the delights at every turn.

Glass Santa Clauses adorned the mantle, and six big stockings hung below it, plus two smaller ones for Moose and Klaus. Candles sparkled in each window, and a massive nativity scene told the story of Christmas on a side table. Next to the fireplace stood a towering tree, wrapped in white lights and shining with beautiful silver and gold and red ornaments. These were different from the mostly handmade ones on her family's tree, but they were perfect for Uncle Curtis's home, so elegant and classy. Beneath the tree were gifts, wrapped in brown butcher paper with beautiful plaid ribbons.

"How very Scottish!" she whispered to Josh, eliciting a little laugh from her delighted friend.

In the kitchen, Liddy removed what smelled like a breakfast casserole from the oven. Decorating the island was a beautifully braided wreath of bread, with raisins in each crevice. "Is it like your mother's?" Liddy said, hopeful.

Jenny nodded, unable to speak. Josh handed her the tissues he had prepared, just in case. "You ... you did all this? Just last night? I mean, it's the only way you could have known." She gestured to the beautiful decorations. "You guys, it's so pretty. It's so perfect." She cried again, just a little cry. "I don't have any gifts for you. I didn't know—and what about Isaac? Is it okay to celebrate while he is stuck with ... her?"

Uncle Curtis cleared his throat. "Jenny, you are a gift to us every day. We did this for you, and for each other, not expecting anything from you except what you have already given us. And as much as we need to get Isaac home, you and Josh need a buffer day between jumps. You need a rest, albeit a short one. And though Isaac is not here, we still have a great deal to be thankful for, and we should spend our rest day celebrating."

He led her to the table, set with Christmas china. Only Uncle Curtis would have such a thing. Lifting her dainty white plate, he scooped a big spoonful of the breakfast casserole and slopped it right in the center. "Bon appetit!" he said, suppressing a grin. Everyone else grabbed a seat and passed the casserole. Liddy brought the bread and laid it before Jenny.

"I don't want to mess it up, Liddy! It's so gorgeous. Please say you took a picture." Liddy nodded and cut a piece for her. Cinnamon and sugar gleamed inside the pastry in such an inviting way, Liddy just had to shove a bite in her mouth before she could serve the next person.

"Oh, that's good," she moaned and grabbed the back of Jenny's chair as if her knees were getting weak.

"I know. It's so good," Jenny said, taking a second bite. Uncle Curtis poured coffee for everyone, and they sat together, talking and eating and laughing, the cold and snowy day tapping on the windows.

Once breakfast wrapped, they made their way, with coffee cups in hand, to the warm den. Sam passed the gifts and presided over the festivities. "Each person has their own pattern of plaid ribbon, so make sure you get the right gifts," he explained. "And remember, we only had a few hours to pull these gifts together, so they will probably be ... creative."

"Ophelia will go first, because I'm in charge, and I love her," Sam said, making her blush.

From her dad, Ophelia received a copy of *Anna Karenina*, her mother's favorite book. She held it close and closed her eyes.

"She used to read this by the window. I remember it so well," Ophelia told them. "Isn't this your favorite book, Dad?" Uncle Curtis nodded but said nothing else. Ophelia hugged him hard. "I will treasure it."

Josh gave her a coupon book of places to take him running. "The gift part is that you will beat me to the finish on each run and feel great about yourself. Merry Christmas!"

Ophelia laughed with him. "So creative, Josh. And yes, I will beat you!"

From Liddy, she received a loaf of her favorite sourdough bread. "I might eat this all right now!" Ophelia told her, tearing off a piece and shoving it in her mouth. "Oh man, so good!"

When she got past the bread, Sam handed her an envelope. "The last one, from me."

Tapping the envelope with her fingers, Ophelia decided to read it in private, peering at Sam through her long lashes.

When Sam managed to pull his gaze away from her, he refocused and said, "Uncle Curtis, you're next. That one is from me! Great first choice." The first package Uncle Curtis selected contained a small, framed picture of his father before color photos. "I found it in a random drawer in the Collection months ago and was waiting for a good excuse to give it to you." Uncle Curtis held the picture, rubbing his thumb over it again and again until he selected another gift.

"Oh, that's from me!" Josh chirped when Uncle Curtis picked a big, square envelope. It contained a thank you card with a long, handwritten letter inside. Uncle Curtis smiled from ear to ear when he read it.

"Thank YOU, Josh," was his response, but with such sincerity. Next, he held up a gift wrapped suspiciously in the shape of a coffee mug. "You know me so well, Ophelia," he said, smiling at his daughter. "Oh, it's your favorite one. You're giving me this? The last time I touched it you nearly tackled me."

"I know. It *is* my favorite, which is why I want you to have it."

"I will think of you with every sip," he said.

And finally, Liddy's gift to him was a set of ceramic measuring cups, hand painted. "I made them specifically for you a few weeks ago," she explained, surprising everyone. "What? I have to do something during the day besides cook for you lot." Pottery was on her list of secret talents, along with baking, cooking, and probably swimming.

"Okay Josh, your turn," Sam said, turning to the Guardian. Josh rubbed his hands together with anticipation.

From Sam, he got a pair of bike shorts. "Uh, thanks?" Josh said, confused since he wasn't much of a cyclist.

"I had an extra pair, and they are new, so it won't be, you know, weird to wear them or anything. I'm promising to take you cycling, once all this Sorceress stuff is finished. We can go anywhere you want, with Jenny or Ophelia's help."

"Oh awesome! I will be thinking about a location! Maybe Australia? Or the Alps?"

"Or both?" Sam said.

"Or both!"

Uncle Curtis's gift to Josh was a French butter crock that allowed butter to stay fresh outside the fridge for several weeks. "I thought it might come in handy in your room. Cold butter is so hard to spread on bread, don't you think?" he said with a wink.

"This is perfect, Uncle Curtis!"

Next came Ophelia's, a new set of throwing knives, simple but well made. He balanced one in his knuckle. "Awesome, Ophelia," he said. "These will be useful."

Liddy's gift smelled amazing even before he opened the box. It contained a dozen cinnamon rolls and the promise of another dozen at any point in the next week. He ate one of them right then and offered them to the others. "Best gift ever, Liddy," he said with his mouth full.

"Okay, Jenny, you are next," Sam said.

"No, I'd like to go last, if it's all the same to you."

"Don't have to ask me twice," he said, diving into the pile at his feet. From Uncle Curtis, he got a pay raise, which cracked him up. No one in the family struggled financially due to the nature of their business, the availability of treasure in endless stories, and wise investments by the Keepers and Guardians in years past, but Sam appreciated the gesture nonetheless.

He picked another envelope labeled *To Sam, from Josh*. It was a certificate good for five climbing sessions. Sam had bugged Josh about going climbing with him, a hobby he wanted to get into. Now Josh had promised to take him, and Sam had it in writing.

"This is perfect," Sam said. "You take me climbing, I'll take you cycling. We will be so fit." Josh gave him an odd stare before Sam remembered how fit Josh already was. "Uh, we will have so much fun while I get so fit and you just be you." His revised statement caused a few giggles.

Liddy gave him a framed picture of Duke Chapel, the beautiful, gothic cathedral on the campus of Duke University, where Sam had attended college. "I took it a few years ago on a trip with Isaac," she said. "I thought you would like to see your alma mater on your desk." *Add church photography to Liddy's list of talents!*

"This brings back memories, Liddy. Thank you."

And finally, from Ophelia, he got a small, plain box. Inside was the ring she'd always worn, a small, silver ring of the Claddagh, a crowned heart held in two hands.

"The Claddagh symbolizes friendship, loyalty, and love. I'm giving you all of these things, always."

"I'll treasure it," he whispered to her, holding her gaze long enough to make everyone else shift uncomfortably, and Jenny cleared her throat to break the tension.

"I'll go now," she said. "Sam, pass me something."

She perused her small pile of presents, her heart swelling with gratitude. The first, from Liddy, was a beautiful shell shining with mother-of-pearl on the inside. She rubbed her fingers across the smooth surface. "To commemorate your brief time in my first story," the former mermaid said.

"Liddy, it's gorgeous!"

From Sam, she got an old key with the word IAM engraved along the edge of the bow, worn from years of people's fingers turning it. "I found it in the Collection, and I feel certain it goes to something there, but I haven't had time to discover what it belongs to. Since you like puzzles, I thought you could perhaps solve this one. Oh, and before you ask, I have no idea what IAM means."

"You know I love a little mystery," she said. "Thank you, Sam. I might head to the Collection later to investigate."

From Uncle Curtis came a French press for making coffee. Jenny had developed a taste for it, and a minor addiction to it, since arriving at his home. Now she had her own means of making it.

"This is lovely, Uncle Curtis. Thank you!"

"Oh, that's from me!" Ophelia said with some excitement when Jenny held her final gift. A collection of hair bands, bandanas, and even a few stylish hats spilled onto her lap. Unlike Jenny's mom, who had tried to tame her hair, Ophelia was helping Jenny embrace it, making the chaos beautiful. "I also want to take you shopping in London once all this stuff with the Sorceress resolves. The boys can go cycling, and we can go shopping."

"That is a fabulous idea, Ophelia!" Jenny squealed with excitement at the prospect of shopping with Ophelia in such a cosmopolitan city.

And last but not least, Josh handed her a soft package wrapped with care. She tore the paper off and, inside, found a bracelet. It was simple—a leather strap that wrapped around her wrist several times and snapped closed. Stamped into the leather were the words *Ynghyd Cryfach*.

"It means 'stronger together' in Welsh. I got the idea from our run up Snowdon. I have one too." He showed her his wrist. "I ordered them right after we ran, but with everything going on, there wasn't a good time to give it to you, until today. So, Merry Christmas, Jen." The Compass warmed against her skin, and she glanced at Liddy, who was flipping through a book and paying them no mind. *I won't, Liddy*, echoed softly in her head, but she ignored it.

"Merry Christmas, Josh. And thank you. Thank you, everyone. This was amazing." Jenny spoke with such gratitude, they all nearly cried.

"We aren't done yet. Though we need to discuss tomorrow's jump into *Jack and the Beanstalk*, we will do so in our pajamas, true to Fletcher family form, and it will be done whilst drinking hot chocolate or coffee—you know which I prefer—and eating more of the delicious braided bread thingy," Uncle Curtis declared with great flair.

They scattered to put away their gifts and reconvened thirty minutes later in the Spare Room to commence talks on the jump. Jenny stopped to place a wreath on Fang's head, a royal Christmas crown for the king. He purred and wished her a very Merry Christmas before turning up his nose at Klaus and Moose, who joined in the party with their giant Christmas bones. Moose waggled his tail at Jenny, and she sat on the floor to pet him. Without fail, he had slept on her bed every night, snuggled next to her, but she had ignored him the last few weeks. And though he had Klaus and some attention from Liddy throughout the day, he still relished love from his person. She whispered a vow to play with him more often in the coming days. Moose sniffed at the Compass, wiggled some more, and returned to his bone.

They assumed their now-familiar places in the room to plan for tomorrow's jump into *Jack and the Beanstalk*. And true to his word, Uncle Curtis remained in his plaid pajamas, sipping coffee in his new mug from Ophelia. She smiled at her dad, resplendent in black silk jammies and her hair wrapped in a red and green scarf. In fact, everyone had kept the Fletcher pajama tradition, and Jenny, from her perch by the black wall, sighed with contentment.

"Shall we begin?" Uncle Curtis said. "Would anyone like to give us an overview of the story?"

"Well, let's begin with what we have to retrieve," Josh suggested. "The ransom letter says we need to get coins like the ones Jack stole, so we need to take a few coins from the massive ogre who lives in a house in the sky only accessible by a giant beanstalk that grows from magic beans. Or we could take a few from the bags of coins Jack throws down the beanstalk after he steals them from the ogre but before he climbs down."

Josh received a few blank stares, but not from Jenny. She knew the story. For everyone else's sake, he continued. "In the story, Jack accidentally grows the beanstalk, climbs it, and steals some bags of coins from the ogre. He then returns and steals a goose that lays golden eggs, and then the third time, a magical golden singing harp."

"He's got some sticky fingers, eh? This *Jack*," Sam said.

"For real! Now the ogre, eventually wise to Jack's schemes, chases after him and the harp, through the sky and down the beanstalk, but Jack chops the beanstalk before the ogre reaches the ground, effectively ending the pursuit as well as the ogre's life. Jack's mother, who is initially angry about the magic beans, is now happy as a jaybird because they're rich, and Jack goes on to marry a princess. Oh, and the ogre has a wife who helps Jack at first but then begins to despise him because he keeps stealing from them. I mean, can you blame her?"

Jenny giggled, then added her own thoughts. "I say we jump in right before Jack throws down the bags of coins, at the bottom of the beanstalk, and steal a few before he gets back to civilization. In and out in no time."

"Jenny," Uncle Curtis warned, "You know there is rarely an 'in and out in no time' scenario when it comes to the Compass. But in this case, it might actually happen. Let's make our lists." He tossed a piece of chalk to Jenny, and she went straight to the black wall.

*Needs*

*Compass*

*Guardian Sword*

*Guardian Ring*

*Healing Dagger*

*Bow and Arrows*

"I can't think of much else we need. We can put the coins in our pockets," Josh said, brow furrowed in a grimace.

"Are you in pain?" Jenny asked him.

"Oh, yeah. Sometimes I do that when I'm thinking hard about something," Josh said.

"Sometimes thinking hurts," Sam said. "I get it. My brain never stops."

Jenny added *pockets* to the list with a smiley face by it before moving onto the "must not" section.

*Must not*

*Let a bag of coins fall on you*

*Run into Jack*

*Run into Jack's mother without a convincing reason to be there*

*Run into the ogre or ogre's wife.*

"I guess I should add *A reason to be there* on our *Needs* list, huh?" Jenny said, and then wrote it just below *pockets*.

*Obstacles*

*Jack?*

*Jack's mother*

*The ogre and ogre's wife*

*Plan*

*Jump in*

*Grab coins*

*Go home*

Uncle Curtis was hesitant. "It just seems too simple," he said, rereading the list.

Jenny gave her uncle a squeeze. "If it all goes crazy, we will deal with it, like we always do."

He stood. "You guys find some appropriate costumes for the period," he added. "We'll get some lunch ready."

ooooo 🐾 ooooo

After lunch and a long nap, Jenny asked Josh to go with her to the Collection to find whatever might fit the key Sam had given her for Christmas. It had burned a hole in her pocket all morning.

He agreed with a high five, and, with a quick hello to Fang, they passed through the Spare Room and into the organized, musty immensity of the Collection

# Chapter Thirty-One

"Where should we start?" Jenny said. "*Mundane Furniture? Trick Furniture? Storage?*"

"How about *Trick Furniture* first?" Josh suggested. "Mostly because I want to see what's there."

"I know, right? This way."

They walked past rows of clothing, weapons, horse gear, and potion books before arriving at the large *Trick Furniture* section. "Okay, so what are we looking for?" Josh said.

Jenny inspected the key. "Anything old with a keyhole this might fit into. Duh," she said, winking at him.

"Yes, thank you for stating the obvious."

"Um, I'm thinking we should focus on old desks, trunks, chests, or chests of drawers. Those have a lockable drawer sometimes."

He commenced the search, working through the various pieces of furniture packed together. "Why do you think it says IAM?" he said with a grunt, surprised at the weight of a small but extremely heavy box he had attempted to scoot out of the way.

"I don't know. Maybe the company who made the key, or maybe a biblical declaration? It's all part of the mystery." Her voiced bubbled with excitement. "Isn't it great?" Josh grinned at her enthusiasm.

They dug their way through the furniture, discovering secret door bookshelves, trap chairs that clamped an unwitting person's arms and legs with the push of a button, and desks with secret compartments within se-cret compartments within secret compartments.

One small box, hand carved and shining in the light, intrigued Josh for quite some time, and he attempted to unlock it unsuccessfully for far too long. "Josh, does that box have a keyhole?" Jenny said, wiping sweat from her brow.

"Uh, no," he answered.

"Then could you save it for later?"

"Yes, yes I can. I don't want to, but I will. Just for you."

She thanked him with a smile.

"There's nothing in this section," Jenny said, coughing as a cloud of dust wafted into her face when she closed an old wardrobe.

"What now? *Mundane Furniture?*"

"Let's do it!" Her enthusiasm was unending.

The *Mundane Furniture* section spanned an even larger area than *Trick Furniture*, and the beauty and various levels of handicraft in each piece fas-cinated them. "I think '*Mundane Furniture*' is a misnomer," Jenny said, sitting in a carved, curving, very high-backed chair with a soft, upholstered seat cushion and a few tassels on the corners. "This is gorgeous. Fit for a queen."

She let her mind wander through the possible places this chair could have originated. A king's castle, a queen's sitting room, a rich merchant's foyer, a lord's manner—all romantic and perfect. *Surely a lady once sat here, dressed in a long, flowing gown with a simple yet elegant crown atop her head, surrounded by her ladies in waiting. They discussed courtiers, politics, children, and court gossip while sewing needlepoint or eating dainty cookies prepared by the palace cook who ...*

"Hey, what's this?" Josh interrupted her daydream, jolting her awake. She went to see what he had found. In a corner of the *Storage* section, which bled into *Mundane Furniture*, from the bottom of a forgotten shelf, Josh dragged an old trunk, dusty but sturdy. The black paint was worn in places, and one of the handles on the side jiggled, but it was beautiful, large, and, best of all, it had a keyhole.

For some reason, Jenny hesitated to see if the key fit.

"Just try it," Josh said with a grin.

"I will! Just, gimme a second."

The keyhole appeared to be the right size, and when she examined it more closely, her heart pounded harder.

"Why am I feeling your heart racing?" he said.

"Come closer." She waved him in. "Tell me what you see on the lock."

Josh squatted next to her and leaned in, their faces close to touching.

"Does it say, 'WILL'?" he asked, getting even closer.

She stuck the key in and clicked it to the right, then sat on her heels. "Look at it now. Now it says WILLIAM."

Josh sucked in a breath. "Whoa ... wait, wasn't Arthur Neil's son named William? The one who died?"

"It sure was."

They stared at each other, then to the trunk. "On three, okay?" Josh whispered with anticipation, placing a hand on it. Jenny followed suit. "One, two, three!" Together, they lifted the lid and peered into the trunk. The top shelf held three items, and Josh examined them in turn. A small pocket portrait of a lovely young woman sitting straight and tall, a dried and pressed white lily, and two carved wooden horses. "What do you think these are about?" he said.

"Who knows." Working together, they discarded the top shelf to the side and peered into the rest of it.

"Here's a crocheted blanket," Jenny said, letting the old blue and yellow blanket unfold on her lap.

'Maybe this belonged to William?" Josh said.

"Maybe so." She leaned way in and heaved several hefty books from the bottom of it onto the floor. "Hmm, *Treasure Island*, *The Memoirs of Sherlock Holmes*, *The Brothers Karamazov*, and *Sense and Sensibility*. So, some of the best classics ever, here in one place. And that's it," she said, peeking in one last time.

"We know Arthur Neil was an avid reader, and these were popular books during his lifetime, right?" Josh said. "At least, I think they were. The *Sherlock* book certainly was, and we know he had some serious ties to its author. The books are a good sign this trunk did actually belong to Arthur Neil."

"What about the little portrait?" Jenny asked, holding up the small, circular painting. "Could this be Arthur Neil's wife? William's mother?" She flipped it over. "Ooh! There's an AN etched into the metal here. 'N' for Neil? Arthur Neil? Or what could his wife's name have been? Allison? Ashley? Anna? Arthur and Ashley Neil? Has a nice ring to it."

"I think Ashley was more of a guy name in the 1860s," he said.

"Oh really?"

"Well, my mom made me watch *Gone with the Wind* with her once. It nearly killed me. One of the characters was named Ashley, and he was a man. I'm just assuming based on that."

"Not a bad assumption. Man, that's a really long movie."

"Tell me about it," Josh groaned. "It was torturous." He examined the dried white lily. "What about this flower? Maybe from William's funeral? And the two horses could have been his other children's toys he kept, you know, for sentiment." Josh was on a roll.

"Yes, but all this is circumstantial. And there have been a lot of people named William over the years. It doesn't narrow it down too much, does it? Now, if his son was called Alfred or Llewellyn, it would make things easier. But where we stand now, this may or may not be a trunk that belonged to the first Keeper, and it has a few cool old things, but nothing mind-blowing."

"Should we leave it all here?" Josh asked. "I kind of want a snack."

"Sure."

He set the stack of books in the bottom of the trunk, and one dropped from the top of the pile, hitting the bottom of the trunk with a dull thud. "Wait a second," he said in a muffled voice, removing the big books again. His entire upper body disappeared into the chest, and, after some grunts and scraping, he stood, bringing the bottom of it with him. "False bottom!" he said, a huge grin on his face.

"No way!"

"Oh yes way! And it was hiding something."

She dove into the trunk once more and emerged with two other books, hidden for who knows how long beneath the false bottom.

One book was leatherbound and well-worn, like the other ones, and also a classic, though less convivial than *Sense and Sensibility*. "Ooh, Bram Stoker's *Dracula*. Eek, kind of a scary one," she said, handing it to him to peruse. "I read it once, and it freaked me out."

Josh flipped through *Dracula* while Jenny inspected the second book. Though thick with pages, its cover gave in Jenny's hand, soft and floppy, like a journal. When she flipped to the first page, she gasped. It *was* a journal, and not just any journal.

Josh peered over her shoulder at it. "Whoa," he said. "*October 18, 1872, The Compass Comes to Me.*" He scanned the entry, and at the bottom of the next page, it was signed, AN. The next entry was October 23, 1872 entitled *Return to The Gilded Coffer.*"

"No way," Jenny said again.

"Oh yes way. This is Arthur Neil's book, Jenny, his Compass journal." He stuck a hand in and flipped to the last page. "It goes on for years. Up through 1897. Almost 25 years of Compass stuff in here, Jenny!" He bounced on his toes with excitement.

"This is insane," she said, flabbergasted and almost lost for words.

"Here, you take it. Read it first. I'll take this one." He held up *Dracula*. "It was worth hiding with the journal, so I'll keep it hidden too, just in case."

She clasped the journal to her chest, staring at it, then at Josh. "Should we tell the others?"

"Yes, like, right now! This'll be the best Christmas present of the day. Come on!" He snapped the trunk shut and returned it to its shelf. With *Dracula* in hand, he offered for her to lead the way.

She walked silently through the Spare Room and into the study. "Hey, you want to know something? *Dracula* is the only book I've ever read that scared me so much I couldn't finish it."

"It's that scary?" Josh asked her, surprised.

"It was to me. Maybe you should read it and let me know if I'm just a wimp," she said with a smile.

He chuckled. "Maybe I will. Don't be surprised if I knock on your door late at night, shaking in my boots and babbling about vampires."

"At least then I'd know I'm not the only wimp in the house," she added. "Just don't come knocking at my window. Once you read the book, you will understand why."

The scents of crackling meat, buttery vegetables, fresh baked bread, and sweet potato casserole met them at the top of the basement stairs, and it drew everyone to the kitchen. Liddy and Uncle Curtis bustled about, resplendent in their matching aprons, transferring platters and bowls to the table. "Oh, it smells so good!" Jenny squealed, placing the journal nonchalantly on the sideboard. "Here, I'll set the table. Josh, could you do the napkins?" She passed him a pile of red and green Christmas napkins with a smile.

"Do we tell them now?" she whispered, sidling in closer to him.

"While we are eating, I think," he said. "Okay with that?"

"Totally," she said, repressing a giggle. "This'll be fun, but I'm also really nervous for some reason."

"I get it," he said. "Me too. Just be cool."

Ophelia and Sam poured drinks before sliding into their places, giving each other a little squeeze while the others joined them. "You guys have outdone yourselves," Ophelia said, awed by the feast before her. "I hardly know where to start!"

"How about here?" her father said, passing her the bread. He then commenced carving the roast. Plates quickly filled, and the clankety-clank of silverware mixed with lively conversation.

"So, any luck in the Collection today?" Sam said, shoving more sweet potatoes into his face. Jenny and Josh glanced at each other, and Josh indicated Jenny should begin their tale.

"Actually, yes!" She placed the key in front of her with a touch of drama. "We found where this little guy fits."

"No way!" Sam somehow managed to speak with food in his mouth and not seem rude. "What was it? Was it cool?"

This time, Jenny offered for Josh to continue the story. "It was pretty cool. In fact, we are pretty sure we found a trunk belonging to the one and only Arthur Neil." The clanking of utensils stopped. Everything grew quiet. Uncle Curtis's eyebrows shot up at this news.

"Oh my!" Liddy breathed.

"That's what we thought. But then all we found were some old classics, little mementos, and a baby blanket," Jenny said. "Kind of a letdown. I mean, cute things, but nothing to write home about."

"Indeed," Uncle Curtis said.

"But then we discovered something else. Something a little more interesting." They all leaned in in anticipation. "The trunk had a false bottom." Gasps around the table brought a grin to Josh's face, and he let the news sink in and percolate.

"Well!" spluttered Ophelia, unable to bear the suspense. "What did you find?"

"Two more books, hidden away for years, it would seem," Jenny said.

Josh put the small copy of *Dracula* on the table. "This was one of them. Just a simple copy of the only book to ever scare Jenny so much she couldn't finish it." She rolled her eyes at him before adding the other book to the pile.

"And this one," she said, plopping the journal into the center of the table. "Which happens to be Arthur Neil's JOURNAL!" More gasps, and Sam even slapped his thigh.

"Get OUT!" he said.

"I KNOW!" Jenny nearly shouted. "It covers like, twenty-five years of his life. I mean, we only glanced at it, but holy cow you guys, this is HUGE, right?"

Uncle Curtis wiped his brow with his napkin, working to contain his excitement. "Jenny, Josh, this is quite a discovery. And since you've discovered it, it is yours to examine and read at length. I'd ask, though, that you share with us all you learn, and once you are done, would you let me have a turn?"

Jenny rushed to hug her uncle, kissing the top of his head. "Well, duh, Uncle Curtis. I'd give it to you now if you wanted it!"

"No, no, you keep it for now. Though I must say I am very curious as to its contents."

"I'll read it as quick as I can," she said. "But I have one more thing to do before I crack this baby open. If you guys don't mind, can I leave you to clear the table? This is important."

"Of course, Jenny. And thank you for sharing your discoveries with us," Uncle Curtis said. "And Josh, keep that copy of *Dracula* close. If it was hidden with the journal, it might be important."

"I had the same thought," Josh said. He tapped his temple. "Great minds think alike, eh?"

"Guardian minds think alike," Uncle Curtis replied with a wink.

∞∞∞ 🜨 ∞∞∞

Just before everyone went to bed, Jenny reappeared, her Compass family lounging in the den enjoying a final cup of hot chocolate and basking in the glow of tiny white Christmas lights. "Before you go to bed," she announced, "I have a few things I'd like to do before Christmas day ends, as a thank you for making today so beautiful. It meant so much to me."

Clearing her throat and pushing her hair from her face, she spoke first to Uncle Curtis. "For you, who have become like a grandfather to me, I can never repay you for all you have done. This is just a little something to say thank you." She passed him a beautiful drawing of the Compass she had worked on for a large portion of the evening.

"Oh Jenny, I knew you liked to draw, but this is very, very good," was all he could say.

For Ophelia and Sam, Jenny had drawn a picture of them together, sharing the sweet moment when Sam had woken Ophelia from her cursed slumber after the unfortunate encounter with a spindle. Ophelia held it with delicate fingers, afraid she might damage it. Sam admired it from behind her, his chin on her shoulder. "Jenny, you nailed this one. I look just as good in this drawing as I do in real life. And Ophelia is perfect, as usual."

She nudged him in the ribs but continued examining the drawing, savoring the emotion it evoked in her. "Thank you, Jenny. We will treasure this."

Liddy's picture was the conch shell sitting in the front seat of Isaac's car Jenny had seen the day she received the Compass, before the Sorceress presumably smashed it on the driveway. Liddy lit up when she saw it and commented on the little details Jenny had included in Isaac's car, like the books he always had stacked on the front seat and the hula dancer stuck to the dash. "Isaac says it reminds him of me, which is ridiculous. I don't hula," she said laughing, attempting to sway her hips.

And last came Josh's gift. First, a fork. "It's from *Cinderella*. Don't worry, I didn't use it to like, stab the toe or anything, but I thought about it. I couldn't find a spoon for scooping it up." Josh hooted, and everyone else was confused. They were not privy to the spoon collection. "Our little secret," she explained with a shy grin.

She had also drawn a picture of the Guardian Sword held in a strong hand, complete with the Keeper Ring. On the wrist of the strong hand, there was a leather bracelet with the words '*Ynghyd Cryfach*' stamped in the leather.

His eyes moved from the picture to his own hand and back again, marveling at the likeness. "Amazing, Jenny," he told her, and thanked her with a big high five. She didn't leave him hanging.

# Chapter Thirty-Two

The day off for Christmas revitalized Jenny and Josh, and they were both up early for a run in the training room, listening to the story of *Jack and the Beanstalk* one more time on an audiobook. "Okay, so we are jumping in right before Jack throws down the gold after his first time up the beanstalk, right?" Josh asked, puffing next to Jenny on the treadmill.

"Uh-huh," she answered. "Then we can swipe a few coins from the bag and head home. Easy peasy."

"Ha, ha!" He increased his pace.

∞∞∞ ❦ ∞∞∞

Breakfast was quick but gourmet, with eggs benedict on Liddy's sourdough, laden with hollandaise sauce, with fruit on the side, of course. Uncle Curtis offered to steam some asparagus for the eggs benedict. Jenny agreed, but Josh shook his head. "Vegetables for breakfast is weird."

They ate in silence, thinking about the mission. Josh glanced sideways at Jenny. "I like your braids," he told her between bites.

She patted the two French braids she had attempted to keep her hair under control, along with a headband Ophelia had given her for Christmas.

"Well thanks, Josh. They took a while. Moose, stop begging." She scolded her dog and nudged him with her foot.

"It suits you. The braids, I mean."

She choked on her orange juice. "It *suits* me? Have you been reading *Dracula*? That sounded so proper and pre-20th Century. And kind of awesome. I love it when you talk Victorian." Josh blushed at her words, and she scrambled to undo the embarrassment she'd caused. "Hey! We only have one more mission until we get Isaac back. That's kind of awesome too."

"It sure is," said Ophelia, who strode into the room like it was an army and she was the general. She sat at the head of the table like she owned it, but she served herself and never demanded anything from anyone else except excellence in the training room and all other areas of life. "Today's mission, the *last* mission before the Sorceress, should be pretty straightforward."

Josh snuck Klaus, who was camped at his feet, a piece of bacon. "That's what everyone keeps saying."

"Even the simplest of plans should allow for things to go wrong. So at least take your weapons, the Chameleon Cloaks, and water and extra food." Ophelia could've killed it in Scouts.

He confessed that he already had a box of power bars in his pack along with the Chameleon Cloaks and a water purifying straw.

"Way to think ahead," Ophelia said, impressed. She bit into a piece of toast, watching her students like a proud mama.

ooooo 🐾 ooooo

Everyone in the Compass family convened in the Spare Room by Sam's desk where he had their packs and walkie-talkies. In addition to the food and cloaks Josh had packed earlier, Sam added a can of what he called "Ogre Off" to each pack, just in case they encountered the giant ogre who played a strong supporting role in this story. "It's kind of like super strong pepper spray. I made it myself. It should work, but do not get it in your eyes, whatever you do. Don't do it. Hear my words." The duo glanced at each other, noting the warning in Sam's voice. Sam always had a warning for them.

"Got it," confirmed Josh, and Jenny nodded too.

"Okay, I think we're ready," she said. Linked with Josh, she approached the book, opened to the appropriate page in the story.

"Good luck!" Liddy said, speaking for those staying behind.

Taking a deep breath, Jenny leaned in, allowing the Compass to float above the page. Just before it touched, Moose and Klaus darted through the Spare Room, and Klaus, uncharacteristically bouncy, bumped Josh, who bumped Jenny, and the Compass fell to the other page, one page forward in the story of Jack and Beanstalk. In a wink, they were gone.

"Well, this should be interesting." Uncle Curtis's words echoed in Jenny's ear, and when they landed, Josh started laughing.

"Looks like we've got a hitchhiker," he said, patting Klaus who wagged his stump of a tail then sat at Josh's side.

"Oh my! Well, I should let them know he's okay." She clicked on her walkie-talkie. "Hey, we're alright, and so is Klaus, but I'm not sure where we are in the story—oh, wait. Here comes Jack with the harp, and the ogre is not far behind him. So, we're in this part. Fantastic! Klaus, sit! If you don't obey, so help me ... okay, good boy. We gotta run, guys! Be in touch!" And she clicked off.

Klaus's bump had landed them at the top of the beanstalk, up in the clouds, staring down a straight road they hoped ended at the ogre's house. Jack, the star of the show, was hoofing it down the road, right towards them, with a giant ogre striding after him shouting, "Fee-fi-fo-fum, I smell the blood of an Englishman!" The ground vibrated from the weight of the monster and his determined footfalls.

He was at least twelve feet tall, maybe more, and nearly as thick, with knobby skin and a head resembling an enormous frog. His huge mouth was full of brown, mossy teeth. The ogre smell hit them first, followed by the shrill voice of the golden harp Jack held, which screeched, "Master, master!" Both were incredibly unpleasant.

With nowhere to hide, Jack called to them when he flew by. "Help me!" he shrieked. "Help! I have gold!"

"That's what we are here for!" Jenny said. With a quick nod to each other, they leapt into action. Jenny pulled her bow off her shoulder and grabbed an arrow. It would likely slow the ogre's progress, giving Jack more of a lead and possibly earn them some of the gold they needed.

Her arrow struck home, and the ogre paused, confused at the protrusion in his shoulder. He tried to break it off. This was just the opening they needed. Josh dashed in front of him, and Jenny ran to Josh, stepping into his open hand. With a great display of strength, he boosted her into the air, right toward the ogre. The villain started in surprise, not expecting a girl to fly toward his face. This gave her a perfect target for the Ogre-Off she held. The ogre roared as the souped-up pepper spray hit him square in the face. Jenny flipped over his head and, just like Ophelia had taught her, extended her arms to the side and kept her legs and feet straight and together, squeezing her eyes shut and praying Josh got there in time.

He darted through the ogre's legs and caught Jenny just before she hit the ground. Racing away from the staggering beast, afraid it might topple on them, he held her tight. "Great move!"

"You too!" she said, breathless.

The harp yelled again, "Master, Master!" when Jack started to descend the beanstalk, no doubt wishing he'd stolen something less vocal.

The ogre shook his head and rubbed his face, trying to rid himself of the tears in his eyes. It seemed to work, for he refocused on his precious harp, retrieving it his only concern. Wiping his eyes one more time, the ogre continued forward, leaving Jenny and Josh in his dust. Jenny made to go after him, but Josh stopped her, pulling her the opposite way. "We can get the gold from his house. Jack didn't steal all of it, remember? The ogre is about to take a plunge after Jack chops the beanstalk down. We can't follow, or we will tumble down and break our crowns, too."

Jenny, still exhilarated from flipping over a giant ogre, took a moment to register his words, and she continued to look from the beanstalk to the opposite end of the road.

"He's right, you know," a little voice said from the trees lining the road. Out of the shadows emerged a boy, not more than ten or eleven, dressed as a peasant with floppy black hair falling in front of big, green eyes. Freckles dotted his turned-up nose and spilled onto his cheeks, and he waved at them from beside a tree, unsure if he should approach them.

Klaus wagged his tail at the boy.

"Oh, who are you?" Jenny said. "There was no mention of another boy in the story."

"I'm, uh, I'm just part of the setting," he answered. "I'm kind of stuck here in the clouds. I don't really like heights." His words rolled round in Jenny's head, raising questions faster than she could vocalize them. "Here, come this way. I know where the gold is that you seek. I can help you get it." He headed away from the beanstalk and, presumably, toward the ogre's home and wife and gold.

Josh and Jenny exchanged uncertain glances, not sure whether to trust this little boy or not. "How did he know we were hunting for gold?" Josh said out of the side of his mouth.

"He must've heard us talking or something," Jenny said. "And anyway, Klaus seems to like him. I trust his judgment." Klaus beamed at Jenny's confidence in him, and Josh gave one nod.

"Okay then, lead the way," Josh said at normal volume, gesturing for the boy to go ahead of them, a role he readily assumed.

The house came into view, and they heard a loud crack and two distant thumps. "That was the beanstalk," the boy said. "One thump was the ogre hitting the ground, and the other was the beanstalk tumbling after him. The harp has a new master now."

With access to Jack's gold cut off since the beanstalk was gone and the reality of having to sneak into the ogre-wife's house to steal some more sinking in, Josh stopped. "I wonder if we should jump home and back again, to the page we first intended to land in," he whispered, eyeing the boy.

"I'm okay continuing this way," Jenny said. "I mean, we're already here. It's a little dangerous, but I'd love to see the ogre's house. Up for the challenge?" He would never say no to a challenge no matter how strange the circumstances were.

"Ha! What do you think?" Josh said, relaxing a bit. "Hey, I have to say it again—awesome move with the jump, pepper spray, and flip thing." He nudged her with his elbow.

"I thought that was killer," the boy said, several paces ahead of them. "You guys must practice a lot."

"Well, it took two to make it happen. He's the only one who could throw me that high, and thanks for catching me, Josh. It would have hurt pretty bad otherwise."

"Anytime," he said. "Okay, so, what happens next?" he said to the boy, keeping a keen watch on the ogre's home ahead. "We probably need a plan to get into the house and get the gold."

"Maybe a distraction to get the ogre-wife out?" the boy suggested.

"I could be a distraction, if needs be," Klaus responded with a thick German accent. He looked just as surprised as Josh and Jenny, who both halted and spun to face him, mouths agape.

"Do it again, Klaus, speak!" Josh commanded. Klaus, ever the obedient Doberman, responded, "Vould you prefer I bark as I usually do or use zee verds I now possess to communicate in a more 'uman way?" Then he barked for good measure and wagged his tail.

"So, I guess dogs can talk in stories," Jenny mused, both shocked and delighted. "I wonder what Moose would have to say."

"Oh zat silly puppy. He vould continually ask you to play ball and rub his tummy. He does not possess ze same level of intellect as me, but fear not, Keeper, I do love heem. I vill not keel heem. Zank you fur bringing me a doggy friend, zo I sometimes do vish he vas less bouncy."

"This is so weird!" Josh laughed, rubbing Klaus's head and haunches. "You've been a good friend to Moose, and to me." The boy watched from behind his hair with a sweet expression and half of a smile.

"Oh, I do love zis part," the dog replied, leaning into Josh. " 'umans are so good to us doggies."

"I hate to break up this sweet moment between you two, but let's get a move on. This mission was supposed to be quick and easy, short and sweet, and, uh…" She couldn't come up with a third thing.

"Fast and furious?" Josh said.

"Sure, that works. Fast and furious. Instead, we are trapped in some magical land in the sky only reachable by massive beanstalks and inhabited by a newly-widowed ogre wife who will probably be quite angry at humans right now thanks to dumb Jack and his thieving ways." The boy giggled at Jenny.

"So, ve must formulate a new plan, yes?" Klaus contributed. "How about my original idea? I vill distract her whilst you grab some of zee gold. Perhaps she has never seen a talking Doberman before. And use zee Chameleon Cloaks. Zey are always a vise choice, no?"

Klaus was quite the strategist. They liked his plan, and, sticking with the fast and furious theme, they decided to get in and out as quickly as possible, "out" being home, out of this story, forever. The lingering smell of ogre was enough for them to never want to return.

"Pardon, but what is a Chameleon Cloak?" the boy asked.

"Watch this!" Jenny said with a grin.

She and Josh threw on their Chameleon Cloaks and disappeared right before the boy's eyes. He gasped. Jenny pulled off her hood with a chuckle. "Cool, huh?" she said.

"Whoa!" he whispered.

Pushing off his hood and lifting a finger, Josh clicked on his walkie-talkie and checked in with home base to let them know the new plan before setting off again with hoods in place. Now, it was just a random dog walking along with his little shaggy-haired owner, sniffing here and there at the trees and bushes lining the straight road leading to the ogre home.

When they approached the cottage, the boy dashed into the woods and disappeared in the shadows. Josh and Jenny, still camouflaged, continued forward with Klaus. The ogre-stench increased with each step, and even Klaus made a face when the wind shifted, wafting more of it his way. The book had failed to mention this aspect of ogres.

The house was an oversized cottage with a thick thatched roof, several chimneys standing high above the thatch, large windows with thick glass, and a massive door at the front. Everything had to be bigger to accommodate such large inhabitants.

Klaus walked to the door and scratched, then barked and whined.

Jenny watched with Josh from behind a tree near the house. When he moved a step to get a better view, a small nudge against her side startled her. The little boy had sidled next to her, somehow sensing her presence. She squatted, pulled her hood off, and whispered, "Are you okay?" He nodded and pressed something into her palm.

"This is for you, in case we get separated or something," he said. "You are even better than we expected."

She stared at him, a million questions running through her head again. *Now is not the time for questions! The ogre-wife is coming!* Heavy steps shook the ground from inside the house.

With one quick motion, she shoved the note into her pocket and pulled her hood up. This was no time to be distracted.

"What is it? Your pulse is speeding up," Josh whispered.

"Later," she said.

At that very moment, the clomping stopped, and the front door creaked, revealing the ogre-wife in all her splendor.

She was identical to her recently deceased husband with the addition of sprouts of sandy blond hair shooting from her head and an apron instead of trousers. Her nails were painted red. *Yikes, what did she use as polish?* Jenny swallowed her rising fear.

Unafraid, Klaus inspected the ogre wife up and down, sniffing her feet as she stared at him with a wee smile on her face. She must have liked dogs. Klaus wagged his tail then promptly bit her right on her massive, dirty, hairy toe. The ogre-wife yelped, and the fast Doberman dashed away before she could get a good kick at him. She thundered after him with a shout, vacating the door to the house and allowing Josh and Jenny to slip in. Klaus slid to a halt to ensure she didn't stop because she smelled any "Englishmen." He lifted a leg and peed on her pumpkins.

"How dare you, you mangy mutt! Get back here!" Her big voice grated like a diesel truck on the highway. She went after him, away from the thieves secretly entering her house.

The duo scanned the room, searching for anything resembling a bag of gold. The sheer size of everything made searching difficult. They climbed onto furniture, peered in massive drawers, crawled under beds—nothing. Their frustration grew, as did their concern for Klaus, the boy waiting outside, and the ogre-wife's return.

"Ugh, where is it?" Jenny groaned, stomping her foot and pulling her hood off for a better view of the room. Josh followed suit.

"Let's think. Does it say in the story where the gold was kept?" Josh said. "Let me think ... the chest!" He said it at the same time as the boy who now stood in the doorway, silhouetted against the bright light outside.

"He kept his gold in a chest, and I bet it's that one," said the little boy. He pointed to an enormous chest, eight or nine feet high, sitting under one of the windows.

"I think you're right! Here, I'll boost you again, Jenny," Josh offered, hoisting her onto the chair stationed conveniently by the chest. He clambered next to her, and, together, they pushed with all their might until it lifted. They peeked in.

A pale, yellow light illuminated their faces. Jenny's hazel eyes shone golden as she breathed out a quiet "whoa."

"We found it!" Josh said. At the same moment, they heard barking, getting louder and louder. Josh saw Klaus booking it towards the house, the ogre-wife hot on his heels with a large branch in her hand, attempting to pummel him every few steps. She was getting winded, which slowed her, but so was Klaus. His tongue hung from the side of his mouth.

"Uh oh," said the boy in the doorway, disappearing into the shadows again.

"We've got to vamoose," Josh said, grabbing a handful of gold coins and shoving them in his pockets. "I hope that's enough." Jenny did the same, just in case. They jumped off the chair and pulled their hoods on. The back door of the cottage slammed against the wall, and they ran into the garden on the opposite side of the house from Klaus and the she-monster chasing him. Josh let out a loud whistle, waiting, listening for Klaus to round the corner. Jenny dropped her hood so Klaus could see them, but Josh stopped her. "He can smell us, don't worry."

"If *he* can, so can the ogre," she said, anxious, the stomping of the ogre getting louder with every step. The ground vibrated beneath their feet. Jenny found Josh's arm, ready to get out of there the moment Klaus was within reach.

"We didn't get to say goodbye to the little boy," she said, searching the trees, hoping to spot him.

"Maybe next time," Josh said, now completely focused on the direction of the chase.

Klaus appeared, tearing through the garden, his nose in the air smelling for his friends. Josh whistled again, and the dog paused, pricked his ears, and sprinted right for them just as the ogre-wife appeared, panting. She stopped, unable to run any further, leaning on the garden wall to catch her breath.

"DOG!" she screeched.

"Good try," Klaus said to her, then vanished.

The trio landed, Josh holding onto Klaus with all his might. "Good boy," he whispered to the big dog, who wanted to respond, his mouth moving. When a simple whine came out, he drooped and opted instead to lick Josh's face and wag his stumpy tail. When Josh released him, he trotted off to his special Spare Room water bowl, drank half of it, and crawled under Sam's desks for a well-deserved nap.

Uncle Curtis watched them with uplifted eyebrows. Liddy asked, "So?"

Josh answered by tossing a handful of gold coins onto the desk where they clattered, almost like applause. "It was not quick or easy, but it's done. The last one." He smiled at Jenny. "We did it. We got everything she asked for."

"Thanks to Klaus, we survived, and mission accomplished," Jenny added. "Oh, and Klaus can talk in stories, at least in this one. How crazy is that?"

They debriefed over some sandwiches Liddy had made. When Jenny mentioned the boy who had appeared and helped them, Uncle Curtis became especially interested. He asked some of the same questions Jenny had thought.

"Uncle Curtis, I don't know where he came from, how he got to the ogre's home in the sky, how he knew about the 'setting', or why he stuck this note in my hand and said I was better than they thought. And, I have no idea who 'they' are." She flipped the paper onto the table, enjoying everyone's surprise. "Should I open it?"

"Duh," Uncle Curtis said with a wink, and Ophelia nodded emphatically.

Jenny unfolded the paper and spread it flat on the table. She read it in silence. Her heart clenched, and the blood left her face.

"Well wee Jenny, what does it say?" Uncle Curtis asked. Scooting the paper toward him, she repeated the words written on the page. "To the Compass Bearer: you are not alone."

# Chapter Thirty-Three

"What does that even mean?" Jenny spluttered, almost speechless. Uncle Curtis pondered it, biting the inside of his lip.

Carefully, he laid the paper flat and pressed it with his hands. "Tell me again of this boy who gave it to you," he asked. "Every detail."

Josh offered since Jenny was having trouble forming any words, her mouth moving but nothing coming out. "He was young, maybe ten, with green eyes and black hair."

"And freckles," she managed to add.

"Yes, freckles. He said he was part of the book, a minor character, but maybe he wasn't. He knew about the setting, which seems fishy to me. Maybe he had a Charm. Jenny, did you notice?"

"No, sorry, I didn't. But he did seem kind of strange—more modern than medieval. I think he used the word 'killer' didn't he, Josh?" He nodded an affirmative. "And, he wasn't surprised we were in the story or totally freaked out by the Chameleon Cloaks. He took everything in stride, and he could like, disappear into the shadows. Really disappear. Is there a Charm that lets people do that?"

"Not that I know of," Ophelia answered. "But we don't know about all of them and their powers."

"We *do* know that there are Charms out there that can do some pretty cool stuff. Letting someone disappear into shadows doesn't sound too farfetched."

"So we think this little guy is a, what, a Charm Bearer?" Jenny said.

"We will have to wait and see," Uncle Curtis said. "We need more information. Whoever he is, he either knows about the Compass, or someone else does and is using him as their messenger. It would seem he knows how to find you, which is a little disconcerting. However, he can only do so in a book. I doubt he'll pop into your room. That said, why don't you take Klaus with you tonight, just in case. Moose won't mind the company, will you, pup?" The little dog wagged at Uncle Curtis before jumping into his lap. "Ophelia and Josh, sleep with your doors open, would you?"

Pushing back his chair to stand while tucking the note into his pocket, Uncle Curtis suggested they take a break, clean up, and get some rest. "For now, put this on the back-burner. The Sorceress is our priority. The second meeting with her is coming. We must be ready."

○○○○○ ✳ ○○○○○

After a long shower to wash off the lingering scent of ogre and calm her mind regarding the mysterious note, Jenny lounged at her desk with a towel turban-wrapping her hair. Legs crossed and her toe scratching Klaus, who'd assumed his guard dog duties from the second she'd left the table after lunch, she found a pencil and lost herself in drawing. Casting her mind to *Jack and the Beanstalk*, she created, to her best ability, a portrait of the little boy, with his big eyes and sweet face. *Who are you? And how did you find me?*

∞∞∞ 🔆 ∞∞∞

That night, Liddy made a simple dinner for everyone, but when she dropped a plate after Ophelia called her name for the third time, Josh asked her what was going on. Leaning on the island, cradling her head, she sighed. "It just feels so close, getting Isaac back, I mean. You are going to the Sorceress. It's what we've been waiting for, what you've been training for."

"If all goes as planned, Isaac could be home tomorrow," Uncle Curtis told her. Liddy's beautiful, ocean blue eyes pooled at his words, light dancing off her engagement ring. Jenny longed to reunite Liddy with her lost love, maybe even more than she wanted Isaac back for herself, and that was a whole, whole lot.

"And after him, you will find our parents," added Liddy, trying to smile. "I miss them all."

∞∞∞ 🔆 ∞∞∞

The bright moon illumined Willowbend Lane, and Jenny sat at her desk again, periodically glancing at her door while she drew a picture of Liddy at dinner, resting her cheek on her knuckles. Jenny intended to give it to Isaac once he returned so he could know just how much Liddy had missed him. Maybe it would help him heal from his ordeal with the Sorceress.

The downstairs clock chimed. It was getting to be bedtime, so Jenny set aside her work and patted Klaus with her foot. She padded to the bathroom to brush her teeth and wash her face, pushing on a headband to keep her hair out of the way. It worked, kind of, making her hair even bigger and wilder. Running her fingers through it didn't help, and she finally relinquished her efforts and finished getting ready for bed.

Toweling off her face, the visitor she'd hoped for tapped on her door. Forgetting about her hair, she tiptoed to it, still holding her towel, her cheeks warm. "Hey," she said.

"Hey. Wow, your hair is amazing!" Josh said.

"I've given up. It's out of control. Guh, I wish it were different." Feeling defeated, she tossed the towel on her desk chair and slumped on her bed, trying to hide her dejection.

"Jen, your hair may be big and wild, but it's perfect. Don't let anyone tell you otherwise."

*Perfect, but not pretty. Why didn't he say pretty? Ugh, I wish he said pretty.* She clenched her jaw. *Jenny, get the heck over it. He likes your hair. I guess perfect isn't that bad.*

"So, what's up?" she said. *I'm sure he wants to talk about the mission. The big one. The Sorceress one.*

He shrugged, flipping a gold coin in his hand. "I, uh, I miss my parents tonight." The coin flew high in the air, and he caught it without even looking before his fist dropped to his side. Such an honest confession from this big, strong warrior. "Seeing Liddy tonight—she was so hopeful. We've succeeded so far in all our missions. And we are so close to completing it, which means *hopefully* finding out more about where our parents are. And then I found this coin on my pillow." His gaze met hers with these last words.

Jenny hugged her knees to her chest and leaned against the headboard of the bed. "I had an extra one and wanted to share," she said. Then she tipped forward, her forehead resting on her kneecaps. "I wish I had the same hope you guys do, but all I land on is everything I'm not. I'm not old enough, smart enough, pretty enough, quick enough—there are probably more. And I'm not begging for compliments or anything. But if we are having 'sharing moments' tonight, then this is me being honest."

He tossed her the coin so she could keep her fingers busy and sat in his chair by the bed. "Jen." His stare possessed an unfamiliar intensity, even for him. "If I have to say this over and over until I die, it will always be true, and I will never get tired of saying it. There is no one I trust or respect more, no one I would rather work with, and no one I'd rather have adventures with other than you, Jenny Fletcher, Keeper of the Compass."

She continued to hide behind her knees, uncomfortable with his kind words. But then she faced him, allowing him to see her tears.

"And may I remind you," he continued, "what your mom said about being brave."

She threw the coin at him with feigned annoyance, repeating her mom's now famous words regarding bravery. "If I have to be reminded of what she said one more time, I might freak out. Maybe I should get it tattooed on my arm so I will always have her words right there to remind me to stop being a coward."

"Your mom knew what she was saying," Josh said. "So be brave, Jen. The rest will follow. And yes, you should get it tattooed. That way I can just point to it when you are scared. And tattoos are cool. Maybe I'll get one too."

"You? Yeah right. You are way too conservative for a tattoo."

"Me? Conservative? I'll have you know I'm the only Korean-American I know with longish hair, at least within fifty miles of here."

"What would your mom say if you got a tattoo?"

"I'll have you know that Amelia Park *does* have a tattoo."

Jenny gasped. "No way! What? Where?"

"It says *I lift my eyes unto the mountains* on her shoulder blade, with a mountain skyline surrounding it. It's cool."

"Ooh, I like that." She smiled, but it quickly faded, and she paled. "Tomorrow's the start of getting her home. And tomorrow, you won't be with me. Tomorrow, I go alone."

"I can't believe you go tomorrow. I mean, we don't even have a plan yet." Josh scooted his chair closer to the bed. "Ugh, I hate that stupid Sorceress." The sound of his fist pounding on the chair's arm reverberated through the room, startling Jenny.

"I'll have to be brave," she said. "And so will you. May I remind you of my mother's saying? Being brave means doing what needs doing even if you are scared."

"Is that how it goes?" Josh said. "I'd forgotten. I guess for me, it means sitting here, waiting for you. Being brave means doing nothing. That's so strange."

He sat silent for so long, Jenny finally nudged him to make sure he was still awake, blushing when their eyes met. Then out of nowhere, he lifted his banded wrist. "*Ynghyd Cryfach,*" he said with a gleam in his eye.

"*Ynghyd Cryfach?*" she replied. "But Josh, I go alone tomorrow. We definitely will not be *Strong Together.*"

"I know," he said. "Don't I know."

ooooo 🪷 ooooo

Once Josh left, Jenny settled into her bed. Despite her best efforts, thoughts of the Sorceress continued to seep in and ruminate behind her eyelids, interspersed with other flickers of her and Josh's previous late-night conversations the last few months, mostly regarding the Network and Book Burners—topics they hadn't had the time or energy to broach since *The Little Mermaid.*

With a sigh, her room came into focus, and for a moment, a random shadow appeared like Josh sitting in his chair by her bed. It startled her, and then she chuckled. *I kind of wish he was still sitting there. He makes everything feel so safe. And he's so fun to talk to and, if I'm honest, nice to look at.* She buried her face in her duvet, embarrassed at her own admission, then searched for anything else to think about besides how his floppy hair rested perfectly against his temple or how his smile never failed to lift her mood.

"Oh!" She dug Arthur Neil's journal from the hamper in the corner of her room where she had hidden it after dinner. No one would want to look in there, she felt certain.

With trembling fingers, she flipped to the first page of the journal and skimmed through the initial entries. Arthur had written about his venture into *The Gilded Coffer*, but he provided little information about his actual time in the book, only about the return to his beloved Annabelle and their children days later, a new man, a renewed man, and man his wife barely recognized.

*She sat with me in the library, once the children were asleep, and demanded the truth. I could think of nothing else to do but take her with me. So, we warned the help we would be out for a bit, barred the library door, and away we went. We returned hours later with more than just another adventure to record. We returned with so much more.*

Jenny read the next few lines, then slammed the book shut, eyes wide and mouth hanging open. "Oh my word!" she whispered, jumped from the bed and scurried on her tiptoes to Josh's room, tapping on the already cracked door. "Josh!" she whispered, sneaking into the quiet dark. "Josh? Wake up!"

A figure shut the door behind her and grabbed her arm. "Are you okay?" he said, flicking a lamp on and holding up his finger with the Guardian Ring. "Your pounding heart woke me up. What's going on?" Jenny sat him on the edge of his bed then paced back and forth, Arthur Neil's book held tight to her chest. In one fluid motion, she threw the journal at him.

"Read the entry marked October 24, 1872. It's like, page 5 maybe?" Jenny suggested.

Josh flipped to the page and found the entry, which he read quickly. His reaction was nearly identical to Jenny's. "Whoa," he said. "Whoa. Whoa!"

"Yeah, I know! What do we do? I mean, this news—this is huge. We have to tell everyone."

"Well, yeah, we do. But ... shouldn't we wait until after we ... I mean *you* ... get back from the Sorceress's house, once we get Isaac home?"

Jenny nodded. "I agree. But we can't sit on this for long. It will change everything."

Josh blew out a long breath, eyes darting from the journal back to her. "So, depending on how things go, we could tell them tomorrow, or the next day. That's not too long to keep it a secret," he said. He ran his hands through his hair. "There's a second Compass, Jenny. Another one. Where is it? Who has it? Holy moly."

"I don't know. The boy from *Jack*, maybe? His note makes a lot more sense with this new information."

"Or the Book Burners or the Network?"

"I don't know! We've got to find the boy."

"How?"

"I have absolutely no idea." She sat down hard on the side of the bed next to him. "No idea whatsoever."

# Chapter Thirty-Four

The next morning, the morning of the jump into *Rapunzel* to take the Sorceress the dagger, toe, and gold, Jenny sipped her coffee at the table, trying to wake up after a late night. Last night's discoveries weighed heavy on her mind.

The clomping of Josh's running shoes on the stairs drew her attention. "Hey guys!" He greeted her and Sam. "Great morning, isn't it?" *Wow, he's in a good mood. Way better than me.* Clunking her coffee cup onto the table and resting her head on her hand, she yawned again.

"Late night?" Sam asked her, dropping into the seat beside her.

"Guh, yes. I stayed up too late talking with happy pants over there," Jenny said, jerking her head to Josh who poured his own coffee while whistling. "And now we're paying for it. Well, one of us is." She rubbed her eyes.

"Oh yeah?"

"Yeah, we do that sometimes," Jenny said, stretching. "It's like, therapy or something."

Sam was quiet for a second, then called across the kitchen, "Hey Josh!

After all this is over, can we plan the rock climbing trip you promised me?"

"Oh, absolutely! I've missed climbing a lot."

At the mention of climbing, Jenny brightened. "You'll love it, Sam. Maybe you guys can go the same time Ophelia and I go to London to shop, though I'd almost rather be climbing if I'm completely honest."

"I was thinking it would be more of a guy trip," Sam whispered to her. "But, I'd love to go with you another time. Would that be okay?" A quick wink communicated his good intentions. "And anyway, Ophelia would be heartbroken to miss a girls' weekend in London. Don't tell her I told you, but there are some people there she wants you to meet."

"Oh! Well, in that case ..."

Josh joined them at the table at the same time Uncle Curtis strode into the kitchen. With a quick clap of his hands, the old Guardian got their full attention. "This morning we plan. And if all goes well, Jenny, you will meet the Sorceress again today. Eat quickly. We have lots of work to do. Oh dear, where is Ophelia?"

"She's in the Collection. Said she'd be back by 8:00. Which is in just a few minutes," Sam said, tapping his watch. "And here she is!"

They all turned to see Ophelia emerge from the spiral staircase, her arms laden with clothing. She heaved them into Jenny's lap with a huff. "Whew, these are heavy." Dusting off her hands, she bent closer to her cousin and whispered, "There's got to be something in here perfect for facing the Sorceress. Want to go see if any of these dresses work? I'll come help you with your hair and makeup too, if you want. For today, being fierce starts with looking the part, okay?"

Jenny dashed up the stairs with the outfits, her fatigue forgotten. Dress after dress swirled around her strong frame then dropped to the floor and was discarded. She frowned at the dwindling pile of possibilities. Nothing felt just right, and, after the last item landed with the other rejects on the floor, Jenny sat on her bed with a huff.

Her eyes fixed on her wardrobe. She crossed the floor and threw open the doors. It only took a second to find the items she wanted. A long, flowy, dark pink dress spilled from her shoulders to the floor. A wide, leather belt cinched it at the waist, and she fixed a brown shawl, with delicate embroidered leaves and flowers, under the belt, adding a layer over the pink wool. A quick spin in the mirror evoked a myriad of memories from the first time she wore that dress so many months ago in Granny Bea's cottage. Her hand gripped the Compass, remembering the thrill and fear she had felt upon discovering its power that night.

A knock on the door returned her to the moment. Thinking it was Ophelia, she called out, "Come in!" and posed to show off the costume she'd chosen for this jump with a sassy hand on her hip and a knee cocked, doing her best to impersonate a model. "What do you think?" she asked, brushing curls from her brow, embellishing her pose.

"Hey, I recognize those," a deeper-than-expected voice answered.

Dropping the fake model pose with an embarrassed giggle, she attempted to hide the rising heat in her face. "Oh, hey, uh, yeah, you should recognize these."

"Lovely," Josh said with half a smile.

"What?" Jenny said. *Why did he say that?*

"To answer your question—I think you are lovely. This is perfect for you."

"Oh, well, thank you," she said, flustered under his scrutiny while simultaneously relishing in his compliment. "Um, why are you here?"

He chuckled. "Ophelia sent me up here to see if you need her. I wanted to tell her to do her own errands, but she and Sam were deep in conversation, and I don't think she even realized how bossy she was being. And honestly, I don't mind seeing you again—before the jump."

Heat crept into her face a second time at his words, and she ducked to sit at her vanity, hiding from his intense eyes and broad shoulders. She fiddled with a curl. "Why are you so cheerful this morning? You were bopping around the kitchen on cloud nine." Her fingers worked the curl into several braids while Josh relaxed into his chair by the bed.

"Last night was something else, Jenny, and after discussing you going alone to see the Sorceress as well as the news of the second Compass, I was wide awake for a while, just lying there in the dark. But once I fell asleep, I slept hard. I think I woke up exactly in the same position I started in. And when I opened my eyes, I had a few things figured out in my head, and my first thought was, 'Jenny is going to be brave.' And I know it's true. I just hate that I won't be there to see it."

With a sigh, she paused her braiding and rested her elbows on the vanity. "What am I going to do without you? The Sorceress is just so, you know, strong and beautiful and powerful."

"Just like you," he said. The air rushed from her lungs, and she met his gaze in the mirror, not quite believing his words or that he actually said them. His eyes crinkled with sincerity and kindness and maybe something else. "And you won't be alone. If you need me, I'm one jump away. But you won't need to come get me. I promise."

Jenny pressed her lips together and picked up where she left off with her hair, and within a minute stuck in the last pin. "There," she whispered, standing with a new measure of authority.

"Cool trick with your hair," he said. "You've definitely managed to get it under control."

She patted her braids and nodded, eyes narrowed with intensity. "I think you're right. For a minute or two at least," she said, facing him. When he didn't look away, she shrugged. "What?"

"You just look so different, so much older," he said.

The way he studied her, and his kind words, burned in her chest—an unfamiliar feeling. *I don't know what to do with this. Is ignoring it an option?* Liddy's off-hand remarks all those nights ago about her and Josh not kissing tapped on her shoulder. *I KNOW, Liddy!* She spotted Arthur Neil's journal on the bedside table next to Josh's chair.

"Oh, Josh!" He jumped at the force with which she said his name. "I forgot to tell you! I read more of the journal last night. I learned a few things." She flipped through the pages. "Apparently, Arthur buried Annabelle with the second Compass when she died, thinking it would disappear with her bones beneath the ground. They never told their children, the next Keeper and first Guardian, about the second Compass."

"So, did someone know it was there and rob the grave?" Josh wondered.

"I guess so." Jenny pulled a disgusted face. "Ew, that's so gross. Grave robbing is, well, it's worse than picking up a dismembered toe, in my book. But I can see someone doing it for the sake of the Compass. I might consider it, maybe, with gloves and a HAZMAT suit."

"And who has it now? Whoever first stole it would be long dead," Josh said.

Jenny threw herself backwards on her bed, hugging the journal into her chest. "The suspense is going to kill me," she groaned. "Unless the Sorceress does first." Sigh. "So, are we gonna tell them today?"

"Let's see how it goes with the jump. I imagine tomorrow might be better."

"I agree. There's already a lot going on." She jerked forward again with a gasp. "I just realized something!" she said, finding the page she was wanted and running a finger down it. "Oh! Here it is." The quiet that followed lasted only half a minute, but it was enough for Josh to squirm in his seat.

"I know what your gift is!" she said with a wry grin.

"My gift?" he said, confused.

Jenny huffed. "Josh, your *gift*. Like, the one the Sword should bestow unto you because of your binding to it. Like my golden ball ..."

"Oh!" He scooted closer to her, trying to read the journal upside down. "Well don't stop!" he said.

"I read this last night, half asleep, and it didn't register until just now. Arthur Neil, in his very old age, after he relinquished his role as Keeper and created the Guardianship, wrote about the first Guardian's gift. It's the gift of protection. Somehow his words could surround and protect whoever needed it, which was almost always himself and the Keeper, but not limited to them."

Brightening, Josh leaned forward, like he had a secret to tell her. "I have felt something almost bubbling in me before we go in for missions, like, words to speak or something. I always thought it was just nerves or adrenaline. But now, I wonder if that's what it was the whole time? Is that my gift?"

"Let's try it before the jump, to see what happens. I mean, it can't hurt, right?" Jenny jumped up with excitement. "Josh, this is huge! Oh, and we should try it in a book to see if we can see it happening."

"Well, it can't be in *Rapunzel*. She expects you to come alone."

Jenny thought for a second. "How about by our tree in the picture book?"

"*Our* tree?" Josh asked, eyebrows raised.

She giggled. "Yeah, you know, the one we ate fish under. It's a good tree."

"I like that idea."

Ophelia called from the bottom of the stairs, wondering if everything was okay. Jenny slammed the journal shut and returned it to her hamper for safe keeping. "Would you tell Ophelia I'll be there in like, five minutes?" Josh agreed and left her alone to finish getting ready. When the door closed behind him, she dug into her makeup bag and got to work.

Dusting powder on her skin, her thoughts wandered to Josh—remembering the way his hair fell on his temple and how he brightened at the news of his potential gift. *He believes I can be brave. He believes in me.* She sat taller, straightening her shoulders and studying herself in the mirror. "I can live with that," she said to herself and grabbed her mascara, jaw set with determination.

Fifteen minutes later, she made her way downstairs, fully outfitted to meet the Sorceress—short sword on her hip, bow on her shoulder, arrows on her back, healing dagger in her belt. The kitchen was empty, and she found everyone in the Spare Room, already deep in planning. Josh was at the black wall, making lists. No one paid her mind when she slipped in and scanned his handy work.

*Needs*

*Compass*

*Healing Dagger*

*Mermaid Dagger*

*Toe*

*Coins*

*Flanklets*

*Ash Cuffs*

"Wait," Jenny said from her corner when she read the last item on the list. "What are Ash Cuffs?"

Uncle Curtis's brow wrinkled at the sight of her in full on Keeper regalia. A hint of a smile tugged at his cheek. Something a little like handcuffs appeared from his pocket. "These are Ash Cuffs. They are coasted with an ash-infused concoction, which traditionally render witches powerless when they wear them. I cannot guarantee they will work on a sorceress or in this particular story, but they are worth a try. They can at least help subdue her physically."

"Sounds promising," she said. Sam took them and stuck them in her pack.

"The dagger, toe, and coins are in here as well," he said, shaking the bag. "Great hair," he added. Everyone else turned to her as she patted the braids wrapped about her head. "You look very ... composed. Well done." The approving nod Sam gave her lifted her spirits even more.

Jenny glanced at Ophelia, unsure if her cousin would approve of her choices. The Searcher stood and examined Jenny's outfit before hugging her. "Not what I would've chosen, but it's perfect," Ophelia whispered in her ear with an extra squeeze before releasing her, jostling her weapons only a little.

Josh still stood at the black wall, chalk in hand. He didn't say anything, but his eyes crinkled again, something that happened when he was happy, and he gave her a wink and returned to his job. "Okay, what's next. Oh yes, the 'Must Not' section."

"Oh wait, have you seen my Flanklets, anyone?" she asked the room. "I can't find them, and I was really counting on those. They are kind of my thing now, you know?" Her disappointment was palpable, but they couldn't linger there. "I may have to go without them."

"We will keep an eye out," Sam said. "In fact, I'll go search right now."

"Okay, thanks Sam. Let's keep planning," Jenny suggested, gesturing for Josh to continue while Sam headed to the house. They talked through each part of the plan. Their lists grew, and things took shape.

Must Not

Die

Kill the Sorceress before finding out more information about parents

Leave Isaac behind

Obstacles

The Sorceress because she's crazy

Snooty Julian

Unfamiliar Magic

Unforeseen Circumstances

No Josh


Plan

Jump into the Sorceress's Garden

Give her the items

Demand Isaac back

Pray she honors her end of the bargain

Come back for reinforcements should she refuse

Plan on her refusing because she's a crazy psychopath


Josh and Ophelia agreed on these last two items. "You get us if it's too dangerous. In fact, plan on it," Ophelia told her. "For your sake and for Isaac's. We'll be ready."

Swallowing, afraid she might cry, Jenny nodded.

"Today is *your* day, Jenny. You will need all your wits about you. And you will need to be brave," Uncle Curtis said. "But we are with you, just a whisper away. Don't forget it." And he hugged her, much he did like the first night they met, tall and strong and wonderful.

"I'm ready anytime," Jenny told them once her uncle had let her go. *At least, I think I'm ready. Ugh, wait, maybe I'm not ready at all.*

"You must eat something first," he said. "And it will give Sam time to find those Flanklets. We need you totally prepared." Jenny agreed, and they made their way to the house, Josh falling in next to her in the hallway.

"Even lovelier than before," he said to her, letting his arm brush against hers. "And sorry about your Flanklets."


Chapter 36


After a quick but delicious lunch prepared by Liddy, Josh towed Jenny away, giving some excuse to talk to her before she made the final jump. His words about it being the "final jump" tossed in her brain. *It's not our final jump, really, but it does feel like the last one of this chapter. We'll get Isaac back and reunite him with Liddy. And we'll get the information we are dying for about our parents. I'm not exactly sure how getting that information is going to happen, but I'm going to give it my very best. I hope that's enough.*

Doubt niggled at Jenny's brain regarding this jump all the way to Josh's room. She couldn't stop the "what if" questions bouncing in her head. They consumed her so much, she didn't register Josh talking to her until he said her name a third time. "Sorry," she said. "What did you say?"

"Are you okay?" he asked.

"No. I'm not. I thought I was, but I'm not. Ugh! What if this all falls apart today?" she blurted, his earlier words about his confidence in her forgotten.

He handed her a tissue from his pocket. "Well, what if it doesn't?" he said. Jenny started, his question surprising her. *I've never considered it going well.* As his words sunk in, her shoulders relaxed, and she sighed.

"What am I going to do without you there? I thought I'd be okay, but now that we're down to the wire, going alone is terrifying."

"It scares me too, if you want to know the truth, but you are brave and strong and fast. She underestimates you because of your age. Use it to your advantage. And you are so clever. You can outwit her. I know it." He ran his hands through his hair. "Jen, I wish I could speak a golden ball of encouragement into your heart, but it's not my gift."

He passed her the Blue Ridge Mountain photo book. "Want to see if we can figure out what my gift is and if I can help you today?"

"I do," she said with more confidence than she felt. Not that she lacked confidence in him, but in herself. Still, if his gift was what she thought it was, it could provide her some measure of protection. *I'll take whatever help I can get.*

She flipped to the page in the photo book and, holding Josh's hand, let the Compass pull them in. The stream and tree were just the same. Josh led her to the tree and stood her against it.

"Okay, be still." He stood in front of her and paused, thinking. "*May no one be as fast as you or trick you with clever lies. May all your plans be well thought through and when you speak, be wise. The Sorceress fights with swords and words, but she herself has weakness. May she underestimate you and see a child of meekness. And when you strike, strike fast and true, fight hard against the beast. She will fight back, she'll hold on fast, her hands, they won't release.*"

His words swirled from his mouth, glowing silver, misting her skin, soaking into her clothing and sinking into her short sword, bow and arrows, and even her healing dagger. Her skin absorbed them, and her vision blurred momentarily.

Josh watched, standing with his arms crossed. "Whoa! Your eyes just went silver."

"Can I move yet?" she squeaked.

"Yep."

She relaxed, a huge smile spreading across her face. "That was awesome!" she said with a high-five. "What did that last part mean? About her hands not releasing?"

"I don't know. It just seemed like the right thing to say. Maybe it means she will hold on tightly to everything she has. Maybe she won't let go of Isaac without a fight?"

"So, am I like, invincible now?" she asked.

"I don't think so. I think you are just covered, kind of like if I were there to fight with you. I can't guarantee you won't be injured even when I'm physically with you, and I don't think my words can provide a guarantee either, but I believe they make it harder to harm you," he said. "Or I could be completely wrong about that."

"I guess we'll find out. You sure you're okay staying back from this jump? I mean, you are kind of a man of action, right? And now you have to sit this one out."

"Man of action, eh?" He chuckled. "I'll be fine. It's not always all about me, Keeper." She smiled and returned them home, holding his arm while they landed though she didn't need it for balance anymore. "And anyway, I have a headache after all that." He grimaced and rubbed his temples. "Gosh, that's bad."

∞∞∞ 🐾 ∞∞∞

In the Spare Room, fully armed, she stood in the center of a half-circle created by her beloved Compass family, except Josh who had said he needed to rest after taking some pain medicine. She had watched him walk away toward his room, her heart torn between feeling bad for him and feeling abandoned by him, though she knew that was a silly and immature notion.

Now, everyone else watched her, half smiling but also obviously anxious. Sam apologized profusely for failing to find the Flanklets. Feeling otherwise well-armed and comfortable, she assured him it was okay and likely her fault for losing them.

Uncle Curtis took a sip of his coffee. "Of all the days to get a headache," he grumbled, glancing at the door, hoping Josh would appear to send her off.

"It's okay, Uncle Curtis. He's done so much for me already. And I know if I really need him, he'll be available. Let's let him rest. I will probably call on him later."

Sam stepped in and handed her the walkie-talkie. "He looked pretty bad, and I'm sure he feels worse about not being here." It was as if Sam could read her mind. And he was right. Josh must be pretty sick to not be there for her. She lifted her chin, and, with determination, shoved away her disappointment.

"Be brave," Ophelia said. "Remember your training. I'm sure Josh will come if you need him, headache or not." She hugged Jenny and whispered, "You've got this."

Jenny gave one nod to everyone else, then turned to the book. "I'll be back soon," she told them, "with Isaac." Liddy nodded amidst her uncertainty.

The Compass, eager to go, pulled hard towards the story. She leaned into the pages, and disappeared in a blink of light, landing with ease in the Sorceress's garden. A small sound startled her, and she swirled around, tense. But nothing else moved or caught her ear.

Knowing she was probably being watched, she faced the sprawling mansion and strode toward it, on a mission. There was no room for fear. She had a job to do.

But when she got to the house, a note was tacked to the door, on the same parchment as the ransom letter, with the same red wax seal.

Jenny ripped it off and tore it open.

*We have moved to greater heights.*

The note dropped to the ground. Jenny turned on her heels and ran, hard, up the path, through the gates, and onto the trail leading to Rapunzel's tower.

She radioed home. "I need my climbing gear. It's in my closet," she said. "Sam, drop it at the tower." And on she hurried, mile after mile. *I wonder if jumping home and then to the tower would be less exhausting.* But she was a good runner and covered the distance with ease. *Jumping back and forth will wear me out, especially if I need to go back again for help.*

Within half an hour, the tower loomed into sight. Her breath echoed in her ears, and a few times, she jumped, hearing a branch snap and rustling behind her. She would have to let it ride, though, her mind solely focused on the mission.

The climbing gear was there, at the base of the tower which reached high into the sky, beautiful and terrible, much like the Sorceress herself. Jenny's eyes climbed the stone wall of the tower, up and up and up. *Of all the days to not have my Flanklets.* But she didn't, so she moved past it and grabbed a harness.

It was tricky to harness in a dress, but she managed it, tying her shawl around her shoulders, hiking her skirts and tucking the back of the dress into the front of her belt. *I'm so glad Josh isn't here to witness this part, or Ophelia. Ophelia would die—this is a fashion faux pas for sure. And these shoes with my dress. Yikes.* She slipped her climbing shoes on, thankful Sam had remembered to drop them.

She slipped the gear sling, which held all her anchors, over her head and across her body, arranging it around her other weapons, then clipped some nuts to her harness.

With a calming breath, she found her first hold. Up the tower she went, calling on all her climbing knowledge, focused on her goal. Despite not climbing in several months, Jenny's body moved without thought. She went from one hold to the next, anchoring a cam every so often just in case she fell, though she knew she wouldn't. She *wouldn't.*

But then she hit the top, where the wall ended and the "house" began. There, the tower jutted over her head, the bottom of the big rooms that had once housed Rapunzel and now the Sorceress and poor Isaac. This wasn't beyond Jenny's ability to climb, but it gave her pause to consider her route. Working against gravity and forcing herself to only think about the next hold, she heaved and hoisted her way around the horizontal portion, shoulders burning, onto the face of the top portion of the tower. There, she rested to catch her breath before making her way to the one large window, knowing what lurked inside.

*What is that smell?* A pungent odor wafting from the window assaulted her nose. When Jenny peeked in, she saw the offending cauldron brewing at the hearth. "Boil, boil, toil and trouble!" The Sorceress danced in front of the brew, her dress flowing, the hourglass pendant jostling against her chest. She paused. "No, that's not quite right. Ah! Double, double, toil and trouble—fire burn and cauldron bubble!"

A caged Isaac sat on his cot, his head low, tired and defeated. The Sorceress gazed at him, slowing her samba, swaying towards the cage. "You read that to me once. Do you remember? Long ago. Shakespeare, right? Yes, I remember it well. Then you left me for that … that … monster of the deep. Wretched little mermaid." She kicked the cage and twirled to return to her cauldron when she skidded to a halt. A long shadow cast across the room from the window, Jenny balanced on its ledge. Her dress shifted in the breeze.

"Hello, Sorceress," she said, hopping into the room, shirking her gear and shaking the dust from her boots.

The Sorceress regained her composure and sidled to the fire. "Ah, our guest! I do hope you came alone, child Keeper. I truly do not wish to kill you. And you've arrived just in time. I've had my potion brewing for a few days in anticipation of your advent." She stirred the pot, allowing further potent fumes waft into the room. "You're smarter than your uncle. At least you do as I say like a good little girl," the Sorceress snapped.

Another gust blew through the window. Jenny shivered. Loath to move anywhere nearer the fire, the Sorceress, or her brew, she opted instead to untie the shawl from her waist and drape it on her arms. The Sorceress watched her, and something hitched in her breathing when she focused on the shawl. Jenny caught it. *What was that about?*

Summoning all the swagger she could, she flopped her pack onto a nearby table and took something from the front pocket. "I've brought the items you requested. If you have any honor, you will return Isaac to me in exchange for them as you promised in the ransom letter." She tried to sound as grown up as possible, and she shook the letter she had brought in the Sorceress's general direction. "You promised. I've upheld my end of the bargain. Will you uphold yours?"

Slinking toward Jenny, the Sorceress sniffed, and Jenny stiffened. She kept a firm grip on the handle of her pack, unsure how to react with her enemy so near. The Sorceress raked a fingernail along Jenny's cheekbone, neck, and arm, giggling under her breath. She grasped the strap on the pack, her fingers brushing against Jenny's. "Did no one ever tell you that bad people lie?" Her lips pressed close to Jenny's ear. "I have no honor, stupid girl." And with one move, she ripped the pack from Jenny's grip and tossed it to Julian, who cowered in a corner.

The Sorceress grabbed Jenny's wrist, dug her nails in, and jerked her close. It was all Jenny could do not to cry out. "Where did you get the shawl, Keeper?" Her face was inches from Jenny's, filled with hate, and something else—a memory, maybe? Guilt? Fear?

Taking a chance, Jenny blinked and grinned. "My friend, Granny Bea."

The Sorceress threw her to the floor. "That's impossible. She has no friends."

"Ah, so you *do* know her!" Granny Bea's words echoed in her ears *My granddaughter had a necklace too*. "Granny Bea is your grandmother! Wow. What are the odds? Hey, she thinks you are dead!"

The Sorceress's nostrils flared. "You will NEVER speak of her again. Never." The quiet rage in her voice shook Jenny, who bit her lip to keep from saying more. "Guards!"

Two men appeared from somewhere else in the tower and pointed their swords at her. "Rise!" they commanded. *Hmm. Not a great start.* Anger boiled under her skin, overtaking any fear she ought to feel, and she wished so hard Josh was there. *I need some freaking back-up!*

# Chapter Thirty-Five

The items in the pack clunked onto the large work table where the Sorceress dumped them with far less care than Jenny would have. The two items Jenny had brought previously appeared from her gown's deep pockets, and she and Julian unwrapped each one. She was giddy with victory, even squealing when she found the toe, nicely preserved thanks to some salt and dry cloth in a vacuum-sealed cannister. Her energy and excitement bubbled, a lot like whatever stewed in the cauldron. Julian leaned away from the toe, disgust on his face. *I get it, Julian. Like it or not, we have this one thing in common.*

They were all there: the bone, the spindle, the dagger, the toe, and the coins. "Isaac didn't mean to tell me he was in love with someone else," the Sorceress said, laying out her items, fondling each one while she talked. "But, silly man, he wrote it in his journal—the one I stole from his bag on one of his visits—my third-most-treasured-possession at the time. See, he was training me, he said, teaching me to read, getting me to trust him, all so he could get my hourglass necklace. It was all a ruse. He *pretended* to be interested in me when his heart was always elsewhere. He loved *her*. It's her fault, the harpy. She enticed him, seduced him. I wanted to punish her. So, I waited and waited, and got to her beloved parents the same night I got him, and your parents, too, Keeper. I could almost feel her heartbreak. It was intoxicating. Her torture. Her fear." The Sorceress wiped a bit of spittle from her lips.

"Imagine how she will feel when Isaac forgets her and declares his love for me." She laughed maniacally, dancing another jig and whisking the pot once more. "Love potions are tricky things, you see, very tricky indeed. But you, child-Keeper, you have brought me the ingredients, for which I thank you." Her black and red hair cascaded almost to the floor when she bowed a disingenuous bow toward Jenny.

Jenny suppressed her desire to yank the Sorceress's hair from her head and stuff it down her wicked throat, clenching her fists instead and fighting to remain calm. "No potion could change a man's heart. He loves Liddy, end of story. Get. Over. It." The ire in Jenny's words was unmistakable, and Isaac glanced up for the first time since her arrival, stirred by the mention of Liddy's name.

The Sorceress clucked her tongue. "Oh, such childish notions of love, Keeper. You know so little. The heart is *easily* changed if you know the right words, the right process." She went all doe-eyed, gawping at Isaac. "He will love me. He must," she whispered.

"Please don't forget her, Isaac! Liddy is waiting for you!" Jenny called to him, her voice breaking. A sword poked her in the ribs, and she jerked. "Watch it, dude," she hissed at the guard.

The Sorceress laughed again. "You must not know about this potion. No, of course you don't, why would you? You know nothing, toddler of a Keeper. Let me educate you, just in case you ever need it yourself, perhaps to win the heart of your handsome, beloved Guardian."

Jenny gritted her teeth. She hoped he hadn't heard that—oh wait, how could he? He wasn't there.

*No, this hateful woman will not get to me!* Instead of wilting at the mention of Josh, she dropped so fast, neither of the guards knew what happened before she spun and kicked one in the shins, knocking his feet from under him. He fell forward into the other one, and Jenny rolled away, sprang to her feet, and kicked him in the nose with a sickening crunch. He collapsed onto the other guard, pinning him to the floor. The one beneath him struggled under the weight of his unconscious partner, but before he could rise, Jenny swung a heavy iron pot off the Sorceress's table right onto his head. Both guards were still.

In one movement, Jenny stood tall, her bow in hand, an arrow pointed at the Sorceress. The woman stared at her, the shock on her face giving way to fury.

"What? Scared of a little girl?" Jenny asked, preparing to square off with her nemesis when cold steel pressed against her back once again, and something cold and clammy clamped over her mouth.

"Leave my mistress be, else I end you, child-Keeper. Leave her be!" Julian's cultured, raspy voice sounded in her ear. "Drop your bow." Jenny had to believe him, though part of her wondered if Julian had it in him to kill anything bigger than a cockroach. Her weapon clanged to the floor. Even Josh's protective wards would not likely stop a knife through the heart.

Chuckling again, the Sorceress continued on as if nothing happened. "Now please stop interrupting so we can complete our potion lesson. This is important. First you need an object of deception to trick the heart into love." She took the chicken bone, waggled it in Jenny's direction, and threw it into the cauldron. Next came the spindle. "And a sharpened point to awaken it." Then the dagger, which she sliced across her palm, squeezing blood into the pot. "Blood spilled from a blade unused to purify the heart." Next the toe. "And a thing discarded to break its other ties." She lifted the coins and dropped them in one by one. "Finally, stolen money to buy the heart's favor." Smoke rose from the cauldron where the potion bubbled and consumed its newest additions. The Sorceress regarded Isaac, who remained on his cot, shaking his head no, no, no. He had heard the last part.

With raised arms and skipping feet, she reveled in her concoction, ladling some into a mug for Isaac. "It's time," she said, then squealed with glee.

Isaac hesitated to take it from her through the bars of his cage. "Drink this or she dies," the Sorceress informed him, and Julian jabbed the end of his knife into Jenny's ribs, causing her to suck in her breath. But Jenny shook her head *no* when Isaac looked to her and then to the Sorceress and then to the mug in his hand, steaming and stinky. He stared at it for a long time.

"Tell Liddy I love her. It's either this or she kills us both," he said with such sadness, it broke Jenny, a sob escaping her throat.

She tried to yell and struggle free from Julian, but the fight left her when Isaac tipped the mug and drank.

"NO!" she said. "Oh Isaac, no." With that drink, the Sorceress had won. She had him, and he would love her. And she would take Jenny captive and force her to give away the binding of the Compass or kill her for it, then escape this book and wreak havoc on the world. And Jenny could do nothing with this blade to her flank. Dumb old Julian. "Don't let me bleed on you, *Julian*," she muttered.

The beautiful, terrible woman, a victory smile replacing the anger on her face, leaned in close to the bars on Isaac's prison. "I'd never kill you, Isaac. You are far too pretty and too much fun to have alive, even if you don't love me. But now, I believe you do, don't you, my darling?" Her freaky voice changed into a quiet, hopeful one, her eyes searching his. "Do you? Do you love me?"

Bile bubbled into Jenny's throat, anticipating his answer.

Isaac stood to his full height, and drained the mug with one last swig, letting out a long "aaaaahhh" at the end. He wiped his mouth with his sleeve and passed the mug to the Sorceress, grazing her wrist with his long fingers and staring deep into her very soul. He pressed between the bars, so close their lips nearly touched. Jenny gagged, thinking they would kiss, and at the last second just before contact, Isaac whispered, "No."

The Sorceress grabbed his head and smashed his face into the bars. Jenny screamed beneath Julian's palm when she saw the blood dripping from her uncle's nose and mouth.

Backing away from the bars, chuckling despite the blood, Isaac returned to his spot on the cot. The Sorceress's rage was palpable, and she paced in front of the cage, muttering. "No, it's not possible. I had everything required.

Everything!" She flew to her work table to consult the recipe once more. "How? *How?*" She spun to face Jenny. "It was you, you stupid chit of a girl. Keeper, you did this. You ruined it!"

The Sorceress flung a book at Jenny, who dropped to her knees, and Julian ducked, gasping. With a screech, she rushed Jenny, murderous and terrifying, then skidded to a halt, rearing backwards with an audible inhale.

A disembodied sword had appeared just under her chin, floating in the air, pricking her throat. Blood dripped from a small slice in her neck, and her head jerked, some unseen force yanking her hair. Fear flashed in her eyes.

It was just the opening Jenny needed, and despite her curiosity and shock over seeing a sword hovering in midair at the Sorceress's neck, it did not distract her for long from the cold steel pressed against her spine. Julian, however, *was* distracted, and Jenny used this to her advantage.

When she had fallen to her knees, it put her bow within reach, and she stretched toward it. With a quick spin, she swung her bow with all her might. It cracked into his body with a sickening thud, the strength of her weapon palpable, its sturdiness enhanced by Josh's wards. Silver flickered through the bow when it connected with Julian, and he doubled over with a groan. Jenny kicked her foot hard into the side of his knee. It collapsed with a crunch, Julian crying in pain and writhing on the floor.

Rolling away, Jenny sprang to her feet and stepped between Julian's shoulder blades. "How you like me now, Julian?" she spat. "Just chill, okay. You lose." She bound his wrists, then sat on him to watch the rest of the drama unfold, her bowstring resting against his throat, daring him to try something.

The floating sword didn't waver in the several seconds it took Jenny to subdue Julian. When everyone's attention had returned to the Sorceress, a male voice spoke with authority. "The dagger unused was your undoing." The sword pressed into her neck, drawing another drop of blood. "I dare you to use magic," the voice rasped. "One hint of it and I relieve your body of its head." The Sorceress's eye bugged at his words, and her arms dropped to her sides, taking the warning to heart.

Tears sprung to Jenny's eyes. *I know that voice.*

Leaping off Julian, the space between her and the Sorceress closed in several strides, and she strapped the Ash Cuffs onto those still, slender wrists. "How do those feel?"

The hateful woman paled. "They burn," she said. "What is with you people and burning me, stealing my magic?"

"What's with you kidnapping everyone we love and being a complete nutter?" Jenny retorted, spying several bright keys hanging on the Sorceress's belt and yanking them off with zero apologies.

She palmed the hourglass pendant and jerked it tight against the Sorceress's neck. "Release the binding." Jenny's voice had no hint of childishness in it. The sword against the Sorceress's throat pressed in even more.

"Fine. Take it. It's brought me nothing but trouble, my first-most-treasured-possession. Keep it."

With a less-than-gentle pull, Jenny relieved the Sorceress of her Charm and shoved it in her pack, zipping the pocket to keep it safe then moving toward the cage holding her uncle.

The key rattled against the iron door when Jenny turned it, and, with a soft click, the door swung open. Isaac stepped out, bleeding but smiling, breathing in the free air. He embraced Jenny. "Welcome back, dear uncle," she whispered.

The disembodied sword and voice ordered the Sorceress into the cage, and Jenny slammed the door, locked it, and stuck her tongue out at her nemesis. Three clicks, shuffle, and light thump sounded, and Josh appeared, pulling his hood off. "Hey," he said.

"Hey," she answered. "How's that headache?" She tried to sound annoyed but was unable to hide her smile. They were silent for a moment, a perfect, quiet moment.

She pointed to his ankles. "Now I know where my Flanklets went. Guardian and thief. Oh, and liar. You're worse than me!" And she leapt into his arms. "Thank you for coming."

"Even crazy sorceresses couldn't keep me away. Sorry I had to feign a headache, steal your Flanklets, and hitchhike in on your jump."

"I thought someone might be following me, but I figured it was one of her minions." She jerked her head toward the now rumpled Sorceress. "I'm so glad it was you instead."

Josh released Jenny and embraced Isaac. Though tired and weak, he returned the hug with enthusiasm. "Good to see you, Josh, I mean, Guardian. Strong work."

The Sorceress interrupted their moment by flying off the cot and banging on the rungs of her prison, demanding their attention. "How? How did it not work?" She seemed almost frenzied. "You said the dagger unused! Tell me, tell me!"

Josh leaned against the table with crossed arms. His hair fell on his brow. Dressed in rough wool pants and a deep red, loose-fitting shirt, his formidable presence made it difficult for Jenny to tear her eyes away from him. *Man, when did he become so commanding?*

"A trade," he said to the desperate prisoner. "I'll tell you what you want to know if you tell me where our parents are."

"Never," the Sorceress said, but Jenny caught her almost imperceptible glimpse at the book she had flung at Jenny in her fit of rage. *Oops.*

"Oh, I think you will," Jenny goaded her, slowing stepping toward the book, the Sorceress growing twitchier by the moment. She lifted the heavy manuscript. "*The Book of Haunting,*" she read. "This is the one, isn't it?" The Sorceress didn't move, prompting Jenny to investigate the two other books on the work table. "Or perhaps it's one of these?" She flipped through them nonchalantly, staring the Sorceress down, watching for any tell.

With a sigh, Jenny stacked the three books and shoved them into her pack. She shook the keys for the cage at the Sorceress and made a show of dropping them into her pack with the books. "You guys ready to go? Liddy is waiting," she said. "We'll be taking Julian with us and dropping him off in some other story. You can stay here and rot. Julian, any suggestions on where we can drop you?"

Still subdued on the floor, he squirmed and twisted, trying to see them. "Take me to the real world. That's where I'm from. Please!"

Jenny huffed. "Yeah right." She stooped and studied the well-groomed, pathetic snob of a man. "How about Snow White? I'm sure the Wicked Queen could use someone to stroke her ego even more. You seem good at that, eh Julian?"

"You can't leave me here alone!" the Sorceress wailed, throwing herself against the bars.

Jenny stood next to Josh, staring at the now pitiful sight before her, the solid strength and warmth of his arm against hers.

"Tell us what we want to know, and we'll take you with us and leave Julian," Josh told her, cleaning his nails with the end of his dagger. The Sorceress brightened at this idea. She eyed her captors, calculating all the risks and possible outcomes.

Jenny grew impatient and gripped Julian by his collar. "You have three seconds!"

"The biggest of the books. The one I threw. That's where they are. All the best in finding them, though. I doubt they are still alive. Now, make good on your promise. Take me!"

"Mistress, no!" Julian whined. "Don't leave me."

"Oh, you silly man. Stay here and die for all I care."

Julian gurgled as if his heart might come out of his mouth, broken into a thousand pieces. The Sorceress turned away from him, forgetting he existed.

"Go ahead and tell her. Put her out of her misery," Jenny said, nudging Josh.

He strutted in front of the cage while he spoke. "Your potion required a dagger unused, and you were correct in thinking the dagger from *The Little Mermaid* would work. In the traditional story of *The Little Mermaid*, the dagger given to the mermaid by the Sea Witch to kill the prince does go unused, for she refuses to kill him. You banked on that. However, the dagger Jenny brought you did not remain unused this time. In fact, a very brave girl sliced it through a man's Achilles tendon to end a very long fight. So, really bad luck, I guess." Josh smirked at the Sorceress, and she flew off the bed and roared against the rails and the Ash Cuffs until she crumpled to the floor crying.

"I was so close!" she moaned.

They watched her, wide-eyed and disgusted. Josh chuckled when Jenny whispered, "Wowsers."

ooooo 🎀 ooooo

Jenny, Josh, and Isaac lounged in the now quiet tower, the Sorceress snoozing in her cage. They discussed what to do next, deciding to return the woman to her original story, into the dungeons of a friend.

"I can't believe she came from that story," Jenny said, still surprised after Isaac told them the origins of the Sorceress. "What are the odds?" Even Isaac snickered at her shock. "I've never jumped from one story to another." She bit her lip, concerned, much like Uncle Curtis often did. "I accidentally jumped from one part of *A Tale of Two Cities* to another once. Is it kind of like that?"

"Yes, exactly like that. It's not hard, but you must concentrate. You can't think of anything else except where you want to go. In fact, that's how she ended up here." He jerked his thumb at the Sorceress. "She hitchhiked out of her story, and instead of taking her to the real world, where I was headed, I brought her here, to this very tower. I had to leave, to come to you, Jenny, and get that mirror. Do you remember?"

"I absolutely remember the day you stole my mirror. It was so weird."

413

"She'd been spying on you through it, and I had unwittingly put you in danger because of it. So I left her here, got the mirror, and when I returned, she was gone from the tower. I never did find out how she did it."

"Well, she is a sorceress," Josh said. "How did she get you back up here?"

"I don't know!" he said, shrugging. "I woke up one day, and we were here. Maybe Julian can shed some light on that mystery." They all glanced at the now droopy defeated man who did not appear up for a chat.

"Maybe another time. We can all agree it probably involved some sort of sorcery, right?" Jenny suggested.

"Indeed," Isaac replied. "I spent months searching for her, but she eluded me, running me all over this cursed story. She's a wily one." Jenny snorted in agreement. "Then, out of the blue, she comes to the real world and kidnaps everyone. All I wanted was to get that Charm from her, and she outwitted me, used me, and hurt everyone around me. But now it's almost over." Isaac slumped.

"Okay, let's get this done. You need to get home to Liddy and to your real bed. I hope I get this right."

"You will be fine," Isaac said. "You just have to transport me and Josh and…"

"An evil and totally unpredictable sorceress," Josh said, trying to keep things light.

"Great." Her sarcasm did not go unnoticed.

"You've got this, Jen," Josh whispered, tickling her ear. *Guh, how can I focus when he's breathing this close to me!* Still, she couldn't help but smile.

"Before we go, want to say hi to everyone?" She reached into her bag to pull out the gorgeous walkie-talkie Sam had placed in her pack for Isaac. Josh's favorite black eagle one was also included. *Had Sam known Josh's plan from the beginning? Schemers!* Isaac's walkie-talkie was a curved copper colored wire tipped with a sword hilt.

"I like swords too," he said to Josh.

Pressing the button by her ear, Jenny checked in with home base. "Hey everyone! Can you hear me?"

Sam's voice came through loud and clear.

"What's the status? Where is Isaac?" Ophelia asked.

"Hello Ophelia," Isaac said with quiet resonance, his voice booming even when subdued with emotion. "Hello everyone!"

"Isaac?" The familiar, cascading voice belonging to Liddy sounded in their ears, and poor Isaac choked on his tears. He could not speak for a full thirty seconds. "Isaac? Are you there? Hello?"

"I'm...." He cleared his throat. "I'm here, Liddy, I'm all right. I'm coming home to you. And everyone else. I'm coming home."

Josh tore a tissue in half and passed one half to Isaac and the other to Jenny. He filled the home base in on their plans and got the okay from Uncle Curtis. Though they did not need his permission at this point, it still helped to have his blessing.

# Chapter Thirty-Six

"Remember, picture exactly where you want to go and when," Isaac said. "Otherwise, you end up in a reset story, one where it's like you've never been there before. You need to land in the story you've already been in, like a video game you saved. Think you can do that?"

"What? We can do that? Uncle Curtis never told us about this option," Jenny said with surprise.

"That's because he's not a Keeper. He only knows what he knows. I know more, at least about what *we* can do," Isaac said. "I got good at getting back into a story after I met Liddy. I could return to her every time by concentrating on the story it was when I was there, not the story before I got there."

"Okay, who wants to wake Scary Cry Baby Sorceress over there?"

Sparing Isaac from any more interactions with his former captor and tormentor, Josh volunteered for the job and resorted to poking her with a long iron tool from the fireplace. The softer jabs didn't work, so he gave her a pretty good poke in the ribs, and she jumped, angry, then masked it with disdain. "Oh goodie, it's time to go."

"We did promise to take you with us, and unlike you, we have honor and keep our word," Jenny said, gripping the chain of the Ash Cuffs like it was her job, which it kind of was. She linked with Josh and Isaac. The Compass whirred to life, the arrow spinning one way and then the other.

"What about him?" the Sorceress asked, tilting her head to Julian, uncuffed and whimpering.

"Julian stays here. He has agreed to manage the tower for me until my return. I have promised to let him out of the tower at a later time. Any shenanigans, and I shave his head and force him to wear camo overalls, right Julian?" Jenny said. He nodded, downcast, rubbing his unbound wrists.

Josh squeezed her arm with one hand and shoved his sword hilt, the blade hidden away, right into the Sorceress's flank with the other.

"One false move, and I end you with the press of an emerald," Josh said.

Jenny had to picture a place in a book she had been to before, getting the timing just right. With her destination firmly in her mind, she said the words, and they blinked out of the tower and landed with a crunch in Sherwood Forest, just after Robin's men had run a herd of deer through this glen, the same one she'd landed in by accident all those months ago.

"Good work, Jenny." Isaac complimented her with a pat on the shoulder.

"This way," she said.

They followed the road through the woods leading to the Castle Fitzwalter where Jenny hoped Maid Marian would take the Sorceress to her jailer and keep her locked away forever. She trusted Marian would remember her good deed earlier in the story and be willing to help.

But they had one stop first.

The Sorceress, recognizing her new surroundings, railed and fought against her cuffs. "No, no, NO! Please don't send me back. You promised me the real world! You have no honor, lying worm."

Jenny lifted a finger. "How dare you insult my honor? I promised to take you with me, not take you to the real world. That is simply what you believed. Today we are going to see Granny Bea. I want to hear what she has to say about you. So, welcome home, Sorceress."

Shoulders drooping, hair falling into her face, the Sorceress said, "Here, I am called Agatha, and this is not my home. This place hated me." Her brows gathered in a worried sort of way, and she stopped fighting against the cuffs.

The village near Castle Fitzwalter buzzed with life and still smelled like a dirty toilet. Granny Bea's hovel remained unchanged, mud and wood and a thatched roof. The old woman tottered into the doorless entry. "Oy, it's me old friend, returned again, and so soon!" she called out with excitement, waving to Jenny. "I see you've brought friends."

"Whew, it worked," Jenny whispered to Josh and Isaac.

"I knew it would, Jenny," Isaac said. "You were destined for this Keeper stuff."

Josh just nudged her.

"I see you're still a'wearin the shawl. 'Tis a pretty thing," Granny Bea said. The group approached, and Granny Bea squinted her already beady eyes. "Bless my soul, could it be? Me granddaughter? Agatha, is that you?"

Agatha approached old Granny Bea, head hanging. "Aye Granny, tis I.

418

I've returned, as you can see. In restraints." She sounded contrite, showing her grandmother the cuffs on her wrists. "I ... I failed. I'm sorry." This was not the same Agatha who'd ruled in *Rapunzel* and cleverly kidnapped five people in one night. This Agatha trembled in the presence of her grandmother.

"Aye, so ya did." Then she turned to the other three and clapped her withered hands together. "Won't you come in for a bit and sit? Just a wee rest before continuing your journey. Would ya let me talk to my grand-daughter for a bit? It's been so long since we've chatted."

Jenny, her heart going out to the old woman who had helped her before, agreed. But Josh, always suspicious, hesitated. "Just for a minute. We need to be on our way. Your granddaughter has an appointment with the jailer." He bent close and whispered in Jenny's ear. "Agatha is shaking." She nodded, trying to ignore his broad fingers against her spine.

They crowded into the small house, though Isaac opted to stay outside, claiming he'd had enough of confined spaces for a while.

Several rickety chairs offered them a less than comfortable place to sit. Jenny stood while Granny Bea wandered into the back bedroom, return-ing with the pretty silver and turquoise bracelet Jenny had traded for the shawl and dress she currently wore.

"See here, Agatha, see what old Granny got fur ya whilst you were away? This lovely thing. Oh, do try it on before ya go. Could she just try it, as a parting gift from her granny? Without the cuffs?"

Josh stiffened. Jenny turned to him. "What harm can happen if it's just for a minute? It would mean a lot to Granny Bea, and she was a good friend to me when I needed help."

He shook his head no. "The risk of her magic is too great, Keeper."

"Just take one side off," Granny Bea offered. "The ash will still work. It'll just be for a moment."

Josh drew his sword, as a precaution, and trained it on Agatha. "Try anything and you will regret it. Just for a minute, and then they are back on both wrists."

Before Jenny unlocked the cuffs, she warned Agatha. "Don't be stupid, or he will kill you. Please." Then with a click, one side of the cuffs released.

Agatha rubbed her wrist. "Those things hurt," she said.

"Here ya go, love." Granny Bea tossed the bracelet to Agatha, and a moment afterwards, threw a knife expertly at Josh, who was so focused on Agatha he did not notice the knife flying toward his chest until Jenny screamed his name.

It struck him in the shoulder, only because, on instinct, he'd moved when he heard the scream. It stunned him, the shock of what happened and seeing a knife hilt protruding from his body. He winced, drawing the blade out and dropping it to the floor.

"Get her necklace!" Granny shouted. It was just the moment the Sorceress needed. She twirled her body, more maneuverable now that she had both hands free, and yanked the healing dagger off Jenny's belt. With all her strength, she lunged at Jenny, the dagger lifted and gleaming in the candlelight. Jenny reached to defend herself, hate raging in every part of Agatha's being. "Jenny!" she heard from far away, muffled by a strange calm binding her heart and mind when she locked in on the healing dagger. Streaks of silver darted in her vision. In a moment of clarity, Jenny dropped her arms to her sides and stepped *forward*, toward the Sorceress, who plunged the dagger into the Keeper's chest, just below her breastbone.

Josh screamed her name again, and Granny Bea flew at him from across the room, shockingly quick and strong for an old woman.

He fought back despite an aching shoulder. "The Ash Cuffs ... You knew!" he spat at her, realizing his mistake. "You knew they were Ash Cuffs, though we didn't tell you. You are more witch than your grand-daughter!"

"You have no idea!" Granny Bea said, cackling, lunging for him, punching, swinging, grappling.

He defended himself against her onslaught, his focus divided between his attacker and his injured Keeper. "If she dies ..." he said, blocking, hitting, forcing Granny Bea backwards, trying with all his might to get to his friend.

With every step, Granny Bea changed, growing younger with each passing second. The gray hair became dark red, her wrinkled, haggard face smoothed and brightened. Within half a minute, he no longer fought a hideous old hag but a beautiful woman in her late forties.

An ear-splitting shriek brought them both to a halt, and they turned as one in the direction of the scream. Jenny lay on the floor, alive but pale and sweating, her breathing ragged. The dagger stood brutally from her chest, the Sorceress's hands still wrapped around it. The horrible scream was coming from the evil woman's throat. She shook, shivering. First her arms trembled, then her teeth clacked together, and finally her entire body shuddered, the cold overcoming her. She blanched, and her lips turned blue.

"Let me go!" screeched Agatha to the dagger. "Let me go! It's so cold ... so ... cold!" She continued to scream. Isaac had stepped in to see what the commotion was.

Josh tried to move forward, to be with Jenny, but a strong hand held him in place. "Wait," Isaac said. He had Granny Bea in a strong hold and cuffed with another pair of Ash Cuffs before Josh even noticed. "I asked Sam to bring some in. Thought we might need them. Hello, Beatrice. Good to see you again." His words dripped with disdain.

Beatrice could not move, though her breathing heaved, watching the Sorceress's life ebb away—the dagger draining her, healing Jenny instead. Glowing silver tendrils had twisted up from Jenny's wound and latched onto the Sorceress's hands, binding her to the dagger.

Josh waited, transfixed. Agatha dissolved to dust, dissipating before their eyes, the dagger repairing the very wound it had made just moments earlier.

"She's getting stronger," Josh said to Isaac. "I can feel her pulse."

With a final wail and convulsion, the Sorceress collapsed into a heap of dust and a pile of clothes on the floor next to Jenny. All was quiet.

The healing dagger dropped to the floor. "Josh!" Jenny's voice was weak, raspy. This time no one hindered him going to her, and he fell to his knees beside her, ripping her dress to reveal what was left of her wound.

"It's almost healed," he said, "but I'll need to finish the job."

Jenny winced. "Don't worry," she said. "I'll take care of you if you pass out, like you took care of me." He snatched the dagger, not hesitating for a second, and placed it on her skin. His own arm grew cold, and he could see her flesh knitting together beneath the blade, closing from the inside out. Blood from the puncture in his shoulder trickled down his arm, warm against the cold of the dagger. She tried to distract him from the cold and pain. "You told me earlier today that I looked lovely. I wanted to say thanks. I probably look not so lovely now." A small laugh shook her tired body.

Josh smiled down at her, her hair curling with sweat, face regaining warmth, and through chattering teeth, he reassured her. "You are always beautiful to me. Always." He peered at her. "Your eyes are more golden than ever."

And then, just as the last of her wound healed, he lost consciousness, collapsing against her. She sat up to catch him. "Oh dear."

A minute later he regained some life, enough for her to help lean him against a chair. "Here, this way," she said. "Now you won't end up face down in sorceress dust, which would be totally disgusting." He still shivered and was bleeding, so she removed the shawl from her waist and draped it on his shoulders, staying close to help keep him warm. She also tore off some of her dress and bound the knife wound in his shoulder.

"Should I heal it?" Isaac asked from behind the now much more youthful Granny Bea.

"No, Isaac, it's all right, I think," Josh said with some effort. "The bleeding is slowing down, and you don't want to feel like this. You just got out of prison. You've been through enough. I'll be fine." But his voice shook with weakness.

"As soon as we're home, I'll tuck you into bed, Josh, and bring you lots of pancakes and bacon and butter. I promise. We will be home soon." Jenny faced the woman in Isaac's grip, sauntering toward her.

"You helped me before. Why?" She maintained the command she'd found earlier with the Sorceress. Granny Bea, or rather, Beatrice, remained silent. Jenny lost her patience and grabbed the knife thrown at Josh earlier, slamming it into the table with such force, the entire hovel shook. "*Tell me!*" she yelled.

Granny Bea's eyes flew wide, staring at the knife that almost murdered her table. They then landed on the Compass.

"You had the pretty necklace, the one he used to wear when he came to visit my ... daughter." She gestured to Isaac. *Daughter, not granddaughter.* "I didna know the powers it had when I first encountered it, but my heart wanted it, oh it wanted it so badly. So, I sent Agatha, to get it from him. I told 'er not to return unless she had it."

Again, pointing to Isaac, she went on. "But she failed. She had 'er own necklace with some kind of power, which she used to her advantage, but that obviously ended quite poorly. She always was a useless girl, so driven by emotions. I'm glad she's gone, less of a burden, though I reckon I will need to sweep up." Beatrice's apathy regarding her daughter's death stunned the other three. "She thought she could get him to love her and obtain the necklace that way. She was a fool." Her foot stomped the floor.

"The day you came to visit, I noticed your necklace as you were changing, but I was not assured it were the same one, so I didna make me move just then. I made you promise to return and visit old Granny Bea, and I'd just bide my time till you came again, in case it were the same one I'd seen the man wearin' before. And I knew you'd return—you had an honestly about ya."

Beatrice tapped her chin. "I can be patient, I can. I followed ya to Maid Marian's garden, and I watched through the gates when ya shot the big man, spoke with the pretty ladies, and then vanished. Then I knew it were the same. I knew my daughter had failed, and now she were gone and someone else had the necklace. And I promised myself, when I saw ya again, I'd take it for me own. I'd have it, no matter what."

"Why?" Jenny asked.

"To escape this horrible place and go somewheres I could be myself, without fear of the stake and fire, and no longer live behind the mask of a harmless old woman with no teeth. Us witches are more suspect if we are young and beautiful. Being old made me invisible. I'm tired of being old."

A hint of sadness in Beatrice's voice nearly moved Jenny to let her go, to let her punishment be remaining in the very place she abhorred. It almost made her say goodbye and good luck to Beatrice without consequence.

But there was Josh, pale and cold, and she remembered him with a knife in his shoulder. She saw Isaac, standing resolutely behind the prisoner with weariness just under his skin and sorrow in his eyes, and she remembered him confined by the Sorceress, defeated and alone. Then she put her fingers just under her sternum, feeling the place her healing dagger had killed and healed her just minutes before. It was scarred and tender, the pain and terror of the experience as fresh as her newly formed skin. All these things, all these horrible things, had happened because this woman wanted the Compass. And she remained dead set on having it.

"For your initial kindness to me, I will grant you your wish, Beatrice. We will leave here, and you will come with us. We will go somewhere acceptable for witches." Hauling Josh to his unsteady feet, she whispered promises of home, with just one quick stop. "Just hold on to me, okay?

425

Isaac, bring her here." Josh gripped Jenny's hand, trying hard to remain strong, and she linked arms with Isaac, who held onto Beatrice.

"Where are you taking me?" Beatrice asked.

"To meet your match," Jenny said. They disappeared and landed smack in the middle of a particularly straight road, leading to a large cottage. Smoke rose from the chimney, and the garden still grew big, pretty vegetables. The large, oversized door rose in front of them, and the ground shook with several thuds from inside the house.

"Fee fi fo fum!" The words echoed from the giant cottage windows.

"What place is this?" Beatrice said, shrinking, being forced to walk towards the cottage by her captors.

"Well, it will either be the death of you, or it will become your new home. I hope you don't mind living alone, in the clouds, with no way down unless some foolhardy Englishman decides to grow another beanstalk. But I expect it will be the death of you. The ogre-wife ... she's big, and she's scary, and she despises Englishmen, or women, at this point."

And then Isaac knocked on the door, a resounding tap, tap, tap.

A thud, thud, thud followed, the ogre-wife clunking to the door, chanting again. "Fee Fi Fo Fum, I smell the blood of an English ... witch?"

Jenny and Josh moved away from the door and linked with Isaac.

"Wait, the cuffs!" Beatrice shouted, fighting against them. "The Ash Cuffs!" Jenny thought for a moment, then rushed forward to unclick one of them, leaving the other wound firmly on Beatrice's wrist.

Then, with her arms entwined with Josh and Isaac, she whisked them away, the big cottage door creaking open.

426

# Chapter Thirty-Seven

They touched down in the Collection, Jenny calling for Sam and Ophelia's help. Josh's weight was too much to manage any longer. The three of them helped the injured Guardian to his room where they got his shoes and bloody shirt off. Jenny, who had been studying first aid as part of her school with Uncle Curtis, doctored his wound, and Ophelia gathered blankets to help warm him. Sam brought a hot water bottle from the kitchen and threw several blankets into the dryer to heat them.

They had both offered right away to heal him with the dagger, but he refused. "I'll survive, and you don't want to feel this cold, I promise. You've done more than enough." They then snuck off to go see Isaac, but Jenny remained by his side, washing his wound with warm, sterile water.

Without batting an eyelash, she stitched his shoulder together, carefully approximating the skin. "Thankfully, this is not a severed toe," she joked, bandaging it with gentle fingers and helping him into a warm shirt stuffed with a hot water bottle. For good measure, she also slapped his knit cap on his head and worked it over his ears.

"There," she said, patting his cheeks. "Now you should be roasting." His fingers gripped her forearms and held her there, near him, and he regarded her through tired eyes. Her toes tingled at his touch, and she remained with him for a moment before breaking free to tidy up her first aid kit.

"Did you see your magic?" she asked him, changing the subject, doing her best to not make eye contact. "It, like, latched onto Agatha's arms. I think it's what saved me after I was stabbed." A shiver traveled the length of her spine, remembering it.

"I did see it."

"Do you remember what you said by the tree when you set the wards? *She will fight back, she'll hold on fast, her hands, they won't release.*" Careful to not jostle the bed, she kneeled next to him and entwined her fingers in his. "That's what I remembered when she raised the dagger. I knew it wouldn't kill me—couldn't kill me—as long as she was holding it, and I knew she wouldn't be able to let go. How did you know to say it?"

He shook his head. "I didn't know it or plan it. I just said what came to mind. Maybe the gift knew?"

"Well, I'm so, so glad it worked. And now she's gone, and Beatrice is either about to become supper for the ogre's wife or she's trapped forever in ogre land above the clouds."

"Good move, Keeper," Josh said, his head relaxing into his pillow, his eyelids heavy.

Jenny stayed with him for hours, eventually falling asleep on the floor beside the bed. She awoke once when Liddy covered her with a blanket and placed a pillow beneath her head. "Thank you both," Liddy whispered before leaving the room. "Thank you for bringing back my love."

Dinner that night was a grand celebration of Isaac's return and the end of the Sorceress. Jenny showered beforehand and joined the party with a smile, in her pajamas, and with her hair as wild as could be. Josh also made an appearance, no longer shivering or exhausted, but with his shoulder still achy. Uncle Curtis passed him some medicine from a particular cabinet he kept well stocked in the kitchen. "Glad you made it, Guardian, both there and back again. Good work," the older man said to the younger one, clasping his good shoulder.

Isaac, clean, shaven, and with a haircut, embraced Jenny again. "You saved me, Jenny. You did it! You all did. How can I ever thank you enough?"

"Just stick around for a while, eh? And marry Liddy as soon as possible. Then help us get Mom and Dad back. I think that'll just about cover your debt of gratitude," she said with a wink.

"I'm so sorry I dumped all this Compass stuff on you," he said with a grimace. "I didn't know what else to do."

"It's okay, Isaac."

"No, I need you to know—it was not my plan to be kidnapped the same day. I never saw it coming. You were thrown into this world instead of eased in, like you should have been."

"I'll be honest, it was horribly terrifying, massively overwhelming, and ridiculously stressful, but I was never alone. Since you gave me the Compass, I've had the most intense, terrifying, and best months of my life. Please don't feel sorry for what you did. What you did was give me adventure, and these people. Best birthday gifts ever."

His downcast countenance lifted at her words. "Speaking of birthdays, isn't yours coming up soon?" he asked, his joy returning knowing she harbored no ill will toward him.

"In a few weeks. I'm not sure it'll be remembered, but that's all right. We have more important things to deal with."

"Indeed, we do," Isaac said. "Indeed, we do. But I still owe you a mirror."

With dessert served, Uncle Curtis raised his glass to make a little speech. "We have had some changes this year. A new Keeper, a new Guardian, two new couples here, and two couples still lost. To you six at the table with me, I cannot think of anyone I'd rather have in this Compass family of ours. It is an honor to know you, love you, and be loved by you. To the four still missing, don't worry, we are coming." They all raised their glasses in agreement.

ooooo 🐾 ooooo

Later that night, Jenny sat on the edge of her bed, considering her room. When she'd arrived here five months ago, her walls had been bare. Now, drawings she'd done of all their missions and adventures and lessons decorated each wall, a visual diary of the moments she never wanted to forget. Alone with each memory, she had her people: Uncle Curtis and Sam and Ophelia and Liddy and Josh. And now Isaac. "I love you all," she whispered.

*The Book of Haunting,* the one the Sorceress had said their parents were trapped in, lay on her desk. "Oh Agatha, I hope you didn't lie." She had wanted to jump into the book right away, but Josh had reminded her they probably needed to at least read it, plan, be a *little* prepared. She had rolled

430

her eyes with a smile and conceded, knowing he was right.

Inside her drawer, her phone had a text—a quick hello from Rae. Jenny's heart clenched. *I've got to do better keeping in touch with her. Maybe Ophelia can help me find her a Christmas gift to send, albeit slightly belated.*

Finally, she checked her hamper where the journal was hidden—the journal that would change everything. "What other secrets do you hold?" she wondered, perching again on the edge of her bed.

And that's when Josh knocked on her door. "Come in," she called to him.

"Hey," he said.

"Hey." He dropped into his chair, their knees inches apart.

A small wooden spoon appeared from his pocket. "I saw this one on Granny Bea's table, I think."

"I'm so sneaky," she said, giggling.

"Thanks for this. I have a memento from every jump we've done except Sleeping Beauty. That's pretty cool."

"Oh, I have something for you from Sleeping Beauty!" Jenny flipped through a thick book from her pile and out dropped a folded paper towel which she handed to Josh. "Be gentle."

Inside was the flower she had picked from the courtyard of sleeping courtiers, dried and pressed flat.

"You need something to remember them all by, right? I wanted to get spoons from each one, but that was impossible. I couldn't find a spoon in *Sleeping Beauty*, and ogre spoons are like, as big as me."

"I love everything. I have enough spoons, anyway." He leaned forward in his chair. "So, when do we tell the others about the second Compass?"

She paused. "Well, how about tomorrow?"

"Tomorrow sounds perfect," he said. "They are going to freak out."

"Yep." Part of her couldn't wait to see their faces at the news.

"Maybe they will start sharing some of their secrets too, now that Isaac is home," Josh said. "I'm so curious."

"Oh, I know! Me too. However, I'm kind of glad they haven't shared too much yet. I really want to know, and I also really don't want to know. I think there's a lot more to all this."

"And after that, we go for our parents." Josh heaved a big sigh. "I think it's going to be hard."

"Yep. But, whatever happens, whatever we find, we deal with it together, right?"

He nodded and met her eyes, clasping her hands between his palms. A little thrill shot through her, and she slowed her breath to keep her heart from betraying her in the Guardian Ring. "I wanted to say thank you for taking care of me after you nearly died," he said. "I almost lost you, Jenny." Those deep, dark eyes welled with tears, and his hands tremble. "I ... I thought ..."

"But I'm fine," she whispered. "Your wards saved me. In a way, we took care of each other. I think that's how this thing works." A curl fell over her eye, and before she could toss it back, Josh brushed it to the side, grazing her temple. She dropped her gaze to her lap, unsure what to say and unable to maintain eye contact any longer. With her thumb, she traced the leather bracelet on his wrist, feeling the letters beneath her fingertip.

"Ynghyd Cryfach," she said.

Josh grinned. "Yes. Ynghyd Cryfach."